# START OVER

## Start Again Series Book 2

## J. SAMAN

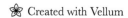 Created with Vellum

# Chapter One

*Ivy*

"NO ONE DRINKS like that unless they're in love," the woman next to me says. I've been drinking in the pub for the past hour, and though I had noticed the nice pair of legs dangling out of the tiny skirt when she'd sat down next to me half an hour ago, I didn't do further research.

I ignore her as I take a sip of my Manhattan, which I only drink during dire situations.

"Oh, come on," she continues, clearly not taking my not-so-subtle hint. "It can't be that bad."

I turn my head to her. She's pretty. Red hair and dark blue eyes, at least that's how they appear in the dim lighting, attached to petite yet soft features.

I shrug a shoulder, turning back to the mahogany of the bar, hoping the heavy bass beat will serve as enough of a buffer between us.

I've never been in this pub before. I guess that really shouldn't surprise me since I've never been much of a boozer—not even in college when you're supposed to hit the turps.

I only live a few blocks away. Staggering distance. That's what they call it, isn't it?

Yes, that's exactly what they call it. I plan on getting good and drunk tonight. I'm sure I'll regret it in the morning, but for now, it seems like an ace of an idea.

My drinking neighbor says it can't be that bad, but she's wrong.

I lost someone today. Not me per se, and it wasn't my fault or anything, but still. It's a life gone. A family devastated. You'd think by this point I'd be used to it and no longer take it personally, but I'm not, and I do.

So I'm getting pissed.

I take a sip of my second Manhattan of the night, admiring the fact that the bourbon and sweet vermouth are now flavorless.

"Breakup or unrequited love?" the girl on my right asks again.

"Neither."

And it's the truth. I'm not in love and I'm not going through a breakup. Sometimes, life just requires a night of drinking in solitude. I don't share these moments of somber contemplation with anyone. Not my colleagues or staff. No one. Which is probably why I don't have a ton of friends. They're all big on commiserating together. I'm not.

Why does everyone always assume that everything has to do with the opposite sex?

"Okay, fine," she says a little dramatically as she sips her . . . whatever the hell that is. "If you don't want to talk about it, I get it."

"Sorry, it's not you."

"Oh right, the whole *it's not you, it's me* line," she laughs. "Your ex must have been a real bitch."

I can't help but laugh with her because this woman is actually a nice distraction—one I could use.

"A bitch?" I turn to face her.

"Yeah, to make you so bitter. Was she whoring around?"

"Whoring around?" I feel like we're playing dirty Mad Libs here, but I can't quite get the punchline. And now I'm mixing metaphors, which tells me I should have eaten dinner before I took to the booze.

Wait, did she say *she*?

Ginger here looks at me equally confused. "The woman you broke up with," the redhead enunciates each word like I'm a child.

"I'm not gay." I tilt my head, wondering why she automatically assumes I am. She should meet my sister, Sophia, then her gaydar would be off the charts. "And I didn't break up with anyone."

She bites her lip, amused as hell. "If you're not gay, what are you doing in a gay bar?"

Her question catches me completely off guard, and I spin on my stool to survey the crowd.

Sure as rain, she's right.

Judging by all the female couples, this is very much a lesbian bar. "Oh." At least I have a good place to take Soph when she comes to visit next month. The drinks are ripper.

She laughs out loud, head tilted back, smacking the bar twice for effect. "It's fine; I'm not gay either. Well, not really anyway."

I swivel back, reaching for the stem of my fancy glass.

"Then why are you here?"

She shrugs a shoulder, "They have the best mojitos in town."

I eye her drink quickly before turning back to my own and finishing it down. "I'm Ivy."

"Claire."

"Nice to meet you."

"Ditto."

Claire downs the rest of her drink in one impressive slurp of the straw before slamming it on the counter and wiping her mouth with the back of her hand. She stands up slowly, adjusting her tiny skirt before slapping a twenty on the bar.

"You ready?"

I furrow my eyebrows. "For what?"

"To get out of here."

"I thought we already established that we're not gay?"

She snorts, "I'm not going to screw you, Ivy, though I do think you're rather babealicious—in a serious, brooding sort of way. I'm headed to a party at a friend's house, and I want you to come with me."

"A party?" I deadpan. "You don't even know me."

"True, but that doesn't mean we can't be friends. Now come on, I'm borderline bitchy late instead of fashionably late."

*What the hell.*

I toss down some money and follow my new friend, Claire, out into the cool misty night. She turns right, immediately setting off at a good clip and crossing her arms over her chest to stave off the cold.

"I like your accent. Australian?"

I nod. "Yes, but I've lived in the States for nearly sixteen years now."

"That explains why you have a slight accent, but don't sound over the top Aussi."

I snicker. "Over the top Aussi?"

"Yup. I would know. I lived in Australia for six months when I was a kid."

I turn to her, taken a back. "Oh, yeah? Where abouts?"

"Sydney. Army brat. My dad was there for training or something."

I can't imagine moving around like that for short stints at a time. Probably explains why she's so affable and outgoing. How else do you meet people or make friends in that sort of situation?

"What about you?"

"Just outside of Melbourne."

"Is your family still there?"

I shake my head, stepping around a couple who decided that the middle of the sidewalk was the perfect place to make out. "My mum and dad are here in Seattle now, and my sister lives in California."

"Nice." Claire stops at the foot of a large craftsman-style home. "This is us."

I angle to her, my eyebrows raised, because the house is completely dark.

There are no lights on and no cars on the street or in the driveway.

"It's a surprise engagement party for my boss and my best friend," she explains, climbing the few cement steps up to the door. "They're getting married in a couple of months, but the ceremony is going to be super small, so one of Kate's work friends set this up so they could celebrate with her."

"Oh, that's a lovely thing to do."

"It is." She looks at me as she opens the front door like she lives here. "But if you say lovely again, we can't hang out."

I snicker, grinning for the first time all day as I wearily follow her in.

"Don't worry, it's just me," Claire calls out, clearly not wanting a houseful of people to yell surprise at her.

"About damn time, Claire," an enticing male voice bellows out from the dark.

"Suck it, Luke," Claire says as she grabs hold of my wrist, seeming to know the way. I allow her to lead me, wondering what the hell I'm doing in a strange house with a strange girl. Around us, people are giggling and shushing one another.

Stumbling over someone, I mutter out an apology as Claire jerks me down to the ground behind a heavy, solid piece of furniture that can only be a sofa or chair.

"If you had gotten here on time, I wouldn't have to give you shit," the same male voice whispers in my ear.

"Sorry?" I whisper back, a little unsettled by his proximity. Our hands are essentially touching as the warmth of his body cascades over mine, his breath brushing my face. He smells like the rain, fabric softener, and some woodsy cologne. It's fantastic, and I practically breathe him in before I can stop myself. It's the sort of scent that women all over the world fantasize about because it's just that good.

"You're not Claire," he says, and I feel his fingers skimming my own in what can only be a purposeful motion. I jerk my hand back to my lap.

"No, I'm not." I don't offer more of an explanation than that. Suddenly I'm embarrassed to be here, practically sitting against a strange man in the dark. His body and face somehow seem closer, though all I can make out are shadows without specific features.

"That's a good thing," he whispers. His breath blowing at a wisp of hair near my neck, sending chills across my skin.

*What the bloody hell was that?*

It's the alcohol. It's making me dizzy and not myself.

He must not realize how close he is to me, so I shift to the other side, abutting Claire's small frame.

As I look around, squinting my eyes against the black, I realize that this isn't just a house party—it's an intimate gathering of friends, and I met the only person I know here twenty minutes ago.

I've never done anything like this, and I have no excuse for my behavior now except that it was a real bastard of a day and I needed the mental diversion.

"Luke," Claire whispers, leaning across me.

She must have bloody night vision goggles or cat eyes or something because she seems to have no difficulty seeing in the dark.

"This is Ivy. I picked her up at Cello's, even though she's straight. Ironic, huh? I meet the only other non-lesbian there and talk her into leaving with me."

"That's fucking hilarious," Luke deadpans. "Now can you shut up so we don't blow the lame-ass surprise? They just pulled in the driveway."

I'm about to ask how he even knows that when I hear car doors slamming shut and a man and a woman talking and laughing.

Keys jiggle in the lock, and I can feel Claire—at least I hope it's her—grab my hand in excited anticipation. The door flies open and someone flips the switch on the lights, and suddenly everyone jumps up, including me, and yells surprise.

I'm temporarily blinded by the sudden transition in lighting, and as my pupils constrict and accommodate, I'm being pulled into the rushing crowd of well-wishers.

Somehow I manage to pry myself away from Claire's ninja grip and maneuver myself to the back of the heap.

The group of about thirty people is laughing and talking animatedly with a woman I cannot see, but her fiancé is towering over the rest with dark, nearly black hair, a thick beard, and glasses.

*Not a bad-looking bloke.*

My eyes scan the room, debating if I should make a run for it out the back when a small blonde woman with an angelic face and light blue eyes approaches me. She looks familiar, but for the life of me I can't place her.

"Ivy Green?"

"Um . . . Yes?" Why does that sound like a question?

"Welcome," she says warmly, and I smile, feeling horrible for not knowing her name when she clearly knows mine. "I'm Kate Taylor. I work at the hospital with you. I'm a nurse in the ICU, but float to the ED sometimes."

And then it all clicks into place.

"Yes, of course," I beam, relieved that I know a second person here, again, sort of. "I apologize for not realizing who you were straight off."

She waves me away like it's nothing. "Claire said you were her date for the night. She's my maid of honor."

That relief from moments ago crashes to the floor, shattering into a million pieces. I'm mortified, because this is clearly *her* engagement party that I'm crashing, and I didn't even know her name.

"Yes, sorry. I hope that's all right?" I look around helplessly. "I realize I'm intruding."

"Not at all. I'm glad you're here. The more people I know at the hospital, the better."

I can relate to that.

Though I've been working there since the start of my residency, I haven't really clicked with many people. But that's all on me. I've been consumed with work and thought of little else.

Scanning around, I see a slew of other familiar faces, including Craig Stanton, who mercifully has yet to notice me.

"It's a bit unexpected that I'm crashing the surprise party of a work colleague."

"I know, right?" Kate laughs out loud.

"What's so funny?" Claire hops over to us. Literally, she's hopping across the room. "You macking my date?"

"No, but I definitely knew her before you did."

"No way," Claire half-yells, pouting with a disappointed jut of her lip.

"It's true, mate," I say, patting her shoulder like she's a small child. "I work at the hospital with her."

"Figgity fuck, Kate. How is it you've met everyone I know before me?"

"Not Luke. You definitely knew him first."

"True, but that dickwad doesn't count."

"Get over it," Kate laughs, before giving a pouting Claire a kiss on the cheek. "I have to mingle, but I'm glad you came, Ivy. I hope we can talk more later."

"Thanks. Me too." I mean that as well. Kate is as sweet as her face.

"Come on, Ivy, let's go hit up the bar and look for unattached men. Something tells me it's slim pickings in that department."

Claire leads me toward the back of the house and into a gorgeous gigantic kitchen where there is a bar set up on the center island and a few people I don't recognize, milling about.

"What's your poison? Another Manhattan?" Claire asks, pulling two red plastic cups off the stack.

"Uh, sure. Why not? I don't have to be on shift until ten tomorrow."

"Atta girl." She pours a lot of whiskey and a splash of sweet vermouth into the cup and hands it to me. No ice. Not even slightly chilled. Just straight up alcohol.

"You're joking, right?" I ask, eyeing the warm, no doubt overly strong, beverage.

"Not at all. This party is lame. We need to get our drink on if we're going to last."

"I can't drink like this. You'll be holding my hair above the toilet in no time."

"Don't tell me I picked up a pussy of a drinker?" she snorts. "Get it? Pussy of a drinker? I picked you up at a *gay* bar."

I really have no words for that one.

I shrug, "Sorry, mate, but yeah."

"At least have a few sips." She drops a couple of ice cubes from the bucket into my cup with a splash. "There, better now?"

"Fine, but if I get sick and make a total mess of myself, you better not think less of me."

"Never. Cross my wicked, black heart." She makes an X over her heart with her finger.

"I'm not sure if that lends itself to trust, but I'll go with it for now."

"Good." She smiles brightly, holding up her own cup filled with some crazy concoction. "To new friends."

"To new friends," I repeat as we crash our plastic cups against each other with a crinkling sound before I take far too large a sip. The liquid burns as it slides down my throat, but for the first time in days, I'm relaxed and happy. Hoping it lasts longer than just this drink. Wondering what else this night has in store for me.

# Chapter Two

*Ivy*

"DR. GREEN," Craig Stanton's unwelcome voice interrupts my mini-drinking session with Claire.

"Dr. Stanton," I reply dryly, rolling my eyes at Claire who is smiling like the Cheshire Cat.

His long, lithe body slides in next to me against the counter, leaning much closer than I'd like. "I didn't expect to see you here tonight, Ivy."

"I didn't expect to be here tonight." I wave a hand in Claire's direction. "Craig meet Claire, my date." I bring my hand back to Craig. "Claire, meet Craig."

"Nice to meet you, Claire." He smiles that charming smile that can only be the product of years of good breeding and money. "How do you know Ivy?"

Claire's smile widens, "I picked her up at Cello's tonight."

Craig's dark-blond eyebrows shoot up to his perfectly coifed hairline. "Is that so?"

I take another sip of my makeshift Manhattan, only to find that it no longer burns my throat, but instead leaves me with a nice warm buzz.

"It is." I turn to Claire with a flirtatious wink. "Evidently, I have a thing for gingers."

Claire bursts out laughing, shaking her head like I'm too much.

"But you're not gay," Craig says, still trying to play catch-up.

"Who says?"

"I say." He points to his chest encased in black cashmere. "In the months I've spent trying to get you to go out with me, you never once gave me the excuse of being gay, and I would assume that would be first on the list if it were true."

I shrug a shoulder, not feeling the need to explain myself.

"You've been trying for *months?*" Claire asks surprised, leaning into us as if we're the best form of entertainment around.

"I have," Craig says with a wry grin. "But she continuously deflects my advancements by saying she doesn't date people she works with."

"That's lame."

I throw Claire a look, and she just throws her hands up in the air with an expression that says, *sorry but it really is*.

"I agree. Especially when I know she wants me." He bounces his eyebrows playfully, his hazel eyes gleaming.

"If that were true, wouldn't I have said yes to you?" I challenge.

"Not if you don't date people from work," Claire oh-so-helpfully points out.

"Our friend Claire here has a point."

"Hi, Craig," a pretty young nurse coos as she passes us on her way back to the living room. Craig naturally offers her a seductive grin and wink.

"That," I point to where the girl just exited, "is why I won't date you."

He shrugs, unconcerned, leaning further against the marble counter in my direction. "I don't even know her name."

I laugh out, rolling my eyes at him. "So I should be flattered that you actually know mine?" I shake my head incredulously before turning to Claire. "Where's the washroom?"

Claire plays with the rim of her plastic cup, an odd gleam in her eyes.

"There are two on this floor, but the closest one is back there." She juts her thumb over her shoulder, pointing behind her toward the back of the house.

"Right," I pat her shoulder. "You two kids enjoy now."

"I'm not that easy to get rid of, Ivy," Craig calls out as I retreat.

"Neither are genital warts, Craig, but I've managed to avoid those all these years. I'm sure I can avoid you too," I smirk to myself, hearing Claire cracking up.

"I'm wounded," he calls back to me.

"You'll live."

I find the washroom in the back between the kitchen and the hall that seems to lead to the back door, but there is a line, so I meander my way back into the front of the house and locate the other restroom.

I use the toilet and wash my hands, thinking about Craig and wondering why he has been so persistent with me.

He is a consummate flirt, but his flawless surgical skills and family name have allowed him to get away with whatever he wants without consequence.

*But it didn't get him a fellowship in Boston,* I remind myself with a smile. And he's still a resident, whereas I'm finishing up my second year of my fellowship before doing a certification year in Boston.

*I* did all of that and landed myself one of the best fellowships around, UW and now one final year in Boston, which I'll be starting next month. Boston Children's Hospital, Pediatric Emergency Medicine Fellow. It has a lovely ring to it, if I do say so myself. Maybe that makes me a bit of a skite, but I really couldn't give a toss.

I reckon Craig's a bit alright in the looks department, and though I've been tempted on occasion to succumb to his wit and charm on particularly lonely days and nights, something tells me that if I did, I would be the butt of the joke and feed for the gossip hens.

I have no interest in being either, especially when I need to prove myself constantly.

I exit the washroom, and am about to return to the kitchen, when I get the sensation that someone is watching me. The hairs on the nape of my neck are standing at attention as I surreptitiously scan the room, trying for casually uninterested.

People are chatting and laughing, drinking and eating, but no one is even so much as glancing in my direction.

An odd aura of relief washes over me, though I still can't seem to shake the lingering sensation. I'm just about to give up and try and find Claire again, when the tides part, and my eyes instantly lock on a set of brown ones in a chair across the room.

And for a moment, everything stops. Everything stands stark still, and time ceases to exist before it comes racing back in full vengeful force as I realize just who this man is.

I jerk back like I've been slapped, because I find myself staring into the eyes that have haunted many a sleepless night for the last ten years.

A small gasp escapes my lips. I take another step back, my hand on my chest over my pounding heart, positive that the alcohol has rendered me deranged and I'm hallucinating.

But as I take a closer examination, staring at him the way he's unapologetically staring at me, I realize I'm not.

I know him. I don't just know him—I went to university with him. But I didn't just go to university with him; he was my first and only one-night stand.

He's sitting in a chair, not speaking to anyone, completely focused on me. Slowly, he rises with an impish grin and mischief in his dark eyes. There may be a little interest too, but there are absolutely no signs of recognition in those fathomless brown depths. And if I thought my heart was racing before, I was so very wrong. Blood thrums in my ears, and my heart is thumping out of my chest in a punishing torrent.

He looks older, as you'd expect to happen after ten years, but those years have been ridiculously good to him. He's exceptional. His tall, drool-worthy muscular frame is showcased in his blue t-shirt and dark wash jeans. Short, thick chestnut hair—the sort that begs to have a woman's fingers rake through it—is well-styled. Chiseled, cut from stone features, and rugged stubble on his jaw make him look like the ultimate cross between GQ and bad boy.

I'm ashamed to admit that I have thought about that night, this man, many times over the years, simply because it was hands-down the best sex of my life. And my memory of his face and body have not nearly done him the justice he so rightly deserves.

But it was only one night.

I like to think it was that way because life was just too real, but I doubt he would have been as interested in a repeat as I was.

He's making his way through the throngs of people, his intention clear as he watches me watch him. I want to move. I want to walk away and leave. I want to run like hell and never turn back. But I do none of those things, because I am completely and utterly paralyzed by his smoldering gaze.

Luke Walker. I can't even . . .

I don't know what to make of tonight.

I end up in a pub I've never been in—a gay one at that—meet a woman who is somehow friends with my work colleagues and my one-night stand from ten years ago.

You just can't make this up. Though I have absolutely no belief in fate, or karma, or retribution, I feel like maybe this is all three.

"I'm Luke. You must be Ivy, Claire's date," he says with a smarmy smile, finally reaching me and standing just a touch too close. His scent engulfs me, knocking me sideways with lust and I feel heat begin to rise up my cheeks. Of course, this Luke is the same man I sat next to in the dark. Of course, he's the one I practically breathed in like a mindless fool.

It was dark. It's really my only excuse.

Oh, and the alcohol too. Yeah, I can blame that as well.

Both do funny things to people. That whole cloak of anonymity mixed with lack of inhibitions makes you brave, and apparently daft.

Luke begins to chuckle, and I realize that it's because I'm

standing here staring at him, like he's the bloody ghost of Christmas past, without responding to his greeting.

"Do you always stare at people you don't know like this?"

I shift, nervously biting my lip because suddenly I feel like I don't know what to say to him. Do I tell him who I am only to feel the overwhelming embarrassment and sting of rejection when he doesn't remember me?

I have no doubt that I was not his first or his last one-nighter, so why do that to myself? I may as well bring out the pathetic flag and wave it in his face.

"No, sorry. Long night is all. I didn't mean to make you uncomfortable or anything." *Shut up, Ivy! Shut the bloody hell up!* Good god, if he wasn't uncomfortable before, he probably is now.

"You didn't," he laughs, taking a step further into my personal space, and though I can claim every bit of five feet, eight inches, my neck has to crane up to see his face. "Actually, I think I like it," he murmurs. My cheeks are flaming again, and I do my best to will it away. "You can look at me like that any time you want."

"Are you always this much of a flirt with women you don't know?" It's a dare, a blatant one, but I don't want to straight out ask him if he remembers me, so this is my not-so-subtle way of going about it.

"That depends."

"On what?"

"On if they're as beautiful as you are."

"Does that line usually work for you?"

He chuckles lightly, a heady raspy sound that makes my toes curl and my eyes desperate to roll into the back of my head. Reaching up, he brushes a strand of a hair behind my ear and I do my best not to close my eyes and lean into his touch.

"You're the first woman I've used it on, so you tell me."

"Fell completely flat," I smirk, but it's more for myself than for him because my voice is calm and steady, hiding the crazed turmoil I'm nearly overpowered with.

"I doubt that," he says knowingly. "We practically kissed in the dark earlier."

I laugh. "Was that you?"

He takes another step. So close and yet not touching. Christ, am I panting? What is wrong with me? Why am I reacting to this man like a simpering halfwit?

"That was me, Ivy. And I have to admit I did not want to be at this party tonight, but that's definitely not the case anymore." His eyes burn into mine, our bodies magnetically drawing closer. The tension between us is tangible and so very hot. Electrified. Pulsing. He feels it too. Hell, I'm sure anyone in a five-kilometer radius can feel it. "I wanted to kiss you as you sat against me in the dark. Even before I saw your gorgeous face. And you know what, Ivy?"

I shake my head, my breath lodged in my chest as his sexy, throaty voice renders me speechless.

His head dips toward mine, mere inches away, as his mouth opens to speak again, Claire catches my periphery, and I jump back, dumping the proverbial—but much-needed— bucket of ice water on my heated body.

"Ivy Pivy!" she calls out to me, dragging a tall, dark-haired man and Kate behind her.

Luke takes a very deliberate step back, as he throws Claire an annoyed scowl that goes unnoticed. He may be miffed, but I'm bloody ecstatic for the timely interruption. How on earth did I let him get to me that fast? *Again.* What was I thinking?

"Ryan . . ." A blotto Claire tosses her arm over my shoulder, her movements sloppy, and her sapphire-colored eyes glassy. "This is my date, Ivy. I picked her up at the bar," she slurs. "She's a hot one, huh? Too bad I don't bat for the vagina league."

I blush, but manage to laugh as I reach out to shake his hand.

"Hi, I'm Ivy Green."

Ryan looks almost surprised for a flash of a moment as he glances quickly at Luke before turning back to me. It was so fast I'm not even sure that's what I saw.

"Ryan Grant, nice to meet you, Ivy. Katie here tells me that you work together."

I nod, shrugging sheepishly. "We do, though I admit I crashed your party."

"Nah," he waves me away, much the way Kate did earlier. "It's really nice to put a face to the name." I furrow my eyebrows, tilting my head at him. "Claire's been going on about you all night," he supplies, but he does that thing again where he looks at Luke.

"Oh w-well," I stammer for some unknown reason. "She is my date, after all. I'd be devastated if our first go wasn't a success."

"I think it's safe to say it was," Kate says. "Are you working tomorrow?"

"I am. In fact, I should probably get going."

Kate steps forward to me with a warm, bright smile that lights up her eyes. "I'm so happy you came, Ivy. I know we just officially met, but if you're free tomorrow night, we're having a pre-wedding dinner here. I mean, it's more to go over details and things, but I'd love for you to join us."

I'm stunned by the offer, and before I can even respond, Claire tugs on my shoulder. "You totally have to come. Wedding planning is *so* boring."

Kate snorts, rolling her eyes. "Thanks, bitch."

"Yeah sorry, that was sort of rude of me, wasn't it?"

"I'm over it," Kate says. "Anyway, we'd really love for you to come, so please say yes."

"Won't I be a blow in?"

"A what?" Ryan laughs out.

I roll my eyes at myself, knowing I must be a little drunk myself. "An uninvited person."

"Oh. Right." He shakes his head. "Not at all," Ryan promises with a smile I can't read.

"Um, okay then. Thanks, sounds like good fun."

Kate knocks Claire's heavy arm from my shoulder. "Hey," Claire complains, but Kate just smirks at her drunk friend.

"How are you getting home?" Luke asks me, taking a deliberate step closer, and out of the corner of my eye, I see Claire and Kate exchange pointed looks.

"Ivy, are you leaving?" Craig asks before I can answer Luke, finding the other side of me.

"Yeah. I have a shift tomorrow."

"Great, I'm leaving too. I'll give you a lift."

I shake my head. "Not necessary, I live close."

"Then it's not out of my way. Come on," he demands, taking my hand and tugging me a bit.

"Fine," I concede with a half-smile before turning back to Claire.

"Thanks for everything tonight, mate," I pull her into my arms for a hug. "You turned a nightmare of a day into something truly special."

"Bitch, you better stop or you're going to make me ugly cry and I don't do that unless I'm drunk."

"You are drunk," I remind her.

She pulls back with a sleepy smile. "Oh, right. Then you should go, but I expect you to put out on our next date."

I laugh, shaking my head. "You got it."

Kate gives me a hug, confirming tomorrow night's dinner with me again, and I wave bye to Ryan and Luke, who's eyeing Craig with an indecipherable expression.

Craig leads me through the door, his hand on the small of my back. "You do realize that this is the first step," he says as he slides into his side, shutting the car door behind him with a click.

"First step to what?"

"You agreeing to go out with me."

"Is it the challenge? The thrill of continuously being shot down? What is it? I just don't get your persistence."

"Maybe I actually like you, Ivy. Maybe I have no other reason for asking you out other than that."

I have nothing to say to that, and we fall silent, both lost in our own thoughts.

I saw Luke Walker tonight, and he didn't remember me.

Worse yet, I'm going to see him again tomorrow and I'd be lying if I said I wasn't looking forward to it.

# Chapter Three

*Ivy*

I HADN'T GOTTEN much sleep before my shift, and it had nothing to do with the amount of alcohol I consumed, or the fact that Craig insisted on walking me to my door before kissing my cheek good-night. It had nothing to do with the fact that I lost a patient yesterday or that I met a new set of friends a month before I'm scheduled to leave Seattle.

The only thing—or should I say only person—that was occupying my thoughts last night was Luke.

It's been ten years since I've seen him, but I knew him instantly.

His face is forever burned into my memory, along with every other detail of that night.

He's someone I never thought I'd see again, and the fact that he didn't even recognize me—even after hearing my name and seeing my face—hurts.

It hurts because I knew him without having to be introduced. It hurts because that night clearly meant so much more to me than it ever did to him. It hurts because no one likes to be forgotten, especially by a man who was inside your body and looks like Luke. There, I said it.

I know, I know, it was a decade and a lifetime ago in a different state, but still.

Which is why I'm anxious as I ring Kate's doorbell. He's going to be here, and I'll have to face him again, and that really shouldn't be something I want. But it is. Christ, that man had my knickers twisted around his finger within five seconds last night.

The door swings open with a flourish, and Ryan Grant is standing on the other side with a big smile and a tilt of his head. "I hope you like Italian," he says by way of a greeting.

"I do."

"Excellent, then you may enter."

He steps back, waving me in, and as I cross the threshold into the house, my eyes are quietly searching around, but all the noise is coming from the kitchen in the back of the house, so I can't see who's here.

"What if I didn't fancy Italian?" I ask as he takes my coat and hangs it up in the closet next to the door.

"Then I'm sorry to say that I would have had to send you packing. Katie worked all day and there was no way I was going to let her cook for everyone so I ordered in. That," he grins, "is my specialty."

"We all need to have one, Ryan, and the fact that you were caring for your fiancée while performing said specialty makes it all the more impressive."

"Then my work here is done." He nods his head in the direction of the kitchen. "Follow me, Doctor. I'm glad you could make it. Claire hasn't shut up about you. If we were in high school, it would almost be endearing."

I laugh, shaking my head. "Am I the last to arrive? Sorry if I'm late."

"Nah, you're fine. Luke just got here." I get a smirk for that, and I'm not quite sure what it means. It's the sort of smirk that says, *I'm in on the joke,* but all that does is make me feel like I'm on the outside of it.

Everyone is crowded around the large center island, and as Ryan and I enter, three sets of eyes glance up at once. "Ivy Pivy," Claire says exuberantly, standing up and throwing her arms around me. "What's shakin' with your bacon?"

"I can't believe you're still standing. I would have thought for sure that you would be nursing the hangover of your life," I say, grinning widely.

"Nope. Kate makes me drink a shit ton of water whenever I commence the consumption of the alcoholic beverages, so it wasn't anything that Motrin and an egg sandwich couldn't cure."

"The consumption of the alcoholic beverages?" Ryan asks, looking at Claire as if her words don't make any sense.

"Yup. That's what I said, boss."

All he can do is stare at her. "Maybe next time you won't get plastered to the point where I have to practically carry you home," Ryan says with absolutely no edge to his tone.

Claire rolls her eyes at him dramatically. "Whatever, Luke was just as roughed up as I was by the end of the night as he brooded in the corner in silence."

My eyes reluctantly make the journey over to his, a place I've avoided since entering the kitchen. He shrugs a shoulder, not bothering to deny it. He didn't seem drunk when he and I spoke, though maybe he's good at hiding it. And the thought that he only approached me because he was drunk makes my chest clench in a horribly uncomfortable way.

"The food should be here soon. Thank you for coming Ivy," Kate says. "Our little foursome needed an addition."

I smile, not really knowing what to say to that. "Claire mentioned that you're getting married in a couple of months?"

"Yup, and lucky for you, we covered most of the boring wedding details before you got here."

"Nothing boring about wedding details," I say, nodding my thanks to Ryan who hands me a glass of red wine.

"That's where you're wrong," Claire says. "Especially when I've been dying to find out what happened when Craig Stanton drove you home. That man is epically hot."

It feels like all eyes are on me, which is a bit unnerving. "He drove me home."

"That's it?" Kate asks incredulously.

"That's it." I take a sip of my wine, trying to deflect the penetrating stares burning a hole into me.

Claire groans. "Boring, Ivy. At least tell me you agreed to a date with him. He's way into you. After you ditched me in the kitchen with him last night, he told me that he's had his eye on you since your first year of residency, but that you were really quiet and guarded, so he held off on asking you out."

I blush furiously, looking down at the marble counter.

"He said that?" Kate asks. "Holy shit. I would never have pegged Craig Stanton as a romantic."

"I can't believe he said that," I whisper, a bit bewildered myself. "That just doesn't seem like him."

"Right?" Kate agrees with a snort. "I wouldn't fall for it, Ivy. That man goes through nurses faster than he does sterile gloves."

"Oh, she's not," Claire says with authority. "She told him she doesn't date coworkers. Is that true, or is that just a way of fighting him off?"

"It's true."

"Why not?" Kate questions like I'm crazy. "You work with so many attractive, eligible doctors."

"Should I be worried about these attractive, eligible doctors?" Ryan asks Kate, kissing the top of her head.

"Obviously not." She holds up her ringed finger at him. "But I don't see why Ivy doesn't go for it."

This is not something I want to discuss with people I hardly know, but going by the overly curious expressions I'm surrounded with, it doesn't seem like they're about to let it go. "I had a bad experience once when I was in medical school."

"What happened?" Luke asks. His voice startles me because it's the first time I've heard him speak since I got here.

My finger traces a pattern in the marble, my eyes unfocused as I stare down. "I was dating a fellow student, and in our last year of school he was . . . getting too serious, and I ended it after a rather large fight we had. He didn't take that well, and things turned a bit ugly, which affected our work at the hospital."

Everyone is silent for a moment, and then Kate gasps. "You're that Ivy?"

My eyes fly up to hers, my brows furrowed. Kate is relatively new at our hospital and was not working there when everything with Jason occurred. That, and it was a long time ago, so I can't imagine it's still the stuff of idle gossip.

"Melinda Crane talked about it once," she explains, and I freeze. Melinda is a nurse who was very much there and even witnessed one of the incidents. "I can't believe that was you."

"She told you about that?"

Kate nods, her expression full of sympathy. "She did. Most of the nurses know about it." I'm bright red; I can't feel it.

"I didn't realize that." I bring my glass up to my mouth, taking a long pull of the crimson liquid, wanting to drown in it.

"Okay, someone better clue me in because I'm dying here," Claire says, exasperated, leaning against the counter, her eyes volleying back and forth between Kate and me.

Kate mouths the word *sorry* to me, and once again, it feels like everyone is watching me.

*Shouldn't the bloody food be here already?*

"It's not as scandalous as it sounds. He just had trouble letting go and made a show of it in the ED, as well as a few other places. Lots of screaming and baseless accusations."

"That's it?" Claire asks Kate who's staring at me.

I shrug. "Things eventually progressed to the point where he stalked me nearly everywhere I went, then he ran me off the road in my car, so I got a restraining order. That seemed to wake him up, and things resolved after that."

"Holy shit," Ryan gasps. "Are you kidding me?"

I take another sip of my wine instead of answering him.

"Jesus," Luke mutters, slamming his fist quietly against the marble. "Where is he now?"

I see Ryan and Luke exchange glances, having some sort of unspoken conversation the way only very close friends can do.

"I didn't track him after he graduated, but he's not in Seattle or Washington State, and that's enough for me." I take a large deep breath.

"Fuckity fuck," Claire says. "That's some looney tunes shit. And I thought Ryan was a crazy stalker for sending Kate those asinine texts every day after she left his sorry ass."

"Such a brat, Claire," Ryan teases while Kate reaches across him to smack her arm.

"I thought they were sweet," Kate adds, reaching up on her toes to kiss his chin. She is so much shorter than him it's almost comical.

"You work for him, right?" I ask pointing between Ryan and Claire.

"Yup," Claire elbows him in the side. "That's the boss."

"And you speak to each other like that? Are you related?"

They both look at each other in horror. "Never," Ryan says. "Claire is the insubordinate pain in the ass I've been stuck with all these years."

"Shove it, Ryan, you'd be lost without me."

The doorbell rings, putting paid to our conversation that still feels strained after my little confession. I don't like talking about Jason, and it bothers me that it's still gossiped about in the hospital. I thought it would have died away over the years, but apparently, a story is still a story.

We fill our plates in the kitchen and sit at the dining room table, our conversation straying away from me as they regale me with stories of how Kate and Ryan met, and a road trip they journeyed on across the country.

Luke has been on the quiet side all night, commenting here and there but not contributing all that much, though every time I look in his direction, his eyes are on me. And when I'm not looking at him, I feel him watching me.

When everyone is finished with their meal, I stand up, grabbing plates and shooing Kate and Claire away when they try to help me clean up. Setting the dishes down on the counter next to the sink, I feel a warm hand touch the small of my back.

"Are you working tomorrow?" Luke asks softly, standing next to me, leaning against the counter as I turn on the water to wash the dishes.

"I've got an early shift tomorrow," I lie.

I'm not working for the next two days straight.

He nods slowly, his arm brushing mine as he helps me load up the dishwasher. We're silent as we clean up, rinsing and washing, before I hand him each dish to be placed in the dishwasher. But he continues to touch me in small ways that I feel throughout my entire body. His hand grazing mine, his hip, his arm—anywhere he can touch, he does.

I'm so acutely aware of his proximity that I nearly drop a plate twice.

Any chemistry? Holy hell do we have that in spades.

I had hoped last night, and ten years ago for that matter, were alcohol-induced episodes, but I was one hundred percent wrong. Two glasses of wine cannot arouse this type of fire inside me. He's everywhere, and I can't help but buzz and hum with nervous energy when I'm in his far-too-sexy presence.

I hand him the final plate, and once he's loaded it, he turns into me, nearly pinning me against the counter. My breath catches, and my heart begins to pound.

He takes my hand, his eyes focused on mine as his fingertips trace up my palm until they reach my wrist. It's such a small action, but it's so very intimate, and I feel that featherlight touch as if it's a bolt of lightning.

His fingers track back and forth against the sensitive skin of my wrist, and I'm having a rough go of concentrating on anything else. Right, that's sort of a lie, his face is pretty captivating as well. Those fingers continue their path up my inner arm, sliding the fabric of my sweater with them and leaving a trail of chills in their wake.

Luke leans in, his eyes holding mine. Just as I think he's about to kiss me, his nose brushes my cheek and goes directly to the spot just beneath my ear where he inhales deeply.

*Oh my god.*

My knees weaken, and I have absolutely no idea how I'm managing to hold myself upright.

I also have no idea why I'm letting him touch me like this. I'm having some sort of out-of-body experience, or temporary insanity, that only this man is capable of conjuring.

*Deep breaths now, Ivy. Deep breaths.*

Yeah, that's not helping since all I can smell is him.

"What kind of doctor are you, Ivy?" he whispers in my ear.

I love the way he says my name. Want to bathe in it before I cuddle it in bed.

"Pediatric emergency medicine," I swallow, my voice oh so very affected.

He pulls back, smiling big, an alluring dimple denting his left cheek.

"Then I guess I can't argue with you about working tomorrow." He smiles lopsidedly. "Too bad, I was readying my case to get you to play hooky. I was hoping to convince you to have lunch with me."

"I guess you'll have to ask someone else." The words taste like acid in my mouth. I have no idea why I'm reacting to him like this.

He shakes his head, his mouth hovering just a few inches from mine. "No, I think you're the only woman I'll be asking out anytime soon."

Who says things like that to someone they've barely spoken to?

Luke Walker, that's who.

It's how he managed to get me into bed the first time a decade ago. His mouth is like my own personal form of kryptonite. If I don't leave now, I will not only be in trouble, but I'll regret it.

"I should go," I whisper. *Why am I whispering?*

"How are you getting home, Ivy?"

Would it be weird if I asked him to stop saying my name? There really is only so much a woman can handle before she's no longer responsible for her actions, and I'm clearly approaching my limit.

"I don't live far. Just a few blocks away."

"Are you walking?" God, he's so close. So very close that if I closed my eyes and leaned up just the smallest amount, our lips would touch.

I swallow, my mouth suddenly so dry as his lips linger just above mine.

I'm surrounded. His smell, the warmth of his breath, the magical fingers dancing on my forearm, his proximity, it's all too much.

"Yes." I take a small step back, but all that manages to do is cause my bottom to hit the counter behind me. I need fresh air that doesn't taste like him to clear my muddled, alcohol-laden, sex-deprived brain.

He shakes his head, dismayed. "Ivy." He rights himself, creating the space I'm desperate for, our intimate moment gone "You can't walk alone in the dark. This is Seattle. It's just not safe," he chastises me like I haven't lived here since university and am perfectly aware of the risks a young woman can encounter when walking alone.

"I'll be fine."

"No. I'll walk you."

I shake my head. "You *really* don't have to. I live right close."

"Then it *really* won't be a hardship for me. Come on." He takes my hand in a firm grip, leading me back out to the dining room where Kate, Ryan, and Claire are still chatting away, contentedly oblivious.

We say our goodbyes to everyone, and more than one look is thrown around when Luke announces that he's walking me home. I try to refuse him again, but that gets me nowhere.

I need to get away from him.

Nothing good will come of us spending time together.

# Chapter Four

*Ivy*

I MAKE it to the bottom step before I hear the door open and shut behind me, forcing a frustrated sigh to escape my lips.

I don't know if I'm elated or irked that he's walking me home. Attraction clearly isn't our issue here. But I'm leaving in a month, and the things I feel when I'm around him are dangerous. They're enticing and seductive, and I'm so unbelievably drawn to him, though we've hardly even spoken.

Like I said, dangerous.

So do I want him walking me home?

On the one hand, it's chivalrous and kind, and I love the fact that he wants me to be safe on my short jaunt home. On the other hand, he turns my stomach into knots and swarming insects, and though it's idiotic and petulant of me, I'm still hurt he doesn't remember me.

"Wait up, Ivy, I told you I wanted to walk you home."

I groan, crossing my arms over my chest before turning to glare at him.

He gives me an odd look I can't decipher, and I realize my hang-ups are my own. I'm behaving like a scorned lover instead of a new acquaintance.

"Sorry, it was just a long, very hard day, and I'm knackered."

"So, it's not me then? You practically running out of the house without me? Because I don't think my ego could take it if it is." He smirks at me as we start to walk on the mostly deserted street.

For a Saturday night in the middle of the city, this street is fairly quiet, which indicates this is likely a family neighborhood. Judging by the size of the houses and the attached lots, I'd say it is.

"Something tells me your ego will be just fine. Might even be beneficial for it to be knocked down a peg or two."

"Ouch," Luke grabs his chest like I shot him. "You wound me, Ivy. Deeply."

I smile over at him, and he moves closer to my side, taking my hand and looping it through the crook of his arm, like we're lovers or the oldest and best of friends.

We're not either, but I don't want to pull away from his warmth all the same.

"Tell me why it was such a hard day for you."

"It just was. Some are worse than others; some are better. Today was one of the more challenging ones, but hopefully, tomorrow won't be."

"Are you always this positive?"

I laugh, shaking my head and looking up at him. "No. Hardly ever." I think on that for a minute. "Let me amend that. Yes, when it comes to my patients and my work. Never when it comes to myself."

"Why is that?"

I shrug, realizing I just revealed far too much of myself to a man that I'm sure after tonight, I won't see again for a long time, if ever.

I am leaving in a month after all.

"What do you do for work?" I ask, changing the subject away from myself.

Luke and I both went to Caltech, though I didn't meet him until our junior year. It was at a pub close to campus, and I was there with a few mates of mine. Luke was alone, sitting at the bar with his head in his hands, and something about him drew me in instantly. I sat down next to him, bought him another round without even speaking to him and got up to leave once our drinks were placed in front of us.

He stopped me, and we ended up talking for the rest of the evening before going home together.

He never explained to me what had him drinking with the most somber expression I'd ever seen on anyone.

I didn't question him either.

But after we had sex for hours—and I do mean hours—we spent the rest of the night talking. Not about our majors, or what we envisioned doing after graduation, or our families. It was the type of conversation you have with a partner or someone you know exceptionally well.

It was about everything and nothing all at once.

It was without a doubt the best night of my life and when I woke up after finally passing out in the wee hours of the morning, he was gone.

He didn't even leave me a note or his number. Nothing. Just gone like he was never there to begin with.

My mate told me a few days later that he had been arrested by the FBI for hacking a bank and had been out on bail the night he and I met. That and his girlfriend had dumped him shortly after the arrest.

So I understood why he ran out, but that didn't mean that I wasn't bothered by it.

A simple explanation or verbal rejection would have been better than waking up to an empty bed after the night we shared. I didn't keep track of the case, though it had been gossiped about by almost everyone on campus.

And I never tried to find him again.

But I always remembered him.

"I work in computers," Luke says after a contemplative beat.

We stand at the edge of the sidewalk, waiting for the light to change so we can cross. The yellow of the street lights creating an eerie halo of light against the fog.

"Ryan and I run an IT security company," he amends. I knew he worked with Ryan, though I figured it was *for* him. I didn't realize he ran the company *with* him.

I turn and smile, somehow relieved that he came out on the other side of the mess he was in.

"That sounds like it keeps you busy."

"It does, but in a good way." I nod, understanding just what that means.

It's how I feel about my work.

He steps into me, his fingers brushing the fog-dampened strands of my hair from my face.

"You have the most beautiful eyes. Has anyone ever told you that?"

*Yes, you,* I want to say, but don't.

"The color of a glacier or an angry ocean. Not quite blue and not quite gray." He's also said that to me before.

I yank my face from his grasp and cross the street without waiting on him to follow or for the light to change.

How can he say these things, know my name, and not remember me?

I hate how disappointed I am. Evidently, he made a much larger impact on me than I ever did on him.

He catches up to me before I reach the other side.

"What did I say? I think you're beautiful. Usually women don't run from me when I tell them that."

"I just want to get home, Luke. It's late and I'm tired. I have to be up before the sun rises, if it even decides to do that tomorrow."

I quicken my pace, able to see my building just up ahead.

"I see my building, so you can go. I'm fine." My words come out as quickly as my footfalls. "Thank you for walking me. It was nice of you."

"Nice of me?" he asks with an incredulous laugh. "Ivy, I am many things, but nice really isn't one of them."

"Point made."

And it is. I get it.

"Have a good night, Luke."

"Ivy, hold up." He reaches out, grasping my forearm and pulling me to a stop as he spins me around to face him. "Why the hell are you running from me?" He looks wounded and bewildered.

And so am I. What am I expecting anyway?

Say he does remember me? It's not like anything can happen between us.

I have one month left on this fellowship, and then I'm finishing up my training all the way across the country.

I sigh out, feeling so utterly foolish. "I'm not running from you."

He raises an eyebrow.

"Okay, maybe I was running from you. I'm sorry. I'm…" *What am I?* "Totally buggered." *Bollocks, I didn't mean to say that out loud.*

He laughs. The sound is deep and resounding and has my face heating instantly.

*What is wrong with me tonight?*

"Ivy, darlin', you're many things, but you're not totally buggered. At least not yet, and something tells me I won't get my shot with that tonight."

Jesus, this guy.

"You can't be serious right now?"

His hands snake around my waist, pulling me into his hard warm chest, clad in thick black leather.

"What if I am serious? What if I say I want you right now? Would that change things?"

I shake my head emphatically, but I'm really saying no to myself.

"Nothing good can come of that. You don't know me, and I don't know you, and this is not happening."

*Again.*

"But you want me, and I really want you."

"Right, so I can wake up tomorrow with you gone?" I can't believe I just said that out loud.

His expression falls, a frown marring his gorgeous face.

"That's not how it would go."

"Right. Yeah. Sure."

"Okay, Ivy. I'll let it go for tonight, but only because I really

32

want to walk you home. I don't mean to come off like a total asshole. Believe it or not, I'm not usually like this."

I find myself smirking up at him. "A *total* asshole? Not so sure I believe that, Luke, but what the hell, right?"

"You took me by surprise. I was not expecting you, but something about you draws me in the way no one has in a very long time."

His gaze turns soft, and for a moment, I'm completely swept away with the promise in those eyes. There's nothing dirty, heated, or sinister in them. They're warm and enticing and so bloody sincere that I'm finding it hard to look away, let alone breathe.

"If I ask you something, will you consider it?"

"Possibly."

"Do you want to hang out with me tomorrow, since you're not working like you said you were?"

How on earth does he know I'm not working? Honestly?

"Don't play coy with me, darlin', I can spot bullshit a mile out, and you're a terrible liar at best. So how about it? Tomorrow?"

I sigh, wondering about the wisdom of this. I'm also oddly tempted.

I'm curious about who this man is and what ten years have done to him. It always felt like I had unfinished business with him. Maybe I can discern some form of closure from one afternoon with him.

"I'm leaving in a month."

"Where are you going?"

"I'm moving to Boston for a year to finish my fellowship certification."

He grins at that. "That's awesome. The fellowship part, not the moving part. Are you coming back after your year?"

I shrug. "I have no idea. It depends on where the job is."

"Okay, Ivy. I get it."

Luke brings my body even closer to his until I'm completely flush against him, chest to chest. And I'm doing absolutely nothing to push him away.

"How's this then?" He smiles like he just had the most brilliant idea. "You hang out with me tomorrow even though you're leaving.

We can be friends, because I really want to spend more time with you. I want to get to know you despite our time constraints, and maybe, just maybe, I can even talk you into some hot casual sex with no strings attached. What do you say?"

A stuttered laugh passes my lips.

Why is that also so oddly enticing?

Never in my life have I chosen sex with no strings.

I've always been austere, focused, and career-minded, but the thought of some casual fun—knowing it couldn't lead anywhere— might just be exactly what I need.

And then I wake up, because that is the biggest load of rubbish I've ever heard.

"You know there is no such thing as hot, casual, no-strings- attached sex, right?"

"Who says? It's absolutely possible."

"Oh yeah? Did the magical fairy who told you that also tell you that processed foods are healthy, smoking won't kill you, and the pull out method is an approved form of birth control?"

He just blinks at me with that cocky, charming smile of his. Damn that dimple.

"You might as well tell me that chocolate has no calories. It's tempting, and I'd love to believe it, but it's just not true. Those things never end well. I really don't even see the point in us spending time together."

His expression falters, but only for a beat before that confidence is back in full megawatt force.

"You're telling me you're leaving in a month, so the option of something other than casual isn't there." Luke's hands cup my cheeks as our gazes lock. "If you were staying, Ivy, something tells me I would be trying a completely different tactic right now. Some- thing tells me I'd be taking you out on a real date and I *wouldn't* be trying to get in your panties on that date either. But I don't seem to have the luxury of time with you, so I'm going to take whatever I can get. So...," he pauses, letting his words marinate in the small distance between us. "I'd like to hang out with you tomorrow. As friends. You in?"

I want this too much to say no, even though I know beyond a shadow of a doubt that this will not end well for me.

"Yes."

Luke smiles so big his entire face lights up. His head dips, and for a moment, my breath catches in anticipation, but his lips press against my cheek and not my lips. Judging by the bereft tingles on my lips, I won't last long as friends.

"You'll never be able to resist me," he says. Clearly, he's telepathic. "And there is no way I can resist you."

"We'll see about that one. Maybe you're right, and maybe you're wrong, but I'm not as experienced at walking away without a wound as you are."

He shakes his head like I've got it all wrong, but I'm really not in the mood to challenge that at the moment.

"You have no idea," he says before releasing my face and taking my hand to lead me the rest of the way home. We pause at the foot of the stairs of my building. He leans down and whispers in my ear, "Or maybe you do. But what you think you know is all wrong, Ivy. That's not how it happened. I never wanted to leave you that night."

I suck in a rush of air as he plants yet another kiss on my cheek. My mouth is partially agape as he rights himself with a huge, knowing grin, his dimple out in full force.

"It was nice seeing you again, Ivy. I'll be here early tomorrow, so get some sleep pretty girl."

And with that, he walks off into the night, swallowed up by the fog almost instantly.

I'll be damned; maybe he does remember me. This thing brewing between us is trouble. I can feel it.

# Chapter Five

*Luke*

10 YEARS *ago*

TOSSING BACK the last of my whiskey, I slide the empty glass away and drop my head into my hands. I can't afford another and that was the cheapest shit they had. The last of my savings just went down my throat, and before that, to pay my bail because no way I was staying in prison another night. But now that means I'm stuck with whatever third-grader the courts decide to stick me with for an attorney.

Not that I would have been able to afford a decent one anyway.

I'm fucked.

Good and fucked. I have absolutely no one to blame but myself.

To add insult to injury, Ronnie was waiting for me when I got home so she could break up with me. Apparently, having a boyfriend who's facing federal charges is too much for her. She didn't seem bothered by my hacking before, but getting caught was her limit.

It's probably for the best anyway, since I'm facing real prison time with no money and no hope.

The bartender slides a drink in front of my downcast face, and as I look up at him, about to tell him that I can't pay for this, he holds up his hands in surrender as if to say it wasn't his idea before jutting his thumb to my left with a smirk.

*What the hell? Did someone just buy me a drink?*

Out of the corner of my eye, I see a flash of light-brown hair and something silver and shiny fleeing.

Instinctually, I reach out to grab her arm and stop her.

Usually, if a girl buys you a drink, they don't do it anonymously. They want you to know it was them. They expect attention and long for other things, but this girl is trying to run before I can even thank her, and that raises my curiosity.

My fingers wrap around her slender forearm, and she's so startled by my touch that she almost drops her drink.

"My bad," I offer by way of an apology as she licks some of the spilled cocktail from her fingers. She hasn't acknowledged me yet, so I'm only getting a half a profile here, but what I can see, I like.

She's tall and slender and her luscious curves are perfectly showcased in the short, silver dress she's wearing. Her hair is long and very straight but looks unbelievably soft and shiny.

This is not the nicest or the trendiest bar in Pasadena, so the fact that she's dressed for a night out in Vegas is amusing.

Finally, almost reluctantly, she moves to face me, probably because I'm still holding her by the arm. But when her eyes meet mine, my goddamn breath catches in my chest. They're the most incredible color. Not quite blue and not quite gray. Like a glacier or an angry ocean, and just as fathomless.

They're the kind of eyes you can't help but stare at. Because of that, it takes me a second or two longer before I get to the rest of her. Her beauty is unmistakable. Impossible to ignore. She possesses a face and body that women envy and men long to claim. She's unwittingly the most erotic combination of innocence and mischief

I've ever seen. Her wine stained lips alone are enough to fill my mind with a myriad of salacious fantasies.

"Did you buy this for me?" I ask, gesturing toward my full glass of amber liquid.

She hesitates again, debating how forthcoming she wants to be with me.

"I, uh . . ." She shrugs. "You looked like you could go for another." Her slight Australian accent is enticing. Just like her. No way in hell am I letting this girl walk away without knowing her name.

Which is unbelievably stupid because I'm going to prison.

Right. I should just let her walk away.

But if this really is one of my last nights of freedom then why not spend it with her?

Selfish? You bet, but I can't seem to muster enough altruism to care at the moment.

"That's really sweet of you." I give her my most charming smile, knowing my dimple will seal the deal. Girls love the dimple. "But why are you running off?"

Her head swivels back into the packed bar, and she points over to somewhere I have no intention of looking.

"I'm here with some mates of mine. I didn't want to interrupt. You looked like you were keen to be alone, but needed a fresh drink to keep you company."

I may, in fact, be in love.

I mean, who the hell does that?

Buys a drink for a stranger without expecting anything in return, just because I look like I could use one?

"I wouldn't mind some company as long as that company is you."

She laughs at my cliché line and shrugs, "Maybe just this one."

"Your friends won't miss you?"

"They'll manage." She leans into me, a smirk playing on her deep-crimson lips. "We're celebrating my birthday."

I motion for her to sit down in the open seat next to mine and she does, crossing her long legs and rubbing her calves together once as if it's a habit of hers.

"Turning twenty-one then?"

She shakes her head with a wink, before bringing her mouth to my ear.

"I'm really only nineteen, but you won't tell, will you?"

I can feel just how big I'm smiling. It's the first genuine one since Tuesday and today is Friday.

"Promise. Your secret is safe with me . . ."

"Ivy Green." She shakes my hand, and I almost want to laugh at just how adorable that is.

"Is that meant to be ironic?" Her brows furrow for a moment before she rolls her eyes. "Because Ivy *is* green."

"Yes, you're a bloody brilliant one, aren't you? I've never heard that before," she says sarcastically, widening her eyes as she waits for my name, which really isn't much better.

"Luke Walker."

And then she bursts into laugher. "Really? Is your middle name Sky?"

"I've never heard that one before, either."

She shakes her head taking a sip of her drink, which looks to be a Manhattan.

"So, we're both unfortunate in the name department."

"Looks that way." I scroll down to her perfect legs that are minimally covered by the short dress and then back up because I really can't stay away from those eyes for all that long. "Happy birthday, Ivy Green."

"Thanks, Luke Walker." She holds her glass up to mine, before we each take a long sip, eyes locked as we do.

"So I take it you're a transfer. What made you come here for school?"

She shrugs. "I'm not really. I've been living in the states since I was thirteen or so. California is similar in climate to Australia—at least this part of it anyway—and my older sister Sophia lives here. Seemed like a good place."

"Freshman or sophomore?"

"Junior."

"Beautiful and brilliant."

She scoffs. "Hardly. Besides, isn't everyone who goes to this school brilliant?"

"Nope. Smart is a decent bet, but I wouldn't go so far as to say brilliant."

She leans into me again, her fingers touching the back of my chair. I wouldn't have pegged her as the forward type, but she is, and I like it. I like it a lot.

"Which one are you then?" Her eyes sparkle, and I find myself leaning in to them.

"Me? I'm as stupid as they come."

She laughs again, and it's the sweetest sound, almost melodic.

I wasn't lying, though. I really am stupid. And arrogant. The epitome of hubris for thinking I was untouchable.

"That's a shame." Ivy shakes her head slowly, only about a foot away from my face. "I don't tend to like stupid blokes. You're lucky I think you're cute; otherwise, I'd go back to my mates."

"*Cute?* That's it?"

She shrugs a shoulder. "Are you a decent dancer?"

"Hell yeah. I'm an awesome dancer."

"Well, if you prove that to me, then you may be elevated to handsome. No promises, though."

"You want to dance with me?" I point to my chest.

"I thought you'd never ask." She winks, tossing down the last of her drink, and I do the same, because there is no way on earth I am not taking this girl into my arms on that makeshift, tiny, pathetic excuse for a dance floor.

"Lead the way, gorgeous." I take her hand, appreciating the warm soft skin against mine and allow her to walk ahead of me so I can watch her flawless ass, because that's just the sort of chauvinist I am.

Once we reach the edge of the dance floor, she turns into me. Tall in her heels, she doesn't have far to go to meet my eyes. Dragging my hands around her waist, I pull her into me, not bothering with gentlemanly pretenses. Ivy doesn't resist as her hands snake around my neck, her fingers finding the back of my hair that is too short for her to twist her fingers into.

We start to move and sway to the music.

It's not a slow song. It's not exactly fast either, but the way we're dancing and holding and grinding is not even close to being in sync with the beat. I don't care, and she doesn't appear to either.

My nose glides down the top of her head into the crook between her shoulder and neck, which just so happens to be one of my favorite spots on a woman.

She smells incredible.

Like vanilla and cinnamon. Like a cookie I would love to devour.

She feels so absolutely glorious in my arms and against my body.

I can't stop myself from placing an open-mouth kiss in that spot, and I hear her breath hitch, and so I wait for the impending stop sign. But she doesn't raise it. She's into this. Into me. And I plan to ride this train as far as it will go.

"You have the most beautiful eyes," I whisper into her ear, enjoying the way her body shivers against me. "They're like glaciers."

"And I'm a sucker for dimples, and though you only have one, I guess I'll count that."

I'm completely and utterly mesmerized by this enticing creature in a way that I have never been before with anyone. *And I only just met her.*

I pull back, cupping her jaw in my hand, our faces so close that our breaths mingle.

"What can I do to make you more sure of me?"

She blinks at me, a small smile curling up the corner of her lips. "I'm sure you can think of something to sway me."

Without thinking of the consequences, I lower my mouth to hers, just for a taste.

I tell myself that it will just be once, and then I'll stop.

But the moment my lips touch hers, I'm a goner.

There's no going back. I have to have more. I *need* to have more. Her lips are soft and malleable and fucking delicious. Like nothing I've ever experienced or tasted before, and suddenly, I'm ravenous for this girl.

Ivy opens for me without my asking, and with that one swipe of her tongue, all reason escapes me.

I've never had a woman kiss me like this. So openly. So possessively. It's like she's offering me a piece of herself in this exchange, and it's heady. A soft moan passes her lips, reverberating into me.

"Ivy," I whisper against her and she smiles against me.

I've seen her around campus before, though we never had any classes together. I noticed her from afar. Also, I dated Ronnie for the last year.

But I did notice Ivy.

She's impossible to miss. And I'm kicking myself for not having made the effort to speak to her before, because I can already tell that one kiss, one night, won't be enough.

I've never hated myself more than I do in this very moment. I've officially blown all chances with this girl before we've even begun.

"Okay." She licks her lips as she draws back with heavy-lidded eyes. "I think you're officially hot. Way past handsome."

I chuckle, dropping my forehead to hers. Her stripper heels make her only a couple of inches shorter than me.

This is it. My one and only chance with her.

Do I take the high and noble road and let her go, or do I do the selfish asshole thing and try to take her home? Decisions, decisions.

She solves my dilemma for me.

"Do you want to get out of here? Have a drink at my flat?"

My eyes shut, breathing in her scent and feeling her warmth against me.

It's the purest form of heaven I've ever known, and I don't know how to say no.

But I have to try.

"I do, Ivy. I really do. You have no idea how much I want you."

She smiles. I can't see it because my eyes are still shut, but I can feel it.

"I'm the wrong guy for you, though. I lead to nothing good."

She shakes her head against mine.

"The wrong guy wouldn't even have given me the warning.

You're a good guy, Luke; you just might be a bit confused with how to go about it."

"Maybe," I sigh. "I like to think I'm not as horrible as it feels I am."

Her fingers run up my jaw until her palms are flat against my face, and another sigh escapes my lips, this one involuntary.

"You feel it too, don't you?"

I don't have to ask her what she's talking about. I felt it the moment I grabbed her wrist to stop her from leaving. I felt it the moment I saw her hair fly by my face, and before that when I noticed her walking across campus. She's different, and we could be something different together. Something astounding. Something you encounter once in a lifetime, if that.

It's been five minutes, and I can already tell that.

But I'm going to prison, and she's going to graduate.

I'm headed in the wrong direction, and she's headed in the right direction.

Life is sort of messed up like that.

"Take me home, Luke. I've never done this before, and it's certainly not my style, but I think I want to break all the rules with you tonight."

"Lead the way, Ivy. Who knows, maybe we can make our own."

And just for once, I can pretend like everything will turn out okay. Even when I know it won't.

# Chapter Six

*Luke*

IVY GREEN. Are you kidding me?

It's that old Humphrey Bogart line, right? *Of all the gin joints, in all the towns, in all the world.*

Yeah, she walked into mine. Twice.

I'm sitting on a bench across the street from Ivy's apartment building. I'm a goddamn creeper. I know I am. But in my defense, I've only ever done this with her. And I did, in fact, tell her I'd be back early.

I stayed up all night, thinking about what she said and what I said and her situation and my situation and everything else I could have possibly thought about.

It was a lot to go through and as I sit here in the early morning, I'm exhausted, and I have one hell of a headache. But I don't want to go home. Not yet anyway.

I want to talk to her just one more time. Spend the day with her if I can. I can't explain what it is about her that I find impossible to turn away from.

Not a good thing, considering she's leaving in a month.

I get that it's fast, but it doesn't feel that way. It feels like a long time coming, and until I see her some more, I can't let go.

So I pull out my phone, open the message window, and send a text. Yeah, I might have stolen her number from Claire. Stop judging!

Me: *Good morning, sunshine.*

I get the message bubble almost instantly.

Ivy: *What? Who is this?*

Me: *Luke. Who else would text you that? You looked really pretty last night. I think I forgot to mention that.*

Ivy: *What are you, six? Who says really pretty? And who texts at this hour?*

The fact that she's texting me back has me smiling like an asshole.

Me: *You're right, but if I said you looked hot in that shirt you wore and that I was dying to strip you out of those jeans, I'd get sued for sexual harassment or something, and I make it a point never to get sued.*

Ivy: *Probably wasn't too brilliant on your part to have typed that to me then. You know, incriminating evidence and all.*

I might in fact love this girl. Seriously. She's fucking awesome. Maybe I am six. Who calls a woman awesome?

Me: *If you read that more carefully, you will see that I used the word IF. You'll note that at no point did I specifically say that I was thinking those things in reference to you. It was more of a general statement.*

Ivy: *Semantics, Luke. Purely semantics.*

Me: *Does this mean it's too late for me to offer up friendship? You know, so I can avoid that harassment suit?*

Ivy: *I suppose I'm willing to hold off on legal action for now, and maybe friends is an acceptable alternative. Not so sure on that yet, seems like it won't work. But you should be aware that my lawyer has already been notified should the harassment persist.*

Now I decide to call her because I feel like it's super sketchy to text that I'm outside her apartment. Some things have to be heard and not read. Especially after what she told us about that fuckwad of an ex last night.

"Why are you ringing me, Luke? It's bloody seven in the morning on one of my very few days off. You said early, but the rules of common courtesy say after nine is an acceptable hour to ring."

"I've never been particularly adept at following rules or being told what to do—and I'm definitely not courteous. No sense in changing that now. Was your accent always this sexy? I think I'd like to hear that accent in my ear every night and morning."

"I'm sorry?" she asks. She sounds confused, and rightfully so. "Have you been drinking?"

I can't help but laugh my ass off at that because no, I haven't been drinking. Not since last night at dinner.

"No, Ivy. I'm merely proposing we spend time together so I can make you speak to me with that sexy-as-sin accent whenever I want. It may be one of your best attributes."

"I'll just hang up on you now. You should get some sleep or eat something or see a doctor other than me."

It's actually the sweetness of her voice mixed with that accent. It's doing something unnatural to my already fucked up brain. Maybe she's just not getting my cracked-out, sleep-deprived humor at the moment.

Or maybe I'm officially insane, and this is just the tip of the mental break.

"Whatever the hell you want, darlin', but I'm outside on the bench across the street from your place."

"Sorry? Where are you?" She's a little alarmed, and I get that. Maybe I'm pushing my luck here. I should slow down so I don't scare her off.

"Where do you want me to be?" I ask, way more suggestive than necessary.

Did I just forget my whole internal monologue about slowing down? Evidently I did. *What the hell is wrong with me?* I can't even seem to curb it. Why didn't I sleep last night?

"I'll be there in ten." I get the hang up beeps and stare at my phone for a solid two minutes, trying to figure out if I should stay or go. And then The Clash's, "Should I Stay or Should I Go" plays in my head. So very fitting. Of course I stay, even though I'm not entirely sure what I'm doing here so early or what I'm going to say.

I just want to see her. It's really that simple for me.

Ten years of curiosity are definitely getting the better of me.

When she sat next to me in the dark Friday night and Claire introduced her, I didn't think anything of it. Many people have the name Ivy. But after I learned her name and heard her soft, sweet voice and that hint of an accent, I knew it was her.

I can't even describe the sensations that ran through me.

Excitement, trepidation, amazement, curiosity, anticipation, they were all there, swirling around inside of me vying for top seed.

So when the lights came on and she didn't even look twice in my direction, I was both relieved and disappointed.

I wanted her to see me. And I was terrified of it too.

But I was desperate for that flash of recognition to blaze in her ice-blue eyes when she realized who I was and that we had been so perfectly intimate once upon a time.

And that night, all those years back, *was* perfect.

Fucking heaven.

By far and away, the most unforgettable, amazing, earth-shattering, best sex of my life.

Seriously. No joke.

It was really that good.

I couldn't get enough of her that night, and she didn't seem to mind it one bit.

But I had to leave. There really was no choice in the matter, though it was absolutely the last thing I wanted to do.

That night in the bar, she was a firecracker. So forward and confident, but when those lights came on at that party and she slipped to the back, far away from notice, I knew something had happened to her. I knew she was a different woman than the one I met all those years before.

And my heart sank.

Not because she was different than I remembered, or even that I wished she was how she used to be, but because I hated the notion that something *had* changed her, and I wasn't there to prevent it.

And maybe I'm just being arrogant here. Maybe I'm assuming too much. But I like to think I could have been her hero, her savior— instead of being the asshole one-night stand who walked out before the sun even came up.

Exactly ten minutes later, she saunters out the front door of her building, wearing a black jacket that skims the spot on her thighs where I want to dig my fingers into, jeans, and Uggs. Her hair is down, slightly damp, and she has no makeup on.

God, she's gorgeous.

Her eyes pierce through the dim light of the early morning, more blue right now than gray.

She takes her time as she descends the stairs of her building and crosses the street to me, trying to appear apathetic, but the way her eyes bounce to me every few seconds betrays her calm.

Finally, she sits down next to me on the cold, hard bench and I immediately take her hand in mine.

She lets me, but I can tell from the heavy sigh that pushes past her lips, I'm trying the last of her patience.

"I don't know what to make of you, Luke," she mutters after a quiet beat. "I really don't. You are a mass of contradictions and mixed messages." She studies our interlaced fingers for a second before turning her gaze on me with deep consideration. "This doesn't seem like friends or even casual. You showing up like this…"

"It's not like I was out here all night. I showered and changed my clothes before I came." She's not amused, and I don't blame her. "I told you I'd be back early in the morning."

She nods, but I really have no defense other than I feel like I was walking through my life by everyone else's rules, and suddenly I wanted to live by my own. I'm involved in something bigger than myself and because of that, I've kept myself detached.

But there *is* no other choice but casual with Ivy. She's leaving, and though that sucks, I get it.

I was half-joking last night at the idea of no-strings sex. I know it's not possible.

She's an all or nothing girl. I knew that the moment she spoke to me that first time, which is why I chose nothing all those years back.

I had to. My life was too uncertain and I was not about to drag her into that with me.

And now the game may be different, but I'm still a key player in it.

Yet, I'm so oddly drawn to this breathtaking creature that my thoughts are consumed by her. I've never wanted to be connected to another human the way I find myself wanting to be connected to her.

"I was hurt when I woke up and you were gone." Her quiet words jolt me out of my thoughts, and her admission stuns me into silence. "But I figured that's what happens after a one-night stand and I should just get over it and remember it for what it was. So I dated other blokes and I went on to medical school, and all was great—until Jason, of course. I did think about you from time to time." I squeeze her hand, and she squeezes back. I can't stop myself from smiling at her, but I don't offer anything more because I can tell she's not done. "I placed as a resident in the hospital here, followed by my fellowship, and that's what I've been doing ever since."

Ivy turns to look at me, and that one simple expression says she gave everything we discussed last night a tremendous amount of thought.

"I've worked unbelievably hard, Luke. Four years of medical school. Three years of residency, two of my regular fellowship, and now a certificate fellowship that I've been dreaming about for the last nine years—for most of my life. It's my goal. The end game of my education that will lead me to the position I want. That's how it works, and I can't let anything get in the way of that."

She pauses, sitting here holding my hand and watching me intently.

I angle my body to face hers, abandoning her hand in favor of her face, which I hold like it's the most precious thing in the world.

"I'd never mess with that. Never in a million years. I think you know that; otherwise, you wouldn't be sitting here with me now. I realize I'm screwed up. That I send mixed messages and do every-thing with you backward. But I want to change that. I do. I tried to tell you last night. I just want to spend some time with you. That's all. Nothing more."

Ivy nods her head, and I release her face, taking her hand again, but whether she understands me or not is something else entirely.

"So, friends?"

"Yup. Friends."

We fall silent again, sitting out here in the freezing cold, watching our breath vaporize into the morning air.

"I'm sorry I left you that morning. It was a chicken-shit thing to do, and even though I think we both know why I did it, it doesn't excuse my actions."

She shrugs a shoulder. "It is what it is and it's fine. Thank you for the apology and it is accepted."

"Awesome. Can we go inside now? I'm freezing my balls off."

"Wouldn't want that, would we?"

She moves to stand up, but before she can get very far, I jerk her back down.

I lower my lips to hers because they're right there and I've wanted to kiss her since I heard that melodic voice in the dark two days ago.

Fuck friends. I've dreamt of this girl for a decade.

I kiss her lightly at first, rediscovering her flavor. The cinnamon and vanilla sweetness is still as intoxicating as it was the first time I pressed my lips to hers. Our soft languid kiss quickly morphs into something fueled by years of pent-up frustration.

That, and I'm desperate and terrified that she's going to push me away any second, so I'm kissing her like it counts. Like I'm fighting the damn clock, because, in a way, I am.

But she doesn't push me away, so I take her lower lip into my mouth, sucking it just a little to get a deeper taste. My memory of her mouth has not done it justice. It's infinitely better. Warm and soft, and so goddamn sweet.

Parting her lips, my tongue sweeps against hers, a groan escaping from the back of my throat. Her mouth conforms to mine, allowing me to lead us. We're at the precipice here. One small shove and we'll be tumbling into an inescapable abyss.

Amazing what one kiss can lead to.

It's sexy as hell. Deep. Passionate. My hands are on her cheeks, and I spin us around so her back is pressed against the back of the cool bench and then I devour her.

I can't get enough.

Her smell, her taste, and the sounds she's making, are all driving me wild.

Ivy's fingers rake through my hair, frantically clinging and pulling like she can't get close enough. And I'm right there with her. Tugging her soft warm body against mine, deepening the kiss, making her moan into my mouth.

"Ivy," I pant against her lips. "Jesus Christ."

She pushes me off, her lips are glistening and her cheeks are flushed, and holy hell is that one erotic sight.

It's an image I want to burn into my brain so I can torture myself with it when she's gone.

"I'm cold and hungry, and have a lot of things to get done," she says, ending our stolen moment.

"What do you have to get done?" I press my lips to the tip of her nose before releasing her face and taking her hand once again.

She gives me a sheepish look. "I still have to pack."

I laugh, leaning into her. "I'm a really good helper, and I take direction surprisingly well for a control freak type A personality. But you do realize you're not leaving for a month?"

She giggles and it's the best sound ever, because it says she's relaxed with me. "Yeah, but I'm type A too. Can you fetch us some brekkie?"

"I'd be happy to. Tea and a blueberry scone?" I ask, and she instantly jumps off the bench away from me. It happens so fast that I'm stunned and stand up too, but her hands fly out defensively, warding me off before I can get close to her.

"How the hell do you know I drink tea and like blueberry scones?" She's not yelling at me, but I think that's because she's too terrified.

*Shit.* I hadn't meant to do that.

"That time in the bar at Caltech? That was not the first time I had seen you. You used to go to Beans & Leaves. I did too. You were ahead of me in line one day and I heard you order."

"And you remembered that all these years later?" She's incredulous.

"I did. I noticed you that day, and I made a note of what you ordered for some reason, hoping I'd see you again there on another day or something."

"I don't know what to think."

I hold up my hands in surrender, wondering if this is a bad time to tell her that I watched her after our night together or if that's a secret better left kept. Going strictly based on her expression, I'm thinking the latter.

"I swear that's how I knew, Ivy. I haven't been following you around Seattle or stalking you—other than showing up here this morning." That's as much truth as I can offer her.

She examines me closely, looking for the lie, but finds none and relaxes.

"I'm sorry, I'm just . . ."

"No need to explain. I get it. I'll go get us breakfast, and I'll be back in a few minutes. Then you can put me to work."

She nods, biting the corner of her lip. "I'm not having sex with you today."

I can't help but laugh. "Just today? So does that mean you will tomorrow?" I tease.

Ivy rolls her eyes, but quickly turns serious. "I don't do the whole falling into bed easily thing. I've learned my lesson one too many times."

"Ouch." I grab my chest like she wounded me. "That hurts. I deserve it, but it still hurts."

"Get over it. I'm starving, and you're wasting time."

"On it. And I promise no sex today or tomorrow. No sex until you tell me I can have it."

"*If,* Luke. And it's a rather large if."

"Nah, it's a when, and you should know that *when* you give me that yes, I might never want to come up for air."

She shakes her head, but there's a definite smile bouncing on the corner of her lips.

I amuse her and she likes me.

Could life get any better than this?

No, I decide. If only there were a way for me to make it last.

# Chapter Seven

*Ivy*

I BUZZ Luke into my flat fifteen minutes later. I really didn't think it would take him that long to get tea and a scone, but when he enters my apartment, he has a triumphant smile spread across his far-too-handsome face.

He really is something else.

"I went to the best bakery in Seattle for your scone, and then around the corner for your tea."

"You really didn't have to do that," I tell him, but I'm smiling all the same.

I still don't know what to make of this.

It's all too much. Too sudden and too unexpected and every-thing else that tells me I should push him out the door before locking it soundly behind him.

I don't know him. Really. I mean, I know nothing about his life or who he is other than the very basics.

It's the same for him, so I don't really get where all of this newfound interest is coming from, but I want to grab hold of it and never let go. And that alone scares me, especially since that's not an option.

There's just something about him that sets me on fire while filling me with the most delicious calm. Try saying no to that; I dare you.

"I did, actually," he says, bringing me back to the moment. "I'm counting this as our first friendship hangout, so I couldn't exactly get a blueberry scone from Starbucks. It's too generic."

He walks past me, dropping a kiss to my cheek before setting everything down on the counter in my kitchen like this is what we do. Like it's all so normal for us to have breakfast together, though we just "met" two nights ago.

Luke's discerning eyes scan my apartment, scrolling over each box before staring at the walls. "Do you own this place?" he asks, popping a piece of scone into his mouth absentmindedly.

"No, I'm renting."

Now my eyes turn to the decent-sized living room, trying to see what he sees. The apartment is open concept. The only thing separating the kitchen from the living room is the island that doubles as a breakfast bar. There is a small space that could be a dining area, but I'm using it as a home office of sorts since this is a one-bedroom.

I've lived here for so many years and have rarely had anyone inside.

"Too bad. It could use some paint."

"I know," I agree with just a touch of regret, taking a sip of my tea. Wanker even got me Earl Grey. I feel like that should be setting off all kinds of alarm bells, but for some reason, it's not. "I hate the white walls, but never had the time to paint them. Too late now." I shrug.

He chuckles lightly, shaking his head. "How long have you lived here again?"

"Nine years," I squeak out, a little embarrassed since nothing, and I do mean nothing, is decorated.

The furniture is here obviously, but everything else is either placed on said furniture haphazardly or packed in boxes. Even the television is sitting on the floor with wires strewn adjacent to it.

"I know it's a mess, but I work a lot and just haven't found the time to get to this." I wave my hand around the space before turning to him and waggling my eyebrows. "But now you're here and promised to be my slave, so…," I trail off with a shrug.

"I had no idea what I was getting myself into. This is going to require some form of payment. I don't work for free you know, darlin'."

"Where are you from?"

He laughs lightly under his breath, probably at my abrupt subject change, but he has an accent. It's subtle, hidden under the covers, but it's there.

"Oklahoma. Does my hint of a twang do it for you?"

"Nope," I smirk. "Incidentally, this really is the best scone I've ever had." I pop another piece into my mouth, chewing and swallowing before continuing. "It's not quite toast and Vegemite, but it may have been worth the trip to wherever you went to get it."

"Vegemite?" His brows knit together. "What the fuck now?"

"Vegemite. Americans can't stand it, probably because it smells like decaying feet and looks like baby poop, but it's so wonderful and I miss it. I usually order it online and have it shipped since there aren't many places around here that carry it."

"I'm sorry, you lost me back at decaying feet and baby poop."

I laugh, sipping my tea. "Just calling it like it is. You ready to get to work?"

"Sure, but after this is done, we're going to discuss payment."

"I already told you sex is off the table."

He grabs my waist, pulling me into his hard chest, his nose burying in my hair before I can even protest.

"I like where your mind is going with that. It means you're thinking about having sex with me. But I told you, I won't even try until you give me the Ivy Green light." He kisses my ear. "You get it? Ivy Green light." He's smiling against my neck, being adorable and playful, and I can't help but laugh at his cheesy joke.

"That's pathetic."

"I know, but you like me anyway." I don't respond to that. "But back to the payment. I may want a really fun day out. Do you ski?"

I snort. "No. I've never been. And before you ask, I don't think standing on two narrow sticks and flying down a mountain at racing speed is an ace idea."

"Okay, no skiing then."

Luke places small, wet kisses from the base of my neck up toward my ear, and my body hums with excitement. His warm breath against my wet skin is driving me insane. It's taking all my self-control not to squirm, or worse yet, tackle him to the ground and have at him.

"Motorcycles? I have one."

"You mean *donor*cycles?" My voice is embarrassingly wanton, dripping with the lust I feel building as his mouth continues its sweet torture.

"Fuck. That's what Duchess Kate calls them too." He chuckles against my skin, making me shiver again. "Is that like a universal medical professional thing?"

I laugh, but swallow it down as he moves across my neck to the other side. How I'm managing to have a regular conversation with him is beyond me. Better yet, why am I not making him stop?

"Maybe, but I'll go for a ride on the back if you give me a helmet. I used to ride with my father when I was a girl."

"Your father rides?"

I nod, and gasp as his hands start to slide up toward my ribs.

"All his life." God, my voice isn't even my own. "Luke," I rasp out a warning as he's getting dangerously close to my breasts.

"I won't cop a feel, Ivy. Promise. I'm just enjoying the touch of you." A moan escapes my lips at his words, and then he pulls back abruptly. "I can't kiss you and not go further if you make noises like that. Holy shit, Ivy." He rakes a hand through his short brown strands. "How could I have forgotten about that? You make the sexiest fucking sounds in the history of sexy fucking sounds."

I swallow down my need and push him away. "Time to work then."

I get a lopsided grin for that, dimple and all, and then he goes straight for the television. Figures, right? I mean, boys and electronics. I don't know how much telly I'll be watching in Boston, but it would be nice to have it off my floor, and it was a bit heavy for me to box up myself. I'd tell him that it's been sitting there for six months since I bought it, but I'm a bit ashamed to admit that.

I go straight for the boxes in my bedroom because I cannot stand having them fill that room a moment longer.

They don't take me that long to go through because it's mostly my summer clothes I'm packing, and linens and things.

For a one-bedroom flat, there is a surprising amount of closet space, which means I've accrued way too much over the years. I even find my vibrator rolled up in some pillow cases and quickly stash that away in the bottom of a box before Luke comes in and discovers it.

As I work in my bedroom, I think about the fact that there is a man in my living room packing up my things, and he may or may not be something more than a friend.

I'm still not sure what to make of him, or this thing going on. I mean, it's been less than forty-eight hours and I've kissed him. And I let him make-out with my neck not even ten minutes ago.

*Not smart, Ivy. Not smart at all.*

But we feel so much more familiar than two people just meeting or getting reacquainted.

It all feels so . . . natural.

Shoving some more items into a box and closing it, I seal it up with clear packing tape. I'm done packing everything in here that can be packed for now, so I close my bedroom door and head for the living room.

Luke is clad in a white t-shirt that clings to his muscular body like a second skin, and low-slung jeans. The light-blue sweater he was wearing is thrown over the back of the chair, as is his jacket. He wipes the sweat from his forehead with the back of his hand like rugged, hardworking men do in commercials.

He's insanely hot. My attraction to him is definitely not in question.

In fact, I've never been this attracted to a man before, ever, which is probably why I practically threw myself at him a decade ago. But I'm not that woman anymore. I've been traumatized, and that sort of thing makes you cautious. It makes you weary and slow to trust.

But that was all a long time ago, and one crazy, stalking ex doesn't mean all men are that way.

But Jason *was* normal. So normal and adorable and smart and funny.

He was just like any old bloke.

And Luke is definitely not.

Luke is complex and has very clear issues packaged up nicely with a questionable past. And yet, I let him into my life and my apartment with very little protest. I can't even say I put up a fight.

He tells me he understands our limitations, and somehow I believe that about him.

He also portrays the overprotective, will-walk-through-fire-for-those-I-care-about vibe. And that is so very alluring.

But there is still something hidden beneath that perfect model façade that I can't quite put my finger on.

Luke gets the television mounted above the fireplace and takes a step back to admire his handiwork.

"Looks good," I say quietly so I don't startle him. "But you do realize it was on the floor so I could *pack* it up, right?" I can't help but grin.

He spins around with a broad smile on his face. "Yeah, but you need a television. I'll pack it up when you're closer to moving." He crosses his arms over his chest. The thick muscles in his forearms and biceps roll with the motion. "And it looks better than good. It looks fucking professional."

I laugh, shaking my head. He's right;he did do a professional job. I don't even see any wires or anything.

"Did you finish in your bedroom?" he asks, and I nod. "We have these boxes to get through and then I can take you out for a proper meal."

I pause, wondering if this is the time to say something…well, not useless, but unhelpful maybe? "We don't really know each other."

He glances up at me, his hand stilling on the top of a box of old textbooks.

"Not really, no." Luke abandons his task, moving toward me with determination. "I know some basics. Good basics. I know you're a doctor who saves children's lives. I know you're beautiful and smart with a quick tongue and a dry sense of humor. I know what you like to drink and eat for breakfast. I know where you went to school and where you're originally from." He places his hands on my shoulders, giving me a good squeeze. "The rest I'll have to learn as we go, but those things I listed?" He looks up at the ceiling as he thinks about this. "Those nine or ten things are a solid start, Ivy. Don't try to avoid this just because you're leaving and we don't know each other." He tilts his head with an impish grin. "And I was a complete gentleman and didn't even mention all of the naughty things that I remember with perfect clarity that you enjoy."

I can't help but grin at that. *Yeah, I remember that too, Luke, but I'm not going there.*

"I don't think I even know ten things about you, though."

He leans into me, keeping his eyes focused on mine. "You know I grew up in Oklahoma. That I went to Caltech but had some trouble with the Feds over a hacking ring I was involved with. You know I work in cybersecurity with Ryan, and that I drink coffee." He laughs to himself. "Okay, maybe you're right. That's really not a lot."

"See what I mean."

"I do, baby, but we're both really attracted to each other, and I don't think a list of all of the things we know about each other is going to change that. Sometimes you just get a feeling about someone and that feeling is worth more than all of the little things put together.

"So you're a Gestaltist then?" I tease, and he furrows his eyebrows like I'm speaking in a foreign language.

"I have no idea what that means." He points to his chest. "Computer nerd."

"The whole is greater than the sum of its parts."

"Sure, however you want to categorize it, but you really can't put attraction or liking someone, or even love, into a theory or neat little package. It's boring that way." He winks at me.

"And boring is bad," I deadpan.

"You're not boring, Ivy. And that's not what I meant. I'm just not a big fan of overanalyzing something to the point of shutting it down. Enjoy the buildup and the newness—and the *fun*." He bounces his eyebrows playfully.

"Are you always this pragmatic?"

Luke laughs, pulling me in for a hug. "Never. Pragmatism is also boring. Seriously, if we keep this up, we'll be eating dinner at five-thirty—just in time for the early-bird special—asleep by eight o'clock *without* having had sex, and lamenting over how expensive everything has become." I smack his chest, eliciting a rumble of laughter to escape him. "I just want to spend time with you and I think you want the same with me."

I pull back to look at him—really look at him. How many nights did I sit up *lamenting him*?

Too many to count. He struck a chord with me that night, which lingered throughout the years. What he's saying isn't wrong. I am overthinking something that probably doesn't require this much thought.

It's not like this is leading anywhere beyond this brief interlude.

"I hate eating dinner at five-thirty."

He smiles, touching his forehead to mine. "I was actually thinking the no sex and in bed by eight was the worst part about that."

"Then I guess we shouldn't be like that."

"Darlin', something tells me we'll never be that boring. Something tells me you'll throw plates at my head when we fight, and we'll have hot, wild sex to make up after." I frown. "Not enough? How's this then? I like all music except country, I hate gin, and if I could do so without drowning or breaking my neck, I'd love to learn how to surf. You can let down your guard with me, Ivy. I'm not going to fuck this up, you'll see."

*More like, we'll see.*

# Chapter Eight

*Ivy*

I startle awake, sitting upright and bringing my thin sheet up to my chest to cover the fact that I'm only in my panties right now. My eyes scan the room, searching for the source of what woke me, but come up empty.

It was loud, almost like a—knocking on my door. Yeah, there it is again.

Climbing out of bed, I pull on a pair of leggings, the bra that I threw over the back of the chair last night, and a tank top that is lying on the floor.

I quickly check the alarm clock on my nightstand, and it tells me that it's eight-thirty in the morning.

*How on earth did I manage to sleep that late?*

Crikey, no wonder I feel so rested.

I think that's the most sleep I've gotten in years.

The knocking is becoming more persistent, and as I approach my door, I hear Luke yell through it. "I know you're in there darlin', no sense in avoiding me."

I laugh, shaking my head.

I really shouldn't be surprised that it's him.

After we finished packing up my apartment yesterday, Luke went home—evidently to shower because he came back with damp hair and clean clothes. I, too, had showered in his absence and then he took me out for Greek food.

Luke called it our first official non-date, and as such, I didn't let him walk me all the way up to my apartment door. I made him kiss me goodnight on the doorstep of the building, much to his dismay.

I figured it was safer that way.

But now he's back first thing the next morning, and as I swing the door open and take him in, I'm hit with a rush of lust.

He's wearing thick dark jeans, black boots, a black sweater with a hot as all sin leather jacket unzipped over it. His hair is in wild disarray, but it's that sexy way that says, *I've been running my hands through it, wanna give it a go?* His jaw is lined with a thick layer of stubble that he still hasn't shaved away from yesterday.

"Can I come in now, or are you still busy eye-fucking me?" He smirks. "I'll wait if you are, it's not like I mind."

I can't stop the blush that creeps up my face, but manage to laugh at myself all the same because he's right. I was completely frozen with the door wide open as I devoured him from head to toe.

"You can come in now." I smile as I step back and wave for him to enter.

I feel like I should be embarrassed for getting busted ogling him, but I'm not.

He knows what he looks like, so why pretend?

"What are you doing here, Luke? I don't recall making plans with you today." I yawn and stretch out my arms and legs, stiff from a solid eight hours in bed.

"It's not raining, and it's not supposed to until late tonight."

I stare at him blankly.

"I have a helmet for you."

"A helmet?" I feel like I should be a little quicker on the uptake here, but I'm not. Too much sleep will do that to a person.

"You said you'd go for a ride on the bike with me."

"I did, but I didn't think we'd be doing it so soon. Isn't it cold outside?" It's been unseasonably cold for May the past two weeks.

He shrugs, "Yes, but it's not terrible, and more importantly, it's dry. We can't go into the mountains yet, we'll have to wait for summer to do that, but we should have no problems going around town and maybe over to the water."

I give him a look, and then he's grinning at me. He knows what he just said.

"I won't be here for that, Luke. I leave in June."

"Right." He snaps his fingers in an aw-shucks manner, oozing sarcasm. "Forgot that for a little bit."

Luke snakes his arms around my waist, yanking me into his chest and burying his face in my hair. Breathing in deeply, he lets out a contented hum.

"Damn, you smell so good. You smell like a cookie I'm dying to taste."

"That's a cheesy line."

He chuckles against me. "It would be if it weren't true." He places a chaste kiss on my mouth. "Oh, before you go get dressed, I got you something."

And then he pulls out the most amazing thing ever.

It's a jar of Vegemite.

A gasp flutters past my lips as I grab it, holding it like it's an apparition that will disappear if I so much as look away.

"Where did you get this?"

He laughs at my reaction. I can't blame him either because I'm treating this like he just handed me the Holy Grail, when in reality, it's a piece of home—which is worth infinitely more to me.

"Do you have any idea how hard that stuff is to find? I mean, I went to like three stores before I found it. Ironically, it was at the specialty grocery store near my place."

I look up at him with watery eyes, because this is quite possibly the sweetest thing anyone has ever done for me. I realize how that sounds; it's only Vegemite, after all. But he went out of his way to search for it, and I know firsthand how difficult it is to find.

"Thank you." I jump up into his arms, wrapping my legs tightly around his waist. With a startled laugh, he grabs hold of me, and then I kiss him. I don't even care that I have morning breath.

He doesn't seem to care either because he's kissing me back with equal ardor.

"Jesus, baby," he breathes against my mouth after we separate. "If I knew this is how you'd thank me for something so small, I would have bought you the biggest thing I could find that would remind you of home. Like a kangaroo or koala."

"They'd be too messy in such a small flat. Vegemite is far more practical."

He grins as he sets me down. "Go change and make sure you wear something warm and good for riding."

"I guess I can't say no to you now, can I?"

"Nope." He smacks my bum. "Now move that gorgeous ass."

I scurry into my room and dig through my clothes as I brush my teeth. I would love a shower, but I don't want wet hair on the bike, and that will take too long anyway.

I locate the dark purple leather pants Sophia bought me as a gag gift for my birthday last year, since they are the best thing I have for a motorcycle ride. Layering them over a pair of tights to keep me extra warm, I throw on a long-sleeved shirt, a sweater, and grab my own black leather jacket.

Securing the elastic around the end of my long braid, I make my way back into the living room toward the man I have no business spending time with. He's leaning against the counter, typing something into his phone and looking impossibly sexy and tousled. Luke may be able to pull off biker hair, but I can't, hence the braid.

"I'm ready."

His eyes feast on my tall black leather boots up to my jacket and then back again.

"It's a good thing you'll be behind me on that bike because, damn, that outfit is all kinds of distracting."

"Then, let's go ride your bike."

I grab my keys, phone, ID, and some cash, tucking them into my pockets because I don't want to carry a purse. We step outside, and sure enough, it is dry, but it's also overcast and chilly.

"Tell me the helmet you have for me has a face guard." The last thing I want is frozen windburn on my cheeks.

"Of course. I wouldn't do that to you, and if you're too cold, we can bag it. I just thought it would be fun."

"No, I'd like to give it a go."

Luke leads me to a sleek black BMW motorcycle with yellow accents. Correction, this looks more like a racer, and no doubt flies like one. "You have a racer?" I don't know why this surprises me. "I don't know what I was expecting, but for some reason, I thought you would be more of an old-school Harley man."

He laughs, turning to me. "Say that again."

"What?" I furrow my eyebrows.

"Racer."

I roll my eyes, but appease him all the same. "Racer."

"I love that. I wasn't lying yesterday when I said your accent may be one of my favorite things about you. I seriously might marry you over it."

"Enough with that. This is only a second non-date, Luke, and as I recall, we both decided this is fun and nothing that will ever lead to more, so stop with all that marrying rubbish."

He nods in agreement. "We did, and clearly, my mentioning marrying you freaks you out, so I'll refrain. But you better start showing me an ugly or crazy side, because as of right now, you're far too perfect."

I grin, looking down and trying to ignore the latest swarm of butterflies I'm feeling.

"Stop being a flirt and let's go."

He hands me a black helmet that has a visor. I put it on and he helps me strap it into place under my chin.

"Ready?" Luke asks as he straddles the bike with grace and ease before reaching out a hand to help me onto the back. I, on the other hand, am the antithesis of graceful. Straddling this massive thing is not as easy as Luke made it appear.

There are a microphone and earpiece inside the helmet, so I can hear him, which is a handy little feature.

"Ready." My voice sounds muffled against the microphone inside the helmet. Although it fits snugly, it isn't uncomfortable. The engine rumbles to life with a deafening roar. As we set off, I wrap my arms around his waist, pressing my body tightly up against his back.

There is nothing to prevent me from catapulting off the back of this bike, and that is a sobering thought. As a child, my father would take me into open, flat land and we'd ride for a bit, but never too fast.

And that was back in Australia.

This is Seattle, and Seattle is neither flat nor open.

There are cars and hills and pedestrians, and continuous starting and stopping. So it's nearly impossible to get a feel for the bike or the rhythm of motion. Maybe it's just been too long since I've been on one of these things, but I'm bloody terrified, holding onto Luke as if my life depends on it. Oh wait, it does.

"You okay back there?" His voice crackles into my ear, reverberating into my pulsating skull. "You're gripping the hell out of me."

"Yes." I think that might be all I can manage.

"I won't let anything happen to you, darlin'. Try to relax and enjoy the city. I bet you haven't explored it much."

"No, I haven't." How weird is that? I mean, I've been living here for nine years, and though I've scouted around some, it hasn't been much.

The seat is vibrating into me, and the engine is a raucous angry cacophony, but Luke is warm and strong and I do my best to take his advice and enjoy the ride and the view. He takes me all over the city, past the Space Needle, Pike Place Market, the university, and the Marina, where several large catamarans and yachts are docked.

The city *is* beautiful, and the more we cruise through it, the more I fall in love with it all over again.

I'm struck with a pang of nostalgia, knowing that I'm leaving so soon and may, in fact, never live here again.

"That's my place." Luke points to a large brick building that looks like it was once a warehouse. Street level is filled with various shops, and the second floor is all open windows with nothing obstructing them from the inside, so that's a little confusing for me.

"That place?" I point where he just was.

"Yup. That's home. I'll explain when we stop. We should be at Myrtle Edwards in a few minutes."

After backtracking through the city a bit, he pulls the bike into a spot on the street and helps me off. My body still feels like it's moving, which is an unsettling sensation, but as we begin to walk into the park and toward the beach, it subsides.

I can only imagine what my hair looks like, and I'm afraid to ask, but he doesn't comment, and I try to forget about it.

Luke guides me over to a small beach area scattered with dark rocks and driftwood.

"Over in that direction," he points, "is Mount Rainier, but you can't see it today. Too cloudy."

"You like living here, don't you?" I ask as I settle myself down into the cold sand. The wind isn't whipping around all that much, making the frigid temperatures more bearable.

"I do." He sinks down next to me, his forearms resting atop his bent knees. "After I left California, I came up here. Seemed like as good of a place as any, and though I was already working with Ryan and he was in Philly, we didn't need to be in the same location to do our thing. He only moved here about a year and a half ago."

I look out over the water, absorbing his words for a moment. "Tell me about your building."

Luke intertwines our fingers, and we sit like that for a quiet moment before he speaks.

"I managed to save up some money after working on a few projects with Ryan, and I bought the building. It was abandoned and not in the best repair. I didn't have a lot of money left after that, so I did the majority of the work myself." I look over at him, and he's grinning out at the water like this makes him proud. "I was able to fix the first floor enough to rent out the spaces, and that provided me with enough revenue to fix up my apartment, which spans the entire second floor of the building."

"That must be a considerable space."

He chuckles lightly. "It is. Probably too large for just me, but . . .," he trails off like maybe there's more to it, but he's not going to tell me.

Suddenly I realize what he's doing. He's opening up to me about himself. About his life. It's restricted and not all that informative as to who he is, but I get the impression that despite its brevity, it's a lot for him to share.

He's trying to make up for the comment I made about not knowing him.

"And you're from Oklahoma."

"I'm from Oklahoma," Luke confirms with a nod of his head, but doesn't offer more. The expression on his face and the tone of his voice suggest that he won't.

"And you don't like country music?"

He laughs. "Can't stand it actually. I realize I'm in the minority with that. Most of this country does, in fact, like it." Luke shifts his position, unexpectedly turning to face me. "You're beautiful," he whispers reverently before taking my face in his hands and pressing his lips to mine for a brief kiss. "I don't know how you're doing it, but you are." I scrunch my eyebrows in confusion. "I don't talk about myself, Ivy. I don't open up to anyone. It's just not me. But I find myself doing it more and more with you."

And then he closes the gap between our mouths once again. Though this time, there's no pulling back, and no more words are needed.

We kiss like this, in harmony with the salty breeze, the sound of seagulls squawking in the air and water lapping against the rocky shore.

It's perfect.

This is only technically a second non-date, but it feels like a lifetime in the making.

It feels like it could lead to forever so effortlessly.

And for this very reason, I should pull away and end this.

But the way he's kissing me, exploring my mouth and creating a labyrinth of emotions and sensations, won't allow me to end it. It's the best sort of trepidation, knowing what could so easily come next and yet needing to resist it. But even if it does end badly—and I think it's probably a safe bet that it will—we're already too far into this.

There's no going back now.

A shiver runs through me, and I snuggle in closer to Luke's side.

"Are you cold, honey?"

I love how Luke has a million names for me. I've never been one to think that terms of endearment are anything but moronic embellishments, but not the way he uses them with me.

"A little," I admit.

"Can I take you home? To my home?"

"Yes."

It's really as simple as that. And that dangerous.

# Chapter Nine

*Ivy*

WE DRIVE ten minutes in Monday morning traffic before he pulls into a driveway adjacent to his building, which is old and brick and beautiful. Luke punches a code into a keypad, and a large black iron gate opens, allowing us entrance to a small parking lot in the back. He parks the motorcycle next to the two back doors and helps me off.

I enjoyed my ride, but I think my days on that thing are done.

"What's with all the keypads?" I ask as he punches in yet another code on one of the back doors before it lets out three beeps and the light turns from red to green. Luke swings the door open, motioning for me to go on ahead of him.

"It's more secure than just a regular lock."

"And security like this is a necessity for you?" I point at the CCTV camera in the top corner of the entrance.

He shrugs, "Isn't security a necessity for everyone?"

It's an evasive answer, but I let it slide for now as he takes my hand and leads me up a well-lit stairwell to another solid oak door.

Yet another camera and keypad. I've never seen a private home equipped like this.

The door opens, and again, he lets me enter before him.

My first thought is that this place is massive. At least four to five thousand square feet of open space. My second is that it's completely different than I had anticipated. I'd expected hard surfaces and modern, sleek, expensive decor.

It's the opposite.

There are warm hardwood floors running throughout the space that look worn and original but seem well-maintained. The exposed brick is juxtaposed with warm-colored plaster walls, and the furnishings are neutral and comfortable looking.

"I love it," I say, mostly to myself, because I really do. It's bright despite the gray sky, and cozy despite its vastness.

And then I realize that this place fits Luke perfectly. On the outside, he's hard, rough, and exceedingly beautiful. But that's just the façade. Much of everything else seems to be held tight to his chest. But once you manage to draw it out, even just a small taste of it, you realize just how precious that really is. Because everything about him is so absolutely remarkable and unexpected in the best possible way.

"I'm glad," he says. "Come in and I'll give you the tour."

Luke takes my hand again and leads me through the large kitchen, dining area and multiple sitting spaces—including one with a ginormous television. His office is one of the few closed-off spaces. We walk into the room, hand in hand, and it is so much grander than expected. Double the size of my bedroom at home and is filled with more computer equipment and monitors than I think I've ever seen before, including the feed for the multiple CCTV cameras. Judging by the numerous images on the monitor, there are several I have yet to notice.

It's an impressive space. I've never seen a room like this outside of television, boasting two large desks, all those monitors I mentioned, as well as a slew of other electronic-looking gadget things that I can't even begin to guess at what they do. His smile is off the charts in this room as his eyes glide over his playthings.

"My Batcave," he says with a smirk. "When I first moved to Seattle after the Feds handed me my ass on a platter and tried to serve it with fries and a Coke, I bought this place," he says, his eyes glued to a monitor, though it doesn't feel like he's focused on it. "I needed somewhere I could keep my stuff that I use to hack-the stuff that wasn't confiscated at least." He gives me a wicked grin. "Computers, laptops, equipment that allow me to jump IP addresses to places all over the world, secure wireless networks, portable firewalls. You name it, it's in this room."

"You still do all of that?" I swallow down a lump because I'm not okay with the illegal stuff. I know he and Ryan run an IT security company, but this. . .

"Nothing I'm getting arrested for. I can promise you that. It's the toys, darlin'." He gives me a boyish smile and a wink. "I'd be lying my ass off if I didn't admit just how much I love my gadgets. They really are half the reason I do what I do."

I notice a half-eaten bag of organic blue corn chips precariously tossed on the side of one of the desks. Nodding my chin in its direction, I raise a mocking eyebrow, making him laugh with his head tilted back, a hand around his stomach as he rumbles with mirth.

"When I was in college, I would have done this," he waves a hand around the room, "with a bag of Cheetos in one hand, and a Monster Energy drink or a Five-Hour Energy in the other. Now that I'm an adult, I hack with fucking organic blue corn chips, gourmet salsa, guacamole, and high-end iced coffee with a double shot of espresso. I feel like a cliché if ever there was one, but I still crunch away on the damn chips while sipping my six-dollar coffee."

"Cliché might be spot-on. Price of being a billionaire, eh?" I tease.

"I really hate that term," he grumbles.

"It's a real beaut of a Batcave or whatever you call it. And while I'm sure this is all heaps of fun, I have no idea what you just prattled on about with networks and the like."

He laughs again. "So I can't convince you to go on a hacking binge with me? Do some penetration testing?" He waggles his eyebrows suggestively, and all I can do is shake my head and roll my eyes.

"You don't want me having a go at your stuff. I'm sure I'd break something just by sitting in your fancy chair. In the hospital, I am relentlessly teased about the fact that I can't even work our EMR."

"No hacking for you then." Luke plants a soft kiss on the corner of my mouth. "Come on, let me show you the rest."

He doesn't bring me to the back of the flat where the bedrooms are no doubt are located. Instead, he directs me over to the sitting area that houses the television and motions for me to have a seat. I do, and I sink right into the plush cream sofa.

"This is fantastic, Luke. How do you ever manage to leave?"

He laughs, "I don't a lot. If I'm not at work, I'm usually here."

"Can't blame you for that."

"Are you hungry?" he asks softly. Standing in front of me, his brown eyes examine me, but in search of what I do not know.

"Yes, I'm famished." I move to stand up, but he stops me with an outstretched hand.

"I'll bring us something. Just relax."

I smile and sink back into the sofa. Luke hits a button on the wall and the gas fireplace comes to life. He hits another button and the soft notes of Debussy fill the room.

If this is a seduction scene he's creating, I doubt I'll last much longer.

I can't tell if I'm drowsy with sleep, or drunk on anticipation of what could come next.

Not even five minutes later, he returns with grilled cheese sandwiches and tomato soup, and I smile at just how adorable that is. "You must do this a lot," I say before I can stop myself.

"Do what?" he asks, mid-chew.

"Bring women to your home to make them soup, turn on the fire, and play classical music."

He looks at me blankly. "Why do you say that?"

"I don't know," I giggle self-consciously. "It just seems like the perfect date. Something that has worked for you in the past." He frowns at me, and suddenly I feel bad for opening my big mouth.

"I'm sorry; that came out wrong. I just meant that this is wonderful and special and I'm loving every second of it."

"I don't really date a lot, Ivy. And I never bring women here. Ever."

"How come?"

He shrugs. "I work a lot, and this is my haven." He turns to me, putting down his half-eaten sandwich and rubbing his hands against each other to remove any excess crumbs. "You're the only woman I've ever brought here, and though I'm sure I'll freak you out, I'm hoping that's how it stays."

"Luke——"

"I know," he cuts me off almost sharply. "I just meant I don't like bringing women here."

I shake my head. "How did this happen so fast?" I whisper to myself. I like him. Dammit all, I do, and that's just so unfortunate.

He smiles lopsidedly, drawing closer. His brown eyes become twin pools of desire, and I'm lost.

Completely and utterly lost in this man.

But more importantly, I don't want to be found.

I'm enjoying our little interlude way too much.

I know I'm in trouble. I know that two days with him aren't enough. I know I'll want more and that I'm already desperate to manipulate time and space so our brief moment becomes infinite. I know I could be doing irrevocable damage to myself by letting him in. I know all of this. But what I don't know is how to make it stop.

"Ivy." Warm, slightly calloused fingers brush my cheek. "It's not fast, baby, it's exactly the way it's supposed to be." He skims his lips against mine. "Because I can't get enough of you. I came home after dinner last night and all I could think about was how much I wanted to see you again. All I could think was more, I need more. I like you. It's that simple for me."

"I hope you know what you're doing with me, Luke."

He smiles big against my mouth. "I haven't a clue, but that doesn't mean I want to stop. I figure I'll go as far as I can with you, and the rest will take care of itself."

"I can't get attached to you."

I'm already attached to him. Who the hell am I kidding?

"Me neither, so we won't delve into anything too deeply. It's just fun, remember?"

With that declaration, his lips smash into mine as his fingers rake through my hair, pulling on my braid to release the elastic and set my hair free.

"Ivy?" he breathes my name as a question, but it's not really a question. It's a desperate plea.

I answer by pushing him back and climbing onto his lap, straddling his large muscular thighs that roll beneath me.

He groans as his arousal rocks into me, his hands sliding up my back under my multiple layers. I feel the hunger of his mouth as it takes mine, exploring and searching, leading me to the brink of insanity with just a simple swipe of his tongue.

I crave him. I thirst for him. I need him so much closer than is humanly possible.

My insides are molten fire, completely liquefied, and yet I don't think I've ever been this nervous in my life. The irony of that is not lost on me. We've done this before after all. But this is so very different. This feels like I'm teetering on a precipice, and with one wrong move, one small slip, I'm going to fall, and there is just no way I'll ever be found again.

His hands continue to slide up my back, taking my clothes with them, though he makes no attempt to remove them. So I do it for him, momentarily breaking our kiss.

Dark brown hooded eyes take me in, a strangled hiss escaping his parted lips. "God, look at you." Luke's hands cup my breasts over my bra, lifting and testing their weight before he squeezes. His thumbs slide over my nipples and the friction is like nothing else.

I moan, tilting my head back before it lulls to the side as his mouth captures my neck.

I want this to keep going. I *need* this to keep going. I want to be in his bed with him inside of me, but I can't get myself there.

I'm paralyzed with fear, knowing all too well where this will take me. Take us.

"Luke," I moan again, but place my hands on his shoulders to try and hold him at bay.

"I know," he murmurs against my neck. "I don't even have any condoms here." He chuckles like this amuses and frustrates him equally. "Just . . ." Lust-filled eyes find mine. "Let me make you feel good. Please, Ivy. I'm dying to taste you."

"Oh god," I cry.

"Tell me you want that."

"Yes. I want that." And I do. I want it more than I want my next breath. He lowers me to the couch on my back, struggling to remove my leather pants and tights, laughing as he goes.

"Next time, less layers."

"Right-o," I giggle.

His eyes find mine from between my spread thighs, and it's the most erotic sight I've ever seen. "You won't believe me, but I've thought about you for ten years. For ten years, I regretted not being able to do this."

His tongue comes out and licks me from my opening up to my clit where he lingers, sucking it into his mouth. My back to arches off the couch as my eyes to roll into the back of my head.

His lips release me, placing a wet kiss to my clit before he flicks it repeatedly with his tongue. "God, you taste so good, Ivy. So sweet and perfect."

A hum emanates from the back of my throat as he slips two fingers inside of me, pumping them in and out.

Within minutes Luke has me writhing and twisting, pulling his hair both closer and further back. His hand plants itself on my lower abdomen, holding me down. Pinning me so he can fully torture me with his incredible mouth and fingers.

I'm consumed. Utterly overwhelmed, and nothing has ever been this good. It's all Luke.

And it's not just his talented tongue or the way he looks at me like I'm the most beautiful woman he's ever seen—though neither of those hurt his cause. No, it's the way he makes me feel free when I have been hiding. Awake instead of dormant. Fearless instead of petrified. Ceaseless instead of temporary.

There are no words to describe that sort of liberation, and if he can make me feel like this after only a few days, then I may never be able to give him up. I want to drown in the sensations he compels. Fill my lungs and my body with this rush, and pray to god that it never ends.

I feel my orgasm begin to build within me. A rush of heat that starts low only to curl its way through my every cell. His fingers twist, angling up and hitting that magic spot within me.

I detonate.

My hips grind against his face, my body needy as it takes and takes and takes all he's giving me.

When he's done with me, when I'm sweaty and smiling so big my cheeks hurt, I return the favor all too happily. Rolling on top of him, I undo his pants, and take him immediately into my mouth. He chuckles at my enthusiasm, but the sound dies on his lips with a deep groan.

His cock is big and hard and I can't help but savor every part of this man. "Chris, Ivy. What are you doing to me?"

His fingers thrust into my hair, clasping it by the roots as I lap at the precum on his tip before diving down as far as I can go, gagging slightly. He grunts and I grin, sucking and moaning, and doing everything I can to drive him as mad as he drives me.

"Fuck yes. Just like that. Damn, your mouth, Ivy. So good. I'm gonna come, baby."

He pulls on my hair in warning, but I dig in deeper, sucking him harder until he explodes in my mouth with a loud groan and a curse on a his lips. I swallow him down, smiling as I pull off, and fall onto his chest in a happy, sated lump.

"Will you stay with me tonight?" he asks, languidly running his fingers through the strands of my hair as we lie breathless and sleepy on his couch, wrapped in each other.

I prop my chin on his chest as he adjusts his head with his arm behind it so he can meet my eyes. "I don't have any of my stuff."

"Doesn't matter. You can borrow what you don't have, and I'll drive you home tomorrow before I go to work."

"You don't think that's a bad idea?" I chew on the corner of my lip nervously.

"Nah." He runs a hand through my hair. "You need to stop worrying about this. I'm good, Ivy. I swear. I hope you are too, because that was the most fun I've had in ten years, and we haven't even gotten to the really good stuff." He grins suggestively.

Giggling, I say, "Okay then, I'd like that."

"We never ate our lunch."

"Oh yes we did." I give him a devilish grin.

He laughs, bouncing me slightly on his chest. "Who knew you were such a dirty girl?"

"Me?" I say with mock outrage. "You're the one who told me over and over again how desperate you were to fuck me. And I'm greatly paraphrasing, leaving out the naughtiest bits."

"I never said *I* wasn't dirty. You have no idea the depravity I have floating around in my head when it comes to you."

"Tell me something real, Luke, something not many people know about you." I have no idea why I just asked him that. It wasn't my intention to turn our playful moment into something serious.

He looks up at the ceiling for a beat before turning back to me with a small smile that has me blowing out the breath I didn't realize I had been holding in. "I hate Indian food. Can't stand any part of it."

I roll my eyes. "That's pathetic."

"Okay, I'd rather read than watch television."

That surprises me, and he nods, correctly interpreting my expression.

"I think it's because I spend so much time in front of a monitor. The idea of watching more doesn't do it for me. Reading soothes me." Who is this man? Never before have I met someone who is more of a walking contradiction.

"What do you like to read?"

"Almost anything. I got really into the Pillars of the Earth series for a while. I haven't had much time to read lately, so I'm a bit behind."

"I like old movies. You know, Billy Wilder, Howard Hawks,

Alfred Hitchcock—blokes like them. I also have a huge thing for eighties films."

He leans up to kiss the tip of my nose because that's all he can reach. "Which eighties movies?"

"Nearly all of them. There was a theater close to us when I was growing up that used to have an eighties night. I would make Dad and Mum take me every week." I grin at the memory. I'm going to miss my parents so much when I move. I don't see them all that often because of work, but I try to whenever I can.

"Sounds like you had a nice childhood." Luke's words are soft and kind, but there's a fleeting flash of heaviness in his eyes. I must have imagined it.

I nod, my chin rubbing against the smooth hard muscles of his flawless chest. "I did. We weren't well off, but that never seemed to matter, and I never felt like I went without. It wasn't until I was an adult that I realize just how much my family struggled. Especially after we moved here when I was a young teenager."

"I bet you were an adorable kid."

"Nope, I was scruffy and more of a tomboy than anything else. Dad was big into sport, especially football, so I played a lot. Was always caked in dirt."

"Football as in soccer?"

I roll my eyes. "No. Not as in *soccer*." I say the word with the most acerbic tone I can muster. "Soccer is soccer in Australia, just as it is here. I'm talking about Australian Football League or AFL. It's huge at home, and Dad loved to watch, so I used to play in our garden a lot with him. You know, since he only had girls and no boys. Not so much once we moved here. Did you play sports growing up?"

Luke looks off, away from me, focusing on nothing. "Not really."

He sits up, taking me with him, and though we've been lying in very little clothing, his abrupt end to our conversation has me feeling exposed.

I pull my shirt and sweater over my head before tugging up my trousers and tights. Luke gets dressed too, and before I can even comment, he walks off toward the washroom.

*What just happened?*

A minute or two later, I hear his bare feet slapping against the wood floors. "You want to order some dinner?" he asks from behind me. I've been stuck sitting on the couch with my hands folded in my lap, just staring down at them, unsure of what to make of the way he shut down on me the second I mentioned his childhood.

*Maybe he doesn't want us to get too intimate.*

Probably for the best.

So I turn to him, plastering a smile on my face that I'm not sure I totally feel and say, "Absolutely. I'm starved." Even though my gut suddenly feels like it's filled with led.

# Chapter Ten

*Ivy*

I'M WARM AND COMFORTABLE, so very comfortable, as the dull outside light fans across my face. Shifting in bed, very strong muscular arms wrap around me, pulling me into an even stronger chest.

"What time is it?" I rasp, sleep still heavy in my voice.

"Time to get up," Luke says, but he's making no move to do so or allowing me to either.

His nose buries in the space between my neck and shoulder, his mouth peppering me with sweet soft kisses. "How is it you can taste so good?" I giggle as he tickles me a little. "I'm serious here, Doctor. I want a medical explanation for it, because my mouth is watering and it's taking all of my limited self-control not to roll you onto your back and devour every single inch of you."

"Um . . ." Did he just ask me a question? Oh, right. "I just taste good?" *Worst response ever.*

He laughs against my fevered skin. "I think I'm muddling your mind."

"I think you're muddling more than just that."

"Good, I like you like this. Thoroughly under my spell and helpless to resist."

"We should get up."

Puckering his lips, he blows cool air on the moist skin he has been kissing, causing chills to rise everywhere.

"Always the voice of reason," he sighs, rolling off of me until he's flat on his back. "I don't want to go to work today," he whines like a small boy would about school. "I want to stay in bed with you."

"Up you go now." I push his heavy side, barely moving his solid mass an inch. "Time to be a responsible adult. You can join me in bed another day."

"I'm holding you to that." Luke sits up in one quick motion before climbing on top, hovering above me on all fours. "Is it weird that I almost don't want to brush my teeth after having you in my mouth last night?"

I laugh, wrinkling my nose. "Not weird, more like gross, and I'll feel sorry for everyone you speak with today."

"Fine," he groans. "I'll brush my teeth, but you should know that you taste so much better than my toothpaste."

I blush everywhere as he dips down to kiss me as if trying to prove his point.

Luke pulls back with a wink and a lopsided grin before hopping off me and heading for the shower. I would join him, but I have a feeling he's already running a bit behind, and I don't think my presence would help that.

Not even ten minutes later, he's showered, dressed, and ready to go.

He hasn't shaved, and the result is the beginning of a scruffy beard. I run my fingers through the bristles as he passes, enjoying the way they tickle my skin.

"Don't get attached to it; I'm shaving later."

"You don't like having a beard?" I ask as we walk out the door and down the stairs that lead us back to the parking lot.

"Not even a little. It itches like crazy and makes me look too much like Ryan, which is something I strive never to do." He pauses as he holds the outside door for me. "Why, do you like it?"

"I don't know. I'm normally a fan of clean-shaven, but it adds a bit to your bad boy mystique."

His eyes widen, finger pointing at his chest. "Bad boy mystique? No way. I'm a fucking prince, maybe even an angel."

"With the mouth of the devil."

I get a wicked grin for that as he opens my car door, allowing me to slip in.

"You like my devil mouth, Doctor Green, don't pretend otherwise." He shuts the door and saunters around to his side, exuding confidence and . . . contentment. He looks so unbelievably happy, like he couldn't wipe that grin off his face if he tried.

I like that I'm the one who put it there. I like that a lot.

We drive the fifteen or so minutes in rush hour to my flat, listening to NPR and lost in our own thoughts.

I still haven't gotten to all the laundry that is waiting for me at home. No doubt that will take up the majority of my day, but I also need to try and get some rest before my night shift tonight. That's really the hardest thing to do—sleeping during the day before you start working a series of nights when your body is still used to the grind of day shifts.

My circadian rhythm is a disaster because of this.

"What time are you working tonight?" Luke asks as we pull up in front of my building.

"My shift starts at eight, so I have to leave around seven-thirty."

"Can I bring you an early dinner?" He laughs lightly. "I know you said you don't like eating at five-thirty, but that may be the only time to do it."

"Sure, dinner would be great." His smile grows even bigger as he undoes his seatbelt, moving like he's getting out of the car too. "You don't have to walk me up. I'm sure you're already late."

"I want to walk you up." It's that simple and I don't argue as I wait for him to open my door. He seems to appreciate playing the part of the gentleman.

I unlock the door, and Luke dutifully trudges up the four floors behind me, his eyes glued to my bottom the entire way.

*Maybe not such the gentleman after all.*

After unlocking my door, I hesitate on the threshold, knowing he has to leave, but not wanting him to go.

It has only been one weekend with him, but the ever-present giddy sensation in my chest, coupled with the fact that I can't get enough of being around him, means I'm in trouble. This feels too much like fledgling relationship excitement. This feels like the start of something momentous and life-altering. This just feels too much.

The longer we stand here, staring at each other with easy smiles, electricity builds, popping and crackling between us, leading us up to a brilliant crescendo. My body is humming with the current, and I know he feels it too. It's pronounced and explicit and if he doesn't leave this very moment I—

"Fuck work, I can be late," Luke growls as he comes at me predatorily. His mouth crashes into mine almost painfully as he wraps his arms around my bottom, lifting me effortlessly and walking us into my apartment. His foot kicks back, slamming my door shut, and before I can even make sense of anything, he presses me up against it. My legs hug his waist, one foot crossed over the other, dangling above his perfect backside.

Our need is primal, our movements sloppy as he tries to rip my jacket off my shoulders without dropping me. I laugh into his mouth, pushing back on his chest for him to release me so I can aid in his effort. My jacket hits the floor with a loud slap, followed by his, and then his mouth is back on mine.

My fingers yank his dress shirt from his trousers, before greedily attacking each button, needing to touch his gorgeous chest and sculpted abs.

My sweater doesn't stand a chance as he rips it over my head, tossing it somewhere behind him. His mouth comes down to the tops of my breasts as his hands cup and squeeze, pinching my nipples through my bra. Heated lips continue to trail down before pausing above the snap of my leather pants.

"No fucking way am I'm going to be able to get these things off of you while you're standing." With that declaration, he scoops me up into his arms, bride-style this time, carrying me across my apartment and into the bedroom, never once removing his mouth from mine.

Tossing me on the bed with a heavy bounce, I laugh before it stutters and dies in my throat. The look he's giving me is like nothing I have ever seen before. This one expression could set the room ablaze with the amount of heat it's producing.

I don't wait for him to go after my leather pants, I do the honors myself as he watches, his eyes at half-mast and practically black with desire.

Never in my life have I ever felt so wanted.

The second everything is off, including my bra, Luke is back on me, everywhere. His fingers slide inside my pussy as his mouth suckles and claims my breasts.

He is relentless and hungry, pumping into me with his fingers and circling my clit with his thumb at an almost punishing pace. It's too much. I'm building too quickly. I claw at his back, whimpering and moaning until I shatter, splintering off into a million tiny pieces.

"What the hell is that?" I laugh as consciousness slowly comes back to me.

"A condom, baby. As a doctor and a woman, I would hope you've seen these before."

"You said you didn't have any."

He lifts a shoulder in a shrug, smiling playfully. "I lied."

I smack his chest, but my ire instantly evaporates as he removes his pants and opens the condom with his teeth.

He hovers above me, his cock nudging my entrance. "So beautiful," he whispers reverently as he slips inside of me, inch by inch until he's so deep I can't tell where he ends and I begin.

The moment he starts to move, everything changes.

His hand cups my jaw, forcing my eyes to his as he slides out, slowly, only to thrust in hard and deep and rough. My legs hike up, one climbing up his shoulder, the other around his waist, needing him so much deeper.

"Ivy. Ivy. Ivy."

This is nothing like the sex we had ten years ago. This is nothing like sex I've ever had with anyone.

Luke is primal yet gentle, tender yet unrelenting. He is everything and everywhere, and as we move together like the practiced lovers we are not, I feel myself letting go completely.

Sweat clings to our bodies, his hand squeezing my breast and pinching my nipple before it slides lower, down my belly until it finds my clit, where he begins to rub in delicious circles in time with his powerful thrusts.

This isn't lovemaking or even fucking.

This is something new we're creating, leading to a finish that I am both urgent for and desperate to stave off. He picks up the pace, adjusting me so I'm half off the bed, cradled in his arms. The sound of skin slapping against skin coupled with our heavy pants and delirious moans are the only sound.

"Ivy. Jesus hell, Ivy," he groans in my ear. "You feel so good. So fucking good." I can only nod, my speaking voice nowhere to be found. "Tell me you feel this. Tell me you feel just how absolutely profoundly incredible this is."

"Yes," I breathe. "Yes," I moan. "Oh, god. Yes," I cry out as my climax spirals out of control. Luke follows me over the edge, an animal as he fucks me until there is nothing left of either one of us.

My eyes cinch shut as I try to steady my racing heart and slow my breathing. I'm smiling. It can't be helped, and there is no sense in trying to hide it.

Luke growls, and I slowly open one lid, peering over at him. "How on earth am I supposed to get anything productive done today?" He props himself up on his elbow, gazing down at me. "All I'm going to be able to do all day is think about the phenomenal sex we just had, and the fact that I'll be able to smell you on me isn't going to help that."

"So this is my fault?"

"Yes. Unequivocally." His lips find mine, but it's just a brushing of them before he draws back and begins to get dressed. "I want to stay here with you so fucking bad, but I have a meeting, and if I don't show for it, Ryan will be pissed as hell."

I sit up, grabbing my lavender robe from the chair and wrapping it around myself. "It's fine; I've waylaid you enough."

"You have, but it was one hell of a waylaying. You can do that to me anytime." Luke jumps off my bed, reaching down and bringing me with him, enfolding me in his arms. "In fact, I plan on waylaying you a lot. Every chance I get. Now that I've had you again, Ivy Green, there is no way I can stop. You're like heroin, crack, and meth all rolled up into one perfect package."

"That's oddly flattering, considering the reference."

He kisses me long and hard, bending me back like they do in old movies for effect. "I gotta go," Luke whispers against my lips. "I'll see you at four-thirty."

I laugh, pushing him back as I walk him to the door. "I thought you said five-thirty?"

"I did," he confirms. "But that was before the mind-blowing sex. I plan to get here an hour earlier and spend that entire time inside of you."

"Who can say no to that?" I muse.

Cupping my face, his lighthearted expression turns serious and genuine. "I'm having way too much fun with you, Ivy. And it's not just the sex. All I seem to want to do is be near you. I can't get enough," he says, mirroring my thoughts from earlier. He kisses me again, conveying something so deep I'm afraid to put a name to it, before pulling back and walking out the door.

"Me too," I whisper to myself, shutting and locking the door behind him. I scrub my hands up and down my face. Suddenly terrified. What am I going to do now?

# Chapter Eleven

*Luke*

"A NIGHT away doesn't fall under the no-strings sex realm, does it?" Ivy asks as we head north toward Mt. Baker. "Especially, to survey a house your best friend is getting married in."

"What do you want me to tell you, sweetheart? Ryan wanted to show Kate the cabin and asked for my opinion as well. You just so happen to have the night off. I'm not missing out on that for this stupid fucking thing, and I can't really say no to him either, so here we are."

"But Kate mentioned skiing. I don't ski, Luke. I thought I made that one clear." She's flustered now. And a little nervous, I think. She considers a night away to be a big deal. Maybe it is, and maybe it isn't, but I believe the real issue is that the good doctor here likes me. In fact, I think Ivy likes me a lot.

But she *really* doesn't want to.

I reach for her hand and intertwine our fingers. "You don't have to ski, baby. In fact, that's not on my agenda."

Out of the corner of my eye, I see Ivy's lips bouncing, though she looks like she's trying to hide her smirk.

"You have an agenda, do you? Why do I get the feeling it will involve me being naked?"

"Because that sort of agenda definitely fits within the realm of no-strings sex, and I happen to like you naked. It's one of my favorite looks for you, and from what Ryan has told me, there are plenty of places I can keep you that way."

Ivy snorts dubiously. "Ryan told you all the places where you can keep me naked?"

I roll my eyes at her as I switch lanes. "No, baby, that would be a ridiculous conversation for us to have. He told me about the private hot tub on our balcony, and the huge walk-in shower in our en suite, and the fur of some sort of animal rug in front of our fireplace, and the giant four-poster king-size bed."

"That seems like a lot of places given our time constraints. We're not even up here for twenty-four hours. At some point, we'll need to eat, sleep, and converse with Kate and Ryan."

"Sleeping, and conversing with Kate and Ryan are overrated, and not high on my priority list." I give her hand a squeeze before bringing it up to my mouth for a light kiss. "You're a doctor, Ivy. You're used to functioning on no sleep. What good is having regular sex with a doctor if I can't take advantage of that small bonus?"

I look over at her quickly, my eyes jumping back and forth between her and the nearly empty highway.

Ivy turns to the window, trying to hide her smile. In reality, she's being a good sport about coming on this little impromptu trip. I know she's exhausted because I picked her up at work after her night shift, which means she hasn't slept.

I also have to get her back to work tomorrow for her next night shift.

And then after that, her schedule picks up and she has virtually no days off for at least another week or so.

It's going to make that whole regular sex thing I just mentioned difficult to continue. It's also going to make seeing her a challenge because our schedules won't coincide unless I blow off work. I'm all for that under normal circumstances, but Ryan and I have a big project in the works, and now is not the time for slacking off. We're in the midst of writing a shit ton of code for some new software we're developing.

Which is why I'm not kidding when I tell her I plan on spending every possible second of the next however long with her, and the more time we can do that naked, the better. But really, I just want to be near her.

Because, well, I'm crazy about her.

I am.

It's a terrible thing and a dangerous thing, and it means I could get really hurt when she's gone in a few weeks. It's not like I can even change her mind and make her stay.

I can't.

This is the direction her life is headed in, and the other night when I casually asked if Boston was the only fellowship to be had, she said it was not only one of the best in the country, but that all the other fellowships worth having have been taken. She said she's finished her two-year fellowship contract here and now to get her certificate she's going to Boston. Evidently, she'd made that arrangement long before I came into the picture and it's too late to change it.

So there you have it folks.

It's a no-win situation.

This is not just her career but her life's work, and unfortunately, it's taking her 3,114 miles away. Yes, I looked it up on Google maps. I'm just that sort of stalker.

And to keep the shit end of things going, Ivy's not coming home for a visit this year. Her parents will be joining her for Christmas, and according to her, she gets no real vacation time. She's there to learn, she reminded me, in a very stern, authoritative voice that I found way too appealing.

So unless I plan on traveling out to see her, which she has not even so much as suggested, we're really sticking with these four weeks and then done thing. And we're already a week in.

I hate it. I fucking hate that idea to the point where I can't even begin to entertain the notion of not seeing her every day.

And here's the ultimate question, how do things like that happen? I mean, I was getting by without an issue before her. Sure, my life wasn't exactly complete or full or whatever, but I managed. I had occasional women that fulfilled my needs, and that seemed to suit me fine.

But now? Now those women seem empty.

Anything other than *Ivy* seems empty and meaningless, and goddamn pointless.

I think about her constantly. She's *always* on my mind. And if I'm not obsessing over her, then I'm probably sleeping, because as I just said, she's always on my mind. So what do I do with that? How do I go from nothing, to Ivy, and back to nothing?

Fuck if I know. So I try not to think about it. I try to live in the moment with her.

Because that's all we have together.

We pull into the 'cabin,' and both Ivy and I look out the windshield at the place and then at each other, and then back at the cabin, and then we both crack up. It's not a cabin so much as it is a multimillion-dollar monstrosity in the mountains that was built to *look* like a cabin.

"You're kidding me with this, right?" I laugh, taken aback, though I feel like I shouldn't be.

I look over to Ivy who's smiling and shaking her head. "This is where they're getting married?"

I shrug, "Guess so. Let's go in and have a look."

Ivy takes my hand, and we rush to the front door. It's cold up here in the mountains, though the snow is gone from everywhere except the mountain peaks.

I open the door with a knock and we walk in, looking around the palatial great room we're instantly greeted with.

"Well, it's certainly big enough," Ivy notes, and I can't help but agree. "I mean, it's gorgeous and grand, but wow. Just wow."

"I know. I wasn't really expecting this, but I don't think I should be fully surprised here. Ryan tends to go over the top when it comes to the Duchess."

"Hey," Ryan's voice startles both of us as he enters, probably because the sound reverberates all around us, echoing off the tall ceilings. "What do you think? Katie says it's too much, but where else are you supposed to fit thirty-five people for a wedding?"

"A hotel?" I deadpan. "Just throwing that out there." Ryan flips me off, but I can see the hurt in his eyes, and I know how much this means to him. "Nah, I'm just messing with you, bro. This place is awesome."

"Yeah?" He looks so damn hopeful it almost makes me want to mess with him more.

"It's aces, Ryan. Truly great. Seeing this gorgeous house makes me heartbroken that I'm going to miss the big event." Ivy walks up to Ryan, giving him a big hug and a pat on the shoulder. She whispers something to him that I can't hear, but it has him smiling and possibly . . . *is he blushing?*

"I hear voices," Duchess Kate calls out in a sing-song voice as she comes from another room on the opposite side of the great room from where Ryan entered. "You guys made it. Thank god."

"Where are we staying, Duchess?" I ask. "I want to throw our things down."

"Upstairs, eighth door on the right."

"Come again? Did you say *eighth?*"

"I did indeed, my fine brown-haired friend. This 'house,'" she puts air quotes around the word, "has twelve bedrooms. I gave you one of five master suites."

"Holy fuck, dude." I look over at Ryan. "I know we do well, but come on? It's one night, right?"

"A very *important* night, Luke," Kate says, enunciating the word like she's telling me to shut up and support my friend because he needs the encouragement. Fucking Ryan. He's lucky I love him as much as I do.

"Okay, well, I'm going to drop off our bags in the eighth room on the right, and then do I get a tour of this palace, or should I just wander around and figure it out as I go?"

"I'll give you the tour." Ryan smiles big before looking over at the Duchess and winking. She giggles at him, slapping his arm playfully and reaching up on her tiptoes to kiss his chin. Kate is unbelievably short compared to him. At least Ivy can kiss me without having to strain herself.

"I'll come with you, Luke," Ivy says through a yawn. "I don't mean to put a damper on things, but I'm completely knackered, and if I don't get at least a little sleep, I'll be entirely useless later."

"And since I can't have you useless later, I think a nap is wise." I take Ivy's hand and lead her in the direction that Kate points us. "Besides, it may take several hours for Ryan to show me the entire place."

Ivy laughs, but I can tell that she's out on her feet. Once we find our room, which really is unbelievable, I leave her to sleep and I go in search of Ryan. I don't have to go far, because the man is waiting for me outside my room.

"Hey, Stalker Joe. What if I had been balls deep inside my girlfriend in there?"

Ryan chuckles, shaking his head. "First of all, I knew that wasn't going to happen with her in that state. Second of all, she's not your girlfriend, and you should get that shit right in your brain now."

*Did I really just call Ivy my girlfriend?*

I didn't even realize I had said that.

"Shit," I hiss out. Ryan leads me down one door before he opens it, showing me another bedroom that is a little smaller with slightly different decor than mine. "I'm in trouble, aren't I?"

"Sounds like it." Ryan pauses in the next bedroom, standing in the center of it staring at me. "What's your deal with her anyway? She's leaving, right? And soon."

"Thanks for the reminder, dickhead. But yeah, she is. And there is dick all I can do to stop it. So," I shrug, "I'm screwed and enjoying whatever time I have left with her."

"But you're falling for her." It's not a question, and the statement gives me pause.

*Am I falling for her?*

"I'm not," I say emphatically. "She's leaving, and I'm . . . me."

Ryan looks at me unimpressed. "What does that even mean?"

"You know what it means."

He sighs, running a hand through his hair. "You could tell her, you know?"

I shrug. "No point. She's leaving."

"I get that she's leaving, asshole, but it's a year and a plane ride, right? You're . . ." Ryan looks away from me for a beat before meeting my eyes. "Different with her."

"Different?" I echo, hating the way that word feels on my tongue.

"Yes, in a good way. In the best way really."

"What is this? Are we going to do each other's nails and discuss the moments of our lives now? I like her. A lot, obviously. It's impossible not to, but she's going, and I . . . have my own shit."

"And that's another thing," he points at me like his mother does when she has a point to make, "You need to stop hiding behind your own shit."

"I'm not," I squeak like a prepubescent boy. "What am I supposed to do, Ryan? There is no point in telling her, and it's not something I share anyway. You shouldn't even know about it, except you're a nosy bastard with insane hacking skills."

He takes two deliberate steps toward me, placing his hands on my shoulders in a way that would seem condescending from anyone else.

"But because I *am* a nosy bastard with insane hacking skills, I *do* know. And I still trust you more than almost anyone on the planet. Something *I* don't do." I swallow hard. "You need to ask yourself if she's worth the fight and the trouble. If she is, then don't let her get away just because she's going to be in Boston for a while, and don't let her get away because you have a past that most people don't."

"And what about my present situation, Ryan? Or are you playing dumb on that one?"

He just stands there watching me.

"If you were me and Kate were Ivy, what would you do about that?"

"I don't have an answer for that, Luke. I know some of what's going on, but definitely not all of it, so I can't really speak to that. But . . .," he sighs, pushing his black-rimmed glasses up the bridge of his nose. "In all honesty, I don't know what I'd do."

I can't say anything back to that. I need to digest that, and it's not something I can do with an audience.

"Come on." He claps me hard on the back the way the fucker always does. "Let me show you the rest of the place where I'm going to trick Katie into marrying me and being mine forever."

"I don't think it's much of a trick if she goes willingly."

"Maybe, but my girl is already freaking out. I caught her crying this morning before we drove up. You know what that means."

I frown. "Do you want me to talk to her? The Duchess and I have a bond you cannot break, not with a thousand swords."

Ryan stops mid-step, turning to face me. "Did you just quote *The Princess Bride*? What kind of self-respecting man does that?"

"The fact that you *know* I just quoted that movie says that you've seen it as many times as I have." I smirk at him as his green eyes narrow at me. "You can't hate on that movie. Besides," I chuckle. "Ivy made me watch it the other day. That girl has a real hard on for eighties flicks."

Ryan shows me bedroom after bedroom, and by this point, I've stopped looking and just nod with an appreciative smile. Like I give a shit about what they look like?

"I can't decide if I like the pussy-whipped version of you or not," Ryan says as we get to yet another goddamn bedroom.

"Said the pot to the kettle. Look at what you're doing right now," I wave my hand in the air indicating our surroundings. "You're showing me bedrooms in the house you've rented for your *wedding*." I point to my chest. "And *I'm* pussy-whipped?"

"I never once said *I* wasn't pussy-whipped. Katie has me by the balls, and she can keep them." He smirks at me. "I like what she does with them."

"And you're saying I should be like this too?"

"That's exactly what I'm saying. Ivy is the best thing to happen to you since I came along, and I'm the master of awesome. Just . . . think about it."

I nod my head and walk on to see yet another boring-ass bedroom that looks absolutely the same as the one before it.

Think about it, he says. I'm different with her, he says. Tell her the truth, he says.

That last one might just be something I cannot do.

# Chapter Twelve

*Luke*

IVY ENDS up sleeping for four hours, and after I wake her up with my face between her thighs—cue wicked smile here—we shower together before joining Ryan and Kate for dinner.

And I have to admit, the four of us together just works.

Ryan and Duchess Kate, and even Claire, are my family. The only one I really have, and well, I sort of feel like I'm living a lie. I mean, I am, but not in the ordinary sense.

In the sense that Ivy and I are a sham.

We're this fake couple with perfect chemistry and symmetry and every other -*try* there is.

So maybe Ryan's right? Maybe I should tell Ivy my dark past and see if she's willing to try long-distance with me?

Crazy, right? Maybe . . .

"So, I told him if he was going to order all that blood and fluids when the patient had an EF of thirty percent, I wasn't going to be the one to hang it," Kate says like any of that was English.

But Ivy fully gets it, shaking her head with a scowl. "Bloody interns. What on earth was he thinking? He would have put that patient into pulmonary edema."

"Right?" Kate slaps the table. "That's exactly what I said. Dammit, I love it when I'm vindicated."

Ivy laughs, but Ryan and I just look at each other, wondering what the hell they're talking about.

Kate pours herself more wine before reaching across the table to empty the bottle in Ivy's glass. This is our second bottle, and I can tell you with absolute certainty that Ryan and I have had a total of two glasses between us. For the mathematically challenged, that means one glass each.

Translation? Our girls are trashed.

Adorably so.

"I think this place is perfect for your wedding," Ivy says, looking around the kitchen that will not be seen by guests. "It's so beautiful and peaceful and . . . romantic."

"Ha," Ryan nudges Kate's shoulder. "Told you, love."

"You don't think it's too much?" Duchess Kate scrunches her eyes like she's trying to see Ivy, or maybe not see double.

Ivy shakes her head slowly. "No, I think it's a fantasy come true. I think your husband-to-be did an ace job."

"I'm sorry you won't be able to come," Kate says to Ivy, before looking at me with an indiscernible expression.

"Me too, but I'm afraid it can't be helped. I leave the week before your wedding," Ivy giggles. "How's that for timing?"

"Do you think you'll ever come back?"

Ivy shrugs a shoulder. "Can't really say." I feel Ivy glance in my direction before turning her attention back to Kate. "I never in a million years thought I'd have a reason to, other than family."

My heart starts pumping like it's trying to outrace my mind.

Is she saying I could be a reason for her to come back?

"Well, if I ever manage to knock Katie up, we could use a doctor," Ryan says before Kate smacks him in the chest. Hard. "What? Why'd you hit me?"

"Because she's a pediatric *emergency* doctor, genius. As talented as she is, I'd rather us not need her medical expertise."

"Fine, point taken. But hitting me that hard means you're drunk. It's time I whisk you away to bed and make you my concubine, since you can't exactly protest." Ryan looks to Ivy with a wink. "Don't worry, Doctor, she likes it."

Ivy holds up her hands, smiling. "TMI, Ryan. I think I officially need to go set fire to my ears."

"Right," Duchess snorts loudly. "Like you haven't heard way worse from that one," she slurs, pointing to me with a wobbling finger that really could be directed at anyone at this table, even people who aren't here. "Or maybe not. Luke's all about the secrets." Then she claps a hand over her mouth with wide eyes and looks to Ryan with an I-didn't-just-say-that expression. "I think you need to take me to bed. I think multiple spankings are in order, and I think I absolutely deserve them."

Kate and Ryan stand, and Kate throws me the most apologetic look in the history of apologetic looks. I just smile, waving her away. What the fuck can I do about it anyway? She's drunk and didn't say too much.

I don't even know if she *knows* all that much.

Ryan isn't usually one to divulge, so I'm guessing my Duchess is going on a hunch. Not a wrong one, but a hunch all the same.

"You ready to go up and try out that hot tub?" I ask Ivy as we stand. Ryan, the stupid rich prick, hired help for our little night away. That help includes a chef and cleaning service, so we don't have to clear our plates or do the dishes.

Personally, I think he was buttering us up with this, but I won't judge.

"Aren't alcohol and hot tubbing contraindicated?" Ivy asks.

"Probably, but I won't let you drown. Promise."

Ivy smiles and allows me to lead her upstairs and down the hall, and I swear it takes us a solid five minutes to make that trek.

But once we enter our suite, I'm blown away. The fire is roaring in the hearth and the hot tub has a layer of pink rose petals floating on the surface.

"Did you knock me unconscious and drag my lifeless body to an over-the-top five-star hotel?" Ivy asks, her jaw slightly agape.

"No, but that would be tempting if this place wasn't amazing."

"So, is this the point in the evening when I get naked and you get naked, and we sit in the boiling hot water while I try to ignore all the thermophiles in there, and we chat about nothing of importance?"

"Um . . . Yes?"

"Good." Ivy turns to me, placing both of her palms on my chest. "Because I'm a little buzzed, Luke. And I think I like you against my better judgment, and I think . . . I shouldn't."

"I know, honey." I lean down to kiss the tip of her cute nose.

"Why did you have to come back now? And why couldn't you have left in the middle of the night again?"

I chuckle, though there really isn't anything funny about what she's saying. In fact, it's so absolutely gut-wrenching that I feel the slice throughout my entire body.

This girl just has me. It's not even wanting. It's way beyond wanting. We're bordering on need here. Big, fat, ugly need.

But how do you say no to the angel of your dreams?

How do you push back from the one you let slip through your fingers a decade ago?

You don't, right? You go for it, even if you know, you fucking *know*, that she'll cripple you. Or worse yet, that you'll cripple her because there is no way we can have a happy ending. It's just not possible for me.

I lower my forehead to hers, staring into her eyes that are almost a smoky gray against the firelight, which serves as the only illumination for our room.

*I'm falling for you*, I don't say.

"I'm in trouble," I choose instead.

"Me too, I think, but I don't want to be, Luke. I'm half-tempted to call this quits and save myself the heartbreak."

Just that simple thought fills me with more dread than I ever thought possible.

"There's no point in doing that. I'd still want you even if I couldn't have you. It's still fun. It's still no strings. Don't overthink this, Ivy." The words burn my throat and taste like battery acid as I swallow them down. I hate lying to her like that. But I can't lose her either. Not yet.

I'm not ready to give her up.

She swallows hard, blinking up at me. "Then let's go soak in the water for a while; it looks heavenly."

She strips down to nothing, standing there naked with the flames of the fire licking an orange glow up her skin. She's so beautiful. So stunningly gorgeous without even the smallest hint of insecurity at her nudity as she stands there, allowing me to drink her in.

"I'm jealous of the firelight."

She tilts her head, a small smirk bouncing on the corner of her lips.

"Those flames are dancing all over your body, every single place I want to touch and kiss." Her cheeks heat, but she doesn't look away.

"Are you ready?" she whispers, this moment too intimate, her desire too great, for her normal tone.

I strip down too, her eyes soaking me in the way mine did with her. Once she's satisfied with my lack of apparel, she reaches a hand out for me.

I accept it, feeling a zing of electricity that is so familiar and yet I never grow used to it. How can it be like this each and every time I'm with her? How can I still possibly crave more?

We sink into the blistering water that smells of chlorine, and I hit the button to turn on the jets. Ivy leans back, resting her head on one of the cushions and closes her eyes. She's content, peaceful even, and I can't stop watching her, wanting to absorb some of that for myself.

"When was your last relationship?" Her eyes don't open as she asks me this, her voice half-lost in the sound of the jets. "Other than that girl in college?"

"No one."

Her eyes open wide at my answer as she regards me with astonishment.

"Really?"

I nod, not wanting to elaborate on the reasons behind all that and praying she won't ask. I'm not ready for that conversation. I doubt I'll ever be.

"That surprises me." It's a simple statement, but the meaning behind it is anything but. She's asking me why without being direct about it, and I refuse to bite. Ivy sighs out when she realizes that. "Do you think you and I would be if I weren't leaving?"

*That's good question, Ivy.*

"I don't know. I'd love to say yes."

"But?" She voices the word I didn't.

"But it's a moot point right now, so why question it?"

She nods, giving a half-shrug, but there's a slight frown marring her expression. "I guess you're right."

I slide through the water, displacing some over the edge as I move to sit directly beside her. "The truth is, I doubt I'd be able to stay away. I can't even seem to do that now, so . . ."

Ivy climbs onto my lap, steam undulating in the air as it rises from her body. Her arms encircle my neck. It's cold out here, but the water makes that experience—the dichotomy between freezing cold and boiling hot—pleasurable.

"Did you know that you're my one and only one-night stand?" I don't respond; I just stare at her. "Did you know that you're also the only man I've ever had no-strings sex with? I don't do this, Luke. I'm a relationship sort of girl, but I'm having fun with you. I really am, and maybe it's time I allowed for that to be okay."

"I didn't mean to make you think I wouldn't want more with you."

She shakes her head, beads of water running down her neck and chest. "No, I'm being serious. I tend to overanalyze everything, in case you haven't noticed," she says, giving me a playful smirk that doesn't quite reach her eyes. "But with you, there's really no need, and that's oddly refreshing. It's like, for once, I don't have to think this through."

Why does that hurt so much to hear?

Why do I want her to beg and plead to be mine?

*I could love you, Ivy. I could love you forever if being with me wouldn't break you.*

"You ready to get out?" she asks, slipping off me and wrapping herself in a giant fluffy white towel. "I'm freezing."

Fun with no strings. What a stupid fucking idea. Especially when I know, *I know*, we're both doomed.

# Chapter Thirteen

*Ivy*

IT'S a rare day for me. Usually, I work twelve to fourteen-hour shifts—if I'm lucky—and those usually end either first thing in the morning or late into the evening. But as I said, today is rare. Today I'm working a swing shift and that has me finishing up at noon. Amazing.

And to add to that, it's an uncommonly beautiful, cloudless day.

So what are my grand plans for the day?

I have none.

Luke is working since it's a Friday, and that's what people with ordinary jobs do during the week. I should go back to my flat and pack. I should make the dozen or so phone calls that I need to make and get things settled for Boston. I moved my plane ticket. I haven't even mentioned that to Luke yet, but I was scheduled to depart on a Monday and I pushed it back to that Wednesday instead.

A little more than two weeks from today.

Crikey, it's coming on fast.

I should be excited. I should be bloody ecstatic because I'm finishing up two grueling years of fellowship that followed three grueling years of residency. So why am I not bouncing off the walls right now? Why am I not jumping for joy and leaving the moment I check out of this program, racing toward the next?

I'll give you a hint. It's a one-word answer.

Luke.

I like him far more than I should.

Which is why when I walk out of the Emergency Department, through the employee exit and toward the parking garage, I'm thinking about him. I think about him the entire three minutes it takes me to get to my car on the second level.

And as if my mind conjured him up out of thin air, he's there, waiting for me, leaning up against the hood of my car and looking as gorgeous as ever.

Luke's wearing a black t-shirt that hugs those impressive biceps to a drool-worthy degree, dark jeans and his typical black boots. His face is clean shaven, but his hair is tousled and windswept.

Sexy bad boy meets GQ.

You'd never know this man is a computer nerd, if I could even dare to call him that.

"What are you doing here?" I can't help the elated surprise in my voice.

"I took the afternoon off." He smiles back, showcasing that dimple to perfection. "And I wanted to spend it with you." His mahogany eyes feast on me and though you'd think they'd be ravaged with heat, since that seems to be our thing, they're not.

They're the unmistakable eyes of a boy who likes a girl.

Damn him.

Goddamn him and those irresistible flutters taking off all throughout my chest.

"I love that," I tell him honestly. "What did you have in mind?"

"Well. . ." He pushes off the hood of my car, meeting me halfway. "It's a beautiful day, Doctor. I was thinking ice cream and a walk in the park."

Oh lord. That's it. I'm a goner. Ice cream is my ultimate weakness. It's like he dialed a direct line into my brain and asked it for the one thing that would make me fall for him. Ice cream and a stroll through the park. Yeah, he nailed it perfectly.

"Ice cream?"

He nods, smiling and looking deeply into my eyes as he wraps his arms around my waist and draws me into his warm body. "I want nothing more than to walk around the city with you and eat an ice cream. It's so juvenile and innocent that I think we may just be able to pull it off."

"Have I told you that ice cream is my absolute favorite food in the whole wide world?"

"Really?"

"Right-o."

"Then I'm really wracking up the brownie points here. A few more of these impromptu dates, and I'll never be able to get rid of you."

I can't help but laugh at that, if for nothing more than the irony that statement presents.

"When do you need to be back here?"

"Tomorrow morning."

He grins wickedly at that. "Then you're mine to do with as I see fit. I'm driving. Leave your car here."

I can only nod because I want absolutely everything he's offering me. Luke takes my hand and leads me back around to the visitor side of the garage since my car is parked in the employee area. Opening my door for me, he waits until I've slipped inside before shutting it.

His car roars to life, the deafening sound of the loud engine bouncing off the concrete walls. "Where are we headed?"

His eyes find mine quickly before turning back to the road, a very satisfied smirk lining his full lips. "I know a place," is all he says before driving us out into a sunny Seattle.

We pull up in front of a shop not too much later, and as he takes my hand, helping me from the car. I can't help but admire the sign that boasts homemade ice cream.

Is he trying to make me fall in love?

I mean, he's not even fighting fair now, is he?

The door jingles with a bell announcing our arrival, and I'm immediately hit with the scent of fresh waffles, vanilla, and of course, ice cream. My mouth instantly waters. I abandon Luke's hand in favor of the glass case that houses so many different and wonderful flavors that I hardly know where to begin.

"May I help you?" a college-age girl with poor skin asks. I'm nearly tempted to offer her a prescription for it before I remember myself.

"Yes," I say without waiting on Luke, who's chuckling behind me, evidently finding my girlish adoration of ice cream amusing. "I'd like. . ." My eyes scroll over the titles and settle on my favorite. "A waffle cone of salted caramel, please."

"What size?"

"Oh." Well, I guess this is my lunch, right? "A medium, please."

"Sure, and for you, sir?" she asks Luke.

He grumbles something under his breath about not liking being called sir but approaches the case with a smile. "Same, only I'd like cookie dough."

"That's bloody unimaginative," I tease, and he looks over at me with a bemused expression. "There are so many other flavors here that are loads more exciting than *cookie dough*," I say, wrinkling my nose up in distaste. In reality, I love cookie dough. It's my second favorite, but I can't resist the urge to needle him.

"Unimaginative, huh?" I nod. "Then I guess I won't give you a taste of it." He leans into me, hovering above my ear. "Too bad, I was hoping I'd be able to taste its sweetness on your tongue."

My face flushes and not from embarrassment.

"God, I love that color on your skin," he growls, causing a series of gooseflesh to rise where his breath passes.

I nudge him with my elbow because if he continues this, we won't make it to the park, and I'm rather looking forward to that.

Luke pays for our cones, and we step outside, licking as we go and groaning out our appreciation. This may, in fact, be the best ice cream I've ever had. Why am I only just now finding this place? It may, in fact, be worse than leaving Luke and my parents behind.

"The park's this way," he says, pointing down the street. Taking my hand, he leads me into the park that is flaunting signs of early summer. Trees and flowers and green grass surround us as we meander deeper in. I'm hit with its appealing aroma everywhere we go.

"In my nine years of living in Seattle, I've never been to this park."

"Not surprising," he says. "You don't have kids or a dog."

"I guess." I shrug, not exactly loving that reminder. As we stroll along, I see his point, noting an area that in the summer is designed to be a splash pad for children to play in and a large gated dog park, where there is small terrier having at it. "You don't either, and yet you seem to know your way."

"I don't sleep so well, and after being attached to a computer for hours, I like to walk around outside. This park isn't far from my building."

"No, I guess it's not." I take another bite of my ice cream, thinking his words through. "But you come here at night? I can't imagine that being a clever thing to do."

He laughs, pulling my hand and my body into his side and leaning his weight against me. "I'm a big guy, Ivy, and so far, I haven't had a problem."

I don't know what to make of that, so I just let it go.

Turning quickly, I lean over and swipe a taste of his ice cream with my tongue before licking the messy cream from my lips. "Hey, what happened to unimaginable?" he laughs, pulling the cone back and out of my reach.

"What happened to you wanting to taste it on my lips?"

"Good point. Come here."

We pause, turning to face each other as his head dips down to mine and our lips meet. It's not a passionate kiss. It's actually rather sweet, no pun intended. It's also quick. Luke pulls back, licking his lips as he goes.

"It tastes better on you."

"Well, then let's see about mine." I practically shove my ice cream into his mouth, making him jump back, chuckling as he goes.

I manage to swipe it on the corner of his mouth and up his left cheek a bit.

I'm laughing so hard, I might actually drop my cone, which would be tragic.

"That was dirty," he says, feigning indignation, but his eyes are sparkling.

"Then let me clean you up." I lunge for him, practically toppling us both over and causing a startled rumble from his chest. I kiss and lick his face until there is no evidence of my crime remaining. "There. Better now?"

"You really are the best kind of trouble, Doctor Green. And in this moment I wish you had gotten a cup instead of a cone. There is something far too erotic in watching a woman lick ice cream off a cone. It's like easy porn for men with weak imaginations. I believe I said juvenile was the goal."

"You don't strike me as someone with a weak imagination, despite your choice in ice cream suggesting otherwise," I smirk as we restart our jaunt.

"With you, my imagination is boundless."

We continue on, approaching a playground that has me smiling broadly. Maybe it's the pediatrician in me, but I could spend hours watching children play. I pull him inside the fenced-off area, and we sit on a bench, watching two young girls who look like twins, swinging on the swings while their mum pushes them.

"What made you want to become a doctor and work with children?" he asks after a few quiet moments, taking my free hand into his.

"My best mate growing up back home had an osteosarcoma. It's a tumor of the bone, and he was always in and out of hospitals. Occasionally when he was doing well, I'd be able to go around for a visit. I knew the moment I saw the doctors tending to him that I wanted to be one."

Luke's eyes are blank, staring out into space, his ice cream momentarily forgotten as it begins to drip down the side of his cone while he thinks on this. "Is your friend okay?"

"Yeah. They did a below-the-knee amputation and chemo, but

he fought the cancer off, and now he manages brilliantly with a prosthetic."

"Wow. That's an amazing story. Do you still keep in touch?"

"Sometimes. He's still over there, so it's hard to match up our time. We email with some frequency though."

He turns to me with a smile, taking up his ice cream again.

"What about you? How did you get into computers?"

His expression falls instantly before he turns away from me, staring unseeingly out into the wooded area just beyond the playpen. He doesn't answer and the longer this silence continues, the more awkward it becomes between us.

*He never answers personal questions.*

Ever.

I don't know if it's a matter of trying to maintain his distance from me or if it's something else entirely, but I'd be lying if I said it didn't hurt, especially when I'm so desperate for more of him.

I'm also dying to ask him if he wants children one day, given that we're sitting in a park watching them play. But I don't dare go there. It's a violation of our no strings, just fun policy. Have I mentioned how much I both hate and love that policy?

So I just ignore the building tension as I finish off the last of my ice cream and enjoy the beautiful day and the happy, healthy children playing.

And then his phone rings.

The second one that he always carries on him, but never uses unless he's being called on it. I've never actually seen such a generic yet high-tech looking phone in my life. But he doesn't answer it. He *never* answers it in front of me.

"We should go," he says, staring at the screen briefly before sliding it back into his pocket. "I have something to take care of quickly, but hopefully it shouldn't take too long, and then I'm all yours."

*Are you?* Yeah, I don't ask that question either.

"Great. Let's go," I say instead. Because nothing good can come of hearing him answer that question. At least not yet.

# Chapter Fourteen

*Luke*

The predawn clouds have that reddish intensity that, at this time of year, can only indicate a storm. Normally that would piss me off, but it's Sunday, and Ivy has a rare day off. She's asleep in my bed, looking so damn beautiful and peaceful it makes me ache.

I'm jealous of her dreams. Of the swirling thoughts floating through her mind because they have her undivided attention all night.

If that makes me a pathetic bastard, then so be it.

In the two plus weeks she's been mine, things have been blissfully quiet. That's not exactly uncommon, but it sets me on edge, because they never stay that way for long. The longer I allow this to go on, the further I get sucked into her.

And she's leaving in fourteen days.

That thought makes me cringe, because who the fuck am I kidding? I'm so gone on this girl it's not even funny.

And that's the thing. It's not funny. It's scary and wrong.

So very wrong, and I have no one to blame but myself. But I keep hoping that everything will take care of itself and that she won't ask me the questions that have been lingering on the tip of her tongue these past weeks.

I know she can see through me.

I know she knows how crazy I am about her. But she doesn't ask, and she's stopped trying to push me away. She did once, and we had a really good fight about it, but I told her, yet again, that we knew what we were getting into.

And I do. I really do.

But that doesn't mean I'm prepared for it.

That doesn't mean that I'm not crafting a plan to try and coax her into believing that a year isn't really all that long, and that somehow, we could make this work.

That we could have a shot at something great. Something real and lasting.

But I'm not stupid. I'm painfully aware of the reality. Which makes me an asshole for taking her into my bed night after night like I'm starving for her. Like I'm racing the clock that's ticking in my head.

The further I allow this to go, the greater the strain in the end for both of us.

I just don't know how to stop it. Fuck that, I don't *want* to stop it.

Soon she'll be gone. Soon, so very, very soon, all of this will blow up, and I'll lose her.

But worse than that, I'll hurt her. Because try as she might, I know she feels the same about me.

Oh, she denies it to an almost pathological degree, but it's there.

I see it in the way she smiles when she doesn't think I notice her watching me. I see it in the way she looks at me. I feel it when I'm inside her.

Every morning I wake up and say, *just one more day and then I'll stop this. I'll let her go because what I'm doing to her is a fucking crime.*

And then that day comes, and I have a new set of excuses.

Then there's the other issue.

The one I have zero control over. And if she were to ever learn all that there is to know, she wouldn't just be gone, she'd hate me.

*What have I done?*

The familiar prickling of panic begins to rise within, like the swell of a wave coming to shore. Ivy is the only one who has ever been able to make the waters recede, to keep them at bay. I need her. I need her now, and I might just need her forever, though there's no way I can keep her that long.

"Ivy, baby," I coo in her ear as I run my nose along her neck, savoring her unique fragrance.

"Mmmm," she groans, pushing me away and making me smile.

"Ivy, wake up. I need to tell you something important."

One of her slate-blue eyes opens, and she peers up at me before blinking twice. "What's wrong?" she mumbles, rolling and stretching out like a cat.

"I need to tell you something important," I repeat.

"You mentioned that already, Luke, but it's dark out, and the fact that I don't have to be up early tells me that this better be bloody life-altering or you're in trouble."

I chuckle, burying myself against her, my nose and mouth perched between her neck and the top of her shoulder. "Happy anniversary."

"Pardon?" She's adorably confused, her voice still thick with sleep, her hair tousled and sexy as hell.

"Today is our two-week sex anniversary. Two weeks ago today we had sex for the very first time since meeting again." I'm smiling like a bastard, waiting patiently for her to lay into me, which no doubt she will.

"Wow, that's unbelievably romantic and clearly worth waking me before the bloody sun. You should have that printed on a card or something; I'm sure it would sell like mad."

I laugh, my chest rumbling against her body, her sweet perfect breasts crushed against me.

"Actually, I was going to hire an airplane to write it across the sky."

"Ooh, I hope the message will include my name. First and last, of course."

"Of course, how else would you know it's for you? You think

we're the only two people in Seattle celebrating a two-week sex anniversary?"

"That's a valid point. I'm sure people all over the world are being woken by their sex partner to celebrate the momentous occasion."

"Is that what you are? My sex partner?" I raise my head, peering down into her beautiful, smiling face. "That sounds awfully clinical, Doctor."

"What would you call us then?"

She's baiting me. I know it, and she knows it, and I can't answer that for her.

But I'm so insanely in love with her. There. I am. I admit it.

I don't even know how or when it happened, but it did. I look at her and I feel a happiness I have never ever known. She's light, a glowing, radiant sun. Pure energy, the most powerful force I've ever encountered.

And I need her. Just a little while longer.

I know it's selfish. I do, but I can't stop.

"I'd call you mine, but that's a ridiculous moniker." I cringe at my words, waiting for her to pounce, but she just looks up at me quietly blinking.

"I guess that's true; we don't really need a title or name anyway. It only complicates matters." She thinks this is just sex to me.

*It's supposed to just be sex to you!*

Right. And as much as I'll hate myself for this later, she still needs to know.

I shift my body so I'm hovering over her, my hands bracketing her head.

"It's been sixteen days since I showed up on that bench outside your building. The best sixteen days of my life, hands down." I stop there, but I'm aching to continue. I can't. She'll end it now, and I'll miss these last fourteen days with her.

Ivy's eyes sparkle with a sheen of unshed tears as she reaches up to run her fingers along my jaw. "Me too," she whispers, almost reluctant to utter the words.

"Hey, none of that." She blinks a few times, trying to hold her tears back. "We're okay, right?"

She nods, but doesn't look all that convinced.

"Not that I'm complaining or anything, but you realize you've only had a series of stolen moments with me, right? I mean, I work insane hours, and I'm rather moody when I'm hungry and tired, which is often and . . ." she pauses, deliberating her next words. "And I don't know you all that well. You don't know me all that well either, because all we've had are these stolen moments."

She's nervous. Ivy chews on the corner of her lip when she is. I doubt she's even aware that she does it. She's afraid and so am I, but I can't change our reality.

"Stolen moments with you are the only kind worth having."

Those tears that had been threatening begin to fall, and I bring my mouth down to capture them before lowering my naked body against hers.

"Is this real?" she whispers against my lips. "I keep expecting to wake up and be gone. This is all a dream. Pretty soon, we'll both have to wake from it."

"I feel the same way."

"So if this were an eighties movie, they'd start playing the cheesy music and we'd kiss and smile to it?"

"Hell yeah. The cheesy music is imperative to our story. How else would we know this was the point where I throw you the epic one-liners?"

"That's a legitimate point." She squirms a little beneath me, and I can't help but love the hell out of that. But she's still apprehensive —so very unsure of this. I am too, way more than she could ever be. "And you're sure about the whole continuing this with me thing?"

*No.*

"Baby, if I wasn't, why would I ever have agreed to try that disgusting Vegemite shit? No one in their right mind would ever do that unless they were getting regular sex. It's probably the only way anyone ever eats it."

Ivy laughs, smacking my shoulder playfully. "Vegemite is what makes us Aussies big, beautiful, and strong. It's a national staple."

"I will not argue that point, but it is the grossest thing I've ever eaten, and I pledged for a frat my freshman year. That's all I'm saying."

She smiles wide, her eyes luminous in the minimal light filtering in from the street. "Do I want to ask?"

"No, you'll think less of me, and I make it a point never to have naked women think less of me."

"I see." Ivy tilts her head to the side, her hair fanned out across my pillow. "Then how about you give me more of you?"

"Like this type of more?" I roll my hips into her and her eyes flutter shut as her lips part in a silent moan. I love it when she does that. It's so goddamn sexy.

"Well, it is our two-week sex anniversary, right? We should celebrate that."

"Whatever you say, darlin'."

My mouth dips to hers, and since it's early and we don't have anywhere to be, I take my time kissing her.

It was never something I ever really cared about. I mean, I like kissing. Who doesn't? But it always led to other things—more pleasurable and crucial things. But with Ivy, I really can't get enough of her mouth. It's the most sensual thing.

I slide inside of her slowly, wanting to prolong this moment.

She is so perfect to me. So absolutely devastatingly perfect.

There is nothing in the world as good as being inside Ivy. Nothing like watching her as I touch and kiss her body. Watching her come undone beneath me, knowing I'm the one who is making her feel that way.

I could be with her forever and never tire of it. I'll always crave more of her sounds and this feeling.

I lust after nothing more than to live in this suspended reality with her, to prolong this dream instead of living the harsh reality where I lose her—where I'm nowhere near good enough to deserve or keep her.

Where she leaves.

We make love, and it's as new as the feelings and sensations swirling around inside my chest. And when we're done, when we're both smiling and sweaty and content, we watch the first of the downpour fall, wrapped in a cocoon of blankets.

"This storm is oddly beautiful, though I still think watching the snow fall is my favorite. It's not something we had back home. In fact, I never saw any snow until I moved up to Seattle," Ivy whispers, enveloped in my arms. "But I like watching the rain and wind whipping past your window from the comfort of your bed."

"I never liked the snow until I moved out here. Or the rain for that matter."

She turns in my arms, away from the window to face me.

"Why not? Does it snow a lot in Oklahoma?"

*Shit.* Here come the personal questions.

"Not a lot, but it does snow on occasion in the winter."

"What was it like there, growing up?"

My body tenses instantly, and I know she feels it because her brows form a small V shape between them. "Hot in the summer and cold in the winter." It's a shit answer, but we are talking about the weather, aren't we? "I'm going to go start some coffee." I kiss the corner of her lips. "Do you want tea?"

Ivy frowns, silently examining me as I slide away from her, pulling on my boxers and sweatpants. I'm going through the motions of getting dressed, but really, I'm cursing myself and waiting for the inevitable.

What would she do if I told her the truth about my past? Would she run away screaming? Would she be afraid of me? God, that thought makes me sick.

"Yes, please," she says.

*What the hell is she saying yes to? Did I ask her question?*

I turn back to her.

"I'd love some tea."

She gets up out of bed and heads straight for the restroom, shutting the door with a quiet click behind her.

Our perfect stolen moment over. And I know it's only a sign of things to come.

# Chapter Fifteen

*Ivy*

ROLLING MY HEAD AROUND, I try in vain to release the tight knots from my neck. Eight hours of non-stop trauma has a way of knocking me on my ass, but the outcome was definitely worth a crick or two.

An eighteen-year-old boy with two gunshot wounds to the chest. A car accident involving a toddler, and a fifteen-year-old who overdosed.

Holy hell, that was horrendous.

But he survived, and hopefully this was enough of a wake-up call to get him off the streets and away from drugs. I am still hopeful despite all the rubbish I've seen in my years of fixing kids.

I am not one to give up on people.

That thought makes me want to laugh for some reason, though it feels anything but humorous. I was blissfully distracted for my entire shift, but now that it's over, my thoughts automatically stray back to Luke.

It's only been a little more than two weeks, but he's all I see, hear, or think about.

He's everywhere all the time, and no matter what I do, I can't seem to think about anything but him.

I should be focusing on my upcoming fellowship. I should be studying in my free time and doing nothing but working every second of every day in preparation for the grueling and demanding year to come.

And though I am doing some of that, all I seem to *want* to do is be with Luke.

We've spent nearly every day of these two weeks together, even if it's just a passing moment we steal like it might be our last. I sleep at his place if I'm not working nights, and he wakes me up at mine if I am.

He comes over after work, and I do the same, and when we're together, we're the only two people in the universe.

I'm mad about him.

I'm also the world's biggest liar, because I'm head over heels in love with him.

And that's just a dog's breakfast, right? I mean, I'm leaving, and he's not following. This is supposed to be fun and nothing more. It's supposed to be fun, dammit! Though I know he feels something for me, I highly doubt it's a tenth of what I feel for him.

Small soft hands cover my eyes from behind me.

I've always hated this trick—even as a child—and it's not something someone relishes when they're standing in the Emergency Department of a hospital. But then I catch the scent of musk emanating from her wrists and I smile so big, my face hurts.

"You derro wanker," I say, and my sister Sophia laughs, removing her hands from my eyes and jumping in front of me.

"Ha. I gotcha, you nubby cunt."

Without warning I launch myself at her, squeezing the life from her small body.

"I can't believe you came up a day early," I squeal. "I wasn't expecting you until tomorrow avro."

"I finished up early with a client and said, fuck it, I'm going to rain on my little sister's parade."

Sophia is wearing her usual all black with bright red lipstick. She is big into the rockabilly style with her short, bleach-blonde hair, done à la Marilyn Monroe from *Some Like It Hot* and black horn-rimmed glasses complete with rhinestones.

"Who was it this time? Movie star in rehab or rock star gone wrong?" I tease, but in reality, I think her job is aces.

She is a publicist to the stars, and the best in her field at that. Sophia is ruthless, and to put it in her words, you don't muck around with a bitch like her.

It's just one of the many, many things I love about my sister.

"Movie star. Such a fuckwit." She rolls her pretty gray eyes, the same color as our father's, and then gives me another hug. "Are you done for the night, or do I need to start drinking by myself?"

"I'm done, but I need a shower and a change before we go out. I'll have to ring around if you want to meet my mates."

"Of course I want to meet your mates," Sophia gives me a look that says I'm an idiot for thinking otherwise. "And I want to meet that bloke you've been getting on with."

"You'll meet him. I have plans with him tonight anyway."

We walk outside into the rainy yet mild evening, and Sophia loops her arm through mine. "I've missed you, Ivy girl. What the hell am I going to do with you all the way across the country?"

"Come visit?" I muse.

"I hate the east coast of this bloody country. It's cold, even when it's hot. The people are not a friendly lot."

I laugh, shaking my head as we slip into my car and drive toward my flat.

"You live in L.A. and are one of the nastiest women I know."

"But that doesn't mean other people have to be rude now, does it? There's a certainty in the deception of L.A. A level of expectation that comes with the lies, but at least people are cordial to your face. On the east coast they're all honest and forthright and cruel. It's unsettling. You'll see."

"Whatever you say." Sophia and I laugh all the way home, chatting like we haven't seen each other in years instead of a few months. She's committed to getting us all decked out for a night out at the pub, and though Cello's is a nicer bar, it's certainly not a club.

"Bloody oath, this one for sure." Sophia walks into the bathroom, the heels of her boots clicking against the tile floor, her hands showcasing a silver dress. Not just any silver dress, but the silver dress I wore the night of my one-night stand with Luke a decade ago.

"No."

"Yes. You'll look scrumptious in this frock."

"Not that one."

She nods her head emphatically, shoving the shiny material at me with determination. "Stop being a prude and put this on. We're running late, and if my liver doesn't get a steady dose of alcohol in the next hour or so, I won't be responsible for my actions." She widens her eyes for effect.

This is really the last dress on the planet I want to wear tonight, but for some odd reason, I don't want to tell her about that. I never once mentioned my one-night stand with Luke, and though I think she'd be proud of me for it, I find I want to keep that night for myself.

I grab the small dress that will show more skin than it will cover and slip it on over my head.

"Gorgeous. Let's go."

I get a ring from Claire just as we're walking out the door, and she informs me that Kate and Ryan are coming as well.

"Just don't bring anyone home to my flat, Soph," I tell her right before we walk in. "It's a one-bedroom, and either you're on the pull-out sofa or in my bed. In either scenario, I don't want some strange woman with us."

"Ivy girl, if I find someone I want to have sex with, I'll be sure to go to *her* place."

"Cheers, mate. Most appreciated."

I open the door for her, and she saunters in with the type of confidence very few people truly have. But Sophia exudes it naturally. She knows precisely who she is and doesn't give a toss if anyone doesn't like it. It's one of the things I admire most about my big sister, and wish I could emulate.

I like to think I have confidence, and with certain things I do.

I am a very good doctor. I excel in my craft with an aptitude and talent that's been mastered through years of education, training, and hard work.

And I feel like once upon a time, I was a brave, self-assured woman. I mean, I still am, but when it comes to men, not so much.

I dated here and there, but my first serious boyfriend turned into some crazy possessive stalker who tried to kill me.

Jason and I were in medical school together, and we were both very focused on our studies. I wanted it to stay casual; he didn't. Slowly, over the months we were together, he began pushing for things in small ways. He didn't like my friends and went out of his way to isolate me from them. He tried to make it so he was the only man around me in a social setting, and would frequently start fights with me over paranoid delusions of infidelity. Like that scene Kate mentioned when I had dinner at her house.

Then he wanted to live together, but went about it passive-aggressively by slowly moving his stuff into my place, and occasionally refusing to leave. Finally, I realized what was really going on, and I ended it.

That's when the fun really began.

He would follow me around to my classes, and make a scene if he saw me speaking to another male—no matter who they were. It began to escalate to the point where he would stalk me everywhere I went, and eventually it all came to a head when he went berserk on a fellow student at a study session who had asked me for my number.

He punched the poor bloke in the face, and when I tried to break things up, I got a nice smack across the cheek for the effort.

That was the wake-up call that I should never have required, and I filed a restraining order that night. The car accident was another matter, and even just thinking about it now, terrifies me.

I've been working tirelessly to recover from all that, and I finally feel like I'm nearly there.

Now I'm "dating" Luke. But that has a very real and fast-approaching expiration date. An expiration date I'd rather avoid, because I'm so mad about him. So absolutely insanely crazy for him that I can hardly see straight, and it scares the bloody hell out of me.

But it also makes me smile as I spot him in the bar waiting for me.

Luke's chocolate eyes take me in, heating with a flash of something else I quickly realize is recognition. I'm wearing the dress I wore the night I met him, and the slow impish grin that spreads across his face suddenly makes me glad I allowed Sophia to force this on me.

"Come on, doll," Sophia pulls me in. Apparently, I stopped moving in the doorway. "I'm parched. I need a bevy before I meet these mates of yours."

"Manhattan, right?" I look over at the bartender and she's smiling at me. "I remember you."

"I'm impressed," I say, a bit astonished. "That was weeks ago."

She gives me a wink and then starts fixing our drinks.

"You slagger," Sophia says to me, playfully nudging my shoulder. "You're sharing your biscuit with that tasty bloke over there, and yet the hot bartender—*female* bartender I should add—knows you." I glare at her, and not for the bartender part. "Oh, come off it. He's delicious enough to make me consider rethinking my anti-dick stance. And those things do absolutely nothing for me."

"Stuff it, you nobby cow," I mutter, gratefully accepting my large drink and taking an equally large sip.

I make the rounds with Sophia, and when she gets to Luke, she gives him a long once-over, inspecting him carefully.

"I've heard loads, though I do have to say you're much larger than my baby sis here let on." She cups the crotch of his jeans and I nearly spit my drink across the room, but settle for choking it down instead.

Luke laughs, not at all disturbed by the fact that a stranger just grabbed his manhood in public.

"I like to think so, though I do wish she had conveyed my size accurately." Luke leans his long frame against the side of the bar, looking at my sister with a broad smile. "Ivy did, however, describe you perfectly."

"Of course she did, I'm by far and away her favorite person ever." She touches Luke's chest, running her bright red nail up and down the center. Suddenly, their little interaction is much more than I can stand.

"That I believe," he says with a wink and a smile that has my tough-as-nails lesbian sister simpering. Luke does have that effect on everyone he meets, so I shouldn't be surprised.

Reaching out, he grabs my hand, yanking me into his chest before leaning down to whisper in my ear, "Is this dress meant to entice or torture?"

I giggle like a little school girl. Apparently he has that effect on me as well.

"Both. Is it working?"

"Like you wouldn't believe. You look so goddamn hot and sexy in that thing I can barely think straight. Please tell me you're staying with me tonight?"

I shake my head, reaching up to run my fingers through his day-old stubble. "Sophia is here."

He gives me a sad smile and a nod of his head. "I know. I just don't like sharing you. Is it wrong of me if I tell you that I miss you when you're not around?"

When he says things like that, my heart clenches and my stomach fills with butterflies.

"No," I shake my head, looking up at him. The way he takes me in, studying my face, resembles love so closely that I have to remind myself it's not. "I feel the same way about you."

Luke leans down, brushing his lips against me before dropping his forehead to mine, his fingers dancing along the exposed skin of my back.

"Jesus, Ivy, how am I ever going to survive when you leave? I'm so addicted to everything about you."

I can't say anything back to that, so I lean up, pressing my lips to his, wordlessly telling him that I feel the exact same way.

"Enough of that lovey-dovey rubbish. She needs a shot of something girly and yummy, because despite the Manhattans she slugs down, she's not a boozer," Sophia informs the bartender, so close to Luke and I that it almost feels like an invasion.

The bartender examines Luke for a beat before turning back to me with a wink. "I'm going to make you two. A pop my cherry, and a bend over Shirley."

I burst out laughing. "You're razzing, right?"

"Definitely not when it comes to sex-themed shots."

"Oh, yummy," Sophia says. "Make mine a tight snatch."

"Bloody hell, Sophia." I'm laughing so hard I have tears rolling down my face. Luke's arms are wrapped tightly around my waist, but he's laughing too and so is everyone else. Only my sister can get away with things like this.

"And what about for me?" Luke asks, leaning forward.

"For you?" The bartender half-sneers, eyeing him closely. "How about a blow job?"

Luke laughs out loud. "There are way too many things I could say to that, but I'll accept it only if my girl here takes it and you make one for all these beautiful women at the bar."

"Coming up." The bartender shakes her head with an amused grin.

"But I wanted a redheaded slut," Claire whines, suddenly joining our small gathering. "It's my calling card."

"I really don't need to hear that," Ryan says with a scowl.

"Lighten up, boss. Last I checked you're not my dad, and if I want to take a pretty lady home with me tonight, I'll do it." Claire sticks her tongue out at him like she's six, and we all laugh some more.

Luckily we're saved by the overwhelming amount of shots that are placed on the bar top, three in front of me—including something with whipped cream on top.

I can only guess at which one that is.

"I can't do all those. I'll be sick."

"I'll take these two," Luke says. "But no way I'm not watching you take that blow job shot. You do know you're not supposed to use your hands, right?"

I shoot him a look, and he throws his hands up in surrender. "I don't make the rules, I just enforce them."

"You want me to put my mouth around that and drink it down without using my hands?" The moment I say the words ,I instantly regret them. Everyone bursts out laughing at my expense. I turn three shades of red, and Luke pulls me into his chest, vibrating with mirth.

"Could you be any more adorable?" he asks, kissing my temple. "That was so much better than you actually taking the shot. Besides, I like it when you use your hands. You have my permission." Now I'm blushing even harder as I push him back and smack his chest. "What?" He feigns innocence. "Just stating a preference here."

"Men," I grumble, before picking up the drink and tossing it down. It's smooth and creamy and delightfully yummy. Licking my lips, I turn to face Luke with a naughty gleam to my eye and a wink.

"You're evil for tempting me like this. First, you come in here wearing the best dress ever created, and now you're taking blow job shots and licking your lips. If I didn't adore you as much as I do, I'd pull you into the bathroom and have my way with you."

"That's oddly endearing," I say.

Everyone else is chatting away and taking their shots and having fun—especially Sophia who is having a field day with Claire and Kate.

"Are we still on for my meeting your parents tomorrow?" Luke asks, his fingers gliding up and down my exposed arms. He can't seem to stop touching me tonight, and I'm certainly not complaining.

I think it's the dress. It must be the dress.

"We are, if you're still interested in meeting them. I've warned you about my dad. He can be a bit . . . much sometimes."

"I want to meet them," he says calmly. "I want to do everything with you."

I'm swooning. I never really grasped the meaning of that word until this precise moment, but that's exactly what I'm doing.

"You mean that?" I can't help but ask, hope burrowing a hole inside my chest and taking up residence there.

"Yeah, baby, I mean that." Luke's hand cups my cheek as he stares intently into my eyes. "I'd say I didn't expect this, but I think I did. Are you okay with that?"

I swallow hard before nodding. "I'm afraid." We're opposites in so many ways. I mean, I guess we also have a lot in common too.

But I never expected to fall this fast and this hard for this man.

"I know, me too. We'll figure it all out. You have another ten days left, and I'm not ready to let you go yet."

# Chapter Sixteen

*Luke*

IVY'S APARTMENT is loud and warm, thanks to the raucous laughter coming from her sister Sophia and Claire. The two of them hit it off instantly last night amongst a fleet of dirty-named cocktails. There may have even been a shared kiss between them, but Ivy will neither confirm nor deny.

Tonight is a pre-wedding party—because apparently we don't party enough as a group—proposed by Claire in lieu of a bachelorette party that Kate was vehemently opposed to having. Ryan doesn't care about having a bachelor party all that much and his brother Kyle, who is the best man, won't get here until the day of the big event anyway.

So that leaves us with this little wine party that Ivy offered to host, since she won't be attending the wedding with me.

The wedding is exactly two weeks away, and though I know Duchess Kate is completely on board with her future with Ryan, she is standing by his side watching everything with the silent observation that can only come from overthinking.

I feel for her, I really do.

I can't begin to comprehend what's going through her mind.

Kate lost her husband and young daughter to a drunk driver almost four years ago, but that isn't a heartache that ever goes away. I imagine that even if this is a happy time, it is also a very painful one.

Ryan, being Ryan, is already attuned to the shift in her demeanor and has kept a protective and comforting hand on her back all night.

It's yet another reason why I love him like a brother.

He is good people—the best really. As I scan the room, I realize I'm stuck in my own form of quiet contemplation. These people, these friends of mine, don't really know me, and yet they've accepted me anyway.

Sure, Ryan knows to a certain extent, but that's because he did his research and pieced together the rest.

I have never told him anything outright, but that never seemed to be a hindrance to his trust or loyalty to me.

Kate too. She loves me unequivocally and without challenge or doubt.

So why do I not trust that their love and acceptance would remain true and intact if it were challenged with all that I have done? All that I am doing and capable of?

And then there is Ivy.

It is amazing how much I love her.

How I have grown to need her in such a short amount of time. The thought of losing her is more than I can endure, and though she's leaving so very soon, it will never fully be over for me.

I met her parents today, which was oddly my idea. They were definitely not what I expected, though Ivy did warn me. Her father seemed to like me enough especially after she introduced me as her friend and promised him that's all we are.

He gave her a skeptical look, clearly reading between the lines.

Can't exactly blame him for that.

I have never witnessed a normal family before. One where the parents love each other and their kids, and no one drinks too much, beats, or degrades anyone intentionally. It was an eye-opening experience and filled me with longing.

That brings me back to my reality. The reality that goes beyond the simple, non-issue of distance. The reality that I'm not who she thinks I am. The reality that she'd leave me for good if she knew. The reality that I love her enough to let her go.

But maybe she doesn't have to know? Maybe we can suspend reality for just a bit longer?

Because she's mine, and as I said before, I need her. In fact, I think she may just own me.

So yeah, I'm going to have to give that one my best shot and hope we come out together on the other side.

Ivy is on her second glass of wine but has yet to take a sip from it.

She's been holding it, letting it linger as more of an extension of her hand than something she is all that interested in. Her eyes are glued to the screen of her phone, a frown staining her beautiful face.

I'd bet money that it's related to a patient. I've never met a doctor who cares more for their patients than Ivy does.

She types something in and then slides the phone back into its resting place in the back pocket of her jeans. Craig Stanton decides this is the perfect moment to make his move, grabbing her attention with some bullshit or another, his intrinsic charm reeling her in.

I let it happen, mainly because I don't exactly see him as a threat.

He's interested in Ivy, but it appears entirely superficial, and well, I trust her.

But I'm still watching, because I'm not a moron either. Who am I kidding? I want to throttle that motherfucker for even glancing in her general vicinity, let alone talking to her.

"You done dicking her around or what?" Ivy's sister Sophia asks, casually sliding in beside me, except there is nothing casual about her slightly aggressive stance. She's an interesting woman, and I'm not quite sure what to make of her. Her love for her younger sister is unambiguous, but she has been merely tepid with me.

"That's not what I'm doing."

She puffs out a dubious breath, the blonde curl dangling from her forehead bouncing in the breeze. "What I'm really asking you here, princess, is if I need to call in my cleaner to take care of you."

Turning to look at her, a wry smile lights up my face. "Your *cleaner*? Is that like some *Pulp Fiction* shit or what?"

"Not exactly. He's more like a problem solver, but he owes me a favor or six, and if you're going to hurt Ivy, I'll make you one of them. And believe me, it would be a piece of piss for him." I want to laugh at that, I really do, but she isn't even so much as smiling. Whatever humor I was feeling dies instantly.

She is absolutely serious.

Yeah, I really don't think she likes me much.

"I'm not a problem for her, big sis, and hurting her is something I find just as abhorrent as you do."

"That's good onya, mate, because you're rather iffy as far as I'm concerned."

"Retract your claws there, Tiger Lily. I may be one of the lost boys on this island, but Ivy is my home, and I'll follow her anywhere."

Sophia observes me for a very long minute. So long in fact that I am resisting the urge to shift my weight out of discomfort. I am rarely intimidated by anyone, but this chick is managing the impossible.

Probably because I am desperate for her approval and know I have a million miles to go until I get there.

"Okay, but screw her over, and they'll find your balls on the side of the road somewhere near New Mexico and your dick in a warehouse in Colorado. The rest of you, I can't really speak to."

"Thanks for the graphic detail on that. Bodily harm and regular old threats aren't enough for you? I get dismemberment and castration?"

Sophia lets out a loud snort. "You're lucky I'm not Dad. Ivy is his baby, in case you missed that today. Anything I can think up; he'll do worse."

"Noted, Soph." I smile, using the familiar nickname Ivy uses for her. "I like you. You're a little scary, quite possibly unbalanced, definitely crazy as fuck, but I love that Ivy has you."

"I know." She sighs. "Ivy is pretty spiffy, and I'm just now starting to see the signs of life that had dwindled for a while." She turns to look at me as she takes a sip of her wine. "That tosser ex of hers really mucked her up, so you can understand my having reservations about you."

I nod, but she's not interested in my response. Her eyes are fixed on Ivy, who's laughing at something good old Craig is saying to her. *Douchebag.* Just the simple idea of him having her sets my teeth on edge. In fact, the idea of any man other than me having Ivy, ignites a torrent of brush fires inside of me that cannot be manipulated or quelled. I am not known for my anger or aggression, but dammit all if that's not what I've got going on right now.

*Dickface.*

"I'd never do anything like that to her. Ivy told me all about Jason, and if she'd allow it, I'd go after him with my bare hands—or my computer, since I'm far more effective with that."

"I know you are, Luke, because though you haven't been fair dinkum when it comes to telling Ivy about yourself, much like your mate Ryan over there, I know everything." My jaw drops, and she grins the grin of the Cheshire Cat who ate the goddamn canary whole. "I told you I have people, and your shit is your own, except that it involves Ivy now, and you need to tell her."

I swallow the lump in my throat that is suddenly cutting off my oxygen supply. This woman has managed to throw me not only off my game, but out of the goddamn park and onto my ass. She's very good. I'll give her that.

"I can't." It's really all I can say, because I'm reeling over here. How on earth do so many people know about me? Okay, it's really only two, but in my very small, limited circle that's like forty percent right there.

"For what it's worth," Sophia turns her attention back to Ivy. "I would have killed the bastard myself too."

I laugh out, probably because I don't know what else to do. That's not exactly what I thought she was referring to.

So much for sealed juvenile records.

"How the fuck do you know so much?" She can't know everything. There's just no way. Ryan suspects because I work with him and have been leaving on my "trips" for years, and has looked into my past with his mad computer skills, but there is no way Sophia could know about that. Right?

Sophia gives me a sardonic look. "Please, bitch, I work in Hollywood. It's my job to know everything about everyone and decide what to say and how to spin it. That's why I'm the best, and everyone knows it. But I also know how to hold onto those secrets, and I won't divulge yours to Ivy. That's not *my* job."

Sophia gives me a half-smile, but the softening in her eyes tells me that her sister is the most important thing in the world to her.

"I know you know this, but she's a regular Joe of a person. She just wants to get up, go to work, do an ace job at it, and come home to someone who will love her. That's it. That's her grand life aspiration, and she fucking deserves it." Sophia takes a deep breath, like just thinking about how ordinary Ivy wants her life to be is exhausting. "If you can't or won't give her that, then walk away."

"Walk away." I test the words on my tongue and they taste like vomit mixed with Vegemite. Probably because in the back of my mind, I know she's right. "She's leaving me soon enough, you know."

"Pft." She rolls her eyes. "You nobby cunt, she's desperate for you to tell her you're willing to try long distance." My eyes widen and a small laugh pops out of my mouth at the name she just called me. "Don't make a face, cunt is a regular insult Down Under. But I mean what I'm saying, so get over yourself for a minute and listen up good. You need to tell her the truth about who you are. All of it. She deserves that from you, especially since I think you love her, and you're what she wants."

"You really don't shut up, do you?"

"That's what you just took from everything I said?"

"Was there more to it than just rambling? I mean, did you tell me shit I didn't already know?"

"Screw you." She flips me off, but smiles as she does it.

"Cool your twisted knickers over there, Secret Keeper Emo Barbie. I'll figure something out."

"Secret Keeper Emo Barbie?"

"No good?"

"Utter rubbish."

"Huh." I rub my chin in contemplation. "I'll have to think of something better. Right now you're too much of a contradiction for me to come up with something more befitting a woman of your caliber."

"You do that, cupcake. In the meantime, I need more booze. My liver is going to shrivel up and implode if I don't feed it properly."

"Isn't it the other way around?"

Sophia shakes her head, her blonde rolled curls bouncing. "No, Ivy informs me that when you have liver disease related to too much alcohol consumption, your liver becomes huge and hard."

"You need help. Seriously. How on earth are you related to Ivy?"

"Brilliant genetics, Luke. Brilliant fucking genetics," she winks at me. "Kisses," she sings as she walks off toward the collection of Australian wine that's assembled on Ivy's kitchen island. I'm smiling like a son of a bitch. I think I love Ivy's sister just as much as she does.

But her insistence on me coming clean is causing a sick knot to form in the pit of my stomach.

I can't do that.

There really is just no way. I'll lose her for sure if I do.

# Chapter Seventeen

*Ivy*

"ALL CLINICAL INDICATIONS POINT TOWARD APPENDICITIS," I tell the parents of the eight-year-old little girl who is lying on the gurney in the emergency department looking miserable. *Poor lamb.* "I'd like to get a CT scan to confirm this and see how far along she is with it. Depending on how inflamed the appendix is, we might be able to give her antibiotics and avoid surgery."

"Is that safe?" her mother asks, looking exhausted. I can't blame her, it's seven-thirty in the morning and they've been here for the last three hours.

"It is, but as I said, it depends on how far along she is with it. From what I can tell given her history and exam, she's pretty inflamed. She has a lot of generalized abdominal pain and positive rebound tenderness in her lower right quadrant. We'll know more after we get a better look at it on the scan. I'm going to place the order for that now, and Doctor Schwartz will be taking over for surgical service. He's excellent, so you're in good hands."

"You won't be doing the medication or surgery or whatever?" the father asks.

"No, sorry. I've been on all night, and Doctor Schwartz is the surgeon. It's always better to have a fresh pair of eyes. If he determines that Michelle needs surgery, which I'm afraid she probably will, he's one of the best."

Both parents sigh out simultaneously. "Okay. Thanks," the mom says weakly.

"Hang in there, Michelle. I'll see if they can give you something for the pain." She offers me a tight half-smile, half-grimace, and I walk out of the room, texting Schwartz as I move toward the nurses' station.

I'm ready to go home. This night was brutal.

Three traumas back-to-back and one of them was a gunshot wound that took the better part of two hours to stabilize before we could even move him up to the OR.

That, and I had a child that I suspected was being abused.

Those cases shake me to my core. It was a three-year-old boy with a broken arm and large bruises on his abdomen and flank that were indicative of being repeatedly kicked. We managed to separate the child from his parents, and he's now in the hands of social services, but still. Those are the types of stories that have me boozing on Manhattans.

"You heading out?" Kate calls to me as I type in the order for the CT scan and morphine for Michelle.

"Yeah." I rub my bleary eyes with the backs of my hands. "I'm knackered. I just have to finish up. You?"

Kate looks equally worn. The ICU got slammed last night and is just now catching up.

"Heading home as we speak. I'm hoping to catch Ryan before he leaves for work." I smile at that. In the weeks that Luke and I have been "having fun," we've spent a lot of time with Kate and Ryan. The three of them together are something rare and special. You don't often see friendships like that.

"Tell him I say hi." I smile, and she throws me a wave and a wink before briskly walking toward the exit.

Cold air brushes across the back of my neck, and I rub it away as I finish typing out my note on Michelle. More cold air, but it feels like someone is blowing on me instead of just passing by, so I turn and find Craig Stanton grinning at me in that buoyant way of his and looking far too good for this hour.

*Why is he blowing on my neck?*

"Morning, Craig. You coming or going?"

"Isn't that my line?"

I scrunch my eyebrows at him. "Pardon?"

He waves me away. "Nothing, just trying to be crass."

"Oh." I roll my eyes. "There's a worthy goal."

"I'm heading out. I was on all night as well." He's smiling at me with his pearly—probably cosmetically whitened—teeth and charming smile. I haven't seen much of Craig in the last couple of days, which is not exactly something I'm complaining about. He's nice enough, I guess, just a little too persistent for my liking.

"Have a good day." I smile slimly and turn back to my computer.

"You interested in grabbing breakfast with me? There's a case I wanted to speak with you about."

"Oh?"

"Yeah. Hypoplastic left heart syndrome that was just born last night."

That gets my attention. "Really? Wow."

He nods with an excited grin.

Don't get me wrong, we're not excited over sick kids or patients, but we are excited over the challenge, the rarity of the case, and the ability to fix the problem. It's what we live and breathe and slave away for.

"I was hoping you'd want in on the surgery."

"Me?" I'm shocked. "I'm ED, not surgery or cardio."

"I know that, but I've seen your work, and it's a rare case. I thought you might like to watch, or whatever."

Why does it feel like he's asking me out on a date? Is it the way he's propositioning me? Or maybe I'm overthinking this.

"I'd love to Craig. When were you thinking of doing the surgery?"

"Are you done here? I'd like to talk more about it, and I'm starving."

"Oh, um." How can I say no to that? He wants to talk surgery, and colleagues catch a meal to discuss a patient all the time. "Sure, but can we not go to the cafeteria? That place is feral."

Craig laughs, brushing his hand against my shoulder for absolutely no reason that I can discern. "There is a really good place close to here. I'll just wait while you finish up."

Ten minutes later, Craig and I are walking out into the bright morning sun, which is finally feeling more seasonably warm. We're headed in the direction of Lake Washington when I hear my name being called. I don't react because it wasn't loud, and I haven't slept. I'm probably just hearing things, but when I hear it again only more emphatically, I turn around to find Luke jogging toward us with a stoic mask on his face.

"Hey, I was calling you. Didn't you hear me?" he asks once he catches up to us and places a kiss on my cheek.

"No. Sorry," I smile. "What are you doing here? I thought we were going to try for a late lunch."

He looks over at Craig for a beat before turning his attention back to me. "I know, but I wanted to catch you after your shift."

"Everything okay?"

"Yeah, um." Luke shifts and looks at Craig again. "Did I interrupt something here?"

Craig and I both speak at the same time, only he says "yes" and I say "no" and now it's just awkward.

"We were actually going out for breakfast," Craig says, looking as cheerful as ever.

"You were going to have breakfast with him?" Luke asks in a tone I can't distinguish. Is he mad or put off by this?

"Yes, Craig wanted to discuss a patient with me." I tilt my head trying to figure this out.

"And you can't do that at the hospital?"

I glance over to Craig who is smiling smugly. I don't like this. Not one bit.

"We're hungry. We just got off a long, grueling shift, and the thought of rank hospital food is not appealing."

"Right," Luke says. I still can't tell what he's thinking, though he's definitely taken a very deliberate and possessive step in my direction.

"Ivy, we should get going so we can eat and get some sleep," Craig says, grasping my elbow. Luke's eyes ignite, and I can see where this is headed.

"*I'm* the only one sleeping with Ivy."

"Hey now." I step toward Luke, as Craig maintains his hold on me. "That's not called for. It's a working breakfast, Luke. Like you've never had those before? Come on. This doesn't have to turn into something."

"Ivy," Luke snarls, pointing an aggressive finger in Craig's direction. "He wants to sleep with you. You may think this is a working breakfast and all professional and shit, but both Craig and I know better."

I look to Craig who still has that damn shit-eating grin on his face, and now I'm just getting annoyed with both of them.

"Well, I'm not interested in playing this game with either of you. If you want to hash it out, then have at it, but I'm tired and hungry. I want to eat so I can go get a few hours of rest before I have to return to the hospital for another shift." My voice ends on a high note as I yank my arm out of Craig's grasp, storming away from both of them.

I hear the two of them chatting behind me, but don't even bother trying to listen. Frankly, I don't care enough.

Craig never mentioned where he was taking me for breakfast, but I find myself standing in front of a posh boutique hotel with both Craig and Luke hot on my heels.

*Was he taking me to a hotel for breakfast?*

That's sort of odd, isn't it? Maybe Luke is right?

"Ivy, can I speak to you for a minute?" Luke asks, glowering at Craig with narrowed eyes. "Alone?"

"Of course," I turn to Craig. "Is this where we're eating?"

"Yes. Best breakfast ever." He crosses his arms over his chest with a satisfied look.

"Okay, I'll be right back. I'll just meet you inside."

"I'll get us a table."

Luke gives Craig a once-over before extending his hand to him, which makes me smile.

"I'll see you later, man," Craig says.

"Later." Luke shakes his hand firmly, and then Craig leaves Luke and I standing alone in the middle of the sidewalk. "I don't like you eating with him in a hotel."

I sigh, far too exhausted to do battle over this, so instead I circle my arms around his waist because he feels good. He always feels so good.

"I know, but it's really just for work. I didn't know he was taking me here."

Luke folds me into his body as he buries his nose in my hair, taking a deep breath the way he always does when he hugs me. "You smell like the hospital," he chuckles. "You still smell like you, but you also smell like that."

"I won't take it personally."

"Ivy, I don't want to leave you here with him."

I peek up at him with a soft smile. "You and I are sleeping together," I raise a challenging eyebrow at him, "so it's not like I'm going to sleep with him."

"Okay, I deserve that look. I'm sorry for saying that to him. I was taken by surprise, is all." He leans down and presses his lips to mine. "I've never been jealous in my life. This is uncharted waters for me. That, and you look unfathomably hot and sexy in your scrubs." I laugh, rubbing my chin against his chest. "No, I'm serious. You really freaking do. If I didn't have a plane to catch, I'd try and talk you into getting a room here."

"Such a perv."

"I'm your perv, and I think you like me that way."

I kiss his warm, soft lips. "I do, it's sort of endearing in an odd way. Hey, wait," I stand up to my full height with a look of censure.

"What do you mean you have a plane to catch? I thought we were having a late lunch? You never said anything about leaving on a trip."

"I know." Luke's expression turns somber and severe. "But I got a call, and I have to go on a . . . business trip. It's just for a couple of days at most."

"Can't someone else go? I mean, I'm leaving soon."

He looks miserable, and I feel bad for asking. "It has to be me."

"Oh, okay." I try to hide my disappointment. *I only have a few days left.* "Where are you going?"

He glances away from me, out into the street.

"New York."

It almost sounds like he's lying. That's my first instinct, but it's an odd one to have. Why on earth would he lie about where he's going on business? Especially when it's so easy to confirm with Kate, Ryan, and Claire.

I'm sure I'm just tired.

He shifts back to me.

"That's why I wanted to come and see you this morning. I won't be landing until late tonight, and you'll already be at work then, so this was my only chance to talk to you."

"It's fine; I'll see you when you get back." I kiss him and he returns it, but it feels off.

He's distant, and maybe it's just because he has this sudden trip and he's preoccupied about it and Craig and whatever else, but it almost feels like goodbye. Like a real goodbye, except I don't actually think it is. Not yet anyway.

I can't describe it.

"Yeah, I should go. I have to pack and get my stuff and head to the airport." He envelops me in his arms again. "I'm going to miss you, baby. I wish I didn't have to go, but I don't have a choice."

"Me too. Call or text me when you land, even if I can't respond."

"Will do." He kisses me good, long and hard, and this kiss feels more the way it should.

More the way his other kisses have always felt.

Like a magic spark inside your chest that spreads throughout your entire body, filling you with the most delicious tingles. Like fire and heat and bewitchment. Like the best kiss you've ever had times ten.

And this isn't even his A-game.

"Now go have breakfast with the douchebag and then get some sleep. I'll call you." He kisses me again and then walks off, leaving me alone, bereft, and empty.

*How'd it get like this so fast?*

*It's only been a few weeks.*

I walk into the swanky black and white lobby and immediately spot the restaurant just off to the right. Sure enough, there is an abundance of people eating breakfast even though it's a workday. Craig is in the back by the window, and when he spots me, he flags me over.

"Hey, sorry that took so long."

"So, are you two a couple now?" he asks far too casually as he peruses the menu, never once looking in my direction.

"I don't know what we are actually. We haven't exactly put a label on anything." *That, and I don't want to tell you it's just sex. Or that I'm in love with him.*

He sets the menu down on top of his place setting, leveling me with the full weight of his hazel eyes.

"Huh. But yet you're here with me."

"This isn't a date, Craig. It's breakfast to talk about a patient." Now it's my turn to make a show of looking over the menu, simply because I'm finding it difficult to maintain eye contact with him.

He's not intimidating me on purpose, it's just that I get a bizarre feeling when I look at him too long. I wouldn't say I'm uncomfortable, but there's just more to that look than simple friendship, and no matter how hard I protest it, we have a certain chemistry together.

"True, and we are going to discuss the surgery because I would like you there in the OR with me, so I'm just going to say this once, and then it will be out there and you can do what you want with it."

I set my menu down, folding my hand on top of it, trying to

appear unaffected though I'm anything but. His words coupled with the tone of his voice set me on edge.

"I doubt you've heard, because it was just finalized the other day, but I was offered a surgical fellowship at Boston Children's." My mouth pops open as my eyes bug out of my head.

Craig smiles at my reaction, leaning closer to me, ever so slightly crowding my personal space.

"It seems I'm coming with you. And you should know that I like you, Ivy. I know I have a bad reputation at the hospital. Some of it is deserved, and some of it isn't, but it's not like that with you. I think we'd make a good team together. We understand the demands of our work, and we have similar interests. I respect the hell out of you and think you're exceedingly beautiful and brilliant and talented. When you tire of Luke the child, *we* can try something real."

I think I just stopped breathing.

"Wow, Craig, I had no idea you felt that way. I, um . . .," I laugh uncomfortably. "I don't really know what to say."

"You don't have to say anything about it right now. I don't like to share, and I definitely don't want to share you with anyone, let alone Luke Walker. So, I'll wait. I'm going to Boston with you, and he's not, so when you're ready, let me know."

Jesus, the way he's looking at me. It's the kind of look you feel everywhere whether you want to or not.

Mercifully, our waiter interrupts our far too intimate and intense moment, and we order our food. Our conversation turns back to work, and all that other business is pushed aside. We talk and laugh and he tells me things and I do the same.

And worst of all, I enjoy it.

# Chapter Eighteen

*Ivy*

IT'S BEEN two days since Luke left, and though he did ring when he landed and then again the following afternoon, I haven't spoken to him. Either I wasn't available when he phoned, or he wasn't available when I did. I've texted a few times only to either not receive any response or get one back saying that he couldn't chat.

I have no idea what he's doing or if he's really that busy, or if he's just blowing me off.

But I think it's strange all the same.

On a different note, I did assist Craig with that hypoplastic left heart patient and it went swimmingly. I mostly looked on while he and another resident did all the work, but it was prodigious to watch. Craig was incredible in action, and though he hasn't brought up our little conversation from the other morning, it's been looping through my mind on constant replay.

Tonight, I have Kate and Claire at my flat, and because I don't have work tomorrow, we're drinking copious amounts of wine and talking and laughing the way girls do. It's wonderful. It makes me miss Sophia desperately. I can't wait for my sister to come and visit me in Boston.

"You must think I'm a raging alcoholic," Kate says as she pours herself a glass of red wine. "I mean, every time you're around me and we're not working, I feel like I'm drinking."

I laugh, holding up my glass as evidence of my own debauchery. "Bloody oath girl!"

Claire rolls her eyes at both of us, before sitting up straight and looking at me with an expression that tells me I don't want to hear what she has to say. We've been discussing Luke for the better part of the evening. For some odd reason, they wanted details, but when I casually mentioned that I haven't spoken to him since he left, Claire started laying into me.

"I don't know why you're so surprised that you haven't talked to Luke since he left," Claire says as she swirls her pinot noir around in her glass. "I mean, it's typical sketchy-ass Luke shit, right?" She looks to Kate for confirmation of this, but Kate just shrugs a shoulder.

"What do you mean by that?" I ask, leaning back on my couch and feigning mild curiosity, though I doubt I'm fooling them.

Claire gives out a rather unladylike snort. "Dude, Luke is the most secretive guy I know."

"Seriously?" I ask, looking at both of them in turn. Claire is looking at me like I'm an idiot for not already knowing that, and Kate just looks sheepish. "Please explain this to me."

"Claire—" Kate chimes in with a cautioning tone, but Claire just waves her away.

"She should know, Kate. I mean, she's screwing him, right?"

Kate throws her hands up in the air like she tried to stop her and it's all out of her control now. None of this is comforting me. Not even a little.

"Luke never talks about himself unless it's in vague generalities. Like, he'll say he grew up in Oklahoma, but never elaborates past that. He's worked with Ryan forever, but also carries two phones and leaves on 'business trips,'" she puts air quotes around the words, "every so often that are not work sanctioned."

"So he's not in New York for business?" I'm way too confused right now.

"Not for Ryan's company, and I have no idea if he's in New York or not," Kate says softly, sympathetically.

"Wow, okay then." I really don't know how I'm supposed to respond to all of this, so instead of commenting further, I drink down the entire contents of my glass before refilling it. "Does Ryan know where he goes, or what he does? It's not like he has a reason to lie about where he is." Can you hear the apprehension in my voice? I sure as bloody hell can.

Kate shrugs a shoulder. "Maybe, maybe not. If Ryan knows, he hasn't told me. And as for being in New York, if he is there, he hasn't been in touch with Kyle, Ryan's brother. They're close friends. You'd think he would reach out, right?"

"What the bloody piss am I supposed to do with this information? No one thought to mention this before I took up with him? Stupid men," I snap, unable to hide my ire. "I mean, I sort of suspected he was dodging my queries, but is he a derro wanker or what?"

"And a derro wanker would be?" Claire asks.

I roll my eyes. "You know, a loser. Someone I should toss. Tell me true blue here, am I making a mistake with him or should I just ask him straight off about what he's up to?"

"Did you know that when you drink, your accent becomes very thick, and you use words and expressions we don't understand? It's not normally like that either. Normally your accent is subtler, so you're throwing me off here," Kate says with a smile, her eyes just as glassy as Claire's—and probably mine too.

"I will try to speak more American, but the accent I can't do anything about." I slap my hand down on my thigh in frustration, nearly spilling my wine. I don't know why their validation of Luke's shifty behavior is upsetting me like this. Probably because I was hoping I was reading too much into it. Because I fell in love with the stupid tosser and now I have confirmation that he's off doing god only knows what, and the people he's closest to in his life know nothing about it.

"I don't think you should get rid of Luke," Kate replies softly. "He's a great guy. He really is. I know he has some private things in his life, but I've never heard him speak about anyone the way he does about you. He might be a touch obsessed—in the best possible way—so just be patient with him."

I nod, absorbing her words. The truth is, I'm not entirely sure what I'm feeling about all of this. I'm leaving in a week, and he's not coming with me. He may have hinted at genuine affection, but has maintained his fun, no-strings banter the entire time. I'm the hopeless idiot, falling for the guy while knowing the reality of our situation.

I'm so resentful for allowing this sort of weakness in myself.

"Or you could ditch Luke's ass and screw Craig—who I happen to think is righteously fuckable," Claire says. I'm blushing like a tomato because I haven't told anyone about the conversation he and I had the other day. "That whole arrogant doctor thing gets me so wet."

"Jesus, Claire," Kate hisses. "The last thing I want to think about is your vagina and its moisture."

"Bullshit, you love thinking about my vag."

Kate rolls her eyes and I do too.

"Maybe *you* should screw him then?"

"No can do, Ivy Pivy. He has zero interest in getting into my glorious panties. I don't know what it is about you, but somehow you spin a spell over every guy you meet. Speaking of vaginas, yours must be made out of gold, or magic, or beer, or something, because men pine for you."

"I really don't know how to respond to half the rubbish you spew, Claire."

She shrugs. "The truth is, you like Luke, so give him the benefit of the doubt and wait until he comes back and then talk with him. Or not," she shrugs again. "I mean, you're leaving in a week or so, right?"

"Yeah, but . . ." *But what?* I take another sip of my wine, unable to finish my hanging sentence. But I was foolishly hoping for more, is what I was thinking. I've never needed a man before and I certainly don't need that sort of distraction before I start my new fellowship. And Luke's the epitome of a distraction. I was hoping he'd be simple and easy, but the deeper I get, the more complicated he becomes. And it's not the relationship part that's convoluted or problematic. That's actually where things are gloriously effortless. It's *Luke* that's perplexing.

No, I definitely don't need a man.

But I still want Luke.

I take another sip of wine as I roll that around my brain. We're already on our third bottle, and I should stop while I'm ahead.

"Did you know that Auburn is in love with Luke?" Claire asks with a knowing smirk, drawing me back to the moment.

I choke on my wine, the alcohol burning the back of my throat. Auburn is not just a color, she's Luke's current assistant, and she's probably ten years his junior. "Really? Is that why she's all cute and blushing around him?"

Kate nods laughing. "It's so adorable. Luke is totally clueless. Every time he tries to talk to her and make her more comfortable, she just gets more flustered."

Now we're all in a fit of giggles because, well, we're drunk, and that seems to be what you do when you're pissed. You laugh over nonsense that really isn't all that funny when you're sober.

"Not to bring up something uncomfortable here, but how have you and Ryan only ever been friends?" I ask Claire.

She wrinkles her nose up in disgust. Her long red locks flow around her bright orange shirt that says, *I like it like that.* "Yes. Because neither of us is the least bit attracted to the other. He views me as a little sister, and he definitely plays the role of obnoxious big brother with me. He's the ultimate cock-block."

"He really is," Kate agrees. "Every time she tries to hook up with someone and he's around, he goes all, 'what are your intentions with her,'" she says in a deep voice, mocking Ryan.

"You're all sort of a cheeky lot, aren't you?" They both nod, grinning. I sit back, thinking on something that randomly pops into my mind. "And Ryan was never arrested when Luke was?"

"No," Kate says, crouching on her knees and leaning forward

with the excitement of intrigue in her voice. Her platinum blonde hair is piled high on her head in a messy bun, which has partially come undone during our little drinking party. "The FBI arrested Luke like thirty seconds after he got into that bank site, but Ryan was already in and they never saw him."

"Interesting and a little odd," I muse.

Claire and Kate both shrug at me as they finish the last of their glasses and Kate lays down on the area rug, intrigue forgotten.

"They must have been watching him or something. How else would they have been there so fast if they weren't?" Kate mumbles, slurring half the words.

She makes a very good point.

"I guess, but I don't remember the FBI looming about campus, and you'd think a regular SWAT team waiting for something to happen would be a bit conspicuous. Something like that would have been the gossip of the school, and none of the other people in the ring got arrested, did they?"

Both of them bolt upright and stare at me with gaping jaws and wide eyes filled with astonishment. It really is adorable how they're so much alike and yet so completely different.

"You went to Caltech?" Claire asks with a high-pitched squeal.

"Yeah? Didn't you know?"

They both shake their heads, again, in unison. "No, we didn't freaking know that," Kate agrees, equally as stunned by the revelation.

"Didn't know that at all," Claire adds. "Did you know him then?"

And now I blush like a grade-school girl with a crush. I blame the wine for that one, because there is no way I could tell a passable lie right now. That, and I figured Luke had spilled the beans to Ryan who had, in turn, spilled them to Kate and so on.

"You total slut," Claire taunts as she gets up on her knees, pointing at me. "You slept with him, didn't you?"

"That explains so much," Kate says, shaking her head in bewilderment. "I mean, that's why he wanted to walk you home that night, and that's why he went after you so quickly."

"Did you date him then or just screw his brains out? Was he any good? I always imagine Luke being good in bed, though I can't explain why."

"Jesus, Claire, do you have any sort of filter?"

"No."

"It was a one-night stand," I explain, staring into the crimson of my wine. "We met in a bar and he came home with me, but he was gone before I woke up." I take a small sip, before drawing my legs up onto the sofa and tucking them beneath me.

"Dick," Kate says, and I point my finger at her because she's spot on with that.

Another thing he and I have yet to really discuss. That list seems to be compiling quickly. But that whole getting busted straight off after breaching the bank's security? Yeah, something about all that isn't quite adding up for me.

"Was it before or after he got nailed?" Claire snickers. "Totally pun intended." Then she starts to cackle, slapping her thigh and everything.

"It was after, on both accounts," I raise an eyebrow at them. "Just a few days, though I didn't know anything about that when I met him, and he didn't talk about it."

"So he did a dick and ditch, a fuck and fly, a jiggy and jog?" Claire asks.

I'm laughing so hard I'm crying. Who the hell comes up with things like this? Claire, that's who.

"How on earth did I manage before I met you, Claire? Honestly. You're like the perfectly dirty equivalent of my mum." My shoulders sag and I'm suddenly so very sad. "What am I going to do when I leave? Doctors aren't this much fun to booze with."

"I'm going to take that as a compliment."

"You should."

"So answer the question, Ivy," Kate continues, annoyed that we got off track. "Did Luke really do that?"

"Yes. He did. Look, I don't really want to talk about Luke or any other bloke for that matter. I'm a brilliant kickarse doctor," I point at Kate, "you're a brilliant kickarse nurse, and you're the badarse mysterious assistant who really runs that place," I finish with Claire. "Men are bloody superfluous."

We all raise our glasses, clinking them together before we finish off our wine. "Even though we're doing that whole women empowerment not needing men thing," Kate slurs, "I totally need Ryan to come and drive me home. I'm so drunk the room is starting to spin, and pretty soon I'll be splatter-painting your walls and floors with red vomit."

"That's colorful imagery right there, Kate, but I think I'm right there with you." Claire says.

"Did you know that I'm thinking about cutting back on my hours?" Kate slurs as she attempts to dial Ryan's number several times before Claire snatches the phone from her hand and does it herself.

"No," I say, surprised, sitting a little more upright.

"Yeah. I hate not seeing Ryan. Our schedules are so opposite, and life's too short to miss time with him."

I nod, aware that she's quietly referring to missing her family that died in a car accident several years back.

"Then, I think cutting back on your hours would be the right call to make."

"Me too, Ivy. And if you marry Luke and I marry Ryan, then we could be like non-related sisters or something."

Claire makes a noise that sounds like a cross between a snort and a burp. "That doesn't even make sense, Kate."

"I know, but that's not really the point, Claire. Stop pissing on my happy parade or whatever I have going on."

"I hate to be the one to break up this moment of love, but I'm not marrying Luke. I'm leaving next week. He and I are just having fun."

"You do know that no one really believes you when you say shit like that, right?" Claire gives me a dubious look, and I can't respond to that, so we all fall silent for a beat before there is a rather loud and demanding knock on my door.

It takes me far longer than it should to reach Ryan, but when I do, I'm swaying, and there are about two and a half of him, which is a bit unsettling really.

"Jesus Christ, Katie. How am I supposed to take advantage of you when you're this drunk?" Ryan asks, cupping his fiancée's face, looking at her like she's the most incredible woman in the world. "Can you walk, love, or do I need to carry you?"

Kate goes to smack his chest, but misses and swats at the air instead. "I can walk."

"That's good, because I may need you to carry me, Ryan. I don't even think I can get off the floor." Claire starts to giggle but instantly stops. "Oh no, I have to pee!"

"You've got to be fucking kidding me," Ryan groans, running a hand through his inky hair. "Remind me to never let them over to your house again for a 'girl's night,' Ivy." Ryan puts air quotes around the words. "Claire, I'm not carrying you to the bathroom, so get your ass up and do your thing before you get in my car."

"Yes, sir," Claire snickers and does somehow manage to pull herself off the floor, which is a good thing, because I don't think I would be much help, and Kate is practically asleep standing up against Ryan's chest.

"Sorry about this. We got to chatting and did more drinking than I think any of us realized." I have no idea if that came out as clear as I intended it to, but judging by the confused expression on Ryan's face, I'm guessing it didn't.

"Whatever, it's fine," he says flippantly. "You should drink some water, Doctor. Don't want a hangover."

"Is he really in New York?" I hate myself for asking, but I have to know, and I have to see his reaction to my question.

Ryan doesn't say anything for a long beat; he just stands there staring at me.

All two and a half of him.

"You know what?" I shake my head, anger and regret oozing from my pores along with the gallon of wine I consumed. "Forget it. I don't want to know the answer to that."

"Yes," he quickly spews, answering me despite my retraction.

But that's all he says and I can't tell if he's lying or not. Damn stupid alcohol messing about my brain.

"Do you know why he's there?"

Ryan looks down at Kate, who is snoring against his broad chest, her mouth hanging open, fast asleep. He chuckles before kissing her forehead tenderly.

"I don't. He never tells me, and I stopped asking a long time ago. I have my theories and assumptions, but they're just that. I figure one day he'll tell me, and then I'll know."

I sigh, holding myself up by leaning against the door. "I don't know how to do that."

"Then you should ask him yourself, but don't be hurt when he either lies or doesn't tell you."

I snort and sway and almost fall over. *Bloody hell!* "That's like trying to place a central line without advancing a dilator over the guide wire to dilate the soft tissue."

"You do know I have no idea what that means, right?"

I nod. "It's not possible. But you're right. I shouldn't be hurt by anything he does or doesn't do."

"Get some sleep, Ivy. Not only are you drunk and about to fall over, but you're ridiculously difficult to understand."

"Right? That's what I said." Claire smacks me on the shoulder and I do practically fall over. Again.

"Yeah," I nod solemnly. "Good night then. Thanks for the fun ladies. Cheers."

They walk out, Ryan carrying a passed-out Kate in his arms, but before I can shut the door, he turns to me with a soft smile. "He's worth it. I know you're leaving, and it's not meant to lead anywhere, but he's crazy about you." Ryan sighs as if he's telling me things he shouldn't. "He may test you, but he's not doing it intentionally. Luke has a lot of issues, and his sense of self-worth is non-existent, but he *is* worth it, and I can promise you that everything he does, he does for a very good reason."

"Thanks." I offer a tight smile, and he gives me an equally tight nod before walking off. Shutting the door, I engage all three locks before leaning my back and head against the wood, staring sight-lessly up at the ceiling.

I don't know why I'm readily exploring all of this.

The simple reality is, I'm going to Boston, and Luke is not coming with me.

So why am I so addicted to this feeling?

Why do I not want to let it go?

The fact that he may or may not be in New York is not exactly what's sticking with me right now. It's not even all the cryptic rubbish about how Ryan doesn't know what Luke's doing or even bother to ask, though there is way more there than Ryan was letting on.

No, it's the weird timing of the FBI raid ten years ago that's burrowing a hole in my brain.

Something about it isn't quite right, and either Ryan is cognizant of it, or he's blatantly ignoring the obvious, because if what Kate was saying is true, he should have been arrested as well. I'm not sure if it's the alcohol swimming in my system, but this is sticking with me, and I can't shake it.

There is more here than meets the eye, I just know it.

# Chapter Nineteen

*Luke*

10 YEARS *ago*

I HAVEN'T SLEPT all night, but I'm the farthest thing from tired imaginable. No, instead of being tired, I'm wired. I'm on fire and jazzed up and angry and frustrated and mad as hell. I realize I'm just using synonyms here, but it's only adding to my point.

Ivy. Beautiful, angelic, sexy-as-all-sin, Ivy, fell asleep in my arms after the best sex I've ever had. After the best sex *anyone* has ever had in the history of sex. Yeah, I'm that confident.

That's how good it was. It was life-changing sex, and I had to leave it all behind because I'm a fucking degenerate who doesn't deserve her.

Worse than that, I'm going to prison.

Not jail, mind you. That's for pansies who have to sleep off a drunken night or douchebags who hit their girlfriends.

I'm going to *prison*.

The official school of hard knocks. I have a hearing set up for Monday with the dean, my advisor, and a few professors, to determine if I can stay in school. What that really translates to is my expulsion.

I could fight it.

Throw out the old, innocent-until-proven-guilty line, but what's the point.

Whether I get expelled or not, I'm still going to be in court for however long that shit takes and then prison. I also got a call from the lead Fed guy and he asked me *again* to roll over on everyone else in the hacking ring.

*Again* I refused.

And not because I'm some do-gooder, benevolent asshole either.

It really boils down to two reasons.

First, I made the choice to get involved with the ring in the first place. That was on me and no one else, so bringing down others to soften my sentence is not only selfish, it's just wrong.

If they do their shit and don't get caught, well, lucky them.

Second, turning on my friends and opponents is exactly something my father would have done to save his measly, pathetic ass, and I refuse to be like him even to the smallest degree.

So that brings me back to Ivy and why I had to run out on her.

It wasn't something I wanted to do. I wanted to wake up with her in my arms before I sank deep inside her again. But I left before she could ask questions and desire things that I was desperate to give her.

It was a chicken-shit thing to do. I admit that fully.

And that's why I'm sitting here in Bean & Leaf, hoping that she comes in so I can talk to her. I couldn't do that while I was wrapped up in her—literally—but she's the kind of woman who deserves better than what I gave her. She's the kind of woman who deserves explanations and excuses and apologies, because the idea of intentionally hurting her is gut-wrenching.

I got all of that from just one night with her. Imagine what days, or months, or years could do.

After two hours of sitting in this chair in the back of the coffee house, Ivy walks in with a friend whom I've never seen before. They're smiling and laughing, and Ivy looks so beautiful in a cream-colored sweater and jeans. Her ice-blue eyes scope her surroundings, but her discerning gaze doesn't find me as I'm partially camouflaged behind a plant.

*Get up and go to her.*

I can't.

I can't move because she looks happy and gorgeous and I want her. I want her so goddamn bad that my fingers ache to touch her again. And what would I say to her anyway? *Oh hey, sorry to run out on you after having the best sex of my life, but I'm facing federal charges and prison time?* Yeah, no. She'll slap my face and I'll deserve it.

*Dammit. Dammit. Dammit.*

I feel like if she notices me, I'll do something, but if she doesn't, I won't.

I'm such a coward, but I can't stand to see the look of disappointment that I'll no doubt receive. That might be worse than anything.

*Stop being a pussy!*

Right.

I stand up, about to approach her when my phone vibrates in my hand. Reflexively, I look down and see it's a number I don't recognize. Just as I draw my eyes up to find Ivy again, I get a glimpse of her back as she walks out.

*Fuck.*

*I could always try again tomorrow.* That's so pathetically lame, I want to kick my own ass.

My phone is insistent, so I open my flip phone, press it to my ear and say, "Hello?"

"Mr. Lucas Walker?" A deep male voice fills my ears and instinctually, I know this won't be good.

"Yes?"

"My name is Michael Sanders; I am an attorney with Sanders, Kaplan, and Cross based out of Los Angeles."

"Okay . . ." I have no idea who this guy is because I'm positive I did not contact him. I'd have to sell every organ in my body to be able to afford a decent attorney, let alone a Los Angeles one.

"I have your file in front of me, and would like to schedule a meeting with you to discuss your case."

"Listen, I can't afford you. I have no idea what your rates are, but I know they're beyond my budget. Unless you're the public defender I've been assigned, I'm going to have to pass."

He chuckles into the phone like my predicament is amusing to him. It's not. Nothing about this is amusing and it pisses me off to the point where I'm about to hang up on the asshole when he stops me short.

"My retainer and services are being covered by a third party who has given me carte blanche for whatever you and your case might require."

"I'm sorry, did you say a third party? Who?" I sit back down, suddenly unable to stand. I'm shaking like crazy, and it's not from the three cups of coffee I've consumed in the two hours I've been a patron in this coffee shop.

"Yes, he asked to keep his identity confidential, for obvious reasons, but he did tell me to let you know—and I'm quoting here— that you were the best adversary he's faced, and that when all of this blows over, he'd like your help with some work he has."

I'm wracking my brain, but coming up empty. Probably because my mind is swirling with the dangerous drug, hope.

"I'm sorry, so you're my lawyer, and I don't have to pay you, and you're going to handle my case?"

"Yes, Luke. That's exactly what I'm telling you," he says this like I'm a child, but right now I don't care about his condescending tone. My acrimony is nowhere to be found, because holy shit, I have a lawyer. "I'd like you to come by my office Tuesday morning first thing. This case is far too sensitive to discuss over the phone, and a lot of the details are being withheld by the FBI. I have a motion in to the judge to get those disclosed, and I should hopefully have them before we meet. But I can tell you that there are a significant number of holes here and that may work out in our favor."

I'm smiling. I can't help it.

This may all turn out to be a dream and not something that will keep me from going to prison, but for the first time since I was arrested last week, it feels like my life might not be so lost.

"Great, I'll be there Tuesday morning. Um, what's your address?"

He laughs that laugh again, but this time, it's not so aggravating.

"I'm going to have some documents couriered over to you by later this afternoon. You don't have to worry about anything, Luke. I'm going to take care of it all."

"Thank you, Mr. Sanders."

"It's Michael, Luke. Call me Michael, and we'll talk soon. Have a good rest of your day." And then he hangs up, and I'm left staring at my phone.

I'm grinning like an idiot, but I don't care.

I have a lawyer.

A real fucking bought and paid for lawyer. And there is only one person I can think of who wouldn't want their identity revealed and who would consider me an adversary. That's the guy I was competing against from MIT with the handle, ThePerfectLie.

According to this Michael Sanders, ThePerfectLie has work for me after I'm cleared of the charges.

I didn't even know happiness could come in this form.

Maybe after I meet with my new lawyer on Tuesday and I have a better sense of things, I could try again with Ivy. Beg for forgiveness and pray she gives me a chance.

Standing up, I slide my phone back into the pocket of my jeans before readying my stuff to leave when two men—clearly not college kids—position themselves in front of me. They're dressed *almost* like everyone else, but it's the small, subtle differences that have the icy sting of paranoia pricking at my skin. They look too normal. Too casual. Like they're trying just a touch too hard to blend in with their designer jeans, black boots, graphic tees, and short coifed hair.

"Luke Walker, have a seat," the blond with green eyes says.

"No thanks," I say, hoping I portray a confidence I don't feel as I move to brush past them.

"We weren't asking," the one with dark hair, dark skin and golden eyes says. "Sit." It's a command and the look in their eyes says not to mess with them. That in doing so, I may be risking my life. Maybe I'm overdramatizing this, but I doubt it and their hard-nosed, authoritarian, all business yet perfectly casual stance and expressions tell me that I'm right.

I sit down.

"Wise decision." They sit too. To any onlookers, we might portray the image of grad students and friends. However, there is nothing friendly about this little impromptu meeting.

"How long did it take you to hack into the federal government's mainframe?"

*Oh shit.*

Neither of them have offered a name or any identification, but they are the type of men who don't have to. Their intimidating presence and irrefutable knowledge imply they're government.

And once again, I'm screwed.

I don't even bother denying it.

"Did you really think that a smashed computer and hard drive would be enough to cover your tracks?"

*Yes, yes I did. Motherfucker!*

"You're good, Luke," the dark-hair guy says. "Very good. And it took us a solid four weeks to find you."

"But we did find you," the other guy adds like it wasn't glaringly obvious.

"I have a lawyer and nothing to say," my voice is surprisingly even, given the workout my heart is getting right now.

"You do have a lawyer, but he won't be able to get the file he wants from the FBI," the blond laughs. "Well, that's not entirely true. He's going to get the one that says you were arrested for hacking into the bank. That's the one we're making public. But your other crimes? You will not be set in front of a judge for those."

"What the fuck?" I bark out.

That's not even legal. *Is it?*

"We've been watching you," he goes on, ignoring my outburst. "Monitoring your activity. We tipped off the FBI about your final challenge in the ring. We had them lined up and waiting, and they arrested you for the bank infiltration on our order, but we're not interested in that. And though you may have a lawyer, you're looking at a lengthy prison stay."

Whoever these guys are, they know I hacked the government and got me arrested for some other charge so they'd have leverage against me.

Blackmail.

That's what this is.

Entrapment.

Another good word.

I swallow hard. This is the part of the game where they play let's make a deal, except this is not a game and there is no deal.

"So what do you want?" I need to get to the punchline here before I have a stroke.

One guy slips me a white business card with a handwritten address on it and nothing else.

"We'll see you there at three p.m. today. If you tell anyone, we'll know, so don't." They stand up in unison and leave without saying anything further.

I stare at the card and then to where they just left.

Then it hits me hard, like a truck being slammed into my chest.

They've got me, and they know it.

And just like that . . . I'm done.

# Chapter Twenty

*Luke*

"WHAT THE BLOODY hell did you do?"

"Oh, come on, you'll love it."

"Rack off, I'm not doing it. I'm going to chunder everywhere if you get me in that thing."

"You do realize I only caught about every other word, right?"

Ivy sighs, but she doesn't look any more relaxed as I pull her up to Seattle's Great Wheel. Truth be told, in all the years I've lived here, I've never done it, but I want to do lame touristy things with her so she'll want to come back after her year away.

It's a pathetic attempt at best. I get that. Fully even, but what the hell, right? Could be fun.

"Now is not the time to make fun of my accent. I don't like heights. That American enough for you?"

"You're locked in there, Ivy." She throws me a look that tells me that didn't help my cause. "Come on," I pull on her hand. "We can make out the entire time. It's beautiful up there. Or so I'm told."

"Luke?" She chews on the corner of her mouth. "Can't we just go eat or do something else?"

"Come on, baby. Live a little. I promise, I won't let anything happen to you."

Ivy's wooden posture relaxes a fraction, and she gives me the slightest of nods.

I got back from my 'business trip' a few days ago. At first, Ivy was distant with me—probably because I didn't call or text her almost the entire time I was gone. That, and two days ended up being four. She never once asked me about the trip. Not even a simple question. That threw me off. I was expecting an onslaught after Ryan filled me on her little drunken night with Claire and Kate, but instead I got nothing.

Her silence is far more disconcerting than the idea of the onslaught.

But the simple fact is, I missed her.

I missed her to the point of near insanity. During that brief hiatus from her, I realized I'm doomed.

I've never experienced this sort of paradox before. There's so much internal strife and conflict, I'm arguing with myself no matter what position I take.

I want to keep this going. I want to be with her and try the whole long-distance relationship thing. A real relationship.

But I don't want to tell her about my past. I don't want to tell her about my family. And I *can't* tell her what I was really doing when I said I was in New York. That last part is non-negotiable, and I assume secrets aren't the best thing for a relationship.

And what I was actually doing could endanger her life if my identity were discovered.

See my dilemma here?

That, and there's the whole issue of me not being good enough for her. Nowhere even fucking close.

The second they lock us in our little space bubble and we sit on the bench seat, she starts to shake.

*Shit. I didn't think she was really that serious about the heights thing.*

"You'll be fine." I wrap my arms around her, holding her close to me and kissing the spot on her neck just above her collarbone. "I promise to feed you after."

"If I sick up, it's on you. Literally."

I can't help but laugh at that. "Would it help if I gave you an orgasm while we were in here? You know, to help you relax."

She's smiling a little now as she elbows me in the ribs. "How will I ever survive without you?" Ivy muses, but I freeze and so does she. Suddenly, this small pod we find ourselves in is suffocating.

I've been putting this off, and Ivy's been avoiding it as well, but I wonder if being stuck in here for however long this thing takes is not a perfect time to bring it up.

Today is Thursday. She leaves on Wednesday, and we haven't said a word about that.

But, screw it.

"When you leave next week, is that it?"

Ivy looks down at her hands that are folded neatly in her lap. "How can it not be?"

"Do you even want to talk about it? I mean, it's only a year, and it's Boston, not Australia."

She shrugs, looking out the window as we start to move, but evidently, she thinks better of that and turns back to her hands.

"Are you saying you want to do that?"

There is so much freaking hope in her voice that my chest clenches at the same time my gut sinks. I inwardly sigh. Why did I bring this up? Can I go back in time thirty seconds and retract my question?

"Maybe."

Ivy laughs humorlessly. "Maybe, huh? Wow, that's glowing. Seriously, I'm overwhelmed by your enthusiasm."

I cup her cheek, tilting her head up until her fathomless eyes meet mine.

"What would you say if I told you that I love you?"

Her eyes grow wide. "Are we speaking in hypotheticals here, or is this an actual declaration?"

"I love you, Ivy," I smile softly, my eyes eating her up. "I do. I tried not to. I swear I did, so you can't be mad at me about that."

"I think I love you too," she says, and I smile so big I'm sure all of my teeth are showing.

"You think?"

"Maybe."

"Maybe?"

"Possibly."

"Possibly?"

She's laughing now and so am I. My lips find hers and we kiss like two people in love as we go up in the damn Big Wheel with the city and water sprawling all around us. It would be one of those idyllic moments. You know, the type they write into cheesy movies.

But the harsh reality is that it's not.

The harsh reality is that even though I want this with her, can I really be that selfish?

"Ivy," I breathe against her. She looks up at me with sparkling eyes, and in this moment, this very freaking moment, I realize I can't do it. I can't destroy her life. The life I know she's desperate for. The life her sister Sophia reminded me that she deserves.

She deserves the world, and that's not something I can offer.

My heart cracks wide open in my chest. I'm bleeding out, and there is nothing she can do to stop it. The pain is unreal, and I'm so very tempted to thrust everything in my life aside and keep her. So very tempted. But how far could we really get that way? How long could we last until she started asking questions and demanding answers that I am incapable of giving?

How long until I make this a million times worse?

Because the simple truth is, I *can't* give her what she wants. And the longer I let this continue, the more I'll hurt her, and if I do that, I'll never be able to live with myself.

"This is all well and good, but there is a very real chance that after my fellowship I won't be returning to Seattle."

Is she giving me an out? It sounds like she is. I should take it, right? I should grab hold of it with both hands.

"My company is here in Seattle. I don't foresee that changing anytime soon."

"I could always try and come back. I mean, I went to medical school, did my entire residency, and most of my fellowship here. They know me. I could probably secure a position."

She sounds so optimistic, and I'm about to obliterate that in three, two, one...

"Ivy, honey, I'm sorry," I say, swallowing down weight of overpowering guilt and fucking despair, knowing that what I'm doing is for her own good in the end.

"For?" she prompts, suddenly nervous, seemingly able to read the change in my disposition.

*I can't be with you. This will never work.* "For not being in touch while I was away," I say instead.

She sighs, exhaustion from a day of working and my unexplained absence making themselves known. Ivy leans into me, silently watching us glide through the world around us.

"I have a lot going on in my life right now, Luke. You made sure to see me almost every day all these weeks. Made your thoughts and feelings for me known every chance you had, and then you disappeared without an explanation. It wasn't even like you told me that you weren't going to be able to stay in touch. You didn't. You just left, and that was it. Maybe it seems ridiculous to expect more given our situation, but I did expect it." Ivy finally fixes her attention on me. "And I know there's a lot you're hiding from me. A lot you never intend to tell me?" That last one is a question, and it's asking so much more than the simple one she poses.

"I can't."

Her eyes close slowly like she was afraid that was going to be my answer.

"I love you, Luke, but I don't think I trust you."

Wow, that may have just killed me.

"I know I've given you no reason to trust me, Ivy, but I care so much about you. So much and I don't want to lose you again."

I need to shut up now. I can't even stop the contradictions.

She shakes her head back and forth. "Were you in New York?"

"Yes and no."

"Is what you're doing illegal?"

"Not technically."

When she opens her eyes, they're glassy with her unshed tears as she stares at me, patiently hoping I'll change my answer and open up to her the way she needs me to. The way I have no intention of doing. Finally, when I don't offer her what she's searching for, she folds into herself and I know what's coming.

And all I can do is let it happen, because this is the way it's supposed to be.

"I don't expect a free pass into your life, but what you give me is so superficial. What you give me is the bare minimum. I know you, yet I don't know you at all. You're asking if this is ending when I leave? You're hinting that you don't want it to, but I want a real relationship and I don't think you can give me that, can you?"

I shake my head, my gut twisting with the regret that chokes me.

"I want you. And I want to be with you. I really do, but I don't know how to do that. I don't know how to keep you and give you what you're looking for. I've done things. Things you know nothing of, but even if I *were* interested in telling you, and you decided to stay with me by some miracle—which you wouldn't—there will always be the other thing. There will always be the very real, dark, and looming presence that I'm forever beholden to. And that I can't change, even if I wanted to. I get how sinister and cryptic that all sounds, but that's probably because it is."

Those tears that were threatening finally spill over, flowing down her cheeks.

"Those phone calls you take?"

I nod. "They're the tip of the iceberg."

"I don't know how to be in a relationship based on secrets and half-truths. I don't need all the details. I don't. I just need something real."

She's pleading. I don't know what to do. I really don't.

This is a hopeless situation. And continuing to straddle the line between loving Ivy and my inability to be forthcoming is only going to destroy us both. Maybe not today and maybe not tomorrow, but eventually it will catch up to us. Eventually, it will end us.

Is it better to do this now and save us both future agony, or do I string her along knowing that we'll never be what she wants us to be? I've had this life going for as long as I can remember, and I don't know how to change that.

Fuck that, I *can't* change it.

"I don't know what to say."

"Tell me I'm not imagining the worst possible scenarios then."

"I can't."

"Fuck you," she snaps, hitting me hard in the shoulder. "I resisted you. I pushed you away from the very start, and you were relentless. *You* pursued *me*."

"I know. I don't even have a good defense, like I tried to stay away or something. I wanted you, and I went after you."

"You selfish bastard. I tried to end this time and time again, knowing that it was leading to heartbreak. But you kept telling me it was fun. You kept convincing me that all would end well. And then you did the worst thing of all, you gave me reason to hope it would never end."

I cover my nose and mouth with my hands, breathing through my palms in ragged torrents, trying to clear my thoughts. She's right. I did that. I am a selfish bastard. I knew the progression of her feelings every step of the way and I did nothing to abate them. I encouraged them because they were the same as my own, and I wanted those fucking feelings of hers dammit.

"I'm so sorry, Ivy."

Her cheeks are flushed and her eyes are bright with her sudden fury.

"Then give me a reason to do this, more than just you love me. Is there a chance at a real future here? I don't mean to put that sort of pressure on you, on us, after this short amount of time, but you're telling me that you love me and I love you back—and that makes me think of forever."

I drop my head into my hands, my elbows on my parted thighs. I have a million reasons for us to try. A million. But none of them are good for her. None of them will work, because it means her life with me will be at risk. It means her life with me will be as she said —superficial.

It means this angel will be with the worst sort of devil.

How could I marry her or give her my babies?

I can't offer her the forever she desires until I work everything out, and I don't know when or if I can even do that.

"I love you." It's all I have left, and it's not nearly enough.

"Then trust me."

"It's not a matter of that, not fully anyway, and I think you know that."

She pulls away, wrapping her arms tightly around her stomach, watching the rain that just started, running down the glass the same way her tears fall against her cheeks.

She's so beautiful. So absolutely exquisite.

And she has me. I'm hers. But she cannot be mine.

She's the woman of my dreams, and I'm throwing her away.

It's all me. I know this, and I'm helpless to stop it, despite how desperate I am for her.

"Do you know what hurts the most about this?" she asks softly, her voice so full of emotion that all I want to do is hold her in my arms and never let go. Promise her anything she needs. Give her everything.

"What, baby?"

She gusts out a half-laugh. "We could have been so amazing. I felt it almost instantly. That night ten years ago, that night at the party, the morning you showed up at my flat, every second of it." Her eyes find mine, and the pain I see in them is more than I can handle. "We could have been epic, Luke. The couple everyone was jealous of. A year would have been nothing compared to the forever."

"I know. I'm sorry. It's not because I don't want that. Please," I practically beg. "You have to know that. I want you, Ivy. I want to be with you." I reach for her hand and she lets me take it into mine.

She nods like she's considering this, and it just makes me frantic to think of a way to be with her. To make this work.

Do I want my life for her? It's not like I'm asking her something easy. It would be lies and half-truths, just as she said, and then there's my past. Fuck, how could I ever tell her about that? She'd leave me for sure. I know she would. How could she not?

170

"Ryan said not to give up on you. That you are worth it. Are you? I want to believe that you are."

"God, I want to say yes."

She turns to me, her eyes so very somber. "But you can't?"

"There are things about my life that I cannot alter. Things I'm a part of and stuck with. Things I've done, and those things I will never be able to tell you about or change."

"This has to do with everything that went down at Caltech." It's not a question. It's like she's put it all together, but yet hasn't. She's got her theories, and I'm sure some of them are right, but she doesn't know everything, nor will she.

"Part of it."

"I don't know what I'm supposed to do here. I want a chance at something incredible, but I also want normal. I want a real life with someone. A partnership. Someone who I'm safe with and will put me first. Can you do that with me?"

I can't even lie to her. "No. Not now anyway."

"So let me see if I have everything straight then." Her tone is almost sarcastic, but it's too bitter to fully accomplish it. "You want to be with me and you love me. But you have a million secrets and things that you're unwilling to share, and that's not something that will change. So you're pushing me away when you'd really rather not."

"I have to." I grab hold of her, tugging her into me because even though I'm telling her goodbye, I can't let her go. "It's not that I don't want a future with you. I fucking do. I want you forever like you wouldn't believe, but I'm bad for you. I'm poison, and you're pure and good. I can never tell you what you want to know."

"Just an inch, Luke. I just need an inch." She's grasping onto me so tight, her fists clutching the fabric of my shirt, needing to hold on just as much as I do.

"You deserve so much more than an inch, Ivy. So much more." Her eyes slam shut as she nods her head, tears leaking one after the other. "I love you, and if I can figure everything out one day, maybe you'll still be there." I press my lips to hers, mourning their absence before I even pull away.

I was so arrogant and wrong to drag her into my world.

So now I do the first right thing I've done in ten years. I pull away and let go.

Her head falls, and she shakes with the restraint of holding back everything my words just did to her.

"How did we get this far? This wasn't supposed to happen," she says, more to herself than to me.

Ivy's asked that question before, and just like then, I don't have an answer. But I'd be lying if I said I wasn't heartbroken. I am, but worse than that, Ivy is, and it's one hundred percent my fault. I never knew guilt could come in this form. I never knew love could feel like this. I never knew pain could be so crippling.

This is wrong. So fucking wrong. Ivy is meant to be mine, and I'm meant to be hers.

This is so motherfucking wrong. But I'm going to fix it. I'm going to make this right for her. I can't keep her. Not yet, anyway. Things are too precarious with me, but I will make this right for her. For us. I'll do what I have to do and I'll fix this. I'll let her go now, and I'll change everything I can possibly change. I'll flip my world upside-down. I'll move heaven and earth if I have to. I'll do whatever it takes to deserve her.

And then I'll fight like hell for her.

"So this is it then? The end?"

I can't even speak the words. They might kill me as they rip a hole inside me.

I nod and she nods, and we fall silent, watching a rainy Seattle fly past us with nothing left to be said.

# Chapter Twenty-One

*Luke*

I DRIVE Ivy home after I screwed it all up. *It's for the best*, I tell myself as I start my car and pull away, unable to look at the woman who became my everything in four short weeks, only to leave her for the second time. *I'll make this right.*

But what if I can't make it right? What if I can't change my situation or my life?

Or what if I can, but by that point it's too late and Ivy doesn't take me back?

That thought is a sucker punch to the gut that knocks the breath from my lungs.

I stop at the first open bar I find but make no move to get out just yet. It looks like a total dive, which almost makes me smile. Almost.

"Fuck!" I slam my hands against the steering wheel so many times that the horn blasts, the phone picks up and hangs up, and I turn on the stereo.

"Fucking asshole piece of shit!" I punch my steering wheel one last time for good measure, but before I can shut off the car to go drown my misery in cheap booze, my phone rings.

Hope flutters in my gut, thinking it's Ivy, but it's not. It's Ryan. Of course, it is.

"I'm not talking so don't even ask."

He laughs. "What did you do?"

"Fuck you. Just fuck you and your happy existence."

"Address."

"I don't even know, man. You're good with computers, find me if you need to, but if not, then leave me the fuck alone."

"I'll be there in twenty."

Of course he will.

Shutting off the car, I run through the rain into the bar.

It is exactly as you picture it would be. Dark, dank, and dirty.

It reeks of stale beer and old whiskey. There's a guy smoking a cigarette in the back, and Seattle hasn't allowed smoking inside public establishments for at least ten years. Old-school Metallica plays in the background, as if to prove just how hard this place is.

I walk up to the bar, which has seen better days, and park my ass in one of the many open seats. It's eight p.m., but you'd never know it based on how empty this place is.

"We're not open yet," the female bartender who looks as worn and weary as the bar she tends, says. Her very bleached blonde hair is teased a mile high, and her smudged eyeliner is at least from the night before. Her leathery skin and raspy voice betray a long-standing smoking habit.

"You're kidding me, right?"

"We open at eight-thirty."

I pull out my wallet and slap a hundred-dollar bill on the counter. "What about now?"

She eyes the money with equal parts desire and disbelief. "That real?"

"It is. Jack, neat. You can leave the bottle."

She snatches the bill off the counter, examining it, even holding it up to the meager light. Once she determines it's the real deal, she goes for that bottle and a clean glass.

"Wanna talk about it, handsome?" She leans over the counter in a seductive pose that I'd find comical if it wasn't so sad.

"What do you think?"

"I think that with your money and looks, she's crazy for letting you go."

I toss back the smoky bourbon that bites all the way down my throat. "Then I guess you don't know shit."

Her dark eyebrows shoot up to her hairline, creating more wrinkles in her forehead than seems age-appropriate.

"Let me know if you need anything else, sugar."

Nodding, I offer a sheepish shrug, feeling a small tick of remorse for snapping at a complete stranger—especially when she's serving me alcohol. I pour myself another and just as I'm about to sling it back, Ryan's large frame slides onto the stool next to mine.

"May I have a clean glass, please?" he asks without saying a word to me.

The bartender slides one down the wood, and he catches it with an appreciative smile.

"I don't want the lecture."

"I'm not here for that, and you know it."

Ryan pours himself a hefty shot and we silently drink them down.

"I fucked it all up. Again," I say, unable to handle this a minute longer. I'm so angry. So goddamn angry, but so wrecked with despair and bitterness that I can't see anything but her.

"Did she end it or did you?"

"We did a lot of back and forth with that, but in the end, she was just looking for me to give in and open up to her. To be honest with her, and instead of doing that, I pushed her away and left."

It's too bad I don't smoke, because this certainly feels like the time a cigarette would be a good thing. Sort of goes hand in hand with misery, self-loathing, and whiskey, right?

"Why?"

I slam my palm down on the bar, enjoying the small sting that accompanies it. "Why what, man? Why didn't I open up, or why did I push her away?" Ryan just looks at me, patiently and expectantly.

His Zen is starting to piss me off. "Don't give me that look. You know the answer to both."

Ryan pours us each another shot, and then sits back in his stool, holding his glass up like he's examining the color of the cheap whiskey I picked.

"I wouldn't be honest if I told you that I only know what you've told me over the years, because I know more than that." I'm not surprised by this, but it still bothers me that he looked into my past. "I guess I can't blame you in one degree for not telling her some of that stuff. I can't imagine what any of that was like for you, but I don't think she would look down on you for what happened."

I snort incredulously. "What happened? You mean what I *did*."

He shrugs. "You're the one who has to live with that, and I don't think you regret the choices you made that night. I know you, Luke. You don't do anything without thinking it through, even if you know it could end badly."

"See." I turn in my seat to face him, looking at my best friend, wondering just how much he knows, and if he were to know all, would he abandon his loyalty to me. "You say that, but I did something, and I've been paying for it ever since. It all loops together in one never-ending cycle of bad decisions and fuck-ups."

Ryan sighs, just a little defeated with me. Screw him, I'm defeated with myself.

"So you think that if Ivy knew all there is to know, all you *can* tell her, that she'd end it?" I nod. "So you ended it first before she could?" I nod again. "And you're not even willing to test that theory?" I shake my head.

"No, because she's smart and beautiful and sweet, and so goddamn perfect. She deserves way better than someone like me, and though I lived for a brief period of time pretending I could actually be worthy of her, I know I'm not. My past is what it is, and what I did may, in fact, be something she can't overlook. But even if she could, there's the other thing. This past week away taught me that quite clearly, so despite the fact that letting her go feels like death and disembowelment and anything else unpleasant you can think of, in reality, I'm saving her."

"From you?"

"Yeah. From me."

"You're a stupid bastard, Luke."

Ryan downs his drink before slamming the empty glass back on the bar and wiping his mouth with the back of his hand. He spins on me, grabbing my shoulders in an unrelenting grip, forcing my attention.

"That fucking girl loves you. She. Loves. You. And I know you love her, possibly *more* than she loves you. Don't let that go over some preconceived notion of not deserving her. Does your past suck? Yeah, it really does. But that shit in Oklahoma was a long time ago, and I can't picture her leaving you over that. As for the shit at Caltech, do you really think I'm stupid enough to believe you got busted and I didn't for the same crime?"

He gives me a pointed look before continuing on without waiting for my answer to his rhetorical question.

"No. I'm not. It's insulting to my IQ, and we both know I'm a motherfucking genius." He smirks at me, before it falls just as fast, and he turns serious again. "I don't know exactly who you're working for or what precisely you're doing. I don't even know if they've got you for life or not. But you've been doing it for ten years, and so far, you've managed a pretty normal existence. You don't have to tell Ivy all the details. You just have to tell her enough, so she knows you're a team, that you're with her, and trust her."

Ryan lets me go, and instantly I crumble against the bar.

"I don't know if I can do that. I'm desperate to make this right. For her and for us. But what if I can't? What if it's not possible? I want to marry her, Ryan. I've only really known her a month, but that's all I can think about," I laugh without humor. "That's some crazy shit right there. But I'm the bad guy and she's my angel, and instead of being sent to save my soul, redeem me, I'll end up being her downfall."

"How do you figure that, Drama Queen?" Ryan is not impressed with me, and I can't say I blame him. I'm not impressed with me either.

"Pour me another one, would ya?" He obliges me, but I know

he's not going to let my little speech go. "I messed up. I was arrogant, and though I spent four years in juvie, I thought I was untouchable. But I wasn't then, and I'm not now."

"One of these days you're going to have to realize you're not a monster. That you're actually a really incredible man who's made a few bad choices along the way. That doesn't mean you're not worthy of her. That doesn't mean you don't deserve to be happy."

"Maybe," I shrug. "But that doesn't change the world I'd be bringing her into and that," I point at him. "*That* is inexcusable."

"And you can't get out now that you're in?"

"I don't know, Ryan. I don't think so. I plan to try like hell. She's worth everything that will entail. But even if I can, it won't change what I've done. And I don't know how to tell her about that."

"So you're letting her go," he says again.

"I'm letting her go." *For now.*

He sighs, running a hand through his hair and finishing off his drink. "Then why did you go after her again, man?"

"I didn't know how not to. I've wanted her for a decade, and then suddenly, she was there." I wave my hand in the air.

"So you're letting her go," he says *again,* and right now, I sort of want to punch him for it. Just sort of, because I still love the asshole, but come the hell on.

I twist to him, facing him fully and staring him directly in his green eyes. "I asked you once if you were me and Ivy were Kate, if you would try to move forward with things. Do you remember that?" He nods once, but it's short and almost curt. "Your answer was, 'I don't know.' Has that changed or are you just pushing this because you think Ivy and I make a cute couple? I love her enough to let her go. That's the only reason I can do it. I love her more than I love anything in the whole world, and that certainly includes myself. So answer me again, if it were you, would you go forward?"

Ryan deflates, running a hand through his hair and adjusting his glasses. That's his go-to when he's tense or uncomfortable, and clearly, I'm making him both. But it's a legitimate question and I think I want a real answer, so I wait him out.

"I can't answer that. Only you know what you're involved in."

That's a bullshit response, but I don't bother calling him out on it. "For what it's worth, I still think you're wrong about your past. I still think you should tell her and see what she does, because I know she'll end up surprising you."

"Bullshit!" I snap. "My goddamn *mother* still doesn't speak to me."

"I don't know what to tell you on that. I think that could be related to her own guilt, but maybe I'm wrong. I don't want to see this eat you alive, and I have a bad feeling that it will."

I laugh out, the alcohol starting to take over. "Nah man, just give me another decade and I'll be straight."

"What happened this week, Luke? What is it that changed everything for you and Ivy?"

"You know I can't tell you that."

"Did you kill anyone?"

I let out a great big guffaw at that. "No, that's a one and done thing."

He nods, evidently he does know my story.

"Did you steal from people? Cheat them out of anything?"

"Nope. That's one I've never done, believe it or not."

"Are you committing treason? Going against the government or setting our world up for war?"

"Don't be so dramatic, guy. Technically that's what I'm working to prevent."

"Then I can't think of anything that would drive her away."

I laugh at that. "In case you missed the memo, Ryan, she's already leaving. She's gone as of the middle of next week. This wasn't supposed to happen. None of this. It was supposed to be casual and fun, and then she was going to leave, and we were both going to be fine. But I'm not fine. And neither is she. And it's entirely my fault. She will never understand that I'm trying to protect her by doing this."

I pour myself another drink only to slam it back without giving it a moment to rest.

"But that's not what happened. And you *could* be with her, even though it will be long distance."

"If it were all that simple, maybe I would. Maybe if I weren't involved with certain things, but I am. And as we've already established, it can't be changed. At least not yet. And what I do puts me in danger. Imagine that shit on Ivy. You remember that month of my life that I was gone?" He doesn't respond, but I know he does. It freaked him out, big time. He even tried to find me. "That I suddenly vanished without explanation? Let's just say I wasn't living the high life at some resort doing cute and cuddly hacks for shits and giggles." He looks stricken, which tells me my point has been made. "Yeah, not exactly relationship material right there. I need to change it and until I can do that, *if* I can do that, I can't be with her."

My eyes slam shut, and the weight of the last fifteen years of my life crushes my chest. I've never admitted anything to anyone. Never uttered the words once. Not even when I've been questioned directly.

Ryan's not surprised. Not even a little. For some odd reason, that makes me smile. "That was two years ago, Luke. Nothing like that has happened since. All of that sounds worse than your present reality."

"Maybe, but the foundation is true, and that's all that matters where Ivy is concerned. She's too good for me. I don't deserve her."

"You've said that already, and it's still bullshit."

"I've pushed her away too many times. She'll never take me back." Now I'm getting to the self-pity part. I can't think like that. I have to think that she'll take me back eventually.

"I don't know the answer to that," he points at me. "But neither do you. You'll regret this forever."

"That's the funny thing, Ryan," I turn to look my friend in the eyes. "That's all I ever do. I live in a permanent world of regret over stupid choices. Maybe I can redeem myself, and maybe I can't, but the way my life works, the way my luck works, she'll be long gone by then."

Ryan drives me home. I left my car at the bar because I am far too inebriated to drive. I immediately walk into my room, stare at the rumpled sheets of the bed that I never made after the last time

Ivy slept here, and dive face-first into them. I figure if I'm going to torture myself, I might as well do it right.

It's been almost a week, but they still smell like her.

I didn't sleep much in the days I was away. I never do when they have me sequestered on that boat. Boat, ha. I almost want to laugh at that. It's a fucking yacht registered to some rich prick who doesn't exist anywhere but on paper. But the people I work for are very competent at selling a bill of goods and coming out looking squeaky clean.

That is their job after all.

My job is another step in the game.

You read about China hacking some American corporation or Russia hacking our government emails or Israel hacking Iranian nuclear facilities—kudos to them on that one. You hear about all these things, but rarely do you hear about what *our* government does.

We play it off like we're above all that espionage hacking bull-shit, but we're not.

We hack everyone. Foreign governments, private groups like Anonymous who think they're above it all, WikiLeaks—damn those assholes are arrogant, good, but arrogant. You name it, we've got a hand in it and that hand just happens to be mine.

Am I proud of what I do? I'm more ambivalent than proud.

Do I feel like anything I do has even the slightest benefit on national or international security? Who the hell knows?

So why do it, you might ask.

Well, I don't have a choice.

I went to that address at three o'clock in the afternoon, like those motherfuckers in the coffee shop demanded, on a perfect California day and walked into a meeting with the last person I ever expected to see again.

Ronaldo Sanchez.

Even his name is over the top.

I met him when I was fourteen years old on my second day of juvie. The fact that he had that name, was way older than appropriate for a juvenile detention facility, and his Spanish accent wavered, should have tipped me off, but it didn't. This was Oklahoma for Christ's sake. The only accents we breed there are twangs that go with our cowboy hats and tall boots. But I was a kid, so I didn't pay attention all that closely.

Those four years in juvie were not spent idly.

I worked my ass off and graduated from high school. Not a GED, mind you, I fucking graduated. That and Ronaldo took me under his wing, giving me a love and appreciation for computers. An outlet for my restless mind.

The rest I picked up by myself. An innate gift he'd called it. A natural talent.

Maybe. None of that shit was difficult for me. I was released on my eighteenth birthday, and by that point Ronaldo Sanchez was long gone. He was two years older than me, or so he claimed.

And after getting accepted to Caltech—still don't know how I managed that—I took my skills to the next level. So by my junior year, I was the master. The best in the hacking ring. I was cocky as sin. I was invincible and nothing could come close to touching me.

Hack the government? Sure. Why the hell not?

But I didn't stop at the justice department. And I didn't stop at the White House either. They didn't pose much of a challenge, so I continued on, especially since no one came knocking at my door, and I was being so very careful, right?

So the CIA, that could be cool. And it was.

Because no one goes after mainframes. Do you know why?

Because they're old as shit and hard as hell to break into. Companies, and even our government, spend millions securing their servers, cloud system, larger networks and everything else. But those mainframes? Those are like untapped mines filled with gold.

They're bursting at the seams with information, and I was good enough and arrogant enough to gain access.

Sure I went after the other stuff too, but without a lot of challenge I got bored quickly.

I didn't do anything with what I found. I wasn't out for world domination or to bring people—or our government—down. I was there for the fun, for the excitement, for the sick adrenaline rush that is so much better than drugs or sex, or even jumping out of a fucking plane.

But I wasn't as clever as I thought I was. Not as invisible, and though I could have sworn I was lurking solely in the shadows, I was really out in the open for all to see.

Or at least for Ronaldo, who was watching me the entire time.

So they busted me and then they screwed me, because I was Ronaldo's guy. He was the man behind the scenes pulling the strings, and I was nothing more than his new puppet.

Still am for that matter.

Yes, I'm sure some of what I'm doing is important. Yes, I'm preventing a lot of bad shit from happening—at least that's what I tell myself.

But at what personal cost?

I'm not allowed to tell anyone what I do or who I work for.

I'm not allowed to discuss anything I do with anyone.

I am to leave at a moment's notice without complaint, nor am I to offer comment when assigned a task.

And it was made very clear to me that I am a target because of all of this, which means anyone I bring into my life is at risk too. Not necessarily the people I work with or my friends, but a lover, wife, girlfriend? Yeah, they could be in trouble.

Governments can be vengeful fuckers. Private, wealthy assholes can be too.

How could I ever live with myself if something happened to Ivy? I couldn't.

So I pushed her away after pulling her toward me, despite falling in love with her so effortlessly.

My head is spinning, or maybe that's just the alcohol.

All I smell is the whiskey emanating from my pores, permeating the air around me with the pungent stink I love and hate. That smell will always and forever remind me of my father. Fucking moth-erfucker.

*Yes, Dad, I blame you for everything.*

What kind of man beats his wife and children?

What kind of man wants to ruin his daughter?

Ryan was right about one thing though; I do not regret every choice I made.

I just wish it didn't cost me Ivy.

And as if the gods of irony hear my plight, my special black phone rings.

# Chapter Twenty-Two

*Ivy*

ORIGINALLY I WAS SCHEDULED to move on Monday, but then I pushed it back to Wednesday because I figured the more time I got to spend with Luke, the better. But that all went to hell. Now I see no reason in prolonging the inevitable, which is why I moved it back up to Monday.

So here I am with my last day of this fellowship behind me, and it felt nothing but anticlimactic. It felt like a waste of a day and a graduation. Any excitement I should be effusing is non-existent. Any pride I should be showcasing is now not-so-mysteriously absent.

And now that Luke is officially out of my life, again, I am moving across the country in two days. But here's the problem with that. I have absolutely nothing to do until then. I'm packed, all except one small suitcase that I'm living out of. I've had my farewell dinner with my parents and coworkers, and though I could change my plane ticket again, my apartment in Boston won't be ready for me until Monday.

Two days with nothing to do but lament the man I was certain was my future.

But I'm not exactly the type of woman who sits around with a pint of ice cream as I cry my eyes out, listening to a mix of the all-time greatest love songs. I don't torture myself with romantic films or scour the pages of angsty romance novels looking for meaning.

No, I'm the type of woman who works her way through a problem—literally—as in I bury myself in my craft. But I don't have that option for the next forty-eight hours, and that leaves me with nothing but my thoughts.

My very dangerous thoughts.

The kind of thoughts that get women all over the world into trouble.

You know the sort.

Overanalytical, compulsive, self-deprecating and relentless.

The type of thoughts that force you to replay every single second of your entire relationship to try and discern where things went so very wrong. Where the signs were that you blatantly missed, because you felt that this time was different. That you were different together and could eclipse all the rules you so carefully created and assembled into place to safeguard against this very thing from happening.

Kate rang this morning with well wishes and promises of a visit when she comes east. I want to excommunicate myself from everything that even remotely reminds me of Luke, but I can't do that to Kate. I can't do that to Claire either. So I agreed to those visits and did my best to keep my voice as upbeat as possible, knowing that every detail of our conversation—and my demeanor during said conversation—was going to be relayed to Ryan.

The problem is that I miss him. The problem is that I love him and I told him that I did. Worse yet, he told me the same. He even initiated that conversation, only to flip it all around and tell me that he was leaving me for my own good. Maybe he didn't come right out and say those exact words, but that's what he intimated.

It's really difficult to be angry with someone who tells you that they love you, but can't be with you because you deserve better and they're unable to give you what you want.

Exasperated? Of course. Resentful? Absolutely. And maybe they're close in meaning to angry, but they're certainly not the same, and there is a very definite and distinct difference.

Maybe I'll get there. Maybe I'll reach the point of absolute heated rage toward him, but right now, I'm sad and depressed and so very mournful of what we could have had. Because I wasn't lying to him when I said we could have been epic. I wasn't lying when I said I envisioned a forever with him. In fact, I never lied about any of it.

But he did, and that seems to be his way. There is nothing more to be done except move on and start over.

So that's what I plan to do.

Any minute now I'll pull myself off the sofa and do something productive with my day. Any minute now, I am going—to answer the door?

I hate the irresistible fluttery dance my stomach leaps into at the sound of the knock on my door. Hate that I am hoping for it to be Luke on his knees, groveling for me to come back. Hate that when I swing the door open, I am greeted with Craig Stanton and not Luke Walker.

"What are you doing here?" I ask in a tone that comes out much sharper than I intend.

He's not fazed in the slightest as he grins at me with that million-dollar gleam. "I'm bored, and I figured you would be too, so I thought maybe you'd want to go do something and get some dinner after?"

I should say no to him. I should turn him down flat and recommence my wallowing—but I don't want to do either of those things. I want to say yes to him and the distraction he's offering.

"Sure." I step back, allowing him to enter. "What did you have in mind?" I ask as I gather my things and stuff them inside my oversized travel purse.

"I don't know," Craig laughs. "I hadn't really gotten that far. I was actually expecting you to be with Luke, but since I was in the neighborhood, I thought I'd take the chance."

I pause, my hand clutching my keys as I turn to face him. "No," I say, but my eyes lower to the floor automatically, unable to watch his expression when I tell him, "We broke up."

"Oh," Craig says, taken aback. "Stupid bastard," he whispers more to himself than to me. "Should I feign disappointment?"

"It is what it is, Craig. I'm not really in the mood to rehash it."

"Do you love him?"

I can only nod.

"Then I'm sorry you're hurting, Ivy. That's not something I would ever want for you. I know people always say this, but in your case it's true. You deserve so much better."

I raise my eyes to his, somewhere between irritated at the platitude and flattered at the compliment. "Like you?"

He smiles and it lights up his gorgeous hazel eyes. "Maybe, but remember you said it first."

I shake my head, trying to hide my smile. "Enough of this, where did you want to go?"

"To Boston. With you."

I roll my eyes dramatically. "You are going to Boston, but not *with* me. Friends, Craig. That's all I'm offering here."

"That's what they all say at first."

"Rack off," I laugh. "I want to go walk about the city. It's a beautiful day, and we won't be able to enjoy it much longer."

"Then let's go," Craig turns the knob on my door, holding it open and waiting for me to walk through. After locking up and taking the stairs down the four flights, we step out into the bright sunshine. As someone who lives in Seattle, I can't help but soak it in with a smile.

I don't look across the street. I don't even venture a glimpse at the bench, because I know I'll be disappointed when I don't find Luke there. Amazing how I went from one stalker to another. Amazing how one terrified me, and the other made me fall in love.

Craig opens the door for me to his over-the-top Range Rover, and as I slide onto the buttery leather seat, cushioned in luxury, I can't help but laugh. "What?" he asks as he gets in, shutting the door behind him with a click and buckling his seat belt.

"What are you going to do with your car?"

"Have it shipped. I love it too much not to."

"Where are you living? I don't think we've discussed that?"

Craig starts the car without asking where I'd like to go. Pulling away from the curb, he begins to drive us in the direction of the market.

"There is a complex of apartments near the Longwood T stop. That's where I'm moving. You?"

"Yup. Seems to be the place the doctors go. That's where my flat is too."

Craig beams at this. "We can walk to work together, and when it snows, I can drive you."

"I may take you up on that. I have no plans on bringing my car with me. In fact, it's already parked in my parents' garage."

"Seriously?" he asks, and I nod. "You're just going to leave it here?"

"I may sell it. I may not. It's newer than my mum's car and better in wet weather, so I told her she could pretty much have it."

"What about your furniture?"

"No, I actually managed to get a furnished flat there. The landlord of my building here said he'd take what I left behind, and everything I want to keep, I'll ship."

"If we had thought this through, we could have shared a place." He gives me a wicked grin. "You know, to save on expenses."

"Right," I ooze sarcasm. "That would have been an ace idea."

"You can resist all you want, and because you're nursing a sprained heart, I won't push it. But you'll end up loving me in the end."

"Sprained heart?"

"Yup. Definitely not broken. And while you're waiting for it to heal, I'll be around."

He pulls into a parking space, hopping out with a wink and a grin before he gets my door for me. "What if I said that it was broken, and that I was only going to want to be friends with you. Will you beg off or stick around?"

"Stick around. I'm not going anywhere."

He smiles that smile again, the one that you can't help but feel, and we both decide to leave it at that. I get what he's indicating. It's not exactly subtle, and though I have no intention of taking things to the next level with Craig, it's nice to have someone when moving to a new city.

Craig and I end up walking around for hours, to the point where our feet ache and our heads pound. And after dinner, we finally decide to call it a night.

"Thanks for a really fun day," I say, once he pulls up in front of my building.

"It was fun. I'm glad I stopped by this morning. Can I walk you up?"

I shake my head. "No, I'm good. Cheers, though." I lean across the console and kiss his cheek before exiting. Craig waits for me to open and enter the front door of my building before driving off, but once he's out of sight, I exit the way I came in, descending the few steps that lead to the street.

He's there. Sitting. Watching. Waiting.

I stand, motionless on the sidewalk, watching him in return, wondering just what his presence means. Wondering if he saw me leave this morning with Craig only to return hours later.

It's dark out, but the street lights on either side of the bench clearly illuminate him and his expression, though I can't decipher it. Maybe that's the reality of only knowing someone for a month. I don't know all of his expressions. I don't know what every single look he has means.

Maybe I don't really know him at all.

He rises slowly, clearly as torn about crossing the street and the distance between us as I am. There's a large black duffle bag along with his computer bag at his feet, and as my eyes focus in on them, I realize what they signify.

He's going away on another one of his trips.

He's leaving and wanted to make sure to see me one last time.

My heart sputters to a stop for the briefest of moments before taking off at warp speed. Never have I felt such rising panic before in my life.

This could very well be the last time I see him.

Do I want to spend this moment staring at him across the street?

And as I consider at those bags, analyzing them and their meaning, I'd love to say that I get his reasoning behind ending things. That I understand everything clearly and that I'm at peace with it all.

But I don't understand, and I'm not at peace.

I have no real explanation for his actions, and as I refocus on him—on his gorgeous face and tall, strong body—I ache everywhere. I ache for everything he's given up on. Mourn our happily ever after, because I wanted it so badly I could practically taste it.

But instead of that happily ever after, I'm left with crippling, anguishing spasms wracking my insides.

So I continue to stand here. Unwilling and unable to be the one to breach this great divide. Hoping he'll take the initiative, but also praying he'll turn and walk away.

But this is Luke, and he can't leave without his grand moment.

Without warning, he abandons his belongings, running across the street nearly at a sprint until he practically slams into me. His arms surround me, yanking me into his chest with the force of a desperate man. Strong, large hands cup my face as he crashes his lips to mine.

And though this may be the most passionate kiss I've ever experienced, it's also the emptiest. I can feel his apology as his lips move against mine, because though I'm in his arms, and his lips are pressed to mine, this is not a reconciliation. This is not asking for forgiveness or to start over.

This is not asking for another chance.

This is goodbye.

And I realize in this moment just how wrong Craig was. This is so much more than a sprain. So much more than a fracture. This is shattered. This is obliteration. This is total annihilation to the point where I don't think my heart will ever truly recover.

*I may never get over you, Luke Walker.*

And with that hopeless and tragic thought, I push him back, breaking our kiss and all our points of contact. Tears are streaming not only from my eyes, but his as well, and my heart breaks all over again, but this time for him.

"I love you," he whispers, the words barely audible.

"I love you too," I whisper back.

But I know I need to be the one to leave this time, despite how fucking hard it is.

So I take him in one last time, memorizing every single one of his glorious features, before turning around and walking away for good.

# Chapter Twenty-Three

*Luke*

*One year later*

I sit at my palatial mahogany desk with my feet kicked up, hoping to hell I scuff the fine finish. The only problem with that plan is that I'm too antsy to keep my feet where they are and end up turning in my chair to see the view from my office window, moving my feet back to the floor.

Rain and my own goddamn reflection against the darkened night sky beyond the pane. That's my view right now. Water runs down the glass in thin rivers.

Kate and Ryan are out tonight celebrating, but I have no interest in joining. I'm happy for them, I really am, but I'm tired and moody and hating on everything the same way I have been for the last year.

Ivy.

That woman haunts my thoughts.

And it's not because she's gorgeous, because I already know that she is. And it's not because she's brilliant and witty, because I already know that too. No, it's everything else that has my brain going in overdrive. It's everything else that has me sitting in my office on a Friday night a year after I pushed her away.

It's the fact that I'm *still* thinking about her.

It's the fact that she was different, that we were different, that has me going crazy.

I thought I'd be done with this by now.

The ever-present obsessive rotation of questions force themselves to the forefront of my mind. Where is she right now? What is she doing? Who is she with? That one kills me every time. Does she still think about me the way I think about her?

So that's why I'm here and not out celebrating with everyone else. Because I can't make it stop. Because the masochist in me doesn't *want* to make it stop.

I love Ryan. Let me make that clear. He is the brother that I never had, and I thank whatever there is above us for him daily. He saved my ass. He gave me a job when I didn't even graduate college and made it seem like *I* was doing *him* a favor by taking it.

He never made me feel second. I am never the Robin to his Batman.

I am more a Bruce Banner to his Tony Stark, if that makes sense.

We're equals.

He may technically sign my check, but every single business decision he's made has gone through me first. Every single meeting that may change the course of *our* company, I've been present at. My office is right next to his and it is exactly the same size.

What does that tell me?

It tells me that Ryan is the best man I know. It tells me that I will never find a better human being than him. A more loyal one. It tells me that he has my best interests at heart with everything, and that I'm a shit for being here instead of toasting the fact that he and Kate have been married a year and are pregnant with twins.

I had a date tonight, and I think that's what really set me off on this latest round of Ivy torment. She's a girl I met in the grocery store near my apartment yesterday. The same fucking grocery store that carries that godforsaken Vegemite shit.

In truth, she caught me at a weak moment. I was lonely and hurt and disappointed, and whatever the hell else someone is supposed to feel when they're obsessed with the woman they let get away almost exactly one year ago to the goddamn day.

So yeah, this girl flirted, and I flirted back, and before I knew what the hell I was doing, I asked her out. When I called her an hour ago to cancel, she was surprised, but took it like a champ even though it was a dick move.

"Oh," the startled female voice of my assistant, Lyla, snaps me out of my staredown with the rain that is streaking down the glass of my windows. "I'm s-sorry, Mr. Walker. I thought you had l-left for the night." Her thick southern accent is more pronounced, no doubt due to the fact that I scared her by sitting in my own office.

"I had, but I came back." Her brows furrow, but only for a moment. "Please call me Luke, Lyla. Mr. Walker makes me think of my father, and I avoid thinking about him whenever I can." Damn, I'm in a crap mood. I shrug apologetically because I don't mean to take it out on her.

Lyla joined us here just a couple weeks ago.

I seem to go through assistants like tic tacs.

I hate those damn candies, which is probably why I go through assistants the same way. She's young. Like right-out-of-college-first-job-ever young.

She walks to my desk hesitantly, as if she's afraid I might snap at her for moving or breathing in my direction. Her outstretched hand is a little shaky as she places a few pieces of paper on the edge of my desk.

"These are the documents that y-you'll need for the meeting with the Tyson group Monday morning."

I like her accent. It's nice. Sort of rolls around you like warm honey.

I don't like it nearly as much as an Australian accent.

*I'm so fucked.*

"Thank you," I smile, sitting up straight and loosening the damn tie I decided to wear this morning, which now feels like a noose around my neck. "What are you doing here this late?"

Lyla blushes a little, and for the first time, I realize she's dressed differently. She's dressed for a night out, wearing a short skintight black dress that hugs her shapeless figure.

"I u-uh…" She shifts her weight, looking over toward the book-shelf like it will save her from having to answer me. "I was j-just heading out."

I shrug, because I'm not really all that interested. "Well, have a good weekend then." I offer a grin.

"Thank you, s-sir." She looks relieved, and I'm about to call her out on calling me sir again, but she practically runs out of my office.

*Have I done something to make her feel uncomfortable?*

That stutter is new. I don't remember that from when I first met her. I honestly can't think of anything I could have done. Normally, I would automatically say yes because I can be an ass like that, but I feel like I've tried extra hard to be on my best behavior with her since we have to work so closely together and my assistants don't seem to last very long.

*Maybe I'll have a heart-to-heart with her on Monday.* Yeah, I'll do that.

I have little interest in going home, but I'm not exactly in the mood to work either. Instead, I get up out of my comfy leather chair and do something I absolutely have no business doing. I walk out of my office, peer around to ensure I'm the only one left on the floor, and then head right into Ryan's office.

Locating the bottle of very expensive bourbon from the bottom drawer of his cabinet, I pour myself a healthy serving into one of the cut crystal tumblers he has, and go over to his desk to sit down.

It's exactly like mine.

Ryan has no ego or pretension, though his genius and talent certainly could warrant both.

No, instead, I'm the face of the company. A role that works out well for both of us.

My eyes glide over to the framed picture he has on his desk of him holding Duchess Kate.

I love this picture. If I'm being honest with myself, it's the sole reason I came in here. Kate is leaning up against a tree in their backyard, smiling up at Ryan with pure adoration in her eyes like the camera caught them in a private moment.

It's flirtatious and mysterious, and I'm unbelievably jealous of that look she so freely gives him.

Not because I love the Duchess in that way, but because everything just seems so easy for them now. I know they had a rough start and that Kate is still working through her guilt, but they're making it work.

I haven't made anything work with a woman, ever.

I down the rest of my drink, look at the picture for one last fleeting moment and then get my ass up and out of this office.

It's raining out. No big shocker there.

I mean, it is Seattle. That's sort of a given here, but it's annoying me tonight. Probably because I didn't drive here this morning because it was warm and sunny, but now I'm stuck trudging through the cold rain with not even so much as an umbrella to help me out.

I duck under an overhang of a building two offices down, and decide to order up an Uber when my phone buzzes in my hand.

Claire. Of course, it's Claire.

No doubt giving me shit for not being at the bar along with everyone else.

Claire: *Lyla says you're still at work. Get your ass to the bar, Lucas. I have a surprise for you.*

Me: *I don't like surprises, Claire Bear.*

Claire: *Call me that again and I'll make sure my surprise goes home.*

That certainly piques my interest and if I'm being honest, I know I should be there anyway.

Me: *On my way.*

Claire: *Alright, Alright, Alright.*

I laugh out loud. Claire has a thing for Matthew McConaughey, and she's clearly quoting *Dazed and Confused*.

Tucking my phone into the pocket of my jacket, I take off at a good clip, ducking my head in a pathetic attempt to stay dry.

I spot the bar a block or so down. I've never been to this bar before, probably because it looks nice and I tend to be more into dives lately. The door swings open with authority, and the moment I step inside, I regret it.

It's very trendy in here.

Swanky even, with a lot of dim mood lighting, low-profile red leather couches and high-top black wood tables. It's the sort of establishment where women order craft cocktails—whatever those are—and men order single malt scotch.

I'm from farmland Oklahoma where the only things you'll ever find in a bar are sawdust, domestic beer, and cheap whiskey.

And that's exactly how I like it.

But this is Seattle, and trendy mixed with grunge chic is what you get.

When I don't spot them instantly, I'm tempted to walk out, but it's raining its balls off, and I'm wet enough for one evening. Plus, I know I'm not going anywhere until I at least kiss my favorite Duchess and rub her adorable bump.

Reluctantly, I make my way over to the bar, and immediately the bartender walks over, covered head to toe in multicolored tattoos, and a large septum piercing in her nose.

She's cute, but not exactly my type. I tend to like simple, under-stated beauty, and there is nothing simple or understated about this woman.

"What can I get you, baby?" I want to laugh at the endearment coming out of her badass mouth.

"Well, honey," I drawl, letting my country come out for some reason. "I'll take a whiskey neat."

"Any brand?" She leans forward, showing off her ample cleav-age. I can't help but look, but the large tattoo of a butterfly with its wings spanning each breast is distracting me from the goods.

"Whatever you've got that isn't pretentious." She stares blankly at me. "Jack or Jameson if you've got it."

"Coming up."

Leaning back as I wait, my eyes automatically scan the after-work crowd of expensively clad people.

And then something—or should I say *someone*—catches my eye.

Light-brown pin-straight hair. Hypnotic glacier-colored eyes. Bow shaped lips and a slightly upturned nose.

It's Ivy, and my stupid heart instantly goes into hyperdrive.

She's laughing with Claire, Lyla, and Kate. That gorgeous smile has starred in my dreams on an almost nightly basis.

I stare at her, confirming with my eyes what my heart and body already know.

Claire spots me, broadcasting a knowing smirk before she winks and bobs her head in Ivy's direction. Fucking Claire.

My eyes glide past Claire back over to Ivy, and then someone leans in and whispers something in her ear. She turns to him with a sweet smile and a nod of her head. Is that Craig?

My drink slides across the smooth bar top, and I instantly slam it back.

"Make the next one a double," I call out before the bartender can walk off. "I'm going to need all the help I can get," I mutter to myself.

The bartender nods to me, and my eyes go back over to Ivy, who still hasn't looked in my direction.

A million questions swirl inside me. What is she doing here? Is she just visiting or is she back? Did she know I'd be here tonight? That last one makes me chuckle, because how could she not. But now I'm left with more questions. Does she want to see me?

Hope instantly swells in my chest at that thought, followed swiftly by the crushing blow of reality.

She knows nothing of the changes I've made.

She knows nothing, and though I'm desperate to grab her, haul her out of here over my shoulder like a caveman and tell her everything, I can't.

I pick up the glass that has magically reappeared during my preoccupation with Ivy and drink the whole thing down. She's so goddamn beautiful. It's amazing how much I still ache for this woman. Time and distance have been no obstacle or barrier in my affections for her.

Could she ever understand everything and forgive me for all that I have done?

I slap down some money and order another round for my friends.

Moving through the moderately crowded bar, I slowly approach the group. I need a second to go over the moment I've envisioned too many times to count, and suddenly, I have no idea what to say to her. I didn't anticipate this. Seeing her tonight is not at all what I had planned as our reunion, but here it is.

As I get closer, Ryan, being the tall bastard that he is, spots me, and the look in his eyes freezes me instantly. It's the sort of look that no one else would understand if they caught it, but knowing Ryan as well as I do, I see the warning clear as day. He's talking with Craig and though Ryan's mouth is moving in conversation, his eyes are glued to mine.

And my heart sinks.

It may even stop beating altogether.

Ryan nods once, reading the expression on my face as he confirms my worst nightmare. Blinding rage seeps into my bones, weighing me down, anchoring me to this spot and not allowing me to move forward. I'm the world's biggest fuck up.

Sucking in a deep breath and shoving all my fury down, I steel myself to keep moving. Ivy tenses as I approach, though she hasn't noticed me, and I doubt anyone she's standing with has alerted her to my presence.

No, she can sense me.

And that right there makes me smile.

Ever so slowly and with dramatic flair, she turns to me, her lips parted and eyes wide as they glide up my body until they reach my eyes. But once they do, they blink twice before she swallows hard. Her cheeks turn a stunning rosy color, and the hand holding her glass of red wine begins to tremble.

"Took you long enough," Claire calls out as I approach the table, and Kate and Lyla turn to see who she's talking to. But I'm only looking at Ivy who still appears stunned before her expression turns. . . blank.

Well, that's not what I was hoping for.

"I ordered another round for everyone."

"How magnanimous of you boss," Claire says with the slightest drip of sarcasm. She's the only goddamn person I let get away with almost anything. Ryan's the same way. She's like our bratty little sister that you love and hate at the same time.

"Thanks, Claire Bear," I smile at her scowl. "I live to serve you."

"H-Hi Mister eh, Luke," Lyla says. Why do I make this girl so nervous? She's blushing now too.

"Relax, Lyla, I'm really not that scary."

She gulps and nods and turns toward Kate who pats her shoulder like she needs the support. Am I missing something here?

Then I turn my head completely to face Ivy, who is staring into her nearly full glass of red wine.

"I bet right now you're wishing that was a Manhattan," I say, hoping to relieve some of the tension between us, because right now it's so thick I could cut it with a fucking knife.

I get a half-smile for that.

"It would probably help, yeah."

God, I've missed that accent wrapped in her sweet melodic voice.

We stare at each other for a long pulsing beat, and this is the moment where things turn awkward.

Do we hug? Do I give her a kiss on the cheek or a damn hand shake or what?

I opt for the hug, and she does the same. I can't resist breathing in the scent that I've lived without for far too long and press my lips to her forehead. "Hi," I whisper before pulling back.

"Hi," she replies equally as quiet, but her tone warbles, and her eyes refuse to meet mine.

"You look beautiful," I say softly, but loud enough for her to hear. "How've you been?"

She shifts her weight, surreptitiously glancing over her shoulder in Craig's direction before giving me her full attention. God that makes me sick.

"I've been good, Luke," she says tightly. "What about you? You look well." Her eyes continue their protest against mine.

I want to tell her that I'm not well. I want to tell her that I'm a fucking asshole and that I'm sorry. That I miss her like I've never missed anyone or anything before. I want to tell her I finally made the changes that I silently promised her a year ago I would make.

*Look at me, Ivy.* She doesn't.

"I'm okay," I opt for instead. "What brings you to town?"

Again with that look in Craig's direction, but he's still engrossed in conversation with Ryan, who is watching me and Ivy instead of paying attention. "I . . . uh, we . . .uh, moved back a week ago."

Any hope I had spontaneously combusts and the vacuous hole in my chest grows impossibly larger.

"You and Craig." It's not a question, but she nods slowly, chewing on the corner of her mouth the way she does when she's nervous about something.

I want to turn away from her and leave.

My heart feels like it's broken all over again and I just don't have the stomach to stand here and watch the two of them together.

*How did I let this happen?*

"I was going to ring you," Ivy says hastily, shifting her stance. "I didn't want you to hear from anyone else that I was back in town and . . .," she trails off. "I was a complete knob and couldn't do it."

I laugh and try my best to make it sound natural and not as forced as it feels.

But I don't get to respond to her, because fucking Craig douchebag Stanton decides to take this moment to spot me. A big satisfied asshole of a smile spreads across his face, and I want to pulverize him. Jealousy creeps up my spine, licking a path of fire that automatically has my fists clenching and my chest leaning in before I force myself to relax.

"Luke, how's it going, man? Good to see you."

*Asshole.*

"You too, Craig. Welcome back to the west coast." I don't mean that for a second.

We've garnered the attention of everyone else in the small party, and it feels like a million pairs of eyes are focused on me all at once. Like I'm on stage performing—which maybe I am, because I'm smiling instead of beating this man to within an inch of his life.

"Thanks." Craig slides his arm around Ivy's waist, pulling her possessively close to his side. She tenses slightly, her eyes lowering to the floor, not in shame or embarrassment, but in consideration. She's uneasy with his public display in front of *me*.

After everything I put her through, she still cares about how I feel.

Which tells me that she still cares about me.

Which tells me absolutely everything I need to know.

And now I'm smiling like I mean it. Now I stand up tall, allowing my broad shoulders to roll back as I level Craig with my most confident cocky expression. *She's not yours, dickhead.*

"I don't know how long *we'*ll be here." The prick really did just emphasize we. "Ivy's dad isn't doing all that well, so she wanted to be close to him. When he rebounds, I think we'll end up heading back to Boston."

This gets her attention, almost like that little statement is news to her.

Another check for me.

"I'm sorry to hear about your dad, Ivy." I smile warmly at her, my eyes drinking in and absorbing every luminous feature. "I really like him, ballbuster that he is. Is he doing okay?"

Ivy gives a half-smile. "He really liked you, too." *Score!* "I think he'll be fine. Just some kidney issues."

I frown at that. "Well, I'm sure having you close means the world to him and your mom."

"Thanks."

I get a smile that lights up her eyes, and it's like staring into two flawless diamonds.

"On that bright note, Ivy and I need to get going," Craig says with that arrogant smile of his. "It was good to see you again, Luke." He moves forward, pulling me in for some sort of bro hug when he whispers in my ear, "Looks like I got her in the end. No hard feelings, of course, but you can fuck off any time."

Craig smacks my back hard, and when he rejoins Ivy, I smile at him with a look of my own. It's a look that says, *she's not fully yours and you know it*. It's a smile that says, *game on, motherfucker.*

I drag Ivy in for a hug and now it's my turn to whisper.

"I'll see you tomorrow, darlin'."

She doesn't freeze or stiffen, though she maintains her space with an uneasy laugh that tells me she's not surprised by my declaration. That said, she's not exactly thrilled either by the notion of seeing me again, and was clearly hoping it wouldn't turn to this.

And that feels like a knife to the gut.

They leave the bar together after saying their goodbyes to everyone else, his hand on her lower back. It burns too much to watch, so I don't. Instead, I turn back to all the waiting eyes, affixing my smile and backing it up with overconfidence.

"That went better than expected." I smile, and they just stare at me like I'm nuts. Maybe I am, but it's game time, and one thing about me is that I never lose. I may make stupid as all hell decisions, may screw up constantly, but losing is never an option.

# Chapter Twenty-Four

Luke

"DON'T DO IT," Kate says with a stern look on her face that only mothers can get away with.

"Do what?" I feign innocence, but know I'm not fooling anyone. It's probably the stupid grin on my face that's giving me away. Yeah, that must be it.

"She's happy, Luke," Kate continues. "Leave her alone."

"Nah." I wave her away. "No way in hell she's happy with that dick. Did you see her face when she saw me? When he touched her?" I'm looking at everyone in turn, hoping for some sort of acknowledgment that I'm not delusional and fabricating things that weren't really there.

But no one is really looking at me.

They've got these expressions going, and are trading glances back and forth between each other that hint at a deception of some kind, and I'm not digging it. It's never a good thing when your friends hide things from you.

Except Ryan, he looks just as clueless as I am.

"Whatever," Claire says, rolling her eyes. "She's with sex-on-legs Craig Stanton, no way she's going back to you."

"Thanks, Claire," I deadpan. "Always nice to have your support."

"That's what I'm here for, cupcake." She blows me a kiss.

"You don't really think she's happy with him, do you?"

Only Ryan shrugs. Kate and Claire look away. Again. And Lyla who just looks down at the floor with a frown. This whole not-making-eye-contact thing is starting to bother me. Prickles of paranoia are slithering up my skin, and I wonder just how big that thing is that I'm missing.

Are they getting married or something? I didn't see a ring on her finger.

"Whatever the case with her and Craig, I don't think she'll give in to you again." That's Claire, and as always, she's unhelpful.

"You do know that you've been my friend longer, right?"

Claire shrugs. "I like her more. She's fun. When I grow up, I want to be her sister, Sophia."

"I know, right," Kate says, slapping Claire's arm playfully. "Sophia is freaking awesome. I can't wait to see her again. I'm so happy Ivy moved back."

"Traitors. All of you," I point at the people that I previously referred to as my friends.

"I'm still on your side," Ryan offers. "And who knows, maybe third time's a charm for you two." He's teasing me, and it's annoying, but he's also right. I have so much ground to make up with her, and that ground has turned into Mount fucking Everest now that she's with someone. Not just someone—a pediatric surgeon who she works with and is, according to Claire, sex on legs.

I may just be screwed here.

Why didn't I make her see me that day? Any of those days? Why did I allow her to walk away without talking to me?

"You really think I'm done?" I ask no one or everyone or myself.

They're all silent, and though we're in the middle of a crowded bar, I feel like I could hear a pin drop.

"But things are different now," I persist, trying to convince no one or everyone or myself.

"Are they, though?" Claire says. "I mean, we still don't know dick about you, Luke, and I think that was the crux of the problem the last time, if I recall."

"Why are pasts and histories so important to you women?" I point at Claire and Kate, and even Lyla, who is silently watching all of this. "For that matter, why can't you ladies just be happy in the present? I mean, you're all about knowing every damn detail about a man's past, and once he spills that, you're all about the goddamn future. Where is this going? What does this all mean? Shit, just be happy in the fucking moment!" I slam my hand on the hard high-top table with a little more force than I intend, causing some of the drinks to slosh and spill. "Sorry, I'm just aggravated."

"Listen, Luke," Claire says, moving until she's right in front of me, and I'm forced to look down and meet her dark-blue eyes. "Not all women are like that. Personally, the last thing I want is someone's story, but I think I'm unique in that. I still can't imagine how you all go after relationships with outstretched arms like they're the end-all and be-all. But Ivy *is* like that. And if you want a relationship with her, a real one, you need to be willing to give her all of you. Because that's what people do when they're in love and shit." Claire turns to Ryan and Kate looking for backup. "Am I right here? You two are my relationship compass, and you're all about the sharing of stories and *feelings*," Claire says that last word in an acerbic tone.

"You're not wrong," Ryan says calmly, his eyes blazing into mine.

"I pulled back. I managed to get myself out, well, partially out. But I'm out enough that I can be with her. Why can't that be enough?"

"Maybe it is, but maybe it's not," Kate says. "But it's still going to be something hanging over your head no matter what. I don't know your past, but *I* don't need to. If you love Ivy, if you want her the way you say you do, then you need to trust her."

"I know." I sigh, just a little defeated, and a lot sick with the idea of fessing up.

It was something I had hoped I could build up to slowly or not do at all, but something tells me Ivy won't even consider me again unless I'm willing to lay it all out there for her. Unless I *do* give her everything and let her pick. And then there's a real and distinct possibility that she won't pick me.

"Love sucks."

"Right?" Claire snorts. "That's why I don't entertain that emotion. It's nothing but trouble."

"Not for everyone, Claire," Duchess Kate says, maybe a little hurt by her best friend's words as she rubs a tender caress over her enlarged belly. "Love can be painful, and sometimes, indescribably awful, but avoiding it altogether?" She shakes her head.

"Whatever, I'm a lot younger than you love-struck fools, and maybe when I'm old, I'll be there too." Claire turns back to me, giving me her full attention. "Luke, man the hell up. Stop being a pussy and go after her ready to do battle and hand her the keys to your . . . whatever the hell you call that thing."

I run a hand through my short, slightly prickly hair.

"You guys suck, you know that? What's the point of having friends if you're not going to lie to my face and tell me that everything is going to be fine? I mean, what the fuck?"

They snicker and smile, but I'm sort of not joking here. Sort of anyway.

I leave the bar and my friends who think I'm an asshole for wanting to go after Ivy and do something I should not be doing. I hack the GPS on her phone and find out where she lives.

Okay, so maybe I *am* an asshole. In my defense, I felt guilty as shit about it, but there is no way I could ask Claire or Kate where she lives. But I promise to use my powers for good and not evil.

I'm repeating history a little too closely here.

Especially since it's now dawn and I'm sitting in the doorway of a building across the street from her new apartment. Or rather her and *Craig's* apartment. Yeah, that was bitten out, get over it.

But this is exactly what I did after the night I saw her again at Kate and Ryan's dinner party. Only this time, she lives in a high-rise. These buildings aren't really my type. I get people are all about amenities, but the cookie-cutter layouts, small accommodations, and nosy neighbors don't do it for me.

I like my space. I like my *private* space.

So why am I here?

Because I couldn't sleep, of course.

My friends' ugly words have been playing in my mind on repeat, and that made me restless and had me hacking shit, which led me here. I'd love to say my activities weren't illegal, but I'd be lying, and *that* is something I don't do.

Hey, we all have our limits.

Is omitting really the same as lying? I mean, that's sort of a fine line, right? I think I'll walk on the side that says omitting really isn't the *exact* same as lying.

So here I sit on freezing cold steps without the luxury of a bench, waiting for the sun to fully rise—it's scheduled to anyway—and once it does, I need to find Ivy.

I told her I'd see her again today, and she didn't tell me no.

To me that's an invitation.

Does that make me creepy as hell?

Probably, but when you've got nothing going for you, you grasp at whatever you can.

And I'm grasping.

I can't let her go again. I just can't. I need Ivy more than I need anything or anyone else in my life, and though I've fucked up a time or two or six, I'm determined to make it right.

I decide that I'm not going to stalk her—okay, I may already be doing that—but I decide I'm going to text her and ask her to meet me for breakfast at a coffee shop around the corner so we can talk. And even though it's early as hell, I do that and then I wait for her to wake up and respond.

It's mercifully dry, but it's not all that warm yet, so I tuck my hands into the pockets of my jacket and wait, but I don't end up having to do that for very long. But my response is not in the form of a text message. No, before the sun is fully up, Ivy is walking out of her building, looking around like she's expecting someone to jump out of the shadows at her.

What are you willing to bet that someone she's looking for is me?

She's not dressed for work. In fact, she's not even in comfy clothes or pajamas, even though it's barely five in the morning. She's wearing tight-as-sin jeans, leather boots and a leather jacket.

Holy fuck, is my girl going for a ride?

Before conscious thought catches up with me, I'm running across the desolate dark street in her direction. I'm wary of startling her, so I call out, and she freezes, slowly turning to face me, not all that shocked to see me.

"I was hoping to avoid this," she says with a hint of annoyance.

"But you know me too well," I respond, stopping my little jog once I'm a foot or two away from her. It's dark out, not quite pitch black, but the street lights are still on, and they're definitely the only light we can see each other by.

"What are you doing here, Luke?" She sounds tired. Possibly with me or possibly from lack of sleep while she stayed up all night thinking about me.

"Do I really have to explain that or can we just bypass that nonsense where we pretend I don't stalk you in a positive, healthy, non-threatening way?"

Yeah, it's there. That small twitch of her lips that says I can still make her smile. I could live off of that for years, making her smile.

"I don't want to talk to you," she says. I ignore the aggravated edge in her voice.

"Sure you do," I reply confidently. "You just don't *want* to want to talk to me."

"Right, clearly, your ego has remained unscathed in the year since we've seen each other." Ivy turns on me, suddenly full of rage that seeps from her pores as that perfect control she normally exudes slips away. "The real issue is," she holds up a finger halting herself like she just remembered a point, "let me amend that, one of the *main* issues here is that we wouldn't even be talking, you wouldn't even be standing here, if I hadn't run into you at the pub last night."

I'm shaking my head the entire time and this just seems to piss her off more.

"How can you shake your head? How can you stand there and deny that?" She wants to hit me or slap me or shake me or do something violent. I can see it in her eyes. That fire, all that pent-up angst, tells me that she's still mine.

No one can make you this crazy unless you love them.

"Because last night was not the first time I've seen you."

"Bloody liar!" she yells, and now she does shove me. I can see the hurt I've inflicted, rippling off in waves. It crumbles any charm and bravado I was trying to hold onto. It crumbles everything because hurting Ivy breaks me.

I grab hold of her hands, locking them against my chest before I manage to pull her into me. She tries to fight me off, struggling like hell.

"Stop fighting me, Ivy, and listen to what I'm telling you."

"No. I don't want to hear a word. I hate you. I wasn't mad at you before, at least not really, but now?" She shakes her head, blinking back tears that say love and not hate. "I hate you."

"I've been to Boston three times in the last twelve months to see you. I realize that's not a whole lot, but I was there."

"Then why did I never see you there?" Her tone is incredulous, and maybe a little hopeful, but it sounds more like she's hoping I'm lying. Ivy does not *want* to love me. Ivy *wants* to hate me because this sort of hate is so much easier than love.

"Because I suck at life, Ivy." For some odd reason this makes her stop squirming to look at me. "I went the first time a month after you left. I couldn't stand it anymore, being apart from you, so I went. But nothing in my life had changed, so I didn't even see you, because I knew I'd get on my knees and beg, and that wouldn't be good for you. The second time was about six months after that, and that time I did see you, but you obviously didn't see me. I camped out at the hospital and watched you walk in, but you were in a rush and looked anxious. I got a call and had to leave."

"None of this is all that compelling."

"Yeah, I know that. Neither is the last time I went. It was about a month ago." This makes her eyes widen in bewilderment. "But by that time, some things *had* changed. Some big things. And I thought, maybe, just maybe, I wouldn't ruin your life if you took me back. But then I saw you standing in the lobby of the hospital with a tea in your hand in front of that crazy ball pinging thing they have there. You were smiling down at a kid who looked sick, and her parents were talking to you with big smiles on their faces like you were the answer to their prayers. So I watched you, and you seemed happy—so fucking happy. I knew if I approached you with my bull-shit, you wouldn't be so happy anymore, and I chickened out."

"I was happy, Luke. I *am* happy. And I don't want you messing with that."

That hurts like hell to hear. Not that she's happy, I rather enjoy that, but the me messing with her happiness part. That thought sucks, and I won't do that. I won't. But maybe there's a middle ground here that I'm missing.

"Do you love him?"

She stiffens, and then realizes that she's still in my arms and extricates herself from me quickly, pushing off of my chest like I have the plague or something. Ivy doesn't even look at me when she responds, her eyes are focused on the yellow pool of light on the ground from the street lamps, her arms wrapped protectively around her waist.

"Craig is not what you think he is. He's a wonderful man, and I care very deeply for him." It sounds like a standard answer. Like she's rehearsed this over and over again in front of a mirror.

"Do you still love me?" I wince as the words leave my mouth because I know what's about to come next from hers.

Her eyes flash up to mine, and sure enough, she says, "No." And it's an emphatic *no*, definitely not rehearsed. But maybe it's a little too emphatic? Maybe she's trying to convince more than just me when she says that?

Here's hoping, right?

"I really do need to leave."

She runs off into the predawn darkness without another word, and I let her go, because even though I'm hoping she didn't really mean it, it still kills me to hear it.

# Chapter Twenty-Five

*Ivy*

"I CAN'T BELIEVE you told him you don't love him," Sophia says through her laughter. It's a big laugh, so it takes her a little extra time to get the words out.

"Why not?" I ask just a little indignant. I was rather proud of myself for saying it so boldly without the slightest hint of a warble.

"Because, luv, you're the biggest pussy I know when it comes to confrontation, and I just so happen to know a lot of pussies."

"Ugh, Soph. I did not need that visual."

"Maybe not, but it's still all true."

I sigh, as I switch lanes on I-90 heading toward Issaquah where my parents live.

"All that aside, none of it matters. I'm done with Luke Walker, and it would be nice if he got the memo."

Sophia snorts. "Who the bloody hell says memo? No one uses memos anymore when there are email and text."

"You really are missing the point today," I huff, just a little exas-

213

perated. I was hoping for some good, old-fashioned sisterly support, and I'm getting none.

"No, I'm not. I'm proud of you for telling him that, but I'd be even more proud if you meant it."

"You're not helping. I'm almost at Mum and Dad's. I'll talk to you later."

"Aces. Tell them I love them and all that good rubbish. Ring me later."

"Right. Bye." I press the button on my steering wheel to end the call, and then a few minutes later, I'm pulling into their driveway.

My parents moved to the States after dad lost his job back home while I was a teenager. Sophia had just moved here to attend university, and I think my parents took that as an omen to follow. We originally moved to northern California, but after I moved to Seattle for medical school, they came as well. They've been happy since, but considering the house is clad in Australian flags, AFL team Carlton jerseys, and old cricket paraphernalia, I'd say they miss home more than they let on.

I don't knock or ring the bell, I just turn the knob and enter. Mum yells at me if I don't consider this *my* home as well. I missed them while I was away. They did come out to Boston to see me once, but it wasn't nearly enough.

I'm glad to be back in Seattle.

I loved Boston, but this place is home for me. So now I'm a board-certified emergency medicine attending physician in the Emergency Department.

"Mum? Dad?" I call out, but I hear the telly on in the back room, blasting what can only be football, so I head in that direction.

"Oh. Good, you're here," Mum says as she rounds the corner before I reach the kitchen.

I give her a big hug and kiss her cheek. "I'm here." I smile.

I look a lot like her. Her eyes are bluer than mine, but we have the same light-brown hair. She looks tired. My dad's illness has been rough on her, mainly because she doesn't like to leave him all that often but needs to work too. She teaches at a local elementary school.

"How's Dad today?"

Mum waves me off, "He's fine. You know him."

I nod, but hate that answer.

My dad had surgery for a hernia repair about three months ago, and for some unexplained reason, the whole insult to his body threw him into stage four renal failure. They've tried medications and the like, but nothing seemed to help. Now he's on dialysis as well as the transplant list.

I offered him one of mine since I'm a match, but he refused. I told him if he didn't receive a new kidney in the next six months, I wouldn't give him a choice.

My dad is bloody stubborn, so it's been an ongoing battle between us.

"Did he go for his dialysis today?"

"He did, but don't pester him anymore about the transplant. He'll spit the dummy, and I don't want to hear the two of you go on about it."

"I won't upset him. Promise."

She smiles, patting my cheek tenderly. "Oh, that bloke is here. That one you tossed all that while back?"

"Bloke? What bloke?"

*Please tell me it's not him. Please tell him it's not him.*

My mum narrows her eyes at me like I should already know, and I hate that, because of course I do.

"Luke. He's watching the football match with your father."

"Bloody hell, Mum," I whisper-shout, though the telly is so loud I doubt they can hear me. "Why didn't you make him leave?"

"Because he called to see how your father was doing, and since he likes Luke, Dad invited him over to watch the match. It was a nice thing, even if he is a wanker."

Have I mentioned how much I love my mum?

"Go on back now. They're waiting on you." She's smirking at me like this amuses the hell out of her.

"Oh I just bet they are."

I roll my eyes and weave my way through the kitchen into the wood-paneled living room that has seen better days. My dad is sitting in his old beat-up recliner with his feet up, wearing a Carlton Football team sweatshirt, a glass of ice water in his hand that he no doubt wishes was a VB beer.

Luke is sitting on the couch in all his GQ model glory with a faded green t-shirt and dark wash jeans. Both men are engrossed in the screen and haven't noticed my entrance, but when Luke turns his head to say something to my dad, he catches my eye, and his face lights up in a way I wish I didn't feel all the way down in my toes.

"Hi, Dad," I say, ignoring Luke altogether.

My dad's silver head whips in my direction, and he too smiles at me. "Ah, there's my girl now. What the bloody fuck took you so damn long?"

I roll my eyes at him. "Knock it off, Dad." I kiss his cheek before sitting on the other chair on the opposite side from where Luke is. "How are you feeling?"

"Bloody perfect." He gives me a pointed look that says don't mention it. "You didn't say hi to your mate here."

"You're right, I didn't."

My dad laughs a hearty rumble before throwing Luke a shrug. "I told you she wouldn't be happy."

"Dad?" I grin innocently at Luke before looking back to my dad. "Didn't you once mention something about cutting off his member if he messed me about?"

"Yeah, and I already told him that if he were a clever chap he'd leave before your mum fires up the barbie because I plan on roasting his balls on the open flame."

I look to Luke, who just shrugs like he's not all that concerned.

I grin, leaning over to kiss my dad's cheek before sitting back and pretending to be interested in the match on the telly. "I knew I could count on you. Soph says hi by the way."

"She still coming up next month?"

"Don't know, she said—"

"Fucking wanker, kick the blooming ball," my dad yells at the television, cutting me off.

"Ease up, Dad, you'll give yourself a stroke."

"Ivy, my girl, unless I'm under the age of twenty, you are not to give me medical advice. Either you sit here and watch, or you leave," he says in that loving fatherly tone of his.

"She just cares about you," Luke offers with a broad grin that says he knows he's baiting the lion.

"And you'd do well to stuff it, because I no longer like you."

"You're becoming a bit of an old codger in your advanced years, aren't you?"

"Did you just stand up for me?" Luke asks all smiles, his brown eyes gleaming as he points a finger to his chest. "I told you I'm still her favorite person." He pokes my dad in the arm like they had a bet going.

"Go home, Luke, you've paid your visit."

"Nah, your dad invited me over and said I could stay, so I will."

"I did that," my father confirms. "But at the potential risk to his bollocks." I can only smile at that. "Hey, Ivy," my dad says absent-mindedly, his eyes still on the television. "Did your mate and his girl go back to Boston yet, or are they still hanging about?"

*Crap.* I can feel the heat creeping up my skin, and Luke's eyes are boring holes into my skin. "Uh, no. Not yet. They go back tomorrow."

"He's a nice bloke . . .," my dad trails off, but whether he knows what he's doing or not remains to be seen. "His girl too. What was her name again?"

"Darcy," I supply, hoping that this is where it ends.

"Right, Darcy. Craig and Darcy, sweet couple. Too bad they're not locals anymore. She was a—dive for it, you blooming fuckwits!" he screams at the telly, nearly spilling his water and making me jump because I'm far too on edge not to. My dad's eyes have not wavered from the television once, and now mine are firmly affixed to it as well, like it will save me from this moment.

"I'm going to go see how Mum is getting on."

I stand up quickly, nearly falling over as my feet tangle with each other. Who trips over their own feet?

"Sure, ask her if she's going to make me some snags," Dad says without looking up. "I'm bloody starved here."

I nod, though he doesn't see me, and rush out of the room, scanning the halls in search of my mum. It's not exactly a large house, but I hear her humming from her bedroom. Just as I'm about to barge in on her, a hand grabs my arm, pulling me to a stop.

"Let go," I hiss.

"Yeah, not gonna happen," Luke says, ruining my escape as he holds me firmly in place. "What was that in there?" His expression is impossible to read as he walks me backward until my bum and back bump into the wall of the hallway. He's imposingly tall over me, infuriating me with his proximity and smell and heat.

"That's my dad watching Australian football as he always does. You saw him, Luke, which was nice and all, but now you really should go."

Luke's warm brown eyes narrow as his full lips set into a hard line. "Craig and some chick named Darcy? Explain that to me."

"I don't have to explain anything to you about anyone."

Luke slams a frustrated hand on the wall above my head before leaning into me, but not daring to touch me.

I have nowhere to go; he's completely bracketed me in. But I can't breathe or think with him like this, and I'm so very desperate to be able to do both. He's overwhelming me, the way he used to so effortlessly. My heart is pounding its way out of my chest, something I'm sure he can hear—if not feel. His enticing familiarity makes me want to lean in just as much as push him away. I hate him. I hate him so damn much.

Why can't he just leave me alone? He managed it for a year, and in the span of not even a full day, I've had to endure him three times. I was so much steadier without seeing him. "Get away from me!" I push out. I'm so close to tears, and I hate myself for it. "I don't want you here."

Anger is good. Anger is something substantial to cling to.

"Stop dodging this," he growls, inching his face closer before pulling it back. "Are you with Craig, or is he with some girl named Darcy?"

There really is only so long this lie can continue, and honestly, what's the point in maintaining it? It's not like Craig lives here anymore anyway. He still has two more years left on his fellowship in Boston.

"Craig is with my very close friend, Darcy."

Luke's eyes slam shut as a stuttered breath escapes his lips.

"Why did you lie to me?"

"Oh, come off it," I snap. "You know exactly why Craig and I did that, though in all honesty, it wasn't my idea."

"So you and Craig are just *friends*?" he pushes, unconvinced.

"Luke, it really doesn't matter what Craig and I are. None of that matters. Craig and I are close friends, and he didn't want you messing me about the way he thought you would. So we lied. But the simple truth is that I'm not interested in playing this game with you. I mean, did you honestly believe I'd let you into my life a *third* time, only to have you walk away again without a backward glance? I am many things, Luke, but stupid really isn't one of them."

Luke sighs out long and heavy, an internal struggle warring within the brown depths of his eyes. "I don't know what to say to you, Ivy. I know I messed everything up. I know that seems to be my go-to. But things are different with me now. So different and . . . I would never walk away from you again."

"I don't believe you."

"Jesus, Ivy," he groans, sagging forward like my words knocked his breath out. "Please, just give me a chance to explain. *Please*." Luke leans into his arm that is still raised over my head, burying his eyes into his bicep. "I'm sorry. I'm so fucking sorry. You have no idea. I will be sorry forever, and that's not a lie or a ploy, or anything other than the truth. I know I don't deserve another shot. But the flip side of that truth is that I'm totally and utterly lost without you. I know it's been twelve months, and I know you don't believe me, and that I have a million miles of ground to make up, but please, Ivy, please just let me talk this out with you. If you want to walk away after that, then I guess I deserve it, but not before you know all that there is to know."

I don't know what to say to him. I don't know what to think or how to react.

What do you do when you love someone who is bad for you?

What do you do when you love someone who you know will hurt you again given the chance?

"The definition of insanity, Luke, is doing the same thing over and over again, expecting a different outcome. And you are definitely making me insane, but it's a cycle I'm tired of repeating."

"I'll never hurt you again. I swear on everything that I won't. I know it's been a long time and that we need to start over and all that, but give us that chance."

Hope is a ticking time bomb.

Hope may be the most dangerous of emotions known to womankind.

Hope can go fuck itself.

"I can't. I need you to let me go."

He laughs out, but it's devoid of humor as he finally drops his forehead to mine. And that's my total undoing. That one small point of contact completely obliterates any remaining self-control and determination I had, and without warning, the tears I had been holding back, begin to freefall.

His hand comes up to cup my cheek, wiping away my scalding tears with his thumb. A small sob escapes as my lower lip trembles with restraint.

His eyes are bleeding, wounded, and raw as they search my face, agonizing over my tears. "I can't let you go, Ivy," he says softly, his breath brushing across my cheek. "I don't know how. You're inside me and all around me, and the thought of giving you up is the worst sort of pain. It's anguish, and believe me when I tell you that I know pain."

"Please," I plead.

His eyes close slowly as he takes in a deep breath, reopening them on the slow exhale, allowing me to feast on his torment. "Okay, honey," he says in the saddest voice I've ever heard in my life. "I'll leave. I'll let you go, if that's what you really want. If that's what will make you happy. Because in all honesty, that's all I really want for you. But you need to know how much I still love you. How much I'll love you forever. You need to know because I never want you to doubt that. I won't hurt you again, baby. I'd rather die."

His mouth comes down to my cheeks, drinking up my tears. I want to cling to him. I want to take his words and hold on to them. I want to drown in his promise.

But I can't, because hope and trust are not synonymous.

# Chapter Twenty-Six

*Ivy*

MY PHONE RINGS in the middle of the night, blasting me out of a very sound sleep. My head whips around my room, still hazy and disoriented as I fumble around on my nightstand in search of my phone.

This is never a good thing. That's sort of the universal rule about calls after midnight. They're always bad news.

My first thought is that it's about my father, though he looked well and good when I saw him today, but things can change quickly with kidney issues.

The phone stops ringing right as my finger is poised to answer it. It's a number I don't recognize and that alone sets me on alert. Swiping my finger across the screen, I sit up in bed as I bring the phone up to my ear. It rings once, and then a familiar male voice answers.

"Ivy?"

"Yes?" I'm so confused right now. I know this voice, but for some reason, I can't place it, and the simple fact that he didn't address me as Doctor Green tells me that it's probably not work-related.

"Hey, sorry to wake you, I realize it's late." There is a long pause when I don't say anything. "It's Ryan, by the way."

"Oh," I rub a hand over my face, clearing the sleep from my eyes. "Is it Kate? Are the twins all right?"

"Yes," he rushes. "Yes, oh shit, sorry. I didn't mean to scare you like that. The twins are awesome. Baking away. That's not why I'm calling."

"Okay?"

"I need your help. I wouldn't call or ask you of all people, but Katie is away at a nursing conference, and he's refusing to go to the emergency department."

"I'm sorry, I'm missing something here. What are you talking about?"

"Luke," he says like I should have already guessed that. "Who the hell else would be stupid enough to punch a brick wall?"

"Ryan, back up here for a minute," I say, but I'm climbing out of bed, flipping on the bedside lamp, and pulling on my jeans. "Luke punched a brick wall? Why?"

Ryan sighs out, sounding tired with everything.

"Because the stupid bastard told you he'd let you go and he's in love with you, so he punched a wall thinking that would somehow solve all his problems. It didn't, Ivy. Let me tell you, it really didn't, and I need that hand. I need him to be functioning and able to work, and with his hand like this, he can't." Then I hear a muffling sound before Ryan says something that sounds like "shut up and stop bleeding all over the place."

"What do you need me to do? Because if you're asking me to tell him that I'll give him another go, I'm hanging up on you," I tell him, but I'm brushing my teeth as I speak. I say that I want him to leave me alone, yet at the first sign of trouble or him needing me, I fly out of bed in the middle of the night. Even when he does something as asinine as punching a brick wall.

I should be fractious at this imposition. I should be overwhelmed with rage for this intrusive call, but I'm not. I'm worried about

Luke's hand and about him, and I hate myself for that. I hate myself for being weak where he's concerned. I know now I'll always be, despite telling him to sod off.

"No, I'm not saying that," Ryan continues. "I'm saying that the dipshit may have broken his hand and might also need stitches. I'm saying that he won't go to the hospital, and I'm saying that his hands are worth a lot to me. So I'm asking—no, I'm *begging*, for your help."

"Where are you?" I sigh out, standing in the middle of my living room, looking at my reflection in the window.

I shouldn't do this. I shouldn't get involved. I should let him figure this out on his own. Nothing good will come of me seeing him and helping him. I should say no.

"His place."

"I'll be there in ten."

I disconnect the call and go over to my bag of supplies, grabbing what I think I may need. I'm going to help him. I'll clean up his hand and make sure it's not broken, but that's all.

I stare at myself for a moment through the eyes of the window again. "You're right stupid, aren't you?" I glare at my reflection.

*I won't get sucked in. I won't.*

"Right," I mutter to myself, lacking any and all conviction as I throw on my jacket and head for the door.

Fifteen minutes later—instead of ten—I knock on his door. I spent those extra five minutes sitting in my car, deliberating the sagacity of my decision-making when it comes to Luke. But I've thought this out and through, and came up with a game plan.

I am icy. I am Ivy ice. Cold and impenetrable.

God, I feel so bloody foolish.

The door opens, and an exhausted Ryan fills the threshold. He offers me a tight grin as he pushes his dark glasses up the bridge of his nose.

"Thank you, and I'm sorry. He's not drunk or anything, but he's ornery as hell."

"It's fine," I shrug, feigning indifference, relieved that he's not drunk. Nothing about this is fine. Nothing about being here is fine. I should go. I need to go. Dammit!

"Is that him?" I hear Luke call out from inside his flat, and I furrow my eyebrows at Ryan.

"I, uh . . ." He shrugs sheepishly. "I may have told him that you were a friend of Katie's."

I sigh, my shoulders deflating, seriously contemplating turning on my heels and hightailing it out of here. The look in Ryan's eyes is what's keeping my feet grounded firmly in place. He's silently begging me, and for whatever reason, I like Ryan enough to want to help him.

"Let's just get this over with."

Brushing past Ryan, he graciously steps back to allow me entrance. I spot Luke, sitting on one of the bar stools in his kitchen with his hand wrapped in a cloth and a giant bag of frozen peas over it.

Remember seconds ago when I said I was ice? That was laughable, because ice melts—and that's exactly what I just did all over the goddamn floor. Seeing him wounded and broken is a little more than I can bear. *He did this to himself.* Sucking in a deep, resolved breath, I continue on through the dark expanse.

"So, Ryan here thinks it's broken, but I—" he stops abruptly as he glances up, noting that I'm not this other bloke he was expecting. "You called her?" he snaps at Ryan, looking away from me with something close to regret in his eyes.

"I did. We needed a doctor to look at your hand, and since you're too fucking stubborn to go to the hospital, your ex is what you get."

"Asshole," Luke points at Ryan. "I would never have done something like that to you after the Duchess left."

Ryan laughs out. "Bullshit, man. You were on me for weeks to call Katie, or stalk her down and go find her. You would have absolutely done this, so shut up, take the help, and be done with it."

Luke grumbles something unintelligible under his breath, and I take that as my cue to proceed. I pull in a fortifying breath and walk further into the apartment, refusing to look around, and move over to where he's sitting. My bag drops onto the counter next to his injured hand with a heavy thud as I sit down, not touching him.

"What did you do?" I ask calmly, directly, not wanting to come off like I'm scolding an insolent child, though frankly, I'm dying to.

"I'm sure Ryan already filled you in." Why does he sound petulant with me?

"And you're not drunk?"

"No, Mom," he says with a condescending note as he stares down at his hand. "I'm not drunk. Promise. Not even a drop of alcohol since last night at the bar."

I sigh. His ungrateful tone is irksome. I move to stand, not at all in the mood for this. I could be at home sleeping instead of helping this wanker. "Do you want me to leave?"

He pauses for a moment, noting my new position standing next to him, before slowly shaking his head, and then nodding, and finally shrugging like he doesn't care either way.

"Okay then, that's rather unhelpful. I should go."

"No," he and Ryan say simultaneously.

Sighing out again, I sit back down, just wanting this to be done already. "Remove all of that so I can take a look," I clip out.

Reaching into my bag, I pull out gloves, sterile water, and gauze. I don't bother getting anything else out until I see the damage.

As he does this, trying to contain his wince, Ryan saunters over to us. "Well, kids, I'd love to stay and watch this little moment play out, but I'm tired and have to work tomorrow. I'm leaving."

"You can't leave," Luke and I say in unison.

"You see, actually I can, and I am. It's been fun." Ryan gives us a wave and saunters off without another word.

This is not what I was expecting.

"You don't have to stay either. I'm sure my hand is fine. Believe it or not, I am capable of taking care of it myself."

I ignore him, walking around the island and pouring two mugs of coffee from the pot that was apparently just brewed. I don't like coffee, and I never drink it, but right now I need the distraction from being in Luke's apartment in the middle of the night after everything he said to me earlier.

I turn around and Luke's forehead is resting against the cold stone of the counter, his hand resting uncovered. Though the only lights on in his flat are coming from the sitting area directly behind him, I can see that his hand is swollen and bleeding.

I slide the mug over toward his good side, but he doesn't even stir, and I wonder if he's fallen asleep when he asks, "Is it poisoned?"

"Poisoned?" I reply, not grasping his meaning.

He raises his head, giving me a smarmy grin, looking to the steaming black mug and then up to me. "Yeah, you know, with arsenic or Clorox, or something else equally as toxic."

"Oh," I puff out a laugh. "No, but maybe it would be an improvement if it was."

"Ha," he grumbles, but I see humor dancing in his eyes. "Thanks for the coffee," he pauses, "and for coming tonight. I'm sure Ryan woke you up. I feel really stupid about all of this." Luke's eyes abandon mine in favor of the mug, blowing off the rising steam before taking a sip and returning his head to the counter. "You can leave. I'd rather not suffer this embarrassment in front of you."

I hesitate, debating if I should say something or not.

"What, Ivy?"

His tone is only mildly sullen, so I decide to proceed. "Your hand is not only horribly swollen, but it's oozing all over your counter."

"And your point is?"

"Just checking that you were aware of it."

"I am aware of it." He doesn't lift his head or even move to cover up or dab at his hand that's bleeding onto the stone. I can't stand it.

I can't.

Maybe it's the doctor in me—it goes against our nature to leave a wounded patient—or maybe it's the fact that despite my better judgment, I still care about the arsehole. But whatever it is, I know I won't leave him like this.

I round the counter, heading for my supplies that are still sitting out and begin to open what I need, looking down at his hand.

"Please leave, Ivy."

"No," I snap, beyond done with his rubbish.

Luke raises his head, his weary eyes pinned on my movements, but not my face.

It's like he can't look at me. For some reason, that hurts. I hate that he punched a wall out of frustration or anger or whatever it was he was feeling. I hate that Ryan said I was the cause. I hate that I care either way.

"Lay your hand flat here," I command softly.

He does as he's told with no argument for once, grimacing only slightly as I clean the open abrasions, pressing as gently as possible on the tender flesh.

"Why are you doing this?" he asks gruffly.

"Because you're going to get an infection if I don't, and then you'll lose your hand, and then you won't be able to use your computer, and then you'll get sacked and will be out of work, and I'll blame myself, and guilt is not an emotion I particularly enjoy."

He chuckles softly. His brown eyes, impossibly dark in the limited lighting, finally make the journey up to my face. I'm concentrating hard on his hand because now I'm the coward who can't make eye contact. The air between our close proximity is tense and maybe a little charged. Chock-full of broken promises and a litany of unsaid words. It's tangible and crushing, pressing down on my chest and hindering my ability to take in a deep breath.

"So, you tending to my wounds is really about you?" he whispers.

"Yes," I whisper back.

"So none of this is for my benefit?"

"No." I bite my lip to hide my smile as I apply the ointment to the now-clean abrasions, which surprisingly enough don't require sutures, only a few butterfly bandages, before I cover them with gauze.

He leans in closer to me, feigning like he's watching my handiwork, but his face is mere inches from mine. So close that his breath brushes across me, causing me to inadvertently close my eyes.

"I always knew you were a selfish woman."

"Yes."

I swallow back the nervous ball forming in my throat. The fingers on his good hand brush the hair out of my eyes with painfully slow movements, before they skim around the shell of my ear to the sensitive flesh of my neck. My heart is picking up its pace, my body hyperaware of his closeness and touch.

"There," I whisper, unsure of the strength of my voice. "All finished. Can you wiggle your fingers?" He does easily, which is good, so I lightly press on the metacarpals and phalanges. "There is some point tenderness, but no obvious deformity. You may have a small boxer's fracture, but I can't tell without an x-ray."

God, does my voice have to sound like that whenever he's near?

"Thank you."

His breath brushes my cheek again, and I realize just how close he actually is. He's right there, and as I take in a reluctant breath, I'm bombarded with his scent. Mint toothpaste, fabric softener, and his cologne—which I swear I could bathe in happily.

I draw my head back, hoping to create some distance between us.

He's stifling me.

He's everywhere.

Surrounding me, invading me, and I suddenly can't remember why I hate him so much.

Without warning, he grabs my cheek with his now bandaged hand, averting my escape and luring me back to him in a surprisingly affectionate motion.

I gasp at the zing of electricity his hand produces on my skin, and his mouth instantly covers mine. Luke groans out his pleasure and frustration, like he's been deprived of my lips and this kiss for the last year and has finally hit his limit. He groans like nothing has ever been so right or felt so good.

His lips move against mine, slowly at first, tasting and exploring, rediscovering me as if I'm the most exotic, delicious thing he's ever had. He licks his lips against mine before delving back in, our tongues dancing, more demanding and urgent than the first.

Dragging me closer, I melt into him.

It's impossible not to. I've missed his kisses just as much as he's missed mine.

He threads his good hand through my hair to angle and position my head as he wants. Coveting me in his embrace, coaxing my mouth and body into full submission of his unrelenting kiss. Luke moans into me, and I swear my closed eyes roll into the back of my head as my toes curl.

"So sweet," he whispers against my lips, before taking another taste and pulling away, leaving cool air in his wake and a feeling of loss on my humming lips.

He's never kissed me like that. Never made me feel so loved.

In the year we were apart, his kisses might have been one of the things I missed most about him. They were like phantom limb pain. I knew they were gone. That they weren't coming back, yet I still felt the agony their absence produced on a nearly daily basis. My downtime was severely limited, but in the darkness of night, or the quiet beat in between traumas and patients, I thought of Luke and the kisses that always managed to liquefy my insides.

I have no idea what this kiss means, if it even means anything— whether it's a thank you for his hand, or another attempt at reuniting us.

"I shouldn't have done that," he says with regret, his eyes closed tightly.

"Right," I snap out, my kiss-induced fog instantly gone. "Yeah. Clearly a mistake."

I turn my head to hide just how truly angry I am at myself. Just how hurt I am. What am I thinking?

I pack up my stuff and run out of his apartment as fast as my feet will take me.

And he does nothing to stop me.

# Chapter Twenty-Seven

*Ivy*

MY PHONE RINGS the moment I reach the bottom step, but I don't answer it. By the fourth call, I'm done with this as I furiously press the button on my steering wheel, answering the call.

"That's not what I meant," he says through the speakers of my car.

"I'm not following."

"Sure you are, but you can pretend all you want."

"What's your point, Luke? Despite what you say, you didn't even acknowledge I was alive until I came back." I wipe at a tear that has decided to fall, because this all still feels like a fresh wound. "I'm the girl you cast aside when things get too serious and pull toward you when the moment strikes your fancy. I'm done with these games! So I'll ask you again, what the bloody hell is your point?"

"You didn't say 'bloody hell' the first time you asked me."

I growl at him, regretting leaving in such a rush so I could have smacked that beautiful face of his. I hear him take a sip of his coffee, which just irritates me further and suddenly I wish I had poisoned it.

"You're not invisible," he continues. "Not nearly as much as you think you are. I never wanted to push you away, and I didn't do it because things were getting serious. I'm a mess. I've already told you that, but I'm sure you're more aware of it now, but you don't know the full reason."

"Luke," I sigh out, shaking my head in exasperation. I'm done with his cryptic non-answers. "You're the one who keeps going on about this. I'm fine. I'm done. I'm not looking for anything from you. That's all. So get over yourself already."

"I'm trying, Ivy. I'm trying to get over everything, but I can't seem to do it."

I curse under my breath. "How's this, then? I don't want this." I wave my finger back and forth like he's standing in front of me. "I'm tired of trying to manage your mood swings and decipher your enigmatic unhelpful words. I'm absolutely done with the flirting and the kissing and the everything in between. I'm tired of you pulling me in time and time again, only to crush me after. I'm not exactly sure how many times I have to remind you of this, but I'm hoping this is the last."

He laughs out. "That's not what I'm doing with you, baby."

I sigh dramatically, wondering why I'm still talking to him.

"I like kissing you."

I hiss out, but that only seems to amuse him more.

"It's that damn smell of yours, and the fact that you taste the same. Like cookies at Christmas. Sinful and tempting, and so comforting."

"Are you heavily medicated or something?"

"No, but I probably should be."

"I'm never coming back."

Another chuckle. This one gives me chills, and I hate myself for reacting to his voice. For reacting to him. For getting out of bed in the middle of the night for him and expecting a different outcome.

"Of course, you will. I'm far too entertaining, and I know for a fact that you like me."

"I don't. And your confidence is not attractive, it's annoying."

"Wanna have dinner with me?"

"Absolutely not." I shift in my seat, looking out the window before turning my eyes back to the road in front of me. I feel a damn smile creeping up the corners of my lips.

"I want to kiss you again, Ivy. I want to do everything with you, and I'm not only talking about making love to you. I told you before I still love you and want you. I can't seem to stay away. I meant everything I said to you today about things being different. I can't let you go. I lied about that part." He pauses before his tone turns utterly broken. "Don't leave, baby, I'm so lost without you."

"I'm sure you'll manage."

"Maybe," he sighs out, and I hear him sipping from his coffee again "You're not invisible," he says again. "You're far too beautiful to go unnoticed." We fall into silence after that.

"You're messing with my head," I whisper after a quiet beat. "I've never met someone who says one thing and does another so quickly. I haven't asked you for anything other than to let me go. *You're* the one who continues to blur lines. You may think you are god's gift and beyond special, and that every woman you meet should fall at your feet and worship accordingly. I didn't ask for the flirting or the comments, and definitely not for the kiss or words of love. Grow up."

He chuckles lightly at me, finding amusement in something I find none in.

I'm being serious with him, and his laughter comes off as patronizing.

Doesn't he realize how much he's hurting me? How his words cut so deep that my wounds may never close?

"I know I'm an asshole. I would lie and say that's a new habit, but it's not. I should stay away from you because I'm not a good man, and you make me think about things I'd rather not think about. Remember things I wish I could forget. I've breathed in fire and been burned by the flames, but you . . . ." Luke trails off. "I'm in awe of you, Ivy, and that is as addictive as it is seductive. I walk away only to find I glow so much brighter in your light."

How on earth am I to respond to that? There are no words when someone stuns you that deeply.

I'm so afraid of what he means when he says things like he wishes he could forget and that he's a bad man, but I'm far too terrified to ask.

And then there are the other things he said. About me. Things I don't quite fathom and certainly shouldn't care about whether or not they're true. But fuck all, I do care.

I suddenly can't stop the smile that creeps up my face while I simultaneously laugh and cry.

This man . . . I have no idea what to do with him.

"Have you ever noticed that almost all of our conversations are either sexual or really intense?"

He laughs out loud and long. "This conversation was a bloody brilliant idea."

He's trying to mock my accent.

It's terrible. Only Brits say brilliant with regularity.

"Do you know how stupid you Yanks sound when you try and copy our accents?" I shake my head, but dammit all I'm still smiling. "Seriously, it's awful."

"Can you do an American accent then?" he challenges, and all of our solemnity from just moments ago seems to have lifted, leaving us with our first normal conversation since before I left.

"I've never tried one," I admit. I still don't know what to make of this strange and very complicated man, but he's hard to resist. He just is, and I find I relent to him far too easily.

I pull into my parking spot, but don't shut off the car or try and go upstairs yet. I'm desperate for this moment to last, though I know it can't. Not really. Our issues are more than likely insurmountable, but I'm still clinging on, knowing I need to let go.

His torture is the sweetest of punishments.

"Okay. Try saying this then." He clears his throat, and I can only imagine where this is headed. "Luke is the most amazing man ever."

"No."

"That was not the sentence and you clearly still have your accent. Try again."

I snicker, rolling my eyes, but he's waiting on me, so I take a deep breath and try to think about how the words sounded the way he just said them.

"Luke is the most amazing man ever."

He cracks up instantly, probably because my voice was not my own. It sounded far deeper and forced, and the accent was way off the mark.

"Don't quit your day job, darlin'. That was worse than mine."

"I wasn't planning on it, *darlin'*."

"So are we friends then?" he asks.

"No. Absolutely not. *Friends* is what got us into trouble in the first place."

"Aww, come on, Ivy. It did not. Please don't give up on me. Just have dinner with me. Talk to me."

I hate it when he begs. I feel my insides softening to him and I know, *I know*, if I give in to him now, I'll regret it later. He'll have another excuse or issue or well-intentioned reason for pushing me away. He'll say it's for my own good. That he's being benevolent and compassionate, saving me from the big bad wolf, but I can't do it again.

I. Can't. Do. It. Again.

"I feel like we're going around in circles here."

"Me too." He sighs heavily into the phone. "Do you still love me?"

I don't respond. My teeth are sinking into my bottom lip as I shake my head and then nod.

"You don't have to answer that, baby," he says when he realizes I'm not going to.

"I should go. I need sleep, and it's really late."

"Sure, yeah. Thanks again for coming tonight and fixing my hand. I . . . um, can I call you tomorrow?"

I think on this for a moment.

"I don't think that's a good idea."

"It's actually a great fucking idea; you just don't realize it yet. You like me, remember?"

"I do like you, Luke. That's part of the problem."

"Nah, that's not a problem."

"Please don't call me. I need time and—"

"Fine," he interrupts. "I'll give you time, but I'm not giving up, and I'm not leaving you alone. You're stuck with me, Ivy Green. You're mine, and I'm yours. We're it for each other. I know I've fucked it all up and done things so absolutely wrong, I'll show you that, this time, it's all different."

# Chapter Twenty-Eight

*Ivy*

"IT WAS ONLY one month a year ago. It shouldn't still affect me like this," I say to Craig and Darcy, who are gracious enough to listen to my misery, again. When Craig and I first moved out to Boston, he was his usual relentless self. But he was also, as it turns out, a good friend, and he listened to me cry my bloody eyes out.

Then about two months in, he met Darcy.

She's a physical therapist at Boston Children's Hospital, and the two of them became an instant couple. Very Romeo and Juliet without the wonky families and tragic double-suicide thing.

"I knew I wanted to marry Craig the minute I met him," Darcy says rather unhelpfully.

Craig kisses the crown of her black hair sweetly before turning his attention back to me. "If you want me to kick his ass, I will."

"I know." I can't help but grin at that. "Thanks, mate, but your hands are quite valuable. I'd never forgive myself if I were the demise of your brilliant career."

"You wanna go egg his place or something?" Darcy asks, her

Boston accent thick with the idea of mayhem. "Go all Carrie Underwood on his car?"

"Vandalism isn't really my thing," I say. "I could kill him and make it look like an accident? It's not like I don't know how."

"True, but if they catch you, you'll go to prison, and you're not the kind of woman who could make it on the inside," Craig adds.

"Valid point."

I flop down onto my back, staring up at the ceiling of my flat. I'm in a high-rise now. Don't ask me why I went with this, because I honestly don't know. This place is terribly boring and generic, and just not me.

"I'll ignore him, and he'll go away."

"Maybe," Craig muses. "But I doubt it, and so do you. It might just be better if you talk to him, hear what he has to say, and then tell him to go screw himself."

"What if I listen to him and he ends up making sense?"

The two of them fall silent and I roll my head over to look at their expressions. They're as perplexed as I am, which is not really helping.

"Do you still love him?" Darcy asks.

I swallow hard, but end up giving one small nod.

"And you don't believe him when he says that things have changed and that he'll never leave you again?" Craig chimes in.

"I don't know," I say quietly, thoughtfully. "But I do know that if I trust him again and for whatever reason he does leave or ends it with me, I'll hate myself for taking him back. That, and I may never trust someone again. I feel like all I do is make poor decision after poor decision. First with Jason the not-so-friendly-stalker in med school, and then Luke. I mean, I get that they're only two men, but still. The other blokes just didn't last all that long, and I never felt much for them so I can't really use them as a comparison."

"I say hear him out," Darcy suggests, after a very long silent moment. "And then go with your gut."

"You two need to leave for the airport, and I have a date to get ready for," I say, slowly sitting up and putting an official end to the conversation.

"A date?"

"Yeah, it's that bloke that Sophia knows. The one doing the documentary here in Seattle on the tech industry."

"Oh," they say in unison. "I forgot about him," Darcy adds.

"That's because Soph set it up over a week ago."

"Well, our cab is probably waiting for us. We should get going," Craig says. I stand, throwing my arms around both of them. "You'll be fine, Ivy."

"Thanks, mate. I'm going to miss the hell out of both of you. Ring me when you land, yeah?"

"Of course. We'll see you in a few months when you fly out to see us." Darcy smiles, wrapping her arms tightly around me. "Let me know how it all goes."

My friends leave me a few minutes later and I already miss them. I've only been back in Seattle a few weeks or so, but I was used to them. I was the perpetual third wheel, but we hung out a lot. And though I adore Kate and Claire, they're Luke's friends, not mine per se.

So that leads me back to my date for tonight with some guy who seemed a bit into himself when we chatted on the phone the other night. But hey, maybe I'm wrong. Besides, a date is a nice distraction.

By the time he rings the bell an hour later, I'm wearing a simple black dress with a red belt cinched at the waist and red heels. I even took the time to blow-dry my lifeless hair in an attempt to give it some volume. Didn't help much.

I open the door for him, and my first thought is that he's way too good-looking for me. I'm not even saying that in an insecure way either. His looks are almost otherworldly with California golden skin, very strong prominent features, perfectly styled dark blond curls, and bright blue eyes.

He's built, large and muscular, which I think is to make up for the one flaw that I can detect—his stature. He's not short by any means, but he's definitely not tall, and in my heels, we're about the same height.

"Ivy?"

I nod and he goes in for a hug instead of a handshake. He smells like he swam in cologne and it's as jarring as it is unexpected, and not in a good way.

"Roberto, it's nice to meet you." I pull back to grab my purse as quickly as I can, and make it back to the door before he thinks I'm inviting him in. What the hell sort of name is Roberto when he looks like the epitome of a Beach Boy?

I'd bet my hands that his real name is Robert, and I'm quite fond of my hands.

"It was great of Sophia to set this up," he says as we slip into his Mercedes and speed off. "And I'll be able to report back to her that she got it right in the looks department. You're definitely hot and your body is amazing in that dress."

"Um . . . thanks?" It comes out sounding like a question, because really? Did he just say that to me?

"I hope you like sushi. It's all I eat, though I get it with brown rice," he blathers on. "Too many empty carbs in white rice, and I certainly didn't get this body by indulging in empty carbs."

"Sure. Makes sense."

*Kill me now.*

He pulls up to some posh Japanese restaurant and I guess now isn't the time to tell him that I don't eat raw fish. I'm hoping this place has other things on their menu or it's going to be a very long night.

The valet opens my door and by the time I step out and thank him, Roberto is already at the door of the restaurant and walking inside, not even bothering to wait for me. I'm tempted to run in the other direction and call Sophia to yell at her, but at the last minute he turns around and waves me on like I'm holding him up.

By the time we reach our final table, Roberto has declined two others, because he didn't feel the lighting or atmosphere was befitting someone like him. I'm not entirely sure what that means, but it doesn't sound promising.

The waitress goes to hand me a menu and before I can even accept it, Roberto is ordering up a large sake. Something I don't like either, but since I have no intention of drinking around this fool, I let it slide.

"Oh, you won't need a menu," he insists, practically slapping the thing from my hand. "I've eaten here three times in the last week and I know what's good. I'll just order for both of us."

"Actually, Robert, I'd like to order for myself. I don't eat raw fish."

"It's *Roberto,*" he emphasizes, "and what do you mean you don't eat raw fish? Like ever?"

"Ever, but I see other items on here that I'll eat so you just order whatever you want."

He seems completely baffled by this, maybe even slightly appalled, like one plus one suddenly equals three and the world is spinning off its axis.

"Why would Sophia set me up on a date with someone who doesn't eat sushi?"

I hold in my snicker as best I can, but it's hard, and I find I'm grinning. "What *was* Sophia thinking?"

"Well, maybe you'll try something of mine? I can't imagine someone not eating sushi. It's unnatural."

Now I do snicker, but I cover it up as a cough.

"I can see how you'd feel that way, but I really don't like it so I doubt I'll try it. But you go ahead, don't hold back on my account."

"Like I would," he mumbles under his breath, and all I can think about is that this must be a gag. Sophia would never set me up with this man on a real actual date. I'm half-expecting her to jump out from a dark corner, laughing and pointing at me for falling for it.

While Roberto incessantly jabbers on about something I don't care enough about to listen to, I begin to zone out, only to feel like I'm being watched. That prickly paranoia is raising the hairs on the nape of my neck. I casually try to look around without seeming obvious about it.

I don't spot anyone on my left or right who is even remotely glancing in my direction. I turn in my chair, feigning like I'm trying to get something out of my purse so I can peer behind me. There's a woman seated directly behind me with short brown hair, but her back is to me so it's clearly not her.

But just as I'm about to face Roberto again, she shifts in her chair, turning around suddenly to look in my direction. Our eyes lock in a startled moment. I've never seen this woman in my life, yet she's oddly familiar, and when she whispers my name, I freeze. Her curious expression morphs into a bright knowing smile. She adjusts her position as if she's going to introduce herself, when I spy Luke sitting across from her.

My mouth pops open, and I feel bile rise up my throat. He's on a date with another woman not even twenty-four hours after professing his love for me?

That, and he's clearly told this woman who I am, or at the very least my name.

"Ivy, did you hear me?" Roberto asks, tearing my attention away from the staring game I have going with this woman and I spin around to face *my* date.

"No," I say, not bothering to lie.

I need to get out of here. Now. I can't sit and pretend to enjoy a meal with a man I already cannot stand when Luke and his date are directly behind me.

"I need to leave. I'm not feeling well." I don't even apologize to him as I hastily grab for my purse that is slung over the back of my seat.

"Are you okay? Should I take you home? I mean, I ordered that sake and I'd hate to waste it."

I laugh out humorlessly. "No, you stay and enjoy your meal." I stand up carelessly, nearly tipping my chair back onto Luke's date. I realize how this must look to the two of them, but right now, I can't find it in me to care.

*What a bastard.*

And to think I was considering hearing him out.

*God, I'm so stupid.*

I rush past Roberto, heading for the front of the restaurant, so thankful that both Luke and his date were further back than us and I don't have to pass them as I flee.

Bursting through the glass door and nearly knocking over a woman as I do, I realize I need to get a grip. I'm being so overly dramatic, and that's just not me. So what if he's on a date? So what if he's a lying piece of shit wanker arsehole?

So what?

He's allowed to date anyone he's keen on, and so am I. That's all there is to it.

It was an exceptionally warm day today, but with the sun having gone down, any residual heat seems to have gone with it. Wrapping my arms around my waist, I scan the street, desperately searching for a taxi, but come up empty.

*Of course, never when you need one.*

I pull out my phone to order an Uber when I hear my name being called. Luke followed me out. Why would he do that?

I shake my head, running down the street toward the busier intersection, my heels clicking against the cement sidewalk as I go.

"Dammit, Ivy, wait!" he yells after me. "It's not what you think."

I throw my hand up in the air. "I don't care, Luke, it doesn't matter," I call out, increasing my speed. Feeling so absolutely foolish, I just want to get home and soak in the tub with a bottle of wine and pretend tonight never happened.

By the time I reach the intersection, Luke is hot on my heels, but in this moment, I realize God is indeed a woman, because someone is hopping out of a taxi two feet from me.

"Ivy! Fucking wait!" Luke tries again, reaching for my arm, but I manage to yank it away from his grasp, and he just stands there, staring at me in disbelief with grief-filled eyes. "It's not what you think," he repeats, but I hold up my hand again, to stop him from continuing.

"It doesn't matter."

He shakes his head furiously, fisting his hands into his hair like he doesn't know what else to do with them.

He's too late.

I slide onto the nasty plastic back seat and slam the door shut with authority, telling the driver to go. As we drive away, I can't help but crouch down so I can turn and watch Luke without being overly obvious about it.

He's running his hands through his hair still, and it looks like he's cursing up a storm. He pulls his phone out of his pocket and that's when the cab takes a turn and I lose sight of him.

My phone rings in my hand and I realize I'm still holding it.

Of course, it's him. Should I pick up? Hit ignore?

*Dammit!*

I hit ignore because I have nothing to say to him.

I'm so worked up right now. So perfectly enraged that my vision is practically hazy with it.

Sure, I'm livid with him, but that's not what really has me squirming uncontrollably in my seat. I'm so exasperated with *myself* it's not even funny.

When did I become this woman?

When did I allow a man to unhinge me like this? Allow myself to become unglued at the sight of my ex-boyfriend on a date?

Never again, Luke Walker. Never again.

# Chapter Twenty-Nine

*Ivy*

MY PHONE RANG a total of six more times and I ignored every single one of them. I realized last night that I don't have a lot to say to him that hasn't already been said. Our situation is what it is and that's over. But in the back of my mind, in the darkest recesses of that vulnerable place we all like to pretend doesn't exist, I was hoping he'd come to me.

He didn't, of course, and I continuously flipped back and forth between being relieved and disappointed.

So I slept, albeit restlessly, but now I'm awake, antsy, and unsettled.

I debate getting up and heading to the gym in my building, but in the end, decide it would make me feel better to run some of this off in the fresh air. Grabbing my water bottle, keys, phone, and headphones, I open my front door only to have something large and heavy tumble into my apartment.

It takes me a second longer than it should to realize that Luke is the mass that just rolled onto my floor. It seems he slept in the hall outside my apartment last night, because he's still wearing the same clothes I saw him in on his date.

"Jesus Christ, Luke, get up." I nudge him with my foot, and he stiffly pulls himself off the hardwoods, stretching out like a cat. "Did you sleep out there all night?"

He gives me a sheepish grin. "Yup. All damn night. And let me tell you, your door is really uncomfortable. The hall floor isn't much better either."

"And it never occurred to you to knock on the door, say what you needed to say, and go home?"

"No, because I knew you would just slam the door in my face and that wouldn't do. I figured a sneak attack was the best approach."

His eyes rake over me, a wolfish smile slowly creeping up his face as he notes my sports bra and yoga pants.

"Holy hell, you look hot. Are you going for a run?"

"Please go home; I'm late." I head out my door, but he snakes his arm around my waist, pulling me into him, my back to his front. His nose sweeps up my exposed neck as he inhales deeply, making me shiver, and I know he feels my response.

"Cinnamon and vanilla," he hums. "Did you know that's my absolute favorite scent? Probably because it's yours, but it really is something else."

Rolling my neck to brush him off, I yank on his firm grip, trying to get him to release me.

"It's not what you think," Luke whispers into the shell of my ear. "The woman last night, she wasn't a date. But I'd be lying if I said I didn't love the fact that you were jealous."

Jutting my elbow back, I connect squarely with his flank and he lets out a very satisfying oomph.

"I wasn't jealous, you tosser. What you do and who you do it with is your business, not mine."

He chuckles that husky chuckle of his, and I erupt in chills.

Damn him.

"You're a terrible liar, darlin'. Always have been, but I like that about you."

"Leave, Luke, I mean it."

He moves toward my front door, but at the last second, grabs me, pinning me against the wall the same way he did the other day at my parents' house.

"It wasn't a date, Ivy. That woman was my sister, Elizabeth."

Oh. No wonder she looked slightly familiar. I realize now that they have the same eyes.

Oddly, knowing he wasn't on a date doesn't make me feel any better.

Luke's forearms are pressed against the wall on either side of my head, caging me in once again. His face is so close to mine, his eyes dark glowing with desire and desperation.

Tilting my chin up to look him squarely in the eye, I say ever so calmly, "Did you know that I never knew you had a sister?" My eyes narrow. "Are you aware that I know absolutely nothing about you? Nothing."

He sighs like this deflates him completely. "I know. I'd like to change that. I have so much to tell you, baby, and I wish you'd give me that chance. I *want* to tell you. I want to tell you things I've never told anyone. I thought a lot about this all week—all year—and though it won't be easy, I think maybe, *possibly*, I'd like to try. I would have told you sooner, but I was afraid you'd leave me if I did."

I shake my head. "I don't understand."

"Okay, I'm lying. I didn't want to tell you, and I still don't, but I'm willing to if that's what you need. I'm willing to put almost everything out there for you."

"*Almost* everything?"

"This isn't the place for this, and in all honesty, I hadn't planned to have this conversation with you yet. I just wanted to see you. That was all. But I realize the only way you'll ever consider trying again with me is if I tell you. If you decide to leave me for good after that, then I'll understand, and I'll let you go. For real. I want you happy, Ivy, and if you feel that you can't have that with me, then I guess I have to come to terms with that." He's practically rambling now, and I'm having trouble keeping up. "But I can't tell you everything. There are things I may never be able to tell you. That's why I let you leave. I was trying to protect you. I was trying to do the right thing for once. But I'm not noble and I'm not good for you. I'm a danger to be near, and you're so pure and sweet and innocent and I'm . . . not."

"You're not making any sense right now."

"I know." He grins, though this doesn't feel like the moment for levity. "Let me cook you dinner tonight, and we can talk."

"I need to think about it. And I need you to leave because now I'm really running late and I'll hardly have enough time to exercise before my shift."

"I'll walk you down," he says, removing his arms from my wall and taking my hand.

I know I should pull away.

I know I should push him out the door and lock it and never look back.

That's what the smart, responsible Ivy is telling me to do anyway, because his little speech back there? Yeah, that's setting off all sorts of warning bells. He had mentioned some of that to me before when we took that nightmare of a ride on the Big Wheel.

He's afraid I'll leave him if I know the truth.

He's a danger to be near.

He's not good.

All of those should have me running from him, yet I'm oddly intrigued.

It's like solving a mystery or finishing a ridiculously complex puzzle. Certain things are impossible to walk away from until you know how they finish, and Luke Walker may just be one of those things for me.

We step into the empty elevator and I press the button for the second floor where the gym is located, because now I don't have enough time to go out for a run. The second the doors close, I feel that indescribable electric current. That palpable tension that sends your heart into overdrive and the best sort of tingles to hum all over your body.

He feels it too. I know he does, because his breathing has become erratic and his fingers twitch against my hand with restraint. He wants to grab me. He wants to push me into this wall and have at me. He wants to—

"Screw holding back," he mutters before he does every one of those things all at once.

Luke grasps my shoulders, pushing me into the unforgiving elevator wall before he presses his long muscular body against mine. His hands cup my cheeks, drawing my face to his before he slams his lips to mine.

I gasp in a flash of surprise, but that sensation is instantly replaced with passion and desire, and fucking longing. He's kissing me like he's reclaiming me. Like he's branding me to him, removing every single one of my arguments with each pass of his lips.

It's so unbelievably easy to push sensible, sane judgment aside when you want something. It's so unbelievably easy to rationalize why something that feels so right is not a mistake.

So that's what I do, because that's how he feels, like the best sort of mistake.

Moving on from someone or something that feels unfinished is impossible.

And that's what Luke is.

Unfinished.

How do I turn away from that?

"Ivy," he moans against my mouth as he delves deeper, gliding his tongue against mine. Holding me firmly in place, his body and hands shake with need. "Oh baby, I've missed you so goddamn much," he groans against my lips before his mouth consumes mine again, his hard body pressing into me in a way that should be illegal. In a way that's so unbelievably satisfying, I can hardly stay upright.

A moan slips out from the back of my throat, which he greedily swallows down before the bell on the elevator dings, announcing our arrival on the second floor.

I push him back, that bell the slap of realization I needed.

Luke licks his lips as if he's savoring my flavor before taking my hand and pulling me off the elevator like a small child in need of assistance. Maybe I am, because my legs feel like jelly and walking is a chore.

Wordlessly, he leads me down the hall, past the indoor pool and over to the gym before he presses me up against the wall adjacent to the glass door. He's smiling at me like the cat who ate the canary, and though I don't want to, I mean really don't want to, I'm smiling back.

"I'll see you tonight. Eight-thirty?"

"No."

"No?" he chuckles, hovering over me.

"No," I repeat.

"Why not?" He's still smiling, but his expression is incredulous.

"Because eight-thirty is too late. I need to eat before that."

"Okay," he laughs, leaning into my neck and blowing his warm breath against my already heated skin. "What time does my girl want to eat then?"

"I'm not your girl, and I'd like to eat at seven-thirty."

"Seven-thirty it is not-my-girl. Anything in particular you'd like?"

"It's your house, Luke, you decide the food."

"But not sushi," he grins. "Who was the asshole last night?"

I'm shocked it's taken him this long to ask.

"My date," I say simply.

"Elizabeth told me he hit on her after we ran out, so I don't think he's the guy for you."

"Probably not," I muse, thinking back on Roberto. "Will Elizabeth be there tonight? Do I get to meet her?"

Luke shakes his head. "No, she only stopped here because Seattle was her layover. She's on business in Juno, Alaska of all places this week. You can meet her when she stops in on her way back."

I rest my head against the wall, staring up at the ceiling as I let out a sad sigh. Where did my vigor go? Where is my perfectly crafted and calculated resolve to hate this man forever?

"Is she your only sibling?"

"Yes, she is." The hard note to his words has me dropping my chin to read his expression.

"And your parents?" His eyes turn to granite, and I can only watch as he shuts down.

"Not here, Ivy. I can't——" He breathes out harshly. "Fuck, I have to work myself up to that and even then I don't know if . . ." He steps back, lowering his head to look at the tan carpet, his clenched fists perched on his hips. "I don't know if I can do that."

"Do what?" I take a step toward him.

"Tell you about my family. Tell you about *me*." He spins around and slams his fist into the opposite wall–his injured hand at that–but he just shakes it out like it was nothing. Thankfully, the wall is no worse for wear. "Dammit."

"Luke?" He doesn't move, but his shoulders are rising and falling like he just sprinted a marathon. "Look at me, please," I say evenly.

It takes him a moment, but he does.

He twists back around and looks me dead in the eyes. His jaw is locked tight, and his hands are balled into such tight fists that his knuckles are white, except for one that is oozing a little blood again.

"Go home and shower. You're a mess from sleeping outside in the hall all night and your hand could use a new bandage. Then you need to go to work. Then you need to cook me something really fantastic—like lasagna." I get a hint of his lopsided grin, dimple and all. "We'll chat, and you'll tell me some stuff, and I'll tell you some stuff, but there are no promises or guarantees here. This last year was rough, and I don't know if I can look past that."

He nods, but doesn't say anything else before he stalks off down the long corridor and into the elevator that never left.

And once I'm clear of his spell, once I can no longer smell him or feel him against me or see those brown eyes that seem to look into me instead of at me, I regret agreeing to dinner.

He says he wants to talk to me, to tell me things, but he doesn't.

He says he's changed, but he hasn't.

And maybe he does love me. Maybe he's serious when he says that, but I'm not sure it really matters.

The first time he walked out my door, I didn't exactly put too much thought into it, even though I was hurt. I mean, it was a one-night stand after all, and I was foolish for expecting more.

But the second time nearly destroyed me and I can't do that to myself again. I just can't.

I had a professor at university who once told me that love and fear are the only things that make the world work. Of course, being young and impetuous, I challenged that notion instantly, but he explained that oftentimes it's the love of something—like money, material possessions, or power—and the fear of losing them, that command people to act. That love and fear are really the only two things that can forever alter a person, whether for the better or worse.

That theory has always stuck with me, and every now and then, I find myself trying to refute it.

But right now, those are the only two emotions warring inside of me.

Love and fear.

Both equally, because I still love Luke. I really do. I might not fully understand it, but I'm so absolutely terrified of what that love will do to me to the point where I'm nearly paralyzed by it.

So do I try again?

Do I put myself out there and attempt to overcome my fear? Or do I allow it to keep me safely tucked away from its creator?

# Chapter Thirty

*Luke*

I GET a text at five to eight from Ivy saying she's here. She called earlier to tell me she was running late and that was fine with me. I'm anxious to see her, but I needed the extra time to think this through some more.

I've never done this before. I've never told my story. And it's still not something I want to do now. At all.

But the simple reality is that I love her, and if I want her to trust me, to give me another chance, there really can't be anything like this between us.

I'm nervous as hell. My heart is thrashing wildly in my chest and sweat is slicking the skin at the back of my neck.

*I can do this.*

I don't have a choice if I want a shot at a future with her. I want what Kate and Ryan have.

It's funny, I never thought I'd be one of those people. Always figured I'd be single and alone. Not in a depressing, my life sucks and I'm unworthy way, but I just never figured I'd find someone.

Never really believed in love, if I'm being honest.

Happily ever after always seemed like a sucker's bet.

I certainly never witnessed it growing up, and my first real taste of anything remotely embodying love came through Kate. The first time I saw Kate and Ryan together, it was no secret that they loved each other with all their hearts. I saw it when Kate left him and Ryan was a miserable bastard, but I wrongfully assumed it would pass and he'd move on.

I presumed that's what people did when something didn't work out the way they intended. They moved on. That logic makes me want to laugh, because clearly, I have never been so wrong.

But Kate . . . man, that woman set me straight, long before Ivy came into the picture.

She recounted her marriage to her deceased husband Eric to me. How she had been with him since they were just kids and the extent to which they loved each other—*really* loved each other. I scoured through her pictures and listened with rapt attention to her stories, and for the first time in my life, I saw what a real family was supposed to be like.

I saw what love was supposed to be like.

What a marriage actually was.

It's a partnership. It's knowing you're never alone and that you have someone to love you unconditionally. That was also a foreign concept to me, but by watching Kate and Ryan together and hearing Kate's story, I started to get it. Long for it.

And now they're blissfully expecting twins, their relationship stronger than I've ever seen it.

I knew eleven years ago when I met Ivy that she was something special. Something worth committing to and having, but I was twenty and engrossed in uncertainty and felony charges.

Now I'm thirty-one, and I want her forever.

I want my ring on her finger and my baby growing in her belly. I want her here with me every single day, and in my bed every single night. I want that shot at normal that she's so desperate for, and I don't even think it's boring.

Fuck, after more than a decade of too much excitement, boring sounds like a heavenly respite. Like a dream come true. If that's the life my girl wants, I'll do whatever I can to make that happen for her.

I doubt I'll ever be able to fully walk away from Ronaldo or the company, but it's not nearly what it used to be. Truth be told, I sort of enjoy it now, but maybe the middle ground I now exist in can be the perfect compromise.

I don't know, but fuck it all if I'm not going to try.

I buzz Ivy in, unlocking all the doors and watching her enter and head toward the stairs. She's nervous. I can tell because she's chewing on the corner of her lip.

Opening the door wider, I pull her into me, and for the first time in a year, she doesn't pull away.

"You smell like the hospital," I tease.

She playfully smacks my chest. "Not my fault. You told me to come over right after work. I can shower if you'd like."

"Nah, you must be hungry. I can deal with a little hospital stink."

"Good, because it smells amazing in here and I don't think I could wait much longer to eat."

She pushes me away, heading for the kitchen. I smile like a stupid bastard as I shut the door behind her, my nerves on hiatus for the moment. Having her here with me seems to do that. It's been a long time coming.

She pops a piece of cheese into her mouth from the tray I have set out on the counter and pours herself a glass of red wine. I love that she's making herself at home.

"Bloody hell, I could eat the whole house. I haven't had anything since breakfast."

"Then sit your adorable ass down, and I'll feed you."

Ivy moves over to the dining table that I have set and waiting, looking around the apartment as if she's expecting something to be different since she was last here. Nothing is, and once she realizes that, I see a small smile pull up at the corner of her lips.

"I made you that pesto chicken lasagna you like."

She beams at me for remembering, and I can't even begin to describe what that feels like.

Ivy eats everything I put on her plate times two. She's voracious, and I enjoy the hell out of watching her eat like that.

"That was so good." She takes a sip of her wine before setting the nearly empty glass down. Her eyes spot something across the kitchen on the counter by the stove. "Are those . . ." She sits up further, leaning forward against the table that serves as a restraint. "Are those Tim Tams?" She's smiling like a little girl as she gets up and flies across the kitchen. "Is this a bribe, Luke? Are you trying to butter me up here or what?"

"I am." That's really not a lie. I'm hoping to get her high on food so she's content and too full to run away.

"Bugger, this must be bad." She walks back with the entire package in her hand, shoving a cookie into her mouth and groaning out her pleasure as she chews. "Yum, these remind me of home."

"Come and sit with me by the fire." She stops chewing with a mouthful of cookies. It would be adorable if I wasn't so edgy. I've never told anyone the things I'm going to tell her, and just thinking about them makes me want to throw up.

Ivy swallows hard, setting her cookies down on the dining room table almost absentmindedly, her expression stoic and her features wooden. I turn on the fire through the app in my phone and it starts with a whoosh as the flames come to life.

Sitting down on the couch, Ivy follows, taking off her sneakers before sinking down. She lays her head back against cushions, wrapping the throw blanket over her legs and chest. It's like she's settling in for a story, which I guess she is, but her getting comfortable tells me she has no interest in leaving me once she hears it.

At least that's what I'm hoping that means.

My heart is hammering away, and I know hers is too because she takes my hand, resting it on top of her chest so I can feel it thrum beneath my palm. It's such a small gesture, but it means everything to me. She's in this with me and that gives me the necessary courage to start my story.

Taking the deepest of breaths, dread fills my chest and clouds my vision with tormented memories I wish I could forget.

Our eyes lock.

"I grew up in Oklahoma in a small farming town where people had their land, Jesus, and not a whole lot else. My family was worse off than most because my father had a penchant for gambling and a knack for losing,"

I sigh, already needing a fucking break. Jesus Christ this is so damn hard.

"Go on," she whispers.

I nod, my eyes staring sightlessly at the glowing fire. "It's not like you can go on food stamps because your father is a degenerate gambler, and my mother refused to seek help because she was too proud to allow the neighbors to know what they already suspected, so we went hungry a lot." That thought makes me shake my head. I still don't know how my mother did that to us. "My earliest memory were when I was three and my father beat my mother to the point where she was unconscious on our kitchen floor. And the first time I remember him hitting me I was no older than four, though I know that wasn't the first beating I sustained. My mother used to try and intercede a bit, but that stopped after my father beat her into the hospital for doing it."

Ivy gasps and clasps tightly to my hand that is still resting over her heart. It draws my eyes away from the fire and back to hers. There is no pity in them. God, I love this woman.

I shrug a shoulder. "And that's sort of how it went for a long time, and because I never knew another way, it was just our life."

"Did anyone know?" Ivy asks softly.

I suck in more air, suddenly feeling like the walls are closing in on me as I shake my head no.

"That must have been difficult."

I smile at her, but it might just be the saddest smile I've ever given. "As I got older, I realized that this wasn't the way it was supposed to be. I realized my father was evil, not just sick or had a problem, but truly *evil*. That happened when I was fourteen and my sister Elizabeth was eleven."

I shift on the couch, uncomfortable. The back of my neck is sweating and it feels like the t-shirt I'm wearing is strangling me. My fingers pull the collar away from my neck, but it's not helping. I can't fucking do this.

"You can do this," she encourages and I almost want to laugh at just how well she knows me. She doesn't think she does, but Ivy Green gets me whether she wants to or not.

I sigh. "Elizabeth was carrying my father's dinner plate to the table one night when it slipped out of her hands and crashed to the floor. My father had never really gone after Elizabeth before. He'd always had an odd soft spot for her, and took out his aggression on my mother and me instead. Especially if he had been drinking, which was often. But that night, he backhanded Elizabeth so hard, she flew off her feet and careened into the doorframe, cracking her head. The dress she was wearing went with her, and when she landed, it ended up around her waist, revealing her panties."

I pause here, thinking back on that night, and I'm instantly filled with an enmity unlike any other. My body tenses out of reflex, my jaw clenching tight, and my stomach churns with protective need. When I don't continue, Ivy squeezes my hand. "Go on," she whispers again, her voice thick with emotion.

I inhale a deep breath before blowing it out slowly, trying to compose myself in order to finish this horrific nightmare of a story.

"My father stood above her for a few very long minutes, just staring down at her with her dress lifted like that. Finally, he licked his lips and his eyes darkened with dirty fucking intent." I shake my head, so disgusted by the mere thought of it. "I was only fourteen, but I understood enough of what he was thinking, and in that moment, I knew I had to do something or he'd destroy her. Not just hurt her, but destroy everything pure and innocent about her. I didn't exactly know what I was going to do. I had contemplated going to our pastor for help or my friend's mother. Neither were any great shakes and probably wouldn't offer much help. I knew my mother would never do anything—she'd just brush it off as she always did. I even deliberated running away with Elizabeth. But that all changed the following Sunday.

"I was getting out of the shower before church, dressed in my best, too-small, second-hand clothes when I saw my father standing by the doorway to the room Elizabeth and I shared. He was watching her dress through the crack in the door, the sickest, most depraved look on his face as his body made his thoughts known. Then he touched himself while looking at her, pushing open the door to our room before I called out his name, stopping him. In that moment, my mind was made up. I was decided, and that night after everyone was asleep—"

I swallow so hard and loud that the sound reverberates in my ears, not because I regret what I did, but because this is the point that could make Ivy leave. I'm shaking like a leaf in the wind, pressing my hand to her as firmly as I can without hurting her. My eyes close, visions dancing through my mind as I relive the moment that changed everything.

"That night I went into my parents' bedroom, pulled the loaded revolver out of his nightstand drawer, and aimed it at his head."

Ivy draws in a breath, before a startled gasp slips through her lips, and now she's shaking too.

"I stood there, watching my father sleep, my mother next to him, and I couldn't pull the trigger. I had a flash of a memory, one small moment in time, when my father was decent to me. He taught me how to throw a baseball in our yard. That was it. That was the extent of any positive moments my father and I shared, but it was in my mind, and it was strong enough to give me pause. So I stood there, trembling and sick and crying. I must have made a noise or something because he opened his eyes."

I let out a strangled laugh, though nothing about this is funny. I can't even look at Ivy right now, despite being desperate to know what she's thinking. I close my eyes again and I'm bombarded with my father. His face. His expression. His smell. It still nauseates me all these years later.

"He didn't do anything at first, just lay there watching me with that gun pointed at his face. He didn't try to talk me down or ask me what I was doing. Nothing. Until he saw my resolve to kill him falter and fade. His expression twisted into something I can only describe as diabolically cruel. My father went for the gun, trying to pry it out of my grip, but it wasn't to stop me from shooting him. My father was going to kill me. It was written all over his face in murderous contempt, and I knew that if I didn't shoot him, he was going to either shoot me or beat me to death. So I pulled the trigger."

Ivy stands up suddenly, pacing around the living room, going between the fireplace and the window and back again. Her face pallid, nearly gray, and her slate eyes are wild.

"You killed him," she says flatly despite the myriad of emotions swirling across her.

I don't need to answer, but I do anyway. "Yes."

"Fuck," she hisses out, and all I can do is watch her loop back and forth. I can't even go to her because I know, *I know*, she'll push me away.

So screw it, I've come this far.

"It was murder, Ivy." She winces and shudders at the word. "I knew it then, even though I was only fourteen, and I didn't try to hide that from anyone. I wish I could tell you that I regretted it, but I didn't, and I don't. I told the judge why I did what I did and he sent me to a juvenile detention facility until I turned eighteen. My record was sealed after that point, and I managed to graduate high school and go to Caltech."

She nods, absorbing my words, but has yet to comment or run. She actually hasn't run, I realize.

So I let her work through this. Let her make sense of what I just said and hope. Fucking hell this is torture.

Finally, after five minutes—yes, I said five—she stops pacing and joins me on the couch. Her expression is stricken, and I brace myself for the words that will no doubt end me.

"I don't know what to say about all that. I don't judge you or blame you for the decisions you felt you had to make. Do I wish you had chosen a different course? Absolutely. I still can't wrap my mind around that. But you probably saved your sister from a fate worse than death. I can't begin to understand the courage that took, but I have seen the aftermath of girls who end up like your sister could have. I've seen that particular brand of evil and destruction, and those girls are never the same, Luke. Their spirits are broken." Ivy stretches up, kissing the corner of my mouth. I pull her into me, breathing her in the way I need to as I start to lose my shit.

I'm shaking and crying like a baby, but I don't care.

She didn't run.

But I didn't tell her what came next, and there's more.

So much more.

# Chapter Thirty-One

*Luke*

WE SIT LIKE THIS, wrapped in each other and crying for I don't know how long, but it has to have been a while because it's well past dark now.

"Do you have to work tomorrow?" I ask softly, kissing the side of her head.

She pulls back, wiping tears and mascara from under her eyes and nods.

"I should probably go." That hurts, but I understand all the same. It's not like I really expected anything else. "There's more you haven't told me."

"Yes. A lot."

She thinks on this for a minute, chewing the corner of her mouth. "Can you tell me now? I don't know why, but I just want to hear everything all at once so I can go home and not be able to sleep while I think on everything."

I chuckle lightly. "Not be able to sleep?"

"Do you really think sleep would be possible after what you just told me?" She raises a dubious eyebrow.

"I guess not. Sorry about that."

She shrugs, not really all that concerned with her lack of sleep. "I want to hear the rest please."

"Okay."

It's really not okay. I have zero interest in telling her. I don't want to talk anymore, but I can't say no to her if she's willing to hear it. She's here. She stayed, and she didn't judge me.

*Holy hell, why didn't I tell her this before? I'm such a fucking idiot.*

I could have avoided so much pain.

Sucking in a deep breath, I continue on.

"So I spent four years in juvie, which was an eye-opening experience to say the least. I met a lot of different types of people there, learned many useful skills, but it wasn't until I met a particular guy that things changed. I can't give you his name, so don't ask, but let's just say he taught me how to write code and hack, and then I taught myself how to do it with any system I wanted."

Ivy's eyes go wide, but this part really shouldn't be all that surprising for her.

"I was better than good, I was the best, and that got me into Caltech." I shrug. "At least, I think it did. I still don't know how I managed that one, but whatever. I got into Caltech and everything came easy as pie to me, and before I knew it, I was a part of the underground hacking ring that was in direct competition with MIT."

"That's how you met Ryan?"

"Yes," I confirm. "We were up against each other in the finals. Don't let that unaffected hipster façade fool you, that man is a first-rate hacker."

"Continue, Lucas, you're sidetracking now," Ivy says in that wry way of hers that always has me smiling.

"All the bad stuff began before that."

"I figured."

That has my attention. "You did?"

She smiles like she's brilliant and I underestimate her, which I'm sure I do. Screw that, I did underestimate her because she's here, sitting with me and smiling. She's heaven, and I was epically wrong —as usual.

"I knew there was no way you would get caught for that and Ryan wouldn't, especially since he beat you." She raises an eyebrow in challenge.

"He did beat me, but only because I knew shit was going down and I was busy destroying evidence." That earns me a frown. "I was doing illegal things, Ivy. No reason to say otherwise. I'm not especially proud of that. It's one of the reasons why Ryan and I do what we do now, but that bust, that ring, is not what I've been hiding from you."

She sighs, looking tired and beautiful.

"Do you want to postpone this?" *Please say yes. Please say yes.*

"No." Of course, she doesn't.

I take her hand, holding it tight and look her dead in the eyes.

"What I'm about to tell you is partially classified. There are things I will not be able to disclose, and that will never change." She swallows hard but manages a tight nod of acceptance. "When I first got to Caltech, I was angry. I had been angry for four years and had a chip on my shoulder because of it. I felt I had something to prove. That I was more than some punk kid who killed their asshole father and went to juvie for it. So I began to hack government mainframes. They're really old systems that most hackers don't care so much about, but I went after them.

"And I got in and continued from one place to another. That's what I really got busted for, though they weren't after missing information because I stole none of it. But hacking the United States Government is a big deal. A very punishable big deal, so they had me, and they knew it. They wanted to use my skills, and since I could have gone to prison for a very long time for any one of my transgressions, that was used as leverage. My freedom became payment for my services."

"And that's what you were doing when you left that time and didn't ring me? And all those phone calls you took in private?"

"Yes. I can't tell you anything else about that, though. I can't tell you what I do or who I'm with."

"But you said some things have changed?"

"They have. I worked it so that there is less personal risk involved for me and anyone I'm in a relationship with. Don't ask me how I managed that either."

"*Personal risk?*"

I can only cringe and nod.

"So, you're telling me I was in *danger* when we were together before?" She's looking at me in disbelief. Or maybe she's pissed off that I even placed her in that position to begin with. Hard to say, really.

"Not really, darlin'. I mean, there are people out there, governments out there, who would love to get their hands on me, but it's not like I walk around with a sign on my chest that says who I am and what I do. I've only ever been directly targeted while I was actively working."

"What the bloody fuck does that mean?"

I shrug, because I feel like that's pretty self-explanatory and any further comment will be counterproductive, not to mention illegal for me to share. Besides, that's not really the case anymore. I'm more in the background now, after taking down a large international hacking ring and using that to negotiate my breadth of freedom.

"But you're still working for . . . whomever you were working for?"

"Yes, but to a lesser degree and on a smaller scope."

Ivy shakes her head, standing up again and doing that pacing thing that seems to aid her thought process.

"And that's for life?"

"Possibly, yes."

She shakes her head, dismayed, her lips pursed. Apparently that was not the answer she was hoping for.

"So all this rubbish," she waves her hand in the air. "All this rubbish is why you pushed me away before?"

"I didn't want to. You have no idea how much I flipped back and forth on that." I sit up, leaning forward and placing my elbows on my parted thighs. "Being with you is the only thing I've ever wanted, but I am a convicted murderer who is also part of a black ops sect of the government responsible for dangerous and covert hacks. What was I supposed to do? None of that is your world, and you fucking deserved better."

"And now I don't?"

I physically recoil from her words because it feels like she just slapped me across the face and punched me in the gut at the same time. I've heard the expression if looks could kill, but I think her words may have just done the trick.

"I'm sorry." She blows out an angry breath, staring into the fire. "That was cruel."

"But not untrue."

She doesn't say anything, and I hate it when I'm right. She's done. Checked out on me and I can't say I blame her.

"Thank you for telling me all of that."

Her voice is distant, detached, unemotional. She's gone, and I can't think of a damn word that could bring her back.

I knew she'd leave when she heard the whole truth and nothing feels worse than when you tell yourself, *See? I told you so, asshole.* Yeah, that one really sucks.

"I should go," she says stoically, and my head drops into my hands. "It's late and I have an early shift."

"I'll walk you out." My voice is not devoid of emotion. My voice is filled with the anguish that is crashing down on me in heavy tormented waves.

"That's not necessary," she says, and I slam my eyes shut as my breath lodges in my chest. I didn't think anything could hurt this much. Probably because I never allowed myself to believe it was over until this very moment.

"I'm sorry, Luke. I am. I just . . ." Her voice trails off, and I manage enough strength to lift my head and stare into her beautiful face. But her expression is as undemonstrative as her tone, and I lower my head again. "I need time to think about all of this. To absorb it."

"It's fine, Ivy. You can go, and I'll let you do that. I'll stop chasing you," I sigh out so damn heavy and deflated that my body bows. "If that's what you want, I'll let you go."

"I don't know what I want right now. This is just a lot to process in one night. You're asking me to be a part of a world I don't understand and cannot know about, and turn a blind eye to it when you have to leave at a moment's notice to go and do something that could put both of our lives at risk. I just—I need to go."

I can't say anything else. I can't say bye or take care or I love you. I can't get on my knees and beg her either, because she's right. I may have changed the stakes, but Ronaldo made it clear that once you're part of this, it's sort of a lifelong venture.

And if I am able to 'retire' from it . . . well, no one's done that yet, so who the fuck knows what happens then.

Then there's the whole murdering, illegal activity part of my life that's also not so easy to overlook in the sobering light of day.

Maybe that shit with my dad was justified, and maybe it wasn't, but I have zero excuses for everything else. But I like to feel that I've served my time and then some. I like to feel that my penance is making this world a little safer, a little more secure from evil fucked up people who seek to bring it down.

So I rationalize and justify my life.

What the hell else can a person do and continue on without suffocating in their ugly?

But Ivy? No.

She doesn't need to rationalize anything she's done. She doesn't have to make amends for wrongdoing, because everything she does is on the right side of good. She saves sick kids' lives for fuck's sake. She's a goddamn angel, and I may just be the devil in her scenario.

So when my front door slams shut, I'm not surprised.

I don't even wince or start at the sound of it.

I just take this for what it is, and maybe, eventually, somehow, I'll find a way to live without her.

Maybe. But probably not.

And if I can't have her, it's not like I could have anyone else, so I might as well admit that I had perfection once and lost it.

# Chapter Thirty-Two

*Ivy*

I HATE THE UNKNOWN. In medicine, the unknown can mean death or further disease progression. No, I like it when things are visible, tangible, and with a clear and concise solution.

Cut, fix, sew.

That's what I do.

That's my life, and for thirty years, that's worked for me.

Then Luke comes around and throws in the proverbial monkey wrench and messes it all about. Suddenly, everything I thought I knew and needed is upside-down.

I ran out on him, and that makes me feel like a prize bitch, but I just couldn't think. I was suffocating standing there with no room to breathe—and I needed to breathe dammit!

So I drove home, though I don't remember the trip, and now I'm tossing and turning in my bed in the wee hours of the morning, trying to make sense of everything he said.

Luke killed his father. Not just killed him, but shot him at point-blank range.

Holy Jesus Mary Margaret Jones.

I get his thinking behind it. At least, I think I do. It's easy to see where his actions arose from, and somehow I feel better knowing that he stopped before pulling the trigger. Somehow that makes it an easier pill to swallow than believing that what he did was cold-hearted murder.

He was a scared and very abused boy who was trying to protect his sister. So even though I feel like I should condemn him for his actions, I'm having an impossible time doing it. I mean, you hear all the time about how battered women end up killing their abusive husbands, and I sympathize with them readily.

And in my eyes, Luke's situation was even worse than that.

From the way he made it sound, his mother was not helpful or even someone he could rely on and trust.

His father was a nightmare of epic proportions who was going to more than likely violate the one person Luke had left—his sister. And I don't doubt for a minute that Luke believed it was his responsibility to protect her.

So can I forgive him for what he did? Yes, I think I can. I think I already have.

There's that piece solved.

It's really all of the government hacking rubbish that has me so worked up. It's the clandestine operation that he's a part of and the possibility of him risking not only his life, but mine as well.

And who does things like that?

Who actually has something as insane and outlandish as secret black ops—whatever that means—government spy things as part of their life? No one, that's who. It's fantastical, and if I hadn't witnessed some of it firsthand, I wouldn't believe it.

I suppose that explains all the security features he has in his home.

Luke says things are different now. That the risk is minimized, but he's still involved in that world, and from the way he spoke, he always will be. Can I do that? Can I expose myself to that?

I just don't know. I just don't bloody know.

The mere fact that I'm even considering this, thinking about his life in terms of my own, tells me that I'm still in love with him. As if I needed *that* as a confirmation.

Yes, I love him. Yes, I want him despite my better judgment and the pain he caused me this previous year, but what does that actually mean for me?

Could I marry a man who lives that sort of life? Would we be able to have a family and not risk their lives?"

Jesus Christ, I can't even right now.

I am not this girl. This is up Sophia's alley, not mine.

Letting out a loud and exaggerated groan, I roll over and the bright red numbers on my alarm clock inform me that it's just after four in the morning.

I should get up and get ready for work at this point, but I can't seem to concentrate. I'm as preoccupied as preoccupied gets. I'm dangerous to my patients like this, and that infuriates me, because now I feel like I can't even do my job because of this man.

I only have two patients scheduled for today because I'm new on the urgent care service and that's where I'm working today, so I text my colleague and ask him to take those cases. Those children are far safer with someone else at the helm.

But it's not like I can sleep or rest my brain, and I certainly can't sit around my flat mulling over Luke's deeds anymore. Part of me is very tempted to go back to his flat and talk more, but I don't know if I'm ready for that.

I hate the way I left him. Have I mentioned that already? Because I really do.

I know it hurt him, and though he's hurt me, I'm not vengeful enough to want to return the favor.

It's so late that it's nearly early and I bet that there is a six a.m. flight headed where I need it to go. I don't even bother with a bag because I don't plan to stay the night, so I grab my purse, phone, and keys before leaving my apartment in under five minutes flat.

It's nowhere near close to light out, but the road is devoid of traffic, and it takes me twenty minutes to get to the airport.

The terminal is fairly empty, so I stroll right up to the ticket counter, smiling at the perfectly polished attendant.

"I need a roundtrip ticket to Los Angeles, please."

She gives me a look, clearly noting my lack of baggage and the urgency in my voice. After a long pregnant pause, she begins to type away on her screen. "When would you like to depart and return?"

"First available flight out and I'd like to return this evening, please."

Another long lingering perusal as she taps her manicured nails against the keys of the keyboard. Click, click, click. It's an annoying sound, but I don't comment because I'm at this woman's mercy.

"Why the quick turnaround?" she asks, feigning indifference, though she's clearly screening me to ensure that I'm not some sort of terrorist.

"My ex-boyfriend is mucking about with my head, and I need to go see my sister, but I have patients to get to tomorrow, so I need to come home tonight."

"Fair enough," she shrugs, before going back to her screen and typing away. Moments later, I hand her my credit card and photo ID, and she hands me a boarding pass, and I'm on my way.

My flight leaves in a little more than an hour, so I have time, but just as I'm about to enter the meager security line, I hear my name being called.

*Bloody hell, he followed me.*

Of course, he did.

The fact that I was once stalked similar to this by a man should have me on edge, but Luke has never done that to me. But he has managed to annoy the bloody piss out of me.

"Ivy, wait!" he calls out again as I step up to a large disinterested man. I'm about to hand him my ticket and license when Luke reaches me, grabbing them out of my hand.

"Is there a problem here?" the TSA agent asks in a ridiculously deep voice.

Luke and I both speak at the same time, but I say "yes" and he says "no." Then Luke flashes some sort of badge or special ID or something and the guy stands up taller, nodding his head and suddenly looking much more official than he did moments ago.

"I need a moment alone with her," Luke demands in an authoritative tone that could get me aroused if I wasn't so angry. The man points in the direction of something I can't see, and Luke nods, looking as stern as ever.

"No," I protest. "I have a plane to catch. Luke, go home."

"I'm sorry, ma'am, but he has government security access, and until he gives the all-clear, I can't let you through."

"What the bloody hell does that even mean?" I turn to Luke, who's doing his best to hide his smug smile. *Bastard*. "Luke, I have a plane to catch that I don't want to miss. You can't do this."

I'm about to stomp my foot like a petulant child when Luke takes my arm, leading me around a partitioned-off area that I've never noticed before, and into a small space that really has nothing in it other than three walls.

Maybe this is where they frisk people?

"What do you think you're doing following me here and pulling this rubbish?"

"You're leaving?" He looks so hurt, and I feel bad about that. I really do. But stalking me into the airport and pulling some ludicrous security whatever is just not okay.

"I'm going to see Soph for the day."

He sighs, running a tired hand through his disheveled hair. And now that I look at him, really look at him, I can see just how worn and weary he is. I doubt I look much better.

"You're coming back tonight?" he asks, hopeful.

"Yes. I have to work tomorrow. I'm already missing today. Can I go now?"

"No," he says before grabbing me by the shoulders and pulling me into his chest, wrapping me snugly in his arms and burying his face in my neck. "I was so fucking scared, Ivy," he breathes against my skin, and I can feel his body trembling against mine. "I know I told you I'd let you go, and I meant it. I wasn't going to bother you, but I couldn't sleep, and I ended up on those stairs across the street from your building again. And then I saw you leave, so I followed, and once I realized you were going to the airport, I panicked. I'm sorry. I know that's crossing all kinds of lines and boundaries."

Seriously? He did that? He really is the ultimate stalker. I mean, he wasn't pounding on my door and demanding that I open it before he breaks it down like Jason used to, but still.

"I didn't even intend to go to your place," he continues. "I *swear* I didn't. I was just out on one of my late-night walks, and without conscious thought, I found myself at your building. I was going to leave before the sun came up, but then I saw you."

"I didn't mean to scare you, Luke. I'm not fleeing the country or anything. I just . . . I need space and time to think this through. And your stalking really knows no bounds."

He nods, fully aware of just how wrong that all was. "I don't know what to say to you. Part of me knows that I need to let you go because you're better off without me, but I love you so much that every time I try to imagine my life without you, I just can't."

My eyes cinch shut, trying to keep back the scalding tears threatening to fall.

"I understand you need your sister, and I'm sorry for doing this in the middle of the airport. Go, and if by some miracle you decide you need me even half as much as I need you, I'm here waiting."

"I know," I laugh. "You're always lurking about, aren't you?"

"I am. But in a totally non-threatening way."

He laughs, squeezing my body to his and inhaling deeply like he can't get enough of me. Can't get close enough to me. It drives me wild when he does that, and my body shivers involuntarily. His laugh dies in his throat, turning into a groan.

"You need to stop that, or I'll have to pull you into a room for a cavity search. I'm dying for you, baby, and you shivering against me like that isn't helping. You have no idea how sexy that is."

It's impossible to be in Luke's arms and not feel the same way about him.

His warm, muscular, *masculine*, body presses against me. His smell is like home, familiar and safe, yet at the same time so incredibly sexy and seductive. It's a heady mix that suddenly has me clinging to him, unwilling to let him go.

"Ivy?"

The question in his voice is so loaded. It's asking so many things that the three simple letters in my name can't even begin to hold them all.

I don't respond, mostly because I'm so bewildered that I can't make heads from tails.

I love Luke, so very much. And I want him, so very much.

And yet, I feel stuck in this chasm between so many possibilities and nothingness.

Luke pulls back, studying my face, a smirk twisting his lips. "Will you go on a date with me tomorrow night?"

I snort out an incredulous laugh. "Sorry?"

"A date. We never really did that, and it's been a long time since we've spent any real one-on-one time together. I've placed a lot of pressure on this, considering the small amount of time we've actually spent together. So how about a date?" The lopsided grin he's giving me with that damn irresistible dimple. The mischievous glint in his eyes. I'm so done for. "Come on, you know you want to."

I laugh despite myself. "Okay, I'll go on a date with you."

"Awesome," he smiles wide. "Now, you have a plane to catch." He takes my hand and leads me back to the security area and of course, there's a huge line now.

I groan, "I'll never make it."

Luke winks at me. "Of course, you will, baby." He pulls me past the line right up to the scanning machine and over to a TSA agent. "I'm taking her to the gate. She's been cleared," he says, sounding so official I almost want to laugh like it's some joke and they'll kick us right to the back of the line. But he flashes that badge again and the agent waves us through without being screened or questioned.

"What is that thing?"

He grins at me. "It's confidential." I roll my eyes, and he laughs. "Seriously, though," he says holding my hand and leading me through the terminal to my gate. "Go see Sophia. Think about everything I told you last night. Get some sun and vitamin D. I hear that shit is important." He winks at me again. "You've been living in Seattle too long."

I laugh, nudging him with my hip. "I've actually been in Boston, but that's not a whole lot better. Are you saying I'm pale?"

"Yes." He laughs when he sees my frown and then kisses my temple. "But I love you pale, so it doesn't matter." Luke slings his arm around my waist, pulling me into his side. "Actually, I just love you, so thanks for agreeing to the date."

We stop in front of my gate, and my flight has just started boarding.

"Not loving each other isn't the issue. It's all the rest of the stuff I need to learn to accept or understand or live with, or whatever I'm supposed to do with it."

Luke wraps his arms around me again, leaning his forehead to mine.

"The stuff with my father I cannot change. That's something I will always have to live with. But for the last ten years that I've been involved in the other stuff, not once has my *daily* life actually been threatened. I've never had someone trying to hunt me down or come after me, unless I was on the job. I can't lie about that. But that's changed now. I'm very good at what I do, Ivy, and I take steps to keep my world as safe as I can." His hands come up to cup my face as he stares intently into my eyes. "And I would die before I'd let anything happen to you. It's not as horrible as it sounds. I swear."

I lean up, pressing my lips to his, and it feels so right that my whole body seems to come alive. This is different from the kisses he's given me out of desperation or passion. *I'm* the one making this choice and in doing it, I know there is no going back for me.

I'm his, and he's mine. I just have to come to terms with the rest of it.

Can it really be that simple?

# Chapter Thirty-Three

*Ivy*

THE BEACH that directly abuts my sister's condo is glorious, especially in the morning sun. Large waves are crashing against the shore as seagulls fly high in the air, squawking their delight. There are even a few surfers out there taking advantage of the swells.

I miss beaches like this. Where it's warm and bright and you can actually go in the water. I spent a great deal of my time here while I was at Caltech.

It's hard to believe that it's only a little after ten in the morning and I'm sitting here, considering where I started this morning.

I spent the entire flight down thinking about what Luke had said.

Not just from last night, but this morning as well. I believe him when he says no one has come after him. I mean, I have no idea what he's doing exactly, and I'm sure it's serious stuff, but I doubt hitmen—or whatever these people might be called—are standing outside his building waiting to pounce.

I'm sure there's a large dangerous component to his life, hence the secretive nature of it, but as he said, no one has come after him yet. That, and he told me he's taken measures to scale this all back, so really, it's sort of a non-issue, right?

Did I just rationalize all of that away? I think I might have.

I don't exactly love the whole leaving at a moment's notice and having no clue as to where he is or if he's safe. That part is unsettling as hell, but maybe that's something you adapt to. Something you grow to look past and accept as part of life.

I've already accepted what he did as a teenager, so really, what's my hang up?

It's the gravity of everything combined, I think. And not just his history or the complicated world he's still mixed up in.

I came home, saw him, and then he instantly pursued me. Again. He maintains that he came out to Boston on a few separate occasions, but was still restricted by the same obstacles that instigated him to push me away in the first place.

So dating him after all of this? Is it even possible to take so many steps back and give a go at starting over?

Nothing is ever simple, is it?

Though it really does seem to be that way for other people.

I'm sure every relationship has its hardships and challenges, but these seem almost impregnable. They nearly were, and I don't know how to process all of that.

Dropping back into the warm sand, I close my eyes, facing up to the radiant warmth of the heavens while absorbing the sounds of nature around me. It's tranquil and calming, and I understand fully why people pay a large fortune to live in places like this.

"You'll get sand critters in your hair that way, doll," Sophia says from behind me as she comes up to join me.

"Good. I'm hoping they'll burrow into my brain. If I'm really lucky, they'll be the flesh-eating sort, and I won't have to think ever again."

"There's my upbeat girl," she says, sitting beside me with her knees bent, leaning back with her hands in the sand near my head. "I take it this isn't just a friendly visit?"

"I love you, Soph."

"Ah, this is serious. I'd bet big bickies this has to do with your bloke."

I can only sigh. Suddenly I'm exhausted. The lack of sleep and perpetual overdrive my brain is on with all of this is wearing me down. "He told you about his past, yeah?"

I shoot upright, but when my face is next to hers, I can only stare at the knowing, unapologetic look in my sister's beautiful eyes.

"You knew?"

"Yes, of course, I knew. Don't scowl at me; you'll get wrinkles. It's part of what I do. I investigate and probe into people's lives, and when my wee little sister tells me that she's mad over some bloke, I dig."

"Why didn't you ever tell me?" I ask, my voice reflecting the depth of my chafe. I'm not entirely sure I have a reason to be hurt by her withholding, but I am. No, screw that, I have a bloody reason. She's my sister.

"Because you were in love with him, and I was afraid the truth would scare you off from that. Especially coming from me. And I did urge him to tell you, so when he ended things without doing so, I figured it was for the best and you didn't need to know anything else."

"Ah, Soph." I drop back into the sand, raising my forearm over my eyebrows to shield my eyes from the penetrating California sun.

"Don't, *Ah Soph*, me. There was no bloody way I could tell you that story, so ease up. You can hardly blame the wanker for holding that one back from you, though I think he did right."

"You do?"

"Of course I do," she says in earnest. "That father was bad news. A drunk, a gambler, a child and wife beater, and was steadily working himself up to molester. Scum like that deserve what they get, and according the court documents, Luke wasn't going to do the deed when it came down to it."

"How do you get that information?" I'm stupefied right now. My sister—much like everyone else, I'm quickly learning—isn't who she appears to be.

"Information is absurdly easy to procure if you know the right people and have the money to do it. I work in Hollywood, luv bug, so don't play Connie Coy with me. You know very well what I do." Sophia leans back into the sand, propped up on her elbows, staring out into the azure waters of the Pacific.

"So, you don't think the whole government covert piece is an issue either?"

Her bleach blonde curls whip in my direction. "Come again?"

I grin at her, bouncing my eyebrows. "Apparently, your informants are slacking, and you don't know as much as you think." Sophia frowns, narrowing her bespectacled eyes. "And I can't talk about it. But yeah, he's involved in something much larger than his regular nine-to-five."

"Oh, I love this man," she laughs lightly. "You need to marry him straight off. Seriously, Ivy girl, nothing will ever be boring with him."

"I like boring."

"I know, but you like him more."

And that's it, isn't it?

The crux of everything.

I like Luke more.

Amazing how a simple statement like that can settle something so convoluted.

"Yes, I think I bloody well do."

"Then stop all this nonsense. You've always been a chronic over-thinker, Ivy girl, and that's as dangerous as it gets. Sometimes things don't require further analysis. You love him, he loves you, so just get over yourselves already."

Laughing, I reach over and grab my sister, pulling her down on top of me and sinking us deeper into the sand.

She's laughing too, but she's also fighting, pushing me away and attempting to bury my face in the sand at the same time. We must look insane to any passersby, but I don't care, and neither does she.

"What if he hurts me again?" I ask when we're both breathless and our laughter is starting to subside.

"Then you tell me and I have him taken care of. You never even have to be involved."

I roll my eyes. "Hold back there, Hollywood Homicide. You sound eerily serious. While I appreciate your loyalty, that may be taking it a bit too far."

"Suit yourself there, doll, but if that bloke messes you about again, and just so *happens* to disappear, I wouldn't go around asking too many questions." She holds her hands up in surrender. "That's all I'm saying."

"But you think I should give him another go?"

She chews on the corner of her permanently stained red lip, staring out at the surfers in the distance. "Tell me true blue here, Ivy. Do you love him? Do you think he's really going to give you the toss again, or is he wanting a ring and babies in whatever order that may come in?"

"I think the latter."

"And you love him? I mean, I know he's tasty as sin and could probably make a lifelong lesbian such as myself rethink things, but he's the real deal for you?"

I laugh, leaning my head on her shoulder. "Yeah. I love him."

"Then I say go for it, and if he's daft enough to hurt you, then he'll have me to answer to. And probably your mate, Claire, too, because she adores you."

"Thanks, Soph. You're the bestest big sister I know."

"Right?" She grins, looking at me. "I wish I could commiserate with you here on the way men ruin lives, but I can't. Women are so much easier to manage and tend not to have clandestine, top secret, murderous pasts."

"Thanks so much for that," I say sarcastically. "No really, that's so very helpful."

"Aww, you always were way too serious."

"You say that like it's a bad thing."

"Let's just say I go with the flow much more often than you do, and I am happier for it."

"Touché, my love."

Sophia leans over and kisses my temple. "Go home, Ivy girl. It's time you face this nonsense straight on."

"I will," I smile. "After lunch."

Sophia takes me out in Hollywood to one of her 'hotspots.' It's really just another restaurant with overpriced, mediocre food, outdoor seating and a lot of paparazzi hanging about. When I went to Caltech, I rarely came into this area unless I was visiting Sophia.

This world is not for me.

I eat my twenty-five-dollar salad that was little more than grass clippings on a plate with goat cheese, and as we're rounding the corner, heading back to her car, I slam into a tall, hard body that knocks me to the ground on my bum with a heavy oomph.

"Oh, I'm so sorry," someone says, and as I lift my head to see who it is, my mouth drops open, and I freeze on the ground in the middle of the sidewalk.

"Ivy?" he asks, just as shocked as I am and if this were any other ex from my past, I'd get up, give them a hug and a hello. But it's not just any ex; it's Jason, my stalker.

I'm too stunned, and frankly a little scared, to respond.

Sophia hoists me back up, because apparently my legs refuse to work as well. "Keep on moving, Jason," Sophia says with a warning.

"Relax, Sophia," he puffs out slightly aggravated, but his green eyes soften as they turn back to me. "I'm sorry, Ivy. I didn't mean to knock you down. I wasn't watching where I was going." He reaches a hand out like he's about to touch me, but thinks better of it and it drops to his side. "Are you okay?"

"I'm fine," I manage. "I didn't see you there either."

A smirk twists his lips as his eyes dance all over my face and body.

"It's been a long time," he says in that way of his that once upon a time I found so charming. "You look as beautiful as ever. Are you practicing?"

I can feel Sophia's eyes on me, and in truth, it has been a long time, but yet I'm still on edge around him. I wonder if restraining orders count in another state? I doubt it highly.

"I am," is all I offer. "You?" I ask, continuing the pleasantry for some unknown reason, though I'm edgy and desperate to go.

"Yup. Orthopedics here in L.A."

"That's great, Jason. I'm happy for you," I offer a small smile that he feasts on. "Sophia and I should get going."

When I look at him, all I can visualize are the scenes he made in the hospital and in public so long ago. I picture the paramedics' pitying expressions as they hoisted me out of my car after he ran me off the road. I see everything that I've been trying to stay away from all these years.

Sophia and I attempt to maneuver around him, but he intercepts us by grabbing my arm. Instantly I yank it away, alarm bells going off inside my head as my heart races to a punishing rhythm.

He holds his hands up in surrender. "I'm sorry. I just meant to stop you. I won't touch you." He's eyeing me now like I'm a caged animal, and I don't like or appreciate it. "I want to apologize to you, Ivy. For everything." The sincerity in his voice doesn't do much to soften me, but I do stop to listen, because I feel like I need this.

The way things ended between us was so very bad. Restraining orders, a car accident, and me spending the night in the hospital with a concussion.

"I, um . . ." He shifts his weight, looking down quickly before meeting my eyes again. "I was in a bad way when we were in school. The stress of everything was getting to me, and I just felt out of control and overwhelmed by the pressure to perform at a perfect level. I'm sorry for how far things went. I never meant to hurt you. I loved you and I was hurt you didn't feel the same. I'm sorry."

I don't know what to say to that except, "Thank you."

"Are you still up in Seattle?" he asks, far too hopeful for my liking. Jason may have been in a bad place, but no apology or excuse can change what he did.

The fear and distrust he instilled in me has lasted far longer than our relationship did.

"Do you really think she's going to tell you that?" Sophia asks with an incredulous note. "I think you should keep going, Jason. You said what you had to say and now it's done."

Jason's expression falls like Sophia just knocked all the wind out of his sails.

Finally, he nods, but looks forlorn as his eyes sweep over me with such longing that I know if I stand here with him any longer, things could turn in a bad direction.

"Take care of yourself," I say.

"You too," he says with a sad smile before grabbing me quickly and pulling me in for a hug that stuns me paralyzed.

My heart jacks up instantly. My memory is assaulted with all that he's capable of. His mouth comes down to whisper in my ear, and I can feel Sophia trying to pry him off of me, but Jason is large and strong, and she's no match.

"I've missed you," he mutters, sending the most nauseating, stomach-turning, chills throughout my body. "Still to this day I regret everything I did to mess it up with you, and wish we could go back. I'll be in touch."

I push him off, prying myself free of his grasp and then move past him quickly, practically at a sprint. Why didn't I knee him in the bollocks? Why didn't I smack him across the face? *Dammit!*

Sophia is hot on my heels, and as we approach her car, I yell over my shoulder, "Unlock it."

She does with a loud double beep, and I catapult myself into her Mercedes SUV, slamming the door with ferocity behind me. My breaths are coming out in strong, hard pants, and I feel like I can't get enough air.

*I can't get enough air.*

"Breathe, Ivy," Sophia soothes, rubbing my back. "You're hyper-ventilating." I can hear the worry in her voice but I can't slow my response. "You're safe. He's gone, and he won't hurt you again."

"Dammit," I half-yell, once I manage control of myself. "Five bloody minutes and I'm reduced to a weak cowering thing." I'm so angry with myself right now. So furious at my reaction to him. Why didn't I push him away sooner? Why didn't I get up and keep walking?

*Dammit!*

"Ivy, stop this," Sophia says as she pulls into traffic heading for the airport. "You'll probably never see him again. That was a fluke thing. Go home. Return to your life."

She's right. I'll go home and back to my life and the things I know.

But no matter how hard I try to shake it, Jason completely rattled me.

# Chapter Thirty-Four

*Luke*

BY THE TIME I reach my building, I have a headache everywhere. I didn't get out of my coding fest with Ryan until well after six, and I haven't had much to eat or drink since early this morning. It was just one of those days.

That and I sat up all night outside on freaking stairs across from Ivy's building, again.

I really need to quit doing that.

Hopefully now that Ivy agreed to a date I will.

That thought makes me smile as I punch in the code for the back door that will lead me to my apartment. The stairwell is well lit, which is the only way I am able to distinguish the female form slumped against my door at the top of the stairs. Her face is obscured, having found one of the few shadows in here, but I'd know her anywhere.

"Ivy?" I call out, but she doesn't move and she doesn't respond. "Ivy?" I try again a little louder, but still no movement and now my heart is racing as I take the stairs two at a time.

Is she hurt? Is she sick? What is she doing here?

It takes me less than two seconds to reach her, but it feels like two seconds too long.

My panic recedes marginally as I jostle her shoulders and she stirs with a groan. Her crystalline gray-blue eyes blink open, but the fatigue in them is evident and they quickly close again, as her lips curve up into a grin.

"What are you doing here?" I whisper.

"My flight landed, and I didn't want to go home," she says in that raspy, sleepy cadence of hers that drives me wild.

"You okay, honey?" I touch her cheek, looking her over in case I'm missing something.

She nods but doesn't verbally respond, and something about that feels off.

"Do you want to come in, or continue sleeping in the hall?"

She giggles a little and points to my door, but instead of allowing her to stand, I scoop up her slender body into my arms, pulling her against me where she belongs.

"I'm not a child, Luke, I *can* walk."

"But you're tired, and I like carrying you."

She doesn't protest further, just sinks into me, resting her head against my chest over my heart.

"Your heart is racing," she whispers almost to herself.

"I wasn't expecting to find you passed out on my front step."

"Oh. Sorry."

I kiss the top of her head. "It's fine, baby. Just gave me a start, is all. How come you didn't want to go home? Not that I'm complaining or anything."

"I just didn't."

I hate that answer. It's way too vague for someone who's normally very direct.

"Are you hungry? Do you want me to fix you some supper or just tuck you into bed?"

"Bed."

"Guest room or mine?"

"Yours," she says, and I'm smiling like an idiot. "Wipe that smile off your face, Lucas. I'm going to sleep. You're not getting lucky."

"Ivy, baby, anytime you're in my bed, I'm lucky. Even if you're just sleeping."

"Luke Walker, my own personal sweet talker," she snorts out a laugh. "Ha, that rhymes."

I set her down on the edge of my bed before walking over to my dresser and grabbing a pair of boxer shorts and a t-shirt, both of which will be way too big on her.

"Here," I say, handing her the clothes. "I'll go get you a glass of water. Do you need anything else?"

She's sitting on the edge of my bed, staring at the clothes in her hands, so I stand here, waiting, because something is clearly not right.

"I know your past. I know all of the ugly that ran it for so long, but how did you become you from that?" Her eyes make the journey up toward mine and my breath hitches. They're filled with anguish. "How did you end up not hurting or stalking or threatening women?"

The hairs on the nape of my neck stand on end, and I take a small step toward her, desperate to grab hold of her and get to the bottom of her words. But I don't do that, and after a moment of deliberation, I answer her with sarcasm.

"I do stalk you. As frequently as this morning, remember?"

She nods once, her gorgeous face fixed on mine. "And for some unexplained reason that never once frightened me. Yet you have this horribly violent past that could have so easily shaped your character in a different way. And then there are men who come from everything. Normal families, money, opportunity, and somehow manage to become something dark."

"Ivy, what are you talking about? What happened?"

She shakes her head, and I know she's not going to tell me, and that has my blood running cold. I have half a mind to call Sophia, but I know that will piss Ivy off, and we're already on thin ice as it is.

"I just want to go to bed here. Is that okay?" Her voice is

despondent. Isolated. It makes me want to tear the world to shreds, eliminating anything that could possibly hurt her.

"Of course. You can stay forever." That gets a half-hearted grin as she stands up, clothes in hand and walks toward my bathroom without further comment.

By the time I return with her glass of water, she's in bed with the lights out. I don't say anything as I place the glass on the nightstand and kiss her forehead. She doesn't either, but I know she's still awake based on the modulation of her breathing.

Her silence might be the most disconcerting thing of all.

I make myself something to eat, though I hardly touch it, and spend my evening bouncing back and forth between doing work in my office and checking on a sleeping Ivy. I can't stop myself from studying her. Watching her sleep in my bed, in my home, and wondering what scared her enough to make her show up on my doorstep.

She doesn't stir as I climb into bed well after eleven and pull her soundly into my chest, wrapping her tightly in my protective embrace.

Sleep comes for me quickly, mostly because I haven't had her next to me in so long, and both my bed and I have missed her presence.

When I wake up for work, she's already gone, a note left in her place informing me that she expects me to pick her up for our date at seven.

She can have whatever the hell she wants.

I shower and dress quickly, and by the time I make it into work, things are bustling, mostly because it's Ryan's younger brother's first day.

Kyle was a criminal attorney in New York City until recently when Ryan somehow convinced him to move here and take on the role as our new corporate lawyer. Ryan hasn't discussed it much, but I surmise something must have transpired for Kyle to make the drastic change, especially since he's been brushing off Ryan's propositions for a while now.

Kyle is standing with Claire, in front of her desk, as I walk down the hall toward my office. They're having some sort of discussion, and to an outsider, one who isn't as well acquainted with them as I am, it would seem casual. But it's not. I can practically feel the sexual tension radiating from both of them, and that draws me back to their flirtatious interactions at Ryan and Kate's wedding.

I know they're best friends, but it seems like more. Maybe. Who the hell knows.

This could be fun.

"What's up kids?" I call out, announcing my approach as I slap Kyle hard on the back.

*Little shit.*

"Dick," he mutters, pushing my hand away. God, I love this kid. "That any way to greet your new lawyer?"

"Kyle, I've known you since you were in diapers."

Claire snickers, but Kyle just blows it off. "Right, when was that, grandpa? You mean when I was a teenager?"

"It's still amazing to me how much younger you are than Ryan," I muse. "And how much shorter."

"Shove it," he says, but now he's smiling. "I'm only four inches shorter, and Ryan is a freak of nature. People really shouldn't be that tall."

"He's six-three," Claire comments dryly.

"Which is freakishly tall, I maintain," Kyle says, his hazel eyes and sandy brown hair glow under the florescent lights. "Even Luke, who is a couple of inches taller than me, is shorter than him."

"You boys really have a thing when it comes to length." Claire smirks at both of us. "Anyway, I've got work to do and all that good stuff. I'll catch ya later, Kyle," Claire throws him a wink. "Later, dickwad," she says to me and saunters off, and I can only shake my head at the stupid idiot that is my best friend's little brother.

"You didn't."

"What?" he asks absentmindedly, watching Claire's ass walk away.

"Oh, shit. You fucking did," I laugh my ass off, shaking my head again, because this is not going to end well. "Dude, do *not* let your brother know."

"What?" Kyle feigns innocence, but his hazel eyes do not fool me. He's not that good of a lawyer.

"I mean it. If Ryan finds out that you two hooked up, he'll lose his shit. You may be his little brother, and he clearly loves you because he gave you his blood and whatnot, but Claire is like the sister he never had, and he's fiercely protective over her. And," I stick my finger up in the air remembering my next point, "he does not take well to inter-office fraternization."

"We absolutely have not hooked up. We're just good friends," he maintains with a scowl. "But now that we're on the subject, why is he so against that?"

"Because the big guy, Mr. Serious, does not like drama." I wave my finger in the air, gesturing in the direction that Claire just went. "And office romance is drama. *Especially* with Claire."

"It's not even a thing. Friends. That's all."

"Right," I say, oozing sarcasm. "But just so you know, she will rip off your balls, toss them up in the air, and hit them four hundred yards with a bat." Kyle winces at the imagery, but he needs to know all the same. "She eats men like candy before spitting them out, so she doesn't absorb the calories. Get what I'm saying here?"

"Got it. Like I said, not even a thing."

He's frowning, though, which tells me that it is a thing or was a thing, but hopefully, it's not anymore.

"See ya around the funhouse," I say, smacking his back again.

"Yeah, see ya." He's still staring off into space, probably thinking about his nuts, so I leave him to that because I have a shit ton of work to get to before my date with Ivy.

BY THE TIME I finish up, it's a little after six. I've already made a reservation for eight-thirty for dinner, but first, I want to take Ivy to Bathtub Gin for a drink because it's cozy and intimate.

I get a text that might put a kink in those plans as Ivy informs me that she's stuck in a trauma and that I should just come get her at the hospital instead of her place.

I make my way to the hospital, through rush hour traffic and find a spot to park in, and now it's well after seven. But I'm smiling because I have a date with my girl, which in my mind means she's giving me another chance.

Locating the emergency department, I meander toward the waiting room, which used to be our standard pick-up slash meet-up place. But before I even reach the room, I spot her standing over by the bank of large windows in her regular clothes, typing something into her phone. She looks beautiful in her standard jeans and ice-blue blouse that will no doubt bring out the color of her eyes.

"I never would have pegged you for a chess girl."

Ivy looks up, her cheeks flushing instantly. *Busted*!

"H-how did you know I was playing chess?"

I smile, walking closer to her. "Because I know you, darlin'."

She smiles at that, but it's reluctant. Almost like she doesn't *want* to smile at the notion that I know her. I'll win her over.

"So you say."

"No. I do. I know you." I smile, before I turn serious. "Sophia called me this morning and told me about yesterday with fuckface Jason. She called me at work, and well, I was worried about what he said to you about being in touch. So I hacked his phone. And computer."

Should I have mentioned that last part to her? Probably not given the frown on her face. There is nothing on his phone about her anyway, yet, but it allowed me to fill half an hour with fun this morning.

"And let me tell you darlin', that ex of yours is not only stupid, but he's a total perv. I mean, how dumb do you have to be to open an email from an unknown sender and click on the link for a *porn* site? Clearly, our little friend Jason here has never heard of phishing emails." I didn't even get creative with it. I didn't even make it from someone he knows. I sent that malware almost like a joke, never expecting in a million years he'd bite.

But he did and boom, instant access.

Illegal? You bet. But fuck it. No one can trace it back to me anyway.

"Oh." Ivy scoffs a little. "Can you do that with my computer?"

I shrug, "I could, but I haven't." I roll my head to meet her worried eyes. "Why?" I bounce my eyebrows. "Nervous I'll find something good on there? Something incriminating maybe?"

"No. I just don't like the invasion of privacy, and it's a HIPAA violation."

I love what a goodie-goodie she is. Seriously, I've never met anyone other than the Duchess who walks the straight and narrow so much.

"What are you hiding?"

"None of your business. And if you hack my computer, I'll call the police."

"You'd never know if I did it."

She sighs out, exasperated. "Don't you have anything else to do?"

"Nope." I pop the p sound. "I get bored easily. You ready for dinner or do you want to just skip to dessert and go home?"

"If you go home, does that mean I get to as well?"

"With me?" I smirk. "That's one way to pass the time."

She rolls her eyes that look like blue fire against the color of her shirt. "Clearly, you know what I meant."

"Suit yourself." Neither of us moves to leave. "Ivy," I whine. "I'm hungry."

She laughs at me. "I'm in the middle of a rather challenging chess match."

"Oh yeah?" I yank her phone from her grasp and move her piece for her. She reaches out, trying to grab it back from my hands, but quickly realizes she's not going to get it and gives up in favor of watching me play for her. And when the other player moves, I continue, taking their rook in the process I might add.

"Oh my god," she squeals, and I can't hide my smile. "You are such a rat bastard."

"I can't help it if I'm better at chess than you are."

"You are not," she practically shrieks.

"Agree to disagree unless you want to go toe to toe with me, baby?"

"Maybe another time." She shuts off her phone with a smug smile playing on her lips, thinking she just locked me out.

How cute.

"Let's go get an ice cream. I'm fucking starving."

"An ice cream?" she laughs. "What are you, eight? What sort of date is that? Didn't we already do that once?"

"Yes, I'm eight. Now come on. I'll even buy." Ivy shakes her head, crossing her arms over her chest like she's trying to take a stand or something. "Okay, dinner first, then dessert at my place."

"Well, when you put it like that." She winks at me.

Fucking Ivy *winks* at me.

For some reason, I find this to be incredibly awesome and insanely sexy. People so rarely surprise me, but Ivy's brutal honesty mixed with her fiery temper and overt politeness keep me on my toes. It's one of the reasons I fell in love with her so easily.

She's the most fun I've had in three decades and one year.

She's like the most elusive of hacks.

Cagey yet vulnerable.

Able to be penetrated but only after more dedication, balls, and sheer luck than most are willing to play for. But once you get inside, it's the best sort of rush. The highest of highs that no drug can even come close to touching. Once inside, you have the keys to the motherfucking castle, and you own that shit. It's yours for the wielding, but if you push too far or get carried away with the thrill of the prize, you'll crash and burn.

And that, my friends, is worse than never penetrating it at all because you know how fucking amazing it is on the inside. But you also know you could potentially never get there again.

So do I plan to squander another minute of my life without her? Absolutely not.

# Chapter Thirty-Five

*Ivy*

SO, I have a bit of irony for you. Are you ready? Luke hacked Jason. He completely invaded his privacy and did so unabashedly and unapologetically. That, and he ended up outside my blasted building on a bloody step before chasing me down at the airport. That's pretty close to stalking, right? No. That *is* stalking.

And I do not care.

Go figure that one out.

Maybe it's the fact that Luke isn't really a stalker. I mean, some of his actions say that he is, but I don't believe that is his outright goal or anything. I don't think he sits about possessively obsessing over where I am and who I'm with or what I'm doing to the point of insanity and violence.

But Jason? That's exactly what he would do to the point of following me around everywhere I went. To the point of accosting me and others I spoke to. To the point of violence.

The mere thought of him causes bile to creep up my throat.

I like to think that he's gone. That he's done with me. But that weakness in my brain that I absolutely hate makes me feel like he'll always be lurking about. Men like that thrive on vulnerability, and that's something I need to work on. No one can help me with that.

Strength comes from within, right?

But as Luke throws his arm around my shoulder, pulling me securely into his side, I know I'm safe.

He has one of the most jaded pasts I've heard of. The things he's done? Hell, I still can't make heads or tails of them.

But do I condemn or redeem him?

I love him, and I believe he's a good man. He's never shown me otherwise.

So that's what I'm going to go with. That's what I'm betting on, and I don't think that's the wrong choice. I may even feel it's the right one.

"I made us a reservation," Luke says as he opens my car door for me. We're in his car, and I get the feeling that he'll be dropping me back off here at the hospital in the morning. I seem to be okay with that too.

"Where's that? Because I'm keen for Mexican food."

Luke laughs, shutting my door and then hopping in his side before starting his car with the press of a button. "I actually went with sushi."

I slap at him, laughing. "You did not, you savage liar."

"Savage liar? That's a bit strong, don't you think? How about ruthlessly handsome, or roguishly endearing?"

"That could never describe you."

"You wound me, Ivy. Deeply. You should know that."

"If you don't feed me soon, Lucas, I'll wound you superficially as well."

"God, I love your threats," he sighs. "Okay, I might have gone with Mexican, but if you end up smelling like onions and chiles, I might try to take advantage of you before we hit up the ice cream."

"Really? Onions and chiles do it for you?"

"Darlin', you have no idea." He gives me that lopsided impish smile of his, complete with that sexy-as-all-sin dimple. What is it about his smile that gets me every time?

The Mexican place he picked is one of my favorite restaurants in all of Seattle, and though I'm ravenously hungry, my appetite is dwindling.

"My spidey sense is telling me that something is off with you," Luke comments as he pops a chip laden with guacamole into his mouth.

"I'm not following."

"You're not eating, and that's pretty much a sport with you, so what's up?"

"I don't know. Just uneasy is all."

Reaching out for my hand, I happily place mine in his. "Do you want to go out and meet up with everyone? Ryan's brother has joined our little team of merry bandits and I'd bet money on the fact that he's dying for the redhead."

"Claire?"

"One in the same."

"Wow."

"I know," Luke laughs.

"She'll eat him alive."

He shrugs, "Already warned."

"I'd rather just go home."

"No ice cream?"

"Can we take a pint to go?"

"I can pay the check now, order you up some salted caramel, and we can be eating it in bed within the hour."

"You really are the best, aren't you?"

"Without a doubt. But really, what's going on?"

I look down at my half-eaten plate of enchiladas with regret. I love this place and these enchiladas and don't know why I can't shake this. "You know I saw him?"

"Yes," he answers, though it was a rhetorical question. "He won't bother you, Ivy. I've got him by the balls if he even tries."

My eyes find his. "What does that mean?"

"It means I've got access to his systems should I ever need it. It means that if he ever comes near you, I'll have him arrested and destroy his world. It means I'd never ever let someone hurt you."

"Can you offer the same promise against yourself?"

That gives him pause. "Yes. At least, I think so. You're my world, and I will always protect you. No matter what."

Wow. I mean, just wow. What can someone even say to that?

Luke's eyes hold mine, trepidation clear as day in those brown depths. "Do you have questions for me?"

"No. I really don't. I don't know if I'll ever understand everything that comes with you, but I've thought about it, and maybe I'm okay with that. Maybe it doesn't matter."

"Can you say matter again?"

"Matter?"

"Yeah, but you say it like mat-ah. It's cute."

I roll my eyes, ignoring the way he looks at me like I'm the most beautiful woman on the planet. And I definitely ignore the way it makes me feel. "Pay the check. I want my ice cream, and then I need to sleep."

"With me?"

"Yes."

Luke whips out his wallet in one of the fastest moves I've ever witnessed. He doesn't even wait for the check. He just drops down a couple of large bills, way more than what we owe, and then reaches for my hand.

I take it with more ease than I would have imagined.

We make it out to his car, and as we drive through the streets together, I fall into myself again.

"What are you thinking?" Luke tilts his head in my direction, his eyes still on the road.

"I'm not thinking anything."

"You're the worst liar, baby." He reaches out for my hand again. "You can ask me whatever you want to know."

I shrug, feigning indifference. Honestly, I don't know why I'm thinking the things I am. "It's none of my business."

He chuckles, reaching up to cup my cheek, his thumb brushing up and down, eliciting a shiver down my spine. "Sure it is. I told you, you're mine and I'm yours. I know you're wondering about my past."

"I'm not." He throws me a look and my shoulders fall. "Not really anyway. I just still feel like I'm missing so much of you, and . . .," I trail off, not wanting to finish my thought.

"Did you know that I've only ever had one real girlfriend?" I shake my head, not entirely sure where this is headed and a little frustrated that he changed the subject like that. "I dated a girl named Veronica, Ronnie I called her, when we were in college. She split the second the Feds came banging on my door and after that, I met you."

"Right," I draw out the word, because I knew that already.

"I left you that morning, maybe five or ten minutes after you had fallen asleep. You were so exquisitely beautiful, and it was really not a far stretch to picture something more with you, even though we had just met. But Ronnie had just dumped me over the FBI thing, and I knew I was headed in a bad direction, so I left. I left that morning, but that didn't stop me from hanging around Bean & Leaf whenever I could, hoping to see you. Hoping to talk to you and apologize."

I try looking away, suddenly uncomfortable with his penetrating stare. His thumb and second finger possess my chin, forcing my eyes back to his and holding me there as he studies my expression against the lights of the dashboard as we sit at the traffic light.

"I was stuck on you after that one night. Unable to let go, but I knew I had no choice. That seems to be my theme when it comes to you. My inability to see past myself, the things I had done and things I was doing, kept me from you a second time."

I swallow down, overwhelmed by his intensity that I now can't seem to look away from.

"I have people," he continues. "Kate is an incredible woman, and I love her like a sister. Claire, the monster, too. Ryan most of all, and even that little shit, Kyle. I have people in my life. People I love and who love me back, but other than Ryan, no one really *knows* me. Except *you*," he stresses. "You know me. And though you think you're missing a lot, you're actually not. I want this with you. I want a future and a forever, and I'm really not shy about asking for it. I am so sorry for what I put us through, but I need you, and I think you need me too."

"I might need you too."

A slow smile lights up his face before he leans over to kiss me chastely. "Might?"

"Don't push it."

He laughs, driving forward with the change of the light, taking us back to his place.

LUKE TOSSES his keys on the table next to the door before snaking his arms around my waist and walking me in. "I have ice cream in the freezer," he says into my neck, trailing kisses up and down.

"Not interested."

"Then what are you interested in?" he asks with so much suggestion in his voice that my toes curl as I suppress my moan.

Turning around in his arms, I peer up into his soft brown depths, my hands snaking around his neck.

"Hi," he whispers, brushing my hair back behind my ears so he can study my face better.

"Hi," I whisper in return, and now we're grinning at each other like lovestruck teenagers before their first kiss. It's that same feeling. The incredible coil of anticipation mixed with the bubbles of excitement that pervade my chest.

The delicious buzz of desire grows between us, snapping and popping, fizzing and sizzling and I can't get enough. The buildup is almost as good as the real thing. Almost.

His head dips down slightly before pausing, hovering a few measly inches from mine. He's asking me. This time he has no intention of taking something I'm not willing to offer, but little does he know, I want everything.

His kisses, his hands, his body, his mind, his soul, his everything.

"I love you," I whisper.

His eyes slam shut, and a shaky breath stutters past his lips.

"Wow. Who knew three simple words, arranged in that order, coming from your mouth, could sound like the most prodigious symphony ever composed?" When his eyes open again, they're on fire, and everything inside me ignites before it liquefies into a molten pool of lava. "I don't just want you for tonight," he says, like it's a warning.

"I know."

"What are you saying? I need to hear the words, baby."

"I'm saying I'm yours, Luke. I'm saying I always have been."

His hands clasp my cheeks before his mouth crashes to mine, devouring me. We're pulling at each other in frenzied desperation. This is no sweet, gentle reunion. This is need and passion. And did I mention need? Holy god, do I need this man.

My shirt hits the floor, followed by his, and then he's lifting me up, walking me across the flat. His lips never leave mine, not even to maneuver us around, which is why we bump into furniture here and there, laughing against each other as we go.

Luke tosses me down on the bed with a bounce, causing a giggle to bubble up, but it gets lodged in my throat as I see the expression on his face. It's unbelievably raw and exposed, and if I thought I was eager before, I'm a million times more so now. I've never had someone look at me like that. Ever.

"I'm sorry," he says, regret crumbling his features. "God Ivy, I'm so goddamn sorry for everything I've put us through. I still maintain that you're too good for me, and that you deserve a shit ton better, but I love you. I love you so fucking much. I hate that I hurt you."

Luke drops to his knees on the floor in front of my legs, which are dangling off the edge of the bed. His fingers slide under the backs of my thighs, pulling me closer to him before his head drops to the tops of them. Sitting up, I run my fingers through his soft short hair.

"You're my world," he says quietly, lost in thought. "And the way I love you." I see a small smile pulling on his lips. "It's really not even describable. So that stuff with Jason that Sophia called me about? I can't even go there. I can't even think about it, because it makes me want to wrap you up in my arms and never let you leave here again. It makes me feel like a crazy, possessive caveman. And that got me thinking about my situation. So I'm just going to say this and then if you're still with me, I'm going to make love to you until you never question anything again."

"Okay."

Luke raises his head out of my lap, brushing a thumb across my cheek. "I would never let *anything* or *anyone* hurt you. Ever. I would give my life to protect yours. And I'm not saying this to be dramatic. I'm saying this because you need to know that I will ensure your safety if you decide to be with me. I know it comes with a certain amount of risk, though it is less now than it was. I'm not easy and neither is my life, but god, Ivy, I'd do anything to be able to make you mine forever."

His thumbs brush against my cheeks again, swiping at the tears I hadn't noticed falling.

"Okay."

He pushes out an incredulous laugh. "Okay? I bare my heart and soul to you, and all you can say is *okay*?"

"Yeah. I think that really covers everything, don't you?"

He laughs, shaking his head before tackling me to my back and covering my body with his delicious weight. "Darlin', nothing with us will ever be just *okay*."

"All right? Does that work?"

He starts tickling my ribs and though I'm not all that ticklish, he seems to find my one spot. I'm squirming and giggling, trying to push his hands away.

"Bloody hell, Luke! Stop! Please!"

He does finally stop, leaving me panting and breathless, smiling so big my cheeks hurt.

Luke hovers above me, his hands pressed into the mattress on either side of my head. "You're so beautiful," he says reverently, his eyes gliding across my face feature by feature. "And you're mine, so no more of this okay or all right bullshit."

"Okay," I smirk, but instead of more tickles, he gives me a broad smile before dipping his head down and pressing his lips to mine.

After that, we're a mass of lips and hands and moving bodies. "I missed you," I whisper as he slides inside me. We've done this particular dance many times before, but this time is nothing like anything before it.

This time nothing is held back.

Nothing is hidden.

We move against each other as one with our eyes open, knowing full well that this is the beginning, not the end. And it's so unbelievably, earth-shatteringly, torturously good.

He thrusts into me like a man on a mission. Like any space or distance between us is too much for him to bear. He slides out of me slowly, only to push in deeper and harder each time. Over and over again until I lose my mind.

"Yes, Ivy. I'm close. So close, baby. Tell me you're there with me." I nod. It's all I can do. "Come with me. Now, Ivy. Come now. You feel too good for me to stop."

I explode on cue, shattering apart and moaning out his name in one continuous string of sound. He follows me over, growling and groaning, collapsing onto me and covering me with his incredible weight. When we finally crash back down to earth, we're smiling in relief. Luke pulls me against him, my head resting on his chest over his racing heart.

"Will you move in with me?" he asks after a long quiet moment, his fingers gliding up and down my bare back.

"I'm sorry, I must have misheard you."

"Nope. You heard me."

"Impossible. It's far too absurd of a question to have been uttered."

"The thought of you being in your place alone and me in mine is a little much for me. I realize we're trying to start over and that this is sort of new for us, but I want you to live with me."

"Live with you?"

"Yes.

"I don't think that's a good idea."

"Why not? I want you with me. I enjoy having you in my bed every night in my arms. Last night, holding you like that, holding you like this, it's the way it should be."

"We've been back together for what? Five minutes? Absolutely not!" I practically shriek.

"I was just asking."

"Well, you can stop asking."

"Demanding woman." His mouth meets mine, but this time, he's almost aggressive. Maybe he's angry, maybe he's just having fun, I don't care either way. "Oh, Ivy," he groans against my lips before dipping down to my throat. "I'm going to make you come so fucking hard."

My eyes roll back in my head with just his words. Jesus, I'm in trouble with this one. And when he keeps his promise, when I'm crying out his name and begging for him never to stop, he whispers words of love in my ear that bring me to a place I've never been before.

"That was amazing," I say touching his sweaty face.

"No, Ivy, that was so much more than amazing. That was transcendent. That was perfection. That was something entirely new."

# Chapter Thirty-Six

*Ivy*

I WAKE up well before the sun comes up with a heavily sleeping Luke wrapped around me. I hate to leave him, but I have to if I'm going to get home, grab clean scrubs and a shower before my shift. I try to pry myself away from his vise grip without disturbing him, but he stirs, pulling me back into his warm embrace.

"If you lived here, you'd be home, and therefore all of your stuff would be here, and you wouldn't have to sneak out in the wee hours of the morning," Luke rasps, kissing my neck in a very distracting way.

"Don't start with that again. I think we should try being an actual couple for a while before we discuss cohabitation."

"Cohabitation? You make it sound like a disease. You know Kate and Ryan moved in together pretty quickly, and now look at them."

Sighing, I push him off before sitting up and pulling on my jeans from last night. "Please just drop it. I don't want to rush this. I don't want things getting ahead of us."

Luke props himself up, resting his head in his hand as he watches me dress. "Fine, I'll let it go for now. Are you working tomorrow?"

"No, why?"

"Because I was thinking I'd drug you, drag you down to city hall and marry you."

I turn around after securing my bra and face him with a raised eyebrow.

"I'm kidding," he laughs, holding his hands up in surrender, no doubt reading my murderous expression accurately. "Well, sort of. Only really about the drugging and dragging and city hall part. We'll discuss the marrying part another time."

"You just don't quit, do you?"

"There's no fun in that."

I lean over, kissing his lips chastely. "And you're all about the fun."

"I am, which brings me back to tomorrow. Wanna hang out with me?" He bounces his eyebrows playfully.

I laugh, shaking my head, as I search for my shirt, which I suddenly remember leaving by the front door. "Tomorrow is great." I kiss him again. "I have to go."

"Fine," he groans. "Go, but you'll miss me and wish you never left my bed."

"Probably true."

"I love you," he calls out, and I can't stop my gleeful smile.

"I love you too," I holler back as I locate my shirt and throw it on before flying out the door only to realize I don't have my car here. Luke drove last night and I left mine at the hospital. "Bugger!"

"Yet another reason for you to live with me," he says with a smug smirk, walking down the stairs behind me, his keys in hand. "I'll drive you."

Luke lets out a really big yawn, rubbing the sleep from his eyes. He's ridiculously adorable right now with sex—and sleep—tousled hair accompanying that damn playful smile.

I believe him when he tells me that he loves me, because I not only see it, I feel it. He is unabashed about it, and though I love him equally, I can't help but feel the shutter of fear that this will all come crashing down on me at any moment. That we'll be on a date, or talking, and suddenly, he'll be called away or disclose something horrific or explain to me why we can't be together for my own good.

Because all of those things have happened before.

And the scars they left are indelible. I just need more time to heal. For him to prove to me that he's here, and that this thing between us is real and won't disappear at a moment's notice.

Luke patiently waits while I shower and change at my place before bringing me to the hospital and leaving me there with promises of dinner and a sleepover at my flat tonight. My morning starts out great, but by ten-thirty I have a headache and my throat feels scratchy. By the time I get off the phone with Craig and Darcy at the end of my lunch hour, my whole body aches and I have the chills.

I take some medicine—working in a hospital has its advantages —but by late afternoon, I'm miserable. Luckily I'm not in the ED today, I'm simply in clinic and I only have two more patients to see.

I shoot Luke a text telling him that I'm sick with some sort of plague and that he should save himself before he catches it, and we start a city-wide epidemic. I get no text in return, but frankly, I don't have the brainpower to care.

"Sit down, Ivy. You look like death, and I want to check your temperature," Caroline, one of my nurses orders.

"I'm fine. I'll just go home and sleep."

Caroline shoves a temporal scanning thermometer against my forehead and two seconds later declares that I have a fever and need to go home.

Right. No kidding. I could have told her that much.

The thought of driving home in traffic is not appealing, but I have little choice, and as luck would have it, it takes me twice as long because of an accident. My head is pounding, my body wants to shrivel up and die, my throat is on fire, and my stomach may even be getting in on the action.

I need my bed, and I need it now, which is why I'm beyond relieved when I step into my apartment, only to find Luke in my kitchen standing over a pot of something that smells dangerously close to chicken soup.

*How did he get into my flat?*

"Hi, baby," he says casually like him standing in my kitchen with my bloody lavender apron on, stirring soup is the most normal thing in the world.

"What are you doing here?" My voice sounds like I've been eating sand and washing it down with shards of glass.

"I got your text," he says as if this should explain everything.

"Luke, I need sleep. I'm not up for a visit." Dropping my work bag to the floor, I trudge to my room, not waiting for a response, but when I get in there, I see what he's done, and I suddenly feel so horrible for snapping at him.

There's an extra blanket on my bed, one that is not mine, but looks so warm and comfy I could cry. There's a fresh box of tissues on my nightstand, a glass of water, a bottle of Tylenol, a bottle of Motrin, and a thermometer.

"Did you do all this?" I ask, hearing his footsteps approaching.

"Of course, I did. What? Did you think the sick fairy came in and paid you a visit while you were at work?"

"Luke . . ." I can't even finish my sentence because I'm suddenly crying the way I do whenever I'm sick, which only makes my head and my throat ache more.

"Oh baby, no." Luke scoops me up into his arms, before carrying me like a little girl over to my bed. He pulls the covers back before placing me down as gently as possible. He removes my shoes one by one, followed by my trousers and blouse. My body is wracked with shivers almost instantly, so he strips down to his boxers before climbing in behind me and covering us both with the heavy weight of the comforter.

I've never felt this before, not even with my mum when I was a little girl. If this is what being taken care of by Luke Walker feels like, sign me up. Maybe living together isn't such a bad idea after all.

"Are you delirious, or did you actually mean that?" he asks, and I move my head marginally in his direction because I have no idea what he's talking about. "You just said living together wasn't such a bad idea."

*Oops.*

"I didn't mean to say that out loud."

"But you did. When you're no longer sick, I'll convince you, but for now close your eyes and get some rest, baby. It's like lying next to a freaking oven. I'm starting to sweat just from holding you."

"You don't have to," I manage, but I'm praying he doesn't move because he feels heavenly next to me, and I might start crying again if he leaves.

"I'm not going anywhere, but can I talk you into taking some of these wonderful drugs that I procured? The pharmacist explained that you can take both, but should alternate them instead of taking them all at once."

"You spoke to the pharmacist for me?" Now I'm crying again.

He chuckles lightly, kissing the back of my head. "I didn't know what you needed, so yeah, I did. I have other crap too, but here," he rolls away from me for a moment, but before I can protest, he's back, "take this." I'm handed two pills that I don't even care to examine and a glass of water, both of which sting something fierce on their way down my throat.

"I'm probably contagious, you know. It may be strep."

*Why didn't I swab myself at work?*

"Can I get you something for that?"

God, I love this man.

"Sleep. I need sleep, and if I still feel like this when I wake, I'll ring a colleague for a prescription after I check my throat."

Luke presses his lips to the back of my head again, running his hand down my hair in a soothing caress that instantly has my eyes closing and my body relaxing into his.

When I wake up, I'm alone in my bed, but I'm tucked in so tightly I can hardly move. I have no idea what time it is, but I hear the television on low from the living room, so I know Luke must still be here.

I'm sweaty and sticky, and the throbbing in my head has abated somewhat, so my fever must be down.

I crawl out of bed reluctantly, my bladder the driving force behind that, and after using the washroom, I dress in lounge pants and a sweatshirt before heading out into my living room. Luke is watching a baseball game on low volume, and typing away a million miles a minute on his laptop.

He must hear me enter because his fingers pause mid-keystroke and his head rolls back on the sofa to face me. "Hey, baby." He smiles brightly. "How are you feeling?"

"A little better maybe?"

"Is that a question?" he chuckles, patting the seat next to him on the couch, which I accept, drawing my knees up to my chest and curling into his side.

"Not sure. Might be."

Luke kisses my forehead gently. "Feels like your fever is down, which is good because there is something I have to mention to you, and I was hesitant to do it while you were burning with fever."

"Don't be so dramatic."

"Take a look at my screen and then tell me if I'm being dramatic."

The way he says that has me sitting up a little straighter, peering over at his computer, but I can't decipher what exactly I'm looking at. It appears to be a screen within a screen on one side and another vertical rectangle on the other that is black with a bunch of white letters and numbers that are completely nonsensical.

"What am I looking at here?"

"This," he points to the screen within a screen, "is Jason's phone." I give him a look, but he ignores me. "And that is his email." Luke clicks on something and all of his emails pop up.

"And why are you checking his email?" Yeah, I'm annoyed.

"Because your phone rang twice while you were asleep and both times it was the same California number. The first time I didn't pick up, but the second time I figured it must be Sophia, so I answered. It wasn't her."

I'm shaking my head before he even finishes his statement, ignoring the dull throb accompanying the motion, because it's completely overshadowed by the building trepidation creeping its way up my spine.

"He doesn't have my number. No."

Luke cups my cheek, keeping my eyes focused on his. "He does baby. I spoke to him. He was surprised at first when I answered and told me his name when I asked it. I informed him with the utmost civility that if he ever calls you again, I'd rip his heart from his chest *Indiana Jones* style, but all that did was make him laugh."

I don't know what to say. Why is Jason calling me? I ran into him one bloody time in the street and that was the first time I'd seen him in years. How did he even get my number?

"So I hacked his phone again," Luke continues, "and his computer, but that's not how he found you. There are no links to you in his system, other than the phone calls, which is good. I also wiped your contact information from it."

"You do know that I have no idea what that really means, right?"

"It means that he's not hacking you, baby. It means that he found you another way other than through your personal systems. He's in California still. He's not here and I told him that any more contact would result in another restraining order, which we would make public, including to his employer. That shut him up and he hung up on me pretty quickly after my threat. It's not all that difficult for someone to get your cell phone number, and I'm checking into everything so you have nothing to worry about."

I can only stare at him.

"You don't think—" I can't even say the words.

"No, darlin'. I think he took my threat seriously enough that he'll leave you alone, but if he calls you again, please let me know."

"Jesus, Luke." I shake my head and he wraps his arm around me tighter, reassuring me in the best possible way. "I can't even."

"I know, but I'm on it. His system is clean. There is nothing about you, not even a search, so I think he was just testing the waters with that phone call."

"But you think he'll leave me alone?"

"Yes. I do." He kisses the top of my head and I sink further into him.

"How can you even be sure?"

"Because I have access to his system," he points to his screen, "and I will fuck up his entire world with a simple keystroke if he tries anything."

I feel like that should bother me. Him being able to do that to Jason. But it doesn't.

"Do you want me to fix you something to eat?" he asks softly, setting his computer down with the screen open, evidently still engaged in something imperative.

"I'm not hungry."

"A shower?"

I glance up at him, and he's smiling down at me. The icy brick of fear that was weighing me down moments ago, seems to be thawing. Luke makes me feel safe, and everything he said to me about protecting me with his life comes flashing back.

He meant it.

Of that I have no doubt. The fact that he can do the things he can do, well, yeah, that doesn't bother me so much anymore. Nothing else matters except for him and me and us.

So instead of questioning him further, I say, "A shower would be perfect."

Because I think it just may be.

I think we may be perfect, and if we can get through all the craziness of the last year, I think we can get through just about anything together.

Somehow we found our way.

# Epilogue

*Luke*

I HAD the entire day and night planned out to perfection. Everything from going to Bumbershoot with Kate and Ryan to a quiet, romantic dinner later back at our place.

Everything was planned out perfectly.

And then Kate's freaking water broke in the middle of the damn show.

So instead of watching the bands together and exploring the festival, Ivy and I are driving through horrific traffic toward the hospital. It's hard to be pissed at the Duchess for ruining my plans, especially when we're all so uneasy.

The twins are early after all.

Ivy's been on the phone for the last ten minutes, ensuring that all the best people are on the case, since it is Labor Day weekend.

And despite the interruption and the steady stream of panic flowing through me at the potential risk to my future godchildren, I'm smiling. Ivy is too preoccupied to notice, which is a good thing because she'd probably think I'm an asshole for smiling in a situation as precarious as this, but I can't help it. She'll just have to deal with it.

Somehow I managed to convince her to move in with me two months after we officially started dating again. It just made sense. After the small scare with Jason, which turned out to be nothing more than that singular phone call, Ivy didn't want to stay alone, and I was only too happy to offer my services as bed buddy.

We did the whole back and forth thing, but it was tiring and annoying, and our conflicting schedules made it all the more hectic. I asked her to move in with me nearly every day, and eventually my persistence won out because she finally acquiesced and said yes, though she told me it was for no other reason than to shut me up.

I'm okay with that.

The reason is inconsequential as long as I have her with me. Once she moved in, we transitioned from great to awesome. She wanted boring—excuse me, normal—and that's exactly what I give her. Every damn day, I rock her world with the best fucking form of normal you could ever imagine.

We cook dinner together, and watch TV and movies, and read a lot. She's even learning to love baseball. Now that it's going into fall, I'm going to push hard to convert her into an American Football fan. That Australian Football League her dad is so into is just not for me.

And though I've had this plan brewing in the back of my mind practically since I laid eyes on her, I've held off.

Ivy's dad wasn't getting better, in fact, he was getting worse, but two weeks ago a kidney—that was not Ivy's—became available and he had surgery. A successful surgery at that, and he appears to be doing really well with his new organ.

Everyone is happy, so happy that it felt like the appropriate time to rock the boat, just a little.

But now I'm not going to get the chance because I'm parking in the lot at the hospital instead of listening to kick-ass music before eating a perfect dinner with my perfect girl.

"I see you smiling, Lucas, and I know you're razzed about becoming an uncle or godfather or whatever you'll be, but those babies are early. Let's hold our excitement until we know everyone is okay, yeah?"

She has no idea what actually has me grinning like a stupid bastard.

"Did you know that when you're nervous, your accent is a million times thicker than it normally is?"

Ivy rolls her eyes, hopping out of the car without responding to me.

"Did you ring Kyle and Claire?"

"I texted them, and they both said they were on their way. Claire was at the show with a date that she had to dump, but I think Kyle should be here soon."

Ivy nods her head, looking as apprehensive as I've ever seen her.

"Hey." I pull her into my side, wrapping a comforting arm around her. "They'll be fine, baby. You'll see. All of them."

We rush into the hospital as Ivy fishes through her bag looking for her hospital ID, which should hopefully get us past the dictators at the front desk. It does, but once we get outside the trauma room where Kate is apparently delivering the babies, we're stopped by a small and surprisingly intimidating woman.

"There are already too many people in that room and your presence won't help a thing," she says with an air of authority that's begging to be challenged. "You can go back out to the waiting room."

I'm about to open my mouth to set her straight when Ivy grabs my hand, trying to pull me away.

"No way," I bark at her.

"Luke, first of all, Marybeth here is right." I don't give a fuck if *Marybeth here* is right. "There are far too many people in that room. We'll just be in the way. Second of all, Kate is in the process of giving birth."

"And your point is?"

"My point is that she does not want you seeing that, and something tells me that if we walk in there now, Ryan will kick your arse for seeing his wife's vagina."

"Oh." I hadn't thought about the whole seeing Kate's vagina thing. That thought makes me shudder in the worst possible way.

"Yeah. *Oh.*" Ivy manages to tug me into compliance this time, and once we're back out in the waiting room, we take a seat on the hard, unforgiving pleather chairs.

"I can't believe Kate and Ryan are having their babies today." I shake my head, beyond incredulous.

"Do you want that someday?" Ivy asks casually, but something in her intonation has me craning my head to examine her.

"Want what? Babies?"

"Yes."

She's not meeting my eyes as she chews nervously on the corner of her lip.

"Of course, I do, though I think I may prefer one at a time. Two seems like a lot to have at once." I'm watching her absorb my words, trying to figure out why she's gone from apprehensive over Kate and the twins, to edgy and agitated.

She just bobs her head, looking anywhere but at me, and I can't stand this another moment. Shifting to face her fully, the seat squeaks its protest beneath me as I reach out and take her face in my hand, guiding it until her eyes are forced to meet mine.

"What's up?"

"What do you mean?"

"You're the worst liar, so out with it. You're making an already tense situation worse. Are you okay? Is there something I should know?"

Then she breaks down into tears, and now my heart is really hammering away in my chest.

"I'm sorry," she sobs, and I wrap my arms around her, terrified that she's going to say something like she's dying, or we can never have children or even adopt because of some obscure Australian glitch that makes everything impossible. That doesn't even make sense in my mind, but the fact that she's crying the way she is, in my arms, has me thinking all kinds of crazy illogical things.

"Ivy, you're scaring me, darlin'. What's going on? Are you all right?"

"I didn't want to tell you like this, but I'm crying, and I can't make it stop."

"Okay, now you have to tell me, because you wouldn't believe the things going through my mind right now, and I can promise you that all of them are really bad."

More tears.

*Crap.*

"Are you dying?" She shakes her head. "Are you sick or is someone in your family sick?" Another head shake. "Are you secretly in love with someone else or have knowledge that the polar ice caps have finally melted and Seattle is about to be flooded with water?"

She laughs through her tears, and at this point, I'll take what I can get.

"None of that."

"Then, darlin', you gotta tell me. Whatever it is, we'll figure it out, okay?"

She sniffs a little, wiping her face on my t-shirt, before pulling back to look at me with red-rimmed, puffy eyes, and disheveled hair. She's so beautiful.

"I'm pregnant."

I can only stare at her, while those words replay through my head as I try to make sense of them. *I'm pregnant. I'm pregnant.*

"You're pregnant?" This time I get a head nod. "And it's mine?"

She rolls her eyes, "Of course, it's yours, you daft wanker."

And now I'm smiling like a son of a bitch because Ivy, the woman I had planned to get down on one knee and propose to tonight, is pregnant with my baby.

"Hell yeah!" I grab her, pulling her into me and hugging her securely against me until I remember that she's pregnant and maybe squeezing the life from her isn't a wise thing anymore.

"You're okay with this?" She's still sniffing back her tears.

How can she even question that?

"I'm so much more than *okay*. I'm beyond fucking ecstatic. In fact, I think it's safe to say I've never been happier in my life."

Reaching out, I cup the flat expanse of her lower belly in awe. *My baby is in there.* "When did you find out?"

"This morning. I took a test because I missed my period last week, and it came back positive and I've been thinking all day about how I was going to tell you." She shrugs, sniffles, and wipes her nose with the back of her hand. "I thought you'd be mad as a cut snake with me."

I snicker at the phrase, shaking my head.

And even though we're in the hospital's emergency department waiting room sitting on miserably uncomfortable chairs and it smells like bleach and body odor, I can't think of a better time or place to do this.

I lower myself onto the floor, kneeling in front of her and capturing her thighs between my arms before I lock my eyes with hers.

"Ivy, baby, I love you, and this is not how I wanted to do this. Not at all in fact." Her expression drops. She thinks I'm talking about the baby. "I actually had a whole plan for tonight. Nothing outlandish or over the top, but now everything is different. You're pregnant, and we're having a baby, and well, I just can't wait any longer."

Her head is downcast; clearly, she's not picking up on what I'm about to do, which just makes this moment better.

I place the petite black velvet box that I've kept in my pocket for over a week on her lap in front of her fingers, which are twisted into knots. Her eyes widen as she stares at the box before gazing at me, her mouth popping open into an adorable O shape.

"Ivy, darlin', from the moment I met you all those years ago, I knew you were someone special. Life certainly has pulled us in a million different ways, but we came back together despite everything, which tells me that we're meant to be. It tells me that not everything is random, because we're here together. I love you and I will *always* love you. And I will *always* love our child," I press my fingers to her lower abdomen again, "as well as any subsequent children." A sob escapes her throat, but I think this time, it's a happy one. I open the box in her lap, revealing the diamond solitaire that I bought her. "Will you marry me? Because there is no way I can have a happy ending without you."

"Yes," she whispers, her voice thick with tears and emotion, and though it wasn't the shout from the rooftops I was hoping for, this is far better, because Ivy Green just agreed to be mine forever and we're having a baby.

I slide my ring onto her finger, both of us taking it in before I pull her toward me and press my lips to hers, promising her everything.

Seriously, could this get any better?

"Ivy, Luke?" a voice calls out, and we turn to face the nurse who looks startled to see us embracing like this, before she clears her throat and her expression turns completely impassive. "The babies were both born," she says stoically. "Kate and Ryan asked that I tell you."

She looks like she's about to turn and leave it at that.

Is she kidding me right now?

"Hey," I call out, ready to tackle this lady to the ground if she takes another step. "Are they okay? Are they boys, girls, hobbits, what?"

Her stone façade doesn't crack, but I don't care as long as she tells me what I need to know.

"One girl and one boy. Everyone is doing well, but the babies are premature and will have to stay up in the NICU for a few days."

Both Ivy and I sag in relief.

"Can we see them?" Ivy asks.

"Not yet. We're moving Kate up to the postpartum floor. You can visit her there."

"Thank you," we say in unison, and the nurse turns and walks away without further comment.

"I guess I was wrong," I say, grinning like a fool at my new fiancée.

"Wrong about what?" she asks, furrowing her eyebrows.

"I was just thinking that things couldn't get any better after you said yes to me and told me that you were pregnant, but I was wrong."

"How so?"

"Because Kate and Ryan have a daughter and a son, and everyone is doing well, *and* I'm going to be a daddy and a husband." Ivy nods her head like she not only gets it, but agrees.

Life is fucking perfect.

\*\*\* The End

Liked Luke and Ivy's story? Pick up your copy of Start With Me and get lost in Claire and Kyle's story.

# Start With Me

Prologue

*Kyle*

"I WAS WONDERING when you were going to show up," a sweet yet raspy female voice says from behind me as I step into the over-the-top mansion my brother, Ryan rented for his wedding. I spin around and come face to face with a stunning redhead.

*Wow.* My eyes widen on their own volition so I can take in more of her.

"I'm not gonna lie, Kyle my friend, we'd all but written you off for the main event."

"Um," I start, blinking at the woman whom seems to know me though I'm positive I've never seen her before in my life. She's definitely the sort of woman you'd remember. "I'm sorry, do we know each other?"

"You're Kyle," she says to me as her discerning gaze does a full sweep of my body. "I'd know you anywhere."

A laugh bursts out of my chest. "Really? Because I have to be honest with you, cupcake, I have no idea who you are."

The girl laughs and it's like music to my ears. Warm, smooth and sweet. Like hot fudge on ice cream. It's one of those laughs that light up her whole face, and you can't help but join in because it's just that infectious. "Why, I'm the girl you're walking down the aisle tonight." She bats her long eyelashes at me playfully.

"Is that right?" I move to lean into her, but before I can say anything else, I'm enveloped in a bear hug by a tall, broad man that can only be my brother.

"You're late," Ryan admonishes with a half-hearted glare.

"I'm not late," I reply smoothly. "I'm right on time, big brother." I smack his black tuxedo-clad back hard.

He sighs out, looking more relaxed than I would have anticipated considering he's about to willingly hand himself over to one woman for the rest of his life. Though I guess if you are going to do that to yourself, he picked well. Kate is awesome, and I have to admit they're perfect together.

"Kyle, I love you like a brother, but couldn't you have gotten here yesterday instead of waiting until the last fucking minute?"

I snort derisively. "I *am* your brother, asshole, which is why I'm the best man." I raise my eyebrows. "And on time."

"You're really not," the redhead, who is still standing with us and smiling like she's got a secret, says. "If my non-existent sibling showed up late to the wedding I'm never going to have, I'd be pissed." *What?* "But considering the fact that you flew across the country and then drove up into the mountains, I'm thinking you should get a pass."

"A pass, huh?" Ryan shakes his head at her, and the two exchange something with only their eyes, before he turns back to me. "You do know that if you lived in Seattle and worked for my company, you wouldn't have to work eighty-hour weeks? You would have already been up here. You would have been here last night, in fact. Oh, and I pay a hell of a lot better than whatever bullshit you're making now." Ryan pins a purple orchid onto the lapel of my tuxedo jacket like he's my prom date, before stepping back to admire his handiwork.

"That's probably all true," I bristle. "But I am not a corporate attorney."

He nods solemnly. "But you should be," he says pushing the rim of his black glasses up his nose. "Way less stress than being a criminal defense attorney in New York." I decide to let it go. Partially because we've had this conversation no less than a dozen times since I graduated law school and partially because . . . well, it's his wedding day.

"Wow, I totally can't picture Kyle working with us," the redhead says and my eyebrows furrow.

"I'm sorry, how do we know each other again?"

Ryan rolls his eyes at me, as a small smirk pulls up the corner of his lips. "Kyle, this is Katie's maid of honor, my assistant, and all around pain in my ass, Claire Sullivan. Claire, this is—"

"Your brother, Kyle," she interrupts, smiling with amusement, her eyes still locked on me. "Yes, I do believe I already said I knew him. You have a picture of the two of you in your office on your bookshelf."

Claire. Her name bounces around my mind as I take her in. And, now that I think on it, I remember Ryan mentioning her over the years. I just never realized she was also Kate's maid of honor. And breath-takingly gorgeous.

"Then I guess it's about time we met, especially since I haven't had the pleasure before now and I'm the guy who gets to walk you down the aisle." And then I laugh awkwardly like an insecure teenager who's never talked to a girl he thought was pretty before. "You know what I mean," I say and instantly regret it. Jesus, when had I become such an inarticulate bumbling idiot?

Luke, my brother's best friend, snorts as he walks up to us, clearly having overheard. "Way to play it cool there, guy."

I elbow him, which only makes him laugh more. Claire is gazing at me like she finds me adorable and I realize I like being on the receiving end of that look from her. Even if it is at my expense.

"About time you showed up, motherfucker." Luke laughs. Always a nice greeting from him.

"Blow me, bitch," I say back with an overly exaggerated smile plastered on my face.

"Maybe later." He winks as he nudges my side again. "We've got a show to get through first." Luke stands up to his full height, his short brown hair gelled back. "You ready for this, big guy?"

"Why does everyone keep asking me that?" Ryan grouses, looking at each of us. We just shrug in response. "I mean, *I* asked *her* to marry me. Not the other way around."

"You're, right," Claire says with a wink. "So maybe we should all be asking Kate that question? In fact, I think maybe now that the best man has arrived, we should get this party started."

Ryan's smile grows. "Show time," he booms as he and Luke begin to walk to the back of the room where a few other people seem to be lining up for the ceremony.

"Where is Kate?" I ask, my eyes scanning the vast room decorated in twinkling lights, candles and flowers in search of my soon-to-be sister in law. The alluring fragrance of vanilla, cinnamon and pine trees assault my senses. It smells like Christmas in here, even though it's June.

"She thinks it's bad luck for Ryan to see her before the ceremony," Claire says with a shrug, like superstitions are a ridiculous practice. They probably are, but after Kate lost both her husband and toddler daughter in a car accident several years back, I know she doesn't mess around with anything she views as a potential risk. Even on her wedding day. Especially on her wedding day.

"Looks like you're stuck with me tonight," I say with a smile, liking that thought probably more than I should given our situation. I extend my elbow to her so she can loop her arm through mine, and we follow Ryan and Luke to the back of the room.

"Better you than Teen Wolf over there." She gives an exaggerated shudder, nodding her head in the direction of a guy wearing sunglasses, a fedora and more hair on his face and neck than I've ever seen in my life.

I can't help but laugh at that. Claire is . . . well, she's great. Even though *great* seems like an absurdly lackluster word to use when it comes to this creature. She's smart and quick-witted, with the perfect amount of devilry. And she's fucking hot. Long, thick, glossy red hair tumbles in soft curls down her back. Her skin is like porcelain, smooth and creamy with pink-tinted cheeks. Perfect bow shaped lips are stained a deep crimson color, and when she smiles, her white teeth practically glow. But by far and away her best physical attributes—other than her crazy sexy body—are her eyes. They're anime-size big and a deep sapphire blue. Beautiful really doesn't do them justice.

I lead her to the back of the line behind Luke and the girl he's escorting. All the groomsmen are in black and the bride's maids are in purple strapless, knee length dresses. I can feel Claire's body heat and smell her perfume, and I think I want this girl. Actually, I might just want her a lot.

"A grand says you forgot the rings," Luke says with a cocky grin and I roll my eyes, smugly patting the breast pocket of my jacket.

My empty breast pocket.

*Shit.* Panic slams into my chest with the force of a wrecking ball. Where the hell are the rings? I'm positive I put them in this damn pocket when I got off the plane.

"Ha," Luke rumbles out. "I knew it. This is why Ryan should have named *me* best man."

"Fuck," I hiss, and Claire is snickering, not even trying to be quiet. I turn to Luke wide eyed, before looking to Claire, hoping a distracted Ryan doesn't notice our little conversation. He's busy discussing something with a woman I hadn't noticed before. "What the hell am I going to do?" My hands are flying around, digging through every pocket on my body.

Claire just shrugs, but doesn't seem nearly as concerned as I feel she should be. As concerned as I am. Unless . . .

Just as music begins from the other room and right before we start to move, Ryan turns to me with a wide grin. A very *knowing* grin. His green eyes are sparkling with mirth.

"Something wrong, Kyle?" he asks in that way of his.

"You fucker," I snap a little too loud and that woman Ryan was just talking to throws a look of disdain my way.

Claire, Ryan, and Luke all burst out laughing, before Ryan opens his palm to reveal the two platinum bands that he must have swiped from my breast when he put that damn flower on my chest.

*Bastard.*

"Here." He hands them to me and this time, I slip them into my pants pocket so that if one of them wants to try to snag them again, they'll have to practically grope my dick to do so.

"Welcome to the show, baby brother." Ryan winks at me and I flip him off before turning to face the cream satin-covered aisle that is now splayed out in front of us.

"Sorry," Claire whispers, clearly not sorry at all. "But you have to admit, that was a little funny. I mean, could you imagine being the asshole who lost the rings? It would have been epic."

I look over to her and shake my head. "Yeah, considering I just about had a heart attack, I don't particularly find it that funny." Okay, in retrospect, it's a bit funny. I swear, only Ryan and Luke throw me off my game like this.

"Kyle Smile," she sighs. "If we're going to be BFFs, then you have to learn to roll with the punches a bit better."

"Huh?"

"BFFs," she repeats slowly, like I'm a small child. "Best friends forever. Didn't you go to high school? Anyway, I'm an awesome friend, and since you're the best man and I'm the maid of honor, it's really the way it's supposed to be."

"Friends, huh?" I raise an eyebrow to her. "A friend would have given me a heads up on the ring prank."

"Maybe," she muses with a tilt of her head. "But considering it was my idea in the first place, I really couldn't."

"It was your idea?" I say incredulously, my eyebrows hitting my hairline.

She gives me a hip bump, winking one large blue eye at me. "Yeah. It was all me. But Ryan wasn't exactly opposed to the idea."

I just scowl at her. "How's this then, I'll make it up to you?"

"Oh yeah?" I smile wide, unable to stop myself. "How are you gonna do that?"

"Well, it won't be easy. But I've got all night to think of something. And unfortunately for you, it won't be anything naughty."

"That is unfortunate," I whisper as we move slowly down the aisle to the cords of Pachelbel's Canon. "I'm not so easily won over, you know."

"That's what they all say before they're begging me to be their friend for life."

"Is that a dare?" I smile, pulling her into me just a bit closer before I'm forced to release her.

"Kyle, baby cakes, it's a promise." I chuckle lightly, shaking my head. I kiss her hand and then let my new friend, Claire go so we can watch our loved ones get married.

But I think she's right. Our brief encounter has only made me want more of her. More than just tonight. And the sad reality is, she's Ryan's assistant. And Kate's best friend. And I'm leaving tomorrow at first light. I can't sleep with this woman and run. There's just too much here for that.

Suddenly I'm hit with an odd sense of irony. I might have just met my first real female friend. And that's all she can ever be.

\*\*\*

Want more of Claire and Kyle? Grab your copy of Start With Me today!

# Other books by J. Saman:

Wild Love Series:

Reckless to Love You

Love to Hate Her

Crazy to Love You

Love to Tempt You

Promise to Love Me

The Edge Series:

The Edge of Temptation

The Edge of Forever

The Edge of Reason

The Edge of Chaos

Boston's Billionaire Bachelors:

Doctor Scandalous

Doctor Mistake

Doctor Heartless

Start Again Series:

Start Again

Start Over

Start With Me

Las Vegas Sin Series:

Touching Sin

Catching Sin

Darkest Sin

Standalones:

Just One Kiss

Love Rewritten

Beautiful Potential

Forward - FREE

# End of Book Note

So this is the part of the book where I can spew my thoughts, and on this particular story, I happen to have a lot. First of all, let me thank you wonderful readers! Seriously, I couldn't do this without your support and I am grateful for each of you. Leaving a review wouldn't hurt that either ;). Secondly, let me thank my wonderful family, because I love you dearly and appreciate you dealing with me during the writing process.

Special thanks to Jane Blythe for helping me make Ivy sound like an actual Australian and to the beta readers who helped me so much.

So now, this book. Holy hell people, this one was a nightmare to write. I have three versions of it, including this one. All of them made it well into the two hundred-page range, which tells you that I got way further than I should have.

In the first one, Ivy was Luke's assistant who was divorced from a very scary and abusive man. Ivy had basically been sold off as a bride and enslaved by the man. Luke was her savior in a way and his past—which is similar to the one in this story—helped that along. But I stopped it because the story was getting really dark and convoluted, and needed to end with either Ivy or Luke killing the ex-husband. I just couldn't go there with them.

So onto the second story. It was more along the lines of this one, similar story base, but Ivy wasn't leaving for Boston and her ex Jason (the stalker) was in the picture. Again, it ended up turning so very dark and I even had him kidnapping her and it all spun out of control.

So wrote it a third time and am happy I did, because I was so very close to giving up on this damn story. But I didn't, and in the end, it came out with Ivy and Luke and their journey that I fell in love with. It wasn't an easy journey, and their histories and lives seemed to take over for a bit and get in the way. But I'm a true sucker for a HEA and I couldn't not give them one.

Keep reading for a sneak peak at Start With Me - Claire and Kyle's story.

You can contact me at jsamanbooks@gmail.com or Facebook or Twitter or Goodreads. You can also check SUBSCRIBE to my mailing list for updates on promotions, sales, giveaways and new releases. Or my website: http://jsamanbooks.com

Love you all!!!!

Oh yeah, please leave a review. I'm an indie and need all the help I can get.

Made in the USA
Middletown, DE
25 April 2023